PERSONS UNKNOWN

Also by Susie Steiner

Homecoming
Missing, Presumed

PERSONS UNKNOWN

SUSIE STEINER

HarperCollins*Publishers*Ltd

Published by HarperCollins Publishers Ltd

First Canadian edition

HarperCollins Publishers Ltd
2 Bloor Street East, 20th Floor
Toronto, Ontario, Canada
M4W 1A8

www.harpercollins.ca

Library and Archives Canada Cataloguing in Publication
information is available upon request.

ISBN 978-1-44345-362-2

Printed and bound in the United States of America
LSC/H 9 8 7 6 5 4 3 2 1

14 December

Jon-Oliver

Down. Dizzy. Pitching left. He is draining away like dirty water, round and round. Stumbling not walking, the ground threatening to come up and meet him. And yet he presses on. Something's not right.

He is swampy, heavy-footed. His shin is throbbing. A scuffle – like being spun in blind man's buff – so quick that when it was over he thought he'd been mugged, but he patted himself down and his wallet and phone were there all right.

His muscles are soupy, unresponsive. His legs wade, the landscape too broad for him to make headway. The air is close like a wet web. He can barely draw breath.

He stumbles to the right, into a muddy wooded area in a direction he hadn't intended to take and it's as if the ground is reaching for him. Is it quicksand, not mud?

He's really scared now; nervously places a hand to his chest. His shirt is wet through but it's not raining. He looks at his hand. It is glistening dark; the colour unclear because of the dark and the orangey street lighting.

1

He starts to panic, cannot fill his lungs. What is happening to him?

He falls into the mud, feels some arms take him up and cradle him, looks up to see blonde hair. The alien scent of perfume.

Saskia?

'Sass?' he whispers, confused. Is she the cause of this, after all her stupidity? She went too far and he couldn't stop her.

'Sass?'

His sight dims, he is too tired.

The world dips.

MANON

Crisp in one hand, sandwich in the other; the tickle and press of light internal kneading around her pelvis, like butterflies in a sack. Seems typical that pregnancy has brought zero in the way of nausea but has instead turbo-charged Manon's appetite.

She becomes aware of Harriet and Davy talking, urgent and low, on the other side of the open-plan office. Something's up. They're quickening. Manon elongates her neck, craning to hear, but her colleagues are too far away.

As they pass her desk she says, 'Anything up?'

'Job's come in,' Harriet says, but it's clear she can't be bothered to fill Manon in.

'Ooh, who is it?' Manon says, full mouth.

They ignore her.

She looks at Davy, full of himself these days; Detective Sergeant Davy Walker, promoted by the super, Gary Stanton. He might as well call Stanton 'Daddy'. Well, he's welcome to it. Manon is in hot pursuit of the work–life balance: desk job, regular hours, house full of children. She wants to focus on whether to sign up for an organic veg box or whether this

3

would be taking her personal reinvention too far. You can lead a horse to uncooked beetroot . . .

And yet she is straining out of her seat to overhear the conversation between Harriet and Davy.

'I could be special advisor at the scene, brackets, teas,' she offers.

When she'd first begged Harriet for a job back in the Major Crime Unit, determined to leave behind the misery of the Met (awful boss, crushing workload) and the cost of London living, she said she'd do anything, didn't care how boring. Cold cases.

'You don't want to do cold cases,' Harriet said. 'There is no greater career cul-de-sac than cold cases.'

'I do, seriously. Boring dead-end redundancy's where I'm at.'

And cold cases is where she's ended up, while her belly enlarges (now at the five-month mark), spending quite a few of her days following her satnav inexpertly around the Fens – *turn around where possible* – to interview people who couldn't remember much about last week, never mind a decade ago. Telling herself this is fine. This is what's called Having It All (though most of the time, it feels like having small slivers of the duller bits) – home by five, pick up some Persil non-bio. *You have reached your destination on your right.*

Christ, really?

Harriet has marched off in a hurry.

'Davy; oi, Davy,' Manon hisses at him as he thumbs his mobile phone and Davy – who used to work for *her*, who used to do *her* bidding while *she* shushed *him* – shushes her with his finger. Now he's the DS running the job while she . . . Well, she is quite tired to be fair.

'Just tell me what's up,' she says when he's off the phone.

'Stabbing, male, in Hinchingbrooke Park.'

'Nice of him to kark it so local.'

'Actually, he might not even be dead yet,' says Davy, eyes darting with all the thoughts he's having, checklist and scene log and SOCO, no doubt. 'Right by the forensics lab as well. We can all walk it from here. Really couldn't be more convenient.'

And he is back on his mobile, heading for MCU's double doors.

Her Nineties house, squat in its tray of mown turf, the very image of a child's drawing complete with pitched roof and windows like eyes. Not too bright: a stoic face, happy with its lot. Around the lawn is a frill of box hedging, so low you could step over it – and what's the point in that, she wonders, remembering the burglary prevention advice she used to dole out when she was in uniform. Plant prickly bushes under windows. *Halt! This is a shrubbery!*

Her key in the plastic door with its fake leaded lights, letting herself in and noticing that the reality is a step removed from what she'd hoped for, moving back to Huntingdon. She thought it would be all spacious living and glorious rural(ish) childhoods for Fly and Solly.

'I don't want to bring up a black boy in London,' she said to her sister Ellie at the start of her campaign for them to move back to Cambridgeshire. This had followed Manon being summoned to the headmaster's office at Fly's vast, terrifying comprehensive school and an encroaching fear that he was getting in with the wrong crowd, or possibly that he *was* the wrong crowd.

'That's exactly where you should bring up a black boy,' Ellie said.

'And watch him get stopped and searched every five minutes

of his life? Arrested for stuff he didn't do? Looked at by old ladies who think he's going to mug them? I watch them, you know, giving him a double take, and it breaks my fucking heart.'

'So what, you'd rather take him out to the UKIP heartlands, would you, where he'll be the only black boy for miles around?' Ellie said. 'You should see the old ladies out there.'

'We can't afford to stay here. The rent's crippling me. It's crippling you as well. Come on, we could get a big house, the four of us. Fly would never agree to leave Sol, you know that.'

Ellie looked uncertain. 'It *is* astronomical,' she admitted. 'But God, I hate being uprooted. Having to start again somewhere new, making new friends. Makes me feel exhausted just thinking about it. I've got a group of mums I feel comfortably ambivalent about, right here.'

'We could get a mansion in Huntingdon or Ely or Peterborough,' Manon pleaded. 'You could—'

'Start a course of antidepressants?'

'Go back to work.'

Their charmless four-bedroom house opposite police HQ in Hinchingbrooke is costing a fraction of what they were spending on two flats in the capital, and is more than double the size. They each – her, Ellie, 12-year-old Fly (whose trainers alone, like cruise ships adrift, have their own housing needs) and Ellie's nearly-3-year-old Solomon – have a capacious bedroom, hers and Ellie's both with en suites. The house has one of those bolt-on hexagonal conservatories made from uPVC and, beyond, a 150-foot lawn dotted with menacing conifers. The Bradshaws can even boast a utility room (and what says you have arrived more than a utility room?) with grey marble-effect laminate worktops.

Manon calls 'Hello?' into the volume of the house, clattering her keys onto a glass-topped console in the hallway (an irritant none of them could be bothered to remove – whatever domestic improvements are hatched in the utopias of the night are laid to waste in the harum-scarum day). She smells cooking – whatever Solly has just had for tea.

She stands in the doorway to the lounge, already disappointed by the scene in front of her: an oatmeal vista, its candelabra lights descending stiffly from the low ceiling (a persecution of a ceiling – she feels at times as if it is lowering in real time and will one day crush her). The three-piece suite, extra wide and squat, is the most engulfing Manon has ever sat in, so much so that she often feels she is being consumed by it. Everything beige, so that the whole atmosphere is one of porridgy comfort. They've lived here for five minutes, and she's already nostalgic for the high ceilings of Victorian London.

'Oh Fly, don't play *Temple Run* with him,' she says, removing her coat. 'His brain's not even formed yet.'

'He loves it,' Fly answers without looking up from the iPad he is hunched over, Solly nestled in his lap. Manon walks back out to hang her coat on the banister and to drop her bag at the foot of the stairs. *Where is Ellie? At work?* Her shifts run from 7.30 a.m. to 3.30 p.m. or 1.30 p.m. to 8.30 p.m., and this is considered part time. The entire shift usually on her feet, sometimes with no chance for a break. When she's on nights, she'll often have Solly all day the next day because she's trying to save money on the childminder (Ellie's sense of impoverishment is their microclimate). She'll doze on the sofa while he plays in front of rolling episodes of *Peppa Pig*. There has never been a worse time to work for the NHS, Ellie says. The management obsessed with targets and budgets, every shift short-staffed. No love, only constraint and a communal sense of harassment. Yet her sister has also been a master of evasion

7

lately, time thick yet hollow. The stresses and strains mingled with absences unexplained. 'Shift ran over, sorry.' Or, 'Training. Kept me late.'

Manon frowns at the children: 'He'd also love to bury his face in Haribo; doesn't mean he can, does it?' She strides over and lifts the iPad out of Fly's hands and Solly – predictably – howls, launching himself, starfish-shaped, to the floor. The passion erupting from him, their three-foot Vesuvius. Solomon Bradshaw is either happy or angry. There appears to be nothing in between.

'See what you did?' says Fly.

Home three seconds, and already she's the object of hatred.

'Where's Ellie?' Manon asks, keeping hold of the iPad and wondering where she can hide it this time. *Out in the shed? In the freezer?* This is the wonder of parenting: behind every new low is a lower low, to which you thought you'd never stoop.

'Gone out.'

'Out? Where? Working?'

'Dunno.'

'Well, how long did she leave you alone with Solly?'

If she's on a shift, she should have cleared it, made sure Manon could cover her. Or is she having some fun – *heaven forfend!* – leaving Manon sore, bicep straining as she holds aloft her measuring jug of what is owed and what's been taken. A life with children has brought out in Manon her meanest spirit – never a moment when she isn't keeping a tally.

Fly has got up, lifting Solly's stiff body off the floor. 'Not long,' he says. 'Anyway, I don't mind. Come on dude, time for the bath.'

Manon watches them walk out towards the stairs, Solly's puce face, his breathing juddering with outrage, his little splayed fat hands on Fly's close-cut hair.

8

Flumping into an armchair, Manon feels her tiredness mingle with affection for her adopted son; so much older than his years. She's often washed over with it – pride in his reading, in his gentleness, his soft manners, his decency, his care of Solly.

Solly's mission statement, bellowed while trying to climb the cupboard shelves towards the biscuit tin, is MY DO DAT! He can turn purple at the prospect of being denied complete autonomy – for example, not being allowed to start the car or push his buggy blindly into oncoming traffic; eat a snail or run off with the back-door key. Hot cheeks, angry square face torn up with his despair; trousers descending below the nappy-line, impossibly short legs. His unreasonableness smiled at (most of the time), especially when, tears spurting, he rubs furiously at his eyes and shouts 'MY NOT TIRED!' as if the mere suggestion is a gross slur on his toddler honour.

She could sleep right now.

She could sleep walking up the stairs.

She could sleep stirring a pan at the stove.

The baby squirms, bag of eels.

Yes, it's laughable that she should consider herself the author of Fly's best qualities. She's been his mother for such a short time she can no more claim credit for his good qualities than his bad. His goodness is courtesy of his alcoholic mother, Maureen Dent, slumped with her bottle of Magners in front of *Cash in the Attic* (no cash in their attic, in fact no attic), and down to his brother Taylor, who loved him, who took care of him, probably in much the same way Fly cares for Solly now she thinks about it – you love in the way you have been loved, after all. Taylor turned tricks on Hampstead Heath and was murdered because of it – the homicide that brought Manon and Fly together. Perhaps his goodness is down to the genes of a Nigerian father Fly has never met. The more Manon lives with children, the more she believes in the determination of genes.

Neither a child nor a teenager, though if she has to pick, Manon would place Fly closer to the adolescent camp. People who meet him think him nearer 15 than 12. She has come to realise adolescence is not switched on at once – it seeps, gradually, during late childhood. There are glimpses from age 10. Some say earlier, though she doesn't know about that. It's more like a litmus paper turning blue, as the hormones leach.

Fly can read a room before she can. If there is an accident in his vicinity, he acknowledges vicarious feelings of guilt; can trace the root of awkwardness in a conversation. He once said of a rather sadistic PE teacher, 'She's mean to us because she had an injury and now she can't be an athlete.' He can identify envy without judging a person for it. All this he does quietly, and though she has always thought of empathy as imbued or developed, with him it seems innate. Its flip side is heightened sensitivity – an aversion to high collars and the congestion of cuffs under his coat, which means he wears only a fraction of his wardrobe: one beloved pair of tracksuit bottoms and one hoodie – with the hood *down*, Manon is forever insisting, though he takes less and less notice of her. Tall black youth with his hood up? He might as well wear a sign saying 'Arrest me now.'

Stork-like, he is all limbs. Silent much of the time and unknowable. Fly is unhappy – she knows that much, knows too that she is the cause, and this she can hardly bear. She has uprooted him, unfurled his sensitivities like wounds open to the air. He is not himself. She hopes he'll settle in.

Even so, he has his playful moments – has begun taking pleasure in irony: putting his arm around her shoulder,

10

towering lankily above her, and saying, 'I'm just off out,' and her saying, 'No you're not,' and him saying, 'That's right, I'm not, I don't know where that came from.' Both of them smiling at each other. They can begin to enjoy a new kind of conversation, with meanings other than what is said.

'You are *so* down with the kids,' he'll say to her when she puts some kind of easy-listening mum-pop on the iPod.

Not yet old enough for a man, nor young enough for a boy. What is that? Lines from *Twelfth Night* embedded in her brain. Funny that she'd resented all the drumming and drilling at school, the tittering and yawning in uniforms as lines were delivered by lacklustre boys and girls leaning back in their chairs. The essays on *Coriolanus* or *Much Ado*. She hadn't realised those lines would be the ones to comfort her most in the second half of her life. Perhaps the teachers knew; had thought to themselves, 'You'll thank me one day.'

DAVY

It's good to have Manon back, he thinks, striding across the police station car park towards the featureless grass expanse of Hinchingbrooke Park. He plans to cut through to the wooded area where the body has been found – quicker than trying to walk the enormous curve of Brampton Road. That road is gridlocked with rush-hour traffic, the headlights of school-run mums and commuters out of Huntingdon. Only around five-ish – an unusual time of day for someone to meet a violent death. And opposite a school, too.

He's anxious to get there, to be the first. He breaks into a jog. In the distance, he can see blue lights illuminating the trees in a rhythmic sweep, the flash of a couple of fluorescent jackets.

It's good to have her back, but Manon has to understand that things have changed. He isn't her DC any more – she can't sit in a car the way she used to and bark orders at him. He'll likely be leading this case – not as SIO, that'll be Harriet – but on the ground, running the constables. The thought makes him jog faster. He wants to get there, get started. But his excitement – or is it a stitch? – is tugged at from below by

12

something like aversion. His body pushes forward but his inner self pulls back. *He can't do it. He isn't up to it. He's been over-promoted by the super, who thinks of him as a son.*

Davy is panting (it's a wonder he passed his last bleep test); his heart knocking with impatience to master the scene, and with fear also. He might be unmasked at any moment.

'The shallowness deep within,' Manon said, ages ago now – just after his promotion – when he'd discussed his Imposter Syndrome with her. 'You're not the only one, you know.' And he'd wondered whether she meant, 'You're not the only one who thinks you're a useless twat.'

Why does he keep thinking about her? He wishes she was here, that's why. She seems a more substantial person than he does. He slows to a walk because the stitch is really painful now. Even more substantial these days: her breathing laboured, her breasts enormous. He doesn't want to be one of *those* men, but it's like trying to pretend you're looking out to sea when there's a vast mountain range right in your sightline.

He comes alongside the body. Looks around him. Harriet's not here, nothing's started yet. Within half an hour this place'll be crawling with uniforms. Looking down, he sees the clothing has been cut open so paramedics could work on the victim's chest – white shirt, suit jacket, wool coat, *Ozwald Boateng* written on the purple shimmering lining. The eyes are open, mouth too, the chest caked in dried blood and the small incision of the wound itself, evidently from a knife, like a cut in an uncooked joint of pork. Small red opening in waxy yellow flesh.

Davy looks around him again.

He crouches down unsteadily, and a gust of wind nearly pushes him on top of the corpse. He puts a hand out to balance himself. You don't want to contaminate the scene – isn't that the first rule, the only thing they drum into you at training? *Keep your hands in your pockets.*

If only he could cop a glance at that wallet that he can see poking out of the purple silk lining – then he could get started. If he could get a name off a bank card, an ID, then the story can start and this is a whopper. This one'll be all over the news. The pressure, he can feel it already popping at his temples, is going to be massive. *Keep your hands in your pockets, Davy Walker.*

'What the fuck are you doing, Davy?' It is Harriet.

He jumps up. 'Nothing,' he says. 'I'm not doing anything.'

'Yeah, well, step away from the evidence until SOCO gets here,' she says.

'Know who he is?' Davy asks.

'Not yet. But he'll still be dead in an hour after forensics have got what they need so there's no need to be patting him down.'

He takes a step back.

'We need to cordon this section of wood, make it wide,' Harriet says. 'Where's your notebook, Davy? C'mon, or do you not want to run this scene? First priority is hands-and-knees search for a weapon. No point getting the dogs out, too many people around. But we do need community policing down here – I want the public reassured by not being able to move for police officers. We need a community inspector to go into the school, talk to the head, make sure all the kids get home safely. Same at the hospital.'

'We should check Acer Ward,' Davy says.

'Yes, good thought. See if you can track down the consultant psychiatrist, ask him if they had any psychos go walkabout this afternoon. I didn't just use that word, by the way.'

'What about an ARV?'

'No, leave them out – what can armed response do, realis-

14

tically? Let's not blow the budget. I want scene guards on the cordon, not the idiots we had on the last one. There's a lot of footfall, I don't want this scene contaminated, OK?'

'Who found him?'

'Judith Cole, over there,' Harriet says, nodding towards a woman whose hair is matted against her head with blood. It's smeared down her cheek and has soaked the collar of her coat. She has the distant look of a person who has yet to take in what has happened to her. Someone – a paramedic, probably – has placed a foil blanket over her shoulders of the kind used by runners at the end of a race.

'She's significant, obviously – last person to see him alive. We need her clothes for forensics.'

'Why is there blood on her face and hair?'

'She cradled the victim, tried to listen to his last words apparently.'

Davy is writing furiously, his hand cold and shaky. Harriet doesn't stop, *rat-a-tat-tat*. 'Also at the hospital, let's check to see if anyone's self-admitted. Knife wounds.' She nods at the executive detached homes curling around the cul-de-sac adjacent to the school. 'Over there, Snowdonia Way, that's where I want house to house to start. And we can warn them to be vigilant while we're at it. Set up a roadblock. We want witnesses, people who were driving in this direction.'

Davy is writing down Acer Ward while his brain tries to keep a tab on the subsequent items on the checklist. Nothing must fall off the checklist. He's thinking Snowdonia Way, that was next, then – *what?* – something to do with clothes.

At the same time some other part of his brain is thinking, this isn't a tidy one: not the usual kind of murder where the person who did it is lying smashed next to the victim or is making a cack-handed run for it towards a waiting panda car

15

or where their perp is just, well, obvious because of the back-story: in a relationship with the victim, threatened them with it last time, just did a massive drugs deal and owed someone money. Sent a text saying, 'I'll get you, you're for it.' Their perps, often, were not the brightest bulbs in the chandelier and the cases were tidy. Dirty but clean, as in ring-fenced, not leaching towards the executive new builds of Snowdonia Way with their gas barbecues and two-car garages. Davy feels the anxiety reach its fist around his stomach.

'So that woman Judith Cole,' Harriet is saying, while Davy scribbles *hosp – knife wounds?* 'He died in her arms apparently. At least, he was dead by the time the paramedics arrived. They tried to resuscitate him but no luck.'

'Funny place to die,' Davy says.

'Yes. Very public. Who the fuck is stabbed at half four in the afternoon?' Harriet's swearing always peaks at a crime scene. 'Let's start with a statement from Mrs Cole, down at the station. Send someone to get her a change of clothes. She only lives over there, 5 Snowdonia Way.'

'He looks well-to-do, not our usual lot,' Davy says, nodding at the body.

He steps across the seeping ground to take a look at the man's face the right way up. He has pouches beneath his eyes the size of teabags, a Roman nose. In fact the whole head seems Roman: his hair, cut close, curling forwards towards his fore-head like Caesar's crown of leaves. *What was it made of? Manon would know.*

As she walks away, Harriet adds, 'Need to get the CCTV off the road and this footpath, if there is any.'

Time is of the essence, even when your victim is dead. Witnesses move, rain washes fibres away, memories fade. The commuter who might have noticed something vital goes home

16

to his family, eats dinner, watches TV and soon cannot distinguish between Tuesday and Wednesday. CCTV gets inadvertently wiped by a shopkeeper who knows no better; car number plates are forgotten, descriptions blurred with other memories. They don't call them the mists of time for nothing.

Investigations, Davy realises as he looks at his checklist without knowing quite where to begin, run on the energy of time, run against it sometimes if a living person's in danger – a kidnap, say, or a kiddie lost. Other times it's justice that runs against the clock. Given time, your perp can get rid of the weapon, wipe down his prints, cook up an alibi or hot-foot it to somewhere sunny. The Costa Brava is bristling with British timeshare criminals.

Time blunts all.

It's a relief, now, to be in the warmth of the major crime unit: frying drips on the coffee-machine hotplate; the clack of fingers on computer keys; muffled mobile calls saying, 'No I won't be home, job's come in.' There is no one for Davy to call, no one who minds whether he stays out all night. There's been no one since Chloe, and that ended more than a year ago. Not so much that she put him off all relationships, more that he didn't get back on the horse, and now he's not even in the vicinity of a stable.

As with investigations, so it is with heartbreak: time drains the sharpness from the picture. When Davy'd first broken up with Chloe, she was in every thought he had. He cried every day when they separated, even though it was his choice (doom balloon that she was). Nowadays, he can think of her dispassionately as a significant ex, could even bump into her without a rise in his vital signs. The love has run cold, just like it will with the evidence if he doesn't get a shifty on.

17

Davy glances at his watch – 8 p.m. Being outside for three hours has made his checklist damp. He spent it standing in that patch of wood, sometimes taking a break to sit in an unmarked car, receiving updates from his DCs. Nothing from the hospital; nothing from house to house, except varying degrees of alarm; nothing from the roadblock.

He'd spotted a scene guard smoking a fag and throwing it to the ground.

'What's that?' he asked, pointing at the fag butt.

'What? Nothin' to do with me,' the chap said.

'Better not be,' Davy said, 'because it's going to be tested by forensics and if your DNA is anywhere near it, you'll be in big trouble.'

'OK, well, actually it might be mine,' he said, picking the butt up and putting it in his pocket.

'Victim's name is Jon-Oliver Ross,' Harriet told him, when SOCO were done. 'Banking type from London. Business card says Dunlop & Finch Wealth Management.'

'Never had call for a wealth manager myself.'

'No, me neither. I find an overdraft is all the wealth management I need,' Harriet said. 'Anyway, we need to find out why he was in Huntingdon, when he travelled in and how. Fella that did it might not be local either. We've also got a photo of a woman found in his jacket pocket. A four by six of a blonde, real stunner. She'll be an ex, so we better know who she is as soon as possible.'

SOCO discovered drips of blood at wide intervals along the footpath leading away from where the body was found, and these are being analysed. The phone found on the body is an iPhone, latest version, locked with a passcode so as good as useless. Call data from the telecom company will tell them

18

when texts were sent and to which number, but not their contents. For that, you need access to the handset. Same with apps like WhatsApp and Snapchat.

Davy stretches back, trying to release the stiffness in his shoulders. The frenetic atmosphere has calmed somewhat. The Hinchingbrooke School kids have all gone home, there are no other reports of anyone being stabbed, so it's looking less and less like a random psycho on the rampage, which doesn't surprise him because it's almost never a random psycho. Relationships are what drive people to murder, in Davy's experience.

DC Kim Delaney appears before him, her arms arranged like a forklift, piled with folded clothes. 'Change of clothing for Judith Cole,' she says. 'Brought in by her husband. He's downstairs.'

'D'you want to talk to her about changing out of her clothes?' Davy says. 'Better coming from you, really.'

'Why?' Kim asks.

'Oh, you know, you being,' he coughs, 'you know, a woman.'

'So I have to have all the underwear chats, is that it?'

Davy colours up. It'd be just his luck to fall foul of some kind of mishandling of the politics of the sexes.

'No, no, of course not. I'll do it then, shall I?' he says.

'Don't be a twat, Davy. I was only joking.'

'Oh,' says Davy. 'Oh, right.'

MANON

As they turn out the light and close Solly's door, Manon whispers to Fly, 'You're so good with him.'

She can hear her neediness, as well as the distant sound of Sol singing to himself; he will sleep on his front, bottom in the air like the ruck in a blanket.

They stomp downstairs, Manon with one hand on Fly's shoulder. 'Hungry?' she says.

He doesn't reply and she's used to this. She'll often have to say things five or six times before he responds. This is not particular to Fly – she's heard of parents hauling their children for hearing tests, the doctor saying witheringly, 'There's a difference between not being able to hear and not listening.'

'I'll need your help when this one comes,' she says, her other hand on her bump, and even as she says it she thinks, *leave the poor boy alone*, remembers some parent or other at school saying, 'Never plead with children' and the way she nodded, thinking, I'm always pleading with children. It's my base position.

Lighten up, she tells herself. *He's all right.*

And yet he isn't.

Five days ago, the school office called at 9 a.m. to say Fly hadn't arrived at school.

'I don't understand it,' Manon said. 'He left half an hour ago in his uniform. Where is he?'

'I was hoping you'd know the answer to that.'

'Leave it with me,' she said.

First thing she did was run out of the house, jogging the route of his walk to school, all the while on her mobile phone, checking admissions at the hospital, calling Fly's mobile over and over.

She drove around Huntingdon, paced the high street, barging in and out of cafés. She wondered whether to call it in, really scare him with a police search but she had a gut feeling he'd come in for tea. He wasn't a baby, wasn't *her* baby. He had lived without any assistance from her for ten of his twelve years.

Other thoughts tugged at her: he's been mugged, he's in some trouble he can't get out of, he had his buds in his ears as a car mowed him down. She checked the hospital again.

He came in carrying his schoolbag, at a calculated 3.45 p.m. – trying to pass it off. Bag by the banister, shoes off, uniform dishevelled.

'Don't give me that,' she said, her body shaking, wanting to hit him.

'What?' he said.

'Look at your phone.'

He looked at it. 'Twenty-eight missed calls.'

'So what was that performance all about? I've been worried sick.'

He sniffed. Shrugged.

'Where've you been?'

'Home,' he said.

It was like a sinkhole opening up beneath her.

* * *

21

He has gone to watch TV while she puts the pasta on. Endless pasta, endless cooking it, throwing it in the bin, cooking it again, emptying the dishwasher, loading the dishwasher.

He calls her 'Mum' only sporadically – consciously, to please her or as a deliberate expression of connection. When he is unthinking, she is 'Manon'. They are mother and son by degrees, not innately and not to their core.

'How was school?' she asks, serving his spaghetti.

No response.

'Fly, how was your day?'

'Shit, as usual.'

The truancy took her into the head's office – a discussion about how to help Fly settle, in-school strategies (greater teacher focus), support at home (in this she read criticism). Fly promised not to do it again, said he understood it was about his own safety. To be fair, he looked shaken by the adult response. Perhaps he'd never been under such intense adult scrutiny before and he found it unexpected. The trouble with this sort of thing, she thinks now, lying in bed with a book flattened onto her chest, is she can't solve it. She can't solve Fly, can't make him better overnight. She must let his feelings granulate over time and often she finds it impossible to summon the patience to back off. She wants to work on him like a case. She should have more faith.

She's roused from dozing by the sound of Ellie coming in and by a reawakening anger (she is angry so much of the time and it is *exhausting*). She must have words. Ellie cannot leave Sol alone with Fly whenever she wants; Fly who is after all only 12, much as he seems older, and not old enough to bear responsibility for a 2-year-old, certainly not when there is the possibility of the Internet within a thousand-mile radius.

DAVY

Kim has placed the clothes on the table in front of Mrs Cole, saying, 'So, if you could change out of all your clothes. Your husband has brought you some clean things to wear. Put everything in this evidence bag if you wouldn't mind.'

'Evidence bag? You want my clothes?' says Mrs Cole, taking the brown paper bag from Kim with a shaking hand.

'We'll need to send them to forensics, yes,' says Davy.

'What, even my underwear?' she asks, with a brittle laugh.

'Why not your underwear?' Kim says, looking at her very directly. Eyeballing her, Davy would go so far as to say.

'Just seems a bit . . .' Mrs Cole begins. The blood has dried to a crust on her cheek and neck and has made her hair stiff.

'These things can feel intrusive,' Davy says, 'but there's nothing to worry about. Your things will be returned to you in due course. When you're ready, we'll start the interview, OK?'

He and Kim close the door behind them and walk in silence along the corridor. At the turn of the stairs up to the second floor, Kim says, 'What's in her undies that she doesn't want us to look at?'

Would Kim know the meaning of her clothing, Davy wonders, in the way Manon would? Not the clothing sent to forensics – well those, yes, as well – but her clothing in general: the colours, the price bracket, the shop they came from. These were all markers that Manon could 'read'. He's not sure Kim is feminine in that way. Oh Lord, is he being sexist? Not feminine then; *judgemental.* Manon was master of the snap judgement, which often contained a kernel of truth.

The clothes Judith Cole has changed into are smart and unadorned: navy cardigan with a funny wavy edge and no buttons, very white T-shirt, so white it could have come straight from the packet. Dark, well-cut jeans. Everything new-looking. The blood-stained clothes, from what he could tell beneath the dark burgundy discolouration, were in a range of colours he would describe as light brownish, though he's aware that there are more sophisticated words for it. Mushroom? Apart from her jeans, which were white – before she cradled a stab victim, that is.

Judith Cole is well turned out, that much he can see as he returns to interview room one and sets his pad down on the table.

'Is my husband still downstairs?' she asks. He hasn't set the tape yet.

'He is, yes,' says Kim.

'There's really no reason for him to stay. Our house is only a five-minute walk from here.'

Kim remains silent. She told Davy earlier she likes to create discomfort in interviews, said it provides the space for confession. Davy's acute sense of embarrassment can barely tolerate this.

24

'I can't see what help he would be; he wasn't even there,' Mrs Cole adds.

'Right, here we go,' Davy says, as the long beep rings out from the recording device.

He lists the date, time and people in the room.

'Mrs Cole, you live on Snowdonia Way, is that correct?'

'Yes.'

She confirms she's 44 and works in insurance, is married to Sinjun Cole, which she spells more than three times for Davy who cannot understand why she seems to be spelling out 'St John'. Eventually she does it so aggressively, he drops the subject. The Coles have 12-year-old twin boys attending Hinchingbrooke School, situated opposite the crime scene and adjacent to Snowdonia Way.

'Did you know the victim, Jon-Oliver Ross?' Davy asks.

'No, I've never seen him before.'

'Can you describe what happened when you came across the victim?'

'Yes, I was facing the park and he was walking towards me. I saw him swaying, really weaving from side to side and I thought he was drunk, so I started to think of ways to avoid him but then he fell, right there in front of me. Something about the way he fell – his legs literally went from under him – I knew it wasn't right. I could see he was ill. I rushed over to him and saw the blood coming from his chest. He was awake but he was panicking. He was really very distressed. I had his upper body in my lap. I called the ambulance on my mobile and I held him, which is why I got so soaked in his blood.' She puts a hand gingerly to the side of her face. 'His eyes were rolling back in his head, his chest was going up and down. I was trying to comfort him, saying, "Help is coming, hang on in there, stay awake," that sort of thing.

25

He whispered something which I didn't hear so I put my head next to his mouth and he said, "Sass".'

'Sass? S-A-S-S?' says Davy, pen poised on his notepad, not wishing to open up another spelling debacle.

Mrs Cole shrugs. 'I couldn't understand it either. Perhaps it wasn't even a word, more like an exhalation. But he repeated it. I wondered if he was trying to say "mass" if he was religious – a Catholic. But he said it again, "Sass". A name, perhaps?'

'And why were you in the woods at that time, Mrs Cole?' asks Kim.

'You can call me Judith,' she says with a wrinkling of her nose, which Davy supposes is intended to be friendly. 'I was taking the dog out for a walk – I crossed Hinchingbrooke Park Road with the intention of going to the open ground where I can let him off the lead. He can run about there.'

'And what was your dog doing, when you were seeing to the victim?'

'I'm sorry?'

'Where was the dog?' repeats Kim.

'Sorry, I don't understand what you're asking me,' says Judith, shifting in her seat.

'It's a simple question. You drop to your knees to cradle a dying man. Where's the dog?'

'Oh, right, well, I didn't really notice. I suppose he was snouting around the verges somewhere, you know what dogs are like. Sniffing tree roots, that kind of thing.'

'We didn't see him at the crime scene. The dog. Did you lose track of him?'

'No, no, I didn't lose him. He's back at home. My husband must've taken him – picked him up, I mean.'

She has flushed. She flaps at her cardigan to cool herself

down. Is she of an age for a hot flush? Davy isn't versed in such things.

'I'm not under any suspicion, am I?'

'Why d'you ask that?' says Kim.

'Only, you're talking to me as if I were a suspect.'

'No we're not.'

'Why are you asking me all these questions when I'm just an innocent bystander?'

'You were the last person to see the victim alive,' says Kim. 'That makes you a significant witness.'

DAY 1
15 DECEMBER

'Time, everyone – time is of the essence,' Davy says to the 8 a.m. briefing – a semi-circle of grey-faced detectives who haven't been to bed. Priorities—'

Harriet coughs.

Davy looks at her, flushes; steps aside.

Harriet's voice is loud and strong. 'Jon-Oliver Ross,' she informs the team. 'Thirty-eight years old, of Holland Park, west London. Wealth manager to high-net-worth individuals at a private bank called Dunlop & Finch. This victim was well-to-do, probably well connected. First priority while we wait for forensics is his journey to Huntingdon. Did he come by car or train? I want CCTV off the stations including King's Cross. Did he travel alone or did our perp mark him? There will be a lot of financial work on this one and yes, I'm looking at you Colin Brierley.'

Colin is MCU's resident nerd – an expert in technology, the police investigations database HOLMES and the minutiae of financial records. Colin can tolerate vast panoramas of tedious detail, where others glaze over and lose not merely their thread but the will to live. Colin, though, has a childish excitement about the more inanimate side of police work. He doesn't like to leave the office and so is handed laptops and iPads, phone records or reams of bank statements and he can sit and sit, drilling down into them with a kind of prurient glee. Colin is also the least politically correct man in East Anglia, and for this accolade he has seen off stiff competition.

Harriet has finished and the silence gives space for a discussion, so Davy says, 'Who or what is Sass?' Just to open it up, really.

'Person who killed him?' says Kim.

'Judith Cole might have killed him,' Davy says.

'That's a bit of a stretch – they didn't know each other by all accounts,' says Harriet.

'Something about her isn't right,' Kim says. 'Her husband told us he was unexpectedly working at home at four thirty-ish, the time she went to *walk the dog*' – at this Kim makes large quotation marks in the air – 'but he says the dog was lying on his feet the whole time.'

'Should we question the dog?' asks Colin.

'Yeah, let's *ruff* him up,' says Kim, making a little barking sound.

'Where were the children?' Harriet asks.

'At a sports club at the school,' Kim says.

'Ross's next of kin,' Harriet says to the room. 'Gareth and Branwen Ross, mum and dad, from north Wales. I sent plod round this morning to notify them, so we should expect them sometime today or tomorrow. In their eighties. They'll be knocked sideways, so respect and care, everyone, yes?'

In Davy's periphery, Manon ambles in through the double doors carrying her usual paper bag of pastries and a coffee. She has a rolling gait these days, as well as a double chin, as if someone has attached a bicycle pump to her backside and inflated her. She hails team four across the room, saying, 'Don't mind me,' and Davy can tell she's wanting to sidle in on the briefing. She'll perch on a desk and Harriet will be all ears, awaiting her pearls of investigative wisdom. Well, he's not having it.

'Boss,' he whispers to Harriet, nodding in Manon's direction, 'shouldn't we keep it confidential, it is a murder briefing . . .'

'Oh for fuck's sake, Davy, it's only Manon. She'll nod off in a minute.'

'Who was he then?' says Manon, breathless. She is smiling at Harriet and Davy can see the vicarious excitement on her face. 'Your posh stiff,' she says. 'Got an ID yet?'

'Jon-Oliver Ross,' says Harriet, peering into Manon's paper bag. 'Have you got an apricot one of those? Rich banker type, from Lon—'

'Fuck,' says Manon.

'What?' says Harriet.

'*Fuck*,' Manon says again, feeling behind her for a surface on which to perch or steady herself. 'He's Solly's dad. Jon-Oliver is Ellie's ex.'

Manon

'Only met him a couple of times, for like five minutes, but he'd started having contact in the last six months. Wanting to see Solly. That'll be why he was here – in Huntingdon, I mean.'

Her mind is whirring, too full to listen to what Harriet is saying in reply. She must tell Ellie. Should she just blurt it out? Will Ellie be upset? Does some corner of her carry a residue of love for him, like a cupboard shelf that hasn't been wiped? Does she harbour faint hopes of a reconciliation? Or will she not care? Perhaps she'll be relieved that he's out of her hair.

No, she thinks, Ellie had come round to the idea of Jon-Oliver playing a part in Solly's life. Visits once a month had been accommodated, though Manon was usually either working or on her way out when they occurred. The thought of Solly brings tears to Manon's eyes (tears come easily these days) – no chance of a father now. All the potential of that relationship cut down, before it could begin. It is a tragedy for Solly.

The sound of Harriet's voice becomes louder and clearer as Manon rejoins the present. She becomes aware that the three of them – she, Harriet and Davy – have moved into Harriet's office.

31

'Where's Ellie now?' Harriet is saying, pacing behind her desk; coiled spring, hitching at her bra straps. Harriet's body is sinewy, taut because she's a ball of constrained movement – a rubber band at full stretch, wanting to ping. *Physically, Manon thinks, we couldn't be more different. I have no inner spring. I am in constant preparation for sitting down.*

'Home with Sol I guess,' says Manon. 'They were there when I left for work.'

'Let's bring her in for interview,' Harriet says, half to herself and half to Davy. 'What can she do for childcare?' she asks Manon.

'Childminder'll take Sol at short notice,' says Manon. 'Go easy on her. Look, can I break the news to her? I don't know how she'll—'

'You know you can't,' says Davy. 'You're connected to the case. We'll need to keep you away from all future briefings. And you're not allowed to search the database or ask officers about the case.'

'He really needs to calm his tits,' Manon says to Harriet.

'That's enough, you two,' says Harriet.

Manon realises Davy wants to tell Ellie himself so he can watch her, see how she reacts. Everyone close to the victim is a suspect and how they take the news is part of a close-circuit observation that is often disguised as sympathy and support. *We are giving you a liaison officer to keep you informed/watch your every move and report it back to the investigation.*

'One more thing, Manon,' says Davy. 'Where was Ellie yesterday afternoon and evening?'

'Am I being interviewed?' asks Manon, placing a protective hand on her bump. 'Because if I am, I want all the proper gear – recording device and everything.'

DAVY

'Should we put a trace on Judith Cole's phone?' he says, now that he and Harriet are alone. 'See what she was really doing in the woods at that time? Kim thinks she wasn't walking the dog.'

Harriet has closed the door to her office and is pacing, the wings of her jacket pinned back by her hands on her hips. 'Nah, Judith Cole's not the issue. Woman from across the road who didn't know him? Who cares what she was doing in the park? We don't have grounds for a trace.'

'Except her being the last person to see him alive, and also lying,' Davy points out.

'Yes, but she might be lying for some other reason. Just because she called it in, doesn't put her in line for investigation – you know the Samaritan rule. Priority is questioning Ellie Bradshaw. She's the person who can give us the most on Ross – who he was, who might have wanted to stab him.'

'What are our main lines, boss?'

'I'd say financial work and exes – so that's Ellie. And the photo in his jacket – the blonde. We need to find out who she

33

is. Maybe she's Sass. There's a strong money motive, with someone like him.

'Judith Cole has come in for re-interview,' Davy says.

'Has she? Right, OK, you can have another go at her – *gently*, Davy – just to fill in the gaps in her statement while we wait for Ellie Bradshaw to come in. But no more than that – husband's a lawyer, I don't want a complaint. And Davy? Take Kim with you. Sounds like she was doing a very good job last time.'

Davy is upended by jealousy, like a small boy in rough surf, while the adult in him says, 'Righto, boss.'

'Your husband says you weren't walking the dog,' Kim says, as soon as the bleep sounds, without warning or preamble.

Judith Cole blanches to the colour of her semi-sheer white blouse, which has a white vest visible beneath. At her throat is a sparkling pendant, a single diamond on a silver chain. Unlike the last time they saw her, she is freshly blow-dried and wearing immaculate makeup.

'I did have the dog,' she says, though Davy hears uncertainty in her voice. 'He must be mistaken.'

'Why would you walk over a busy main road to Hinchingbrooke Park when there's a nicer one at the end of your road, which is nearer?' Kim asks.

'I don't think it's nicer,' says Mrs Cole. 'I like Hinchingbrooke Park. I can let the dog off the lead and he can run around.'

'It was pitch dark though,' says Kim. 'Seems a bit odd.'

'Yes, it was dark, but it wasn't late – only four-ish. Do you have a dog?' Mrs Cole asks.

Kim and Davy are silent.

'Well, you see, if you had a dog, you'd know that owning one means venturing out in snow, hail, darkness, you name it. A dog's gotta do what a dog's gotta—'

'Davy?' Harriet is at the door. 'A word, please.'

He and Kim step outside.

'CCTV from King's Cross has come in. I'd like you to take a look.'

'Right, so there's Ross,' Harriet says, pointing at the screen. They are standing around Colin's computer, looking at the grainy images of King's Cross station platform as people make their way to board the train.

Davy watches Ross put his ticket into the barrier and walk through it. He strides down the platform with confidence, coat well cut. He looks like a businessman on his way to a meeting that will not challenge him greatly. His face is unfazed, neither angry nor anxious. *How little we know of what lies ahead.*

'Look at this fella,' Harriet says.

'Who?'

Harriet is leaning over Colin and tapping on his keyboard to set the tape back a few frames. 'There.'

She points at a big man, bald with a black smudge at his ear, possibly an earpiece. He wears a bomber jacket and underneath it he is stocky and muscled, causing his arms to sit wide. The image quality is poor. He is coming through the ticket barriers shortly after Ross.

'He's looking at Ross like he's dinner,' Harriet says.

Even on grainy CCTV footage, they can all see the man's focus is on his quarry, who is just ahead of him. He glances down briefly to get his ticket from the barrier, but then his eyes are back on Ross, hurrying to keep up with him and then boarding the same carriage.

'Who is he? That's what we need to find out,' Harriet says.

They all straighten, away from the screen.

'I've looked at the Huntingdon CCTV and this chap does

not get off the train with Ross, so where does he get off? That's question one,' Harriet says. 'And where does he go? It's identifying him that's going to be the problem.'

'What's the timing on that?' Davy asks. 'We need to get the information off that ticket machine.'

'So, Ross goes through the barrier at 3.08 and forty seconds. The other guy is going through twenty seconds later, so at 3.09 p.m. exactly. We're going to need the station staff to identify whether his ticket was bought with a card.'

'Might've paid cash,' says Davy. 'We should also capture the rest of his journey at the London end, off station CCTV and underground, roads.'

'We could email his picture to local forces, see if anyone recognises him,' Kim suggests.

'How about *Crimewatch*?' Davy says. '*Do you know this man?*' Everyone groans.

'I don't think we're ready to be buried in a gazillion false leads just yet,' says Harriet. 'But he's marking him, right? I mean, he's definitely marking him.'

The others nod, Davy regretting he is not more reassuring in the face of her need for it. There is so much to do, so many tiny steps to complete in just this fragment of the case. He can feel himself getting into a state, a feeling of panic which renders him inactive when what he needs to do is hurry up. And forensics will be in tomorrow, which will present them with still more avenues for inspection. And he hasn't even resolved the dog-no-dog question and the small matter of why Judith Cole is lying. Not to mention the fact he's starving. And who, or what, is 'Sass'?

'Are you all right, Davy?' Harriet asks.

He realises he has been rubbing his brow and frowning at the floor.

36

'Yes boss, I'm fine. Just wondering where to begin,' he says, with a weak smile. He wishes his face was more Jack Reacher, less Charlie Brown. 'I'm still curious about what Ross was saying – the Sass thing.'

Harriet lifts her chin – a kind of worried nod – and Davy wonders if his display of anxiety will make her fearful she's put the wrong man on the job. He needs inspiration – the kind of moment when the memory of a phrase in interview, an unconscious connection made, an imaginative idea of an avenue to try, all these coalesce into investigative brilliance. Combined with luck, you can sometimes crack them that way.

But not when you're desperate, overloaded and vaguely panicking.

Kilburn, north London

Bernadette

—sting testing one two three.

Stop. Rewind. Record.

Right, my memo of evidence. Most people would record this on their phones but I can't work mine. It's an android and I've only just worked out how to find a number and dial it. Anyway, Sanjeev had one of these knock-off dictaphones on the market, so here we go. I am Birdie Fielding and this is a true and accurate account of everything that's happened. I apologise now if I go off the point a bit.

I came out like anyone would – to see what all the tooting and commotion was about. I heaved out through the door of the Payless Food & Wine, could see them all gathering on the corner where Iceland is. I turned over the 'Closed' sign and locked up.

And out into the crowd – the rubberneckers eager for a glimpse of misfortune. Wheelie shoppers, niqabs, prams, hoop earrings. A whole mass on the pavement, spilling into the road. The air was soft outside Shoe Zone and Palace Amusements

– this was back in November, ever so mild. I remember thinking, *this is nice, should've got out sooner.*

I pushed through to the centre. I'm not one to loiter at the back. I spotted Nasreen from the cash and carry, who smiled at me. Never liked Nasreen. Competitive. Always asking me how busy I am at Payless. I smiled back as if we were friends.

Now I saw what they were all staring at – a body on the ground, thrown there by a car I shouldn't wonder, but she was coming round, squeezing her eyes as if she was in pain. Not dead then. And people were beginning to shuffle away with their disappointment at her being alive. She lay there, a mass of skirts like an upended toilet doll. Everything black: lace, broderie anglaise, in layers – and DM boots poking out. Her eyes were fluttering, black kohl pencil against porcelain skin, and she must've spotted the few remaining stragglers getting their mobiles out to call 999 because she shook her head saying, 'No, no. I'm OK. I'll get up in a minute.' Then she opened her eyes fully – I could see it was a struggle – and her gaze fell upon me. I was bending right over her by this point. She signalled to me so I put my face next to hers. She didn't smell how you expect Goths to smell – no cheapo joss sticks or Body Shop musk. She smelled expensive. Citrussy.

'No cops,' she whispered to me, 'no ambulance. Can you get me into your shop?'

Why was she asking me? Well, it wasn't the first time we'd met, was it?

It's not at all like me to help somebody. My gut instinct is to keep out of the way of other people's needs and wants. I live by a policy of non-intervention: I don't want to send in ground troops and never be able to get them out. So I was already out of my comfort zone when Nasreen's dad, Sathnam, helped me carry the Goth into Payless, depositing her at the foot of the stairs to my flat.

She was slumped and I wondered if she was losing consciousness. I put my arms around her neck and tried to hoist her up the stairs like a body in a life jacket – me being the life jacket.

She grimaced, pushed her head to one side. 'I can't breathe . . .'

'You think you've got problems,' I said, panting.

I was forced to change position. I tried the bridal lift and let me tell you, it required Herculean strength to get all 20 stone of me and all of her up those stairs. Each step was a heaving stomp, the kind Frankenstein's monster would take. At the top, once the front door was flung open (and that was a world of pain, her propped against the wall while I fumbled for my keys), I pitched towards the sofa and deposited her down on it with some force.

I collapsed to my knees, panting, then looked up at Tony, there on the wall, and crossed myself – I don't know why, I figured it's what he would have wanted – and said, 'Sweet Jesus, Tony, I hope she doesn't die on me. Not in my flat.'

She didn't die.

She slept. For a couple of hours, as it goes. Then she seemed to come round, though her eyes were still closed, and she shook her head from side to side, saying 'They're coming to get me. They're going to get me.'

I gave Tony a look, which said, 'We've got a right one here.' Because there's only one thing worse than a Goth, and that's a paranoid Goth. A Goth with conspiracy theories.

Why did she pick me? Well, she'd been coming into my shop for a few months, since the heatwave last summer. I recognised a kindred spirit because despite it being 30 degrees, she wore a long-sleeve black T-shirt, black trousers with all manner of rips and rivets, and DM boots. I, too, was clad from my wrists to my ankles and nearly dying in the heat. Anyone who is fat will recognise the reluctance to bare flesh, even in tropical temperatures. Perhaps it wasn't flab she was covering up – impossible to know the state of her physique under all that garb – and anyway, who knows why Goths keep it under wraps? But I nodded at her capacious sleevage and said, 'Sweltering, isn't it? Still, nice day for Lambrini, that'll be £2.50 please,' and handed her bottle of sweet pear wine back to her across the counter. It was to be a couple more weeks before she said a word to me.

At first it was just a faint, 'Hiya,' from under a canopy of kohl black eye pencil. Then, come September, she shivered, and said, 'Season's turning.' Quite the poet.

She always bought Lambrini – the drunkard's tipple of choice. Even the millionaire bloke who invented Lambrini drank himself to death, cheap and swift. I assumed she was taking it to a bench in Kilburn Grange, to join the other winos congregating there. They sit slumped, talking shite, seeping piss, and watching the ladies in hijabs on the outdoor gym equipment.

Then, about a month before the incident that flattened her in front of the Payless Food & Wine (so this would've been October), she came into the shop swaying, approached the counter with her bottle as usual, and promptly sank to the floor. I leaned over it, said, 'Are you all right?' but there was no response.

She was out cold.

I dragged her to the back of the shop, where there's a frayed old armchair (which I'll be honest, doesn't smell too good) and allowed her to sober up out there. So by the time the accident happened in November, we were quite close really.

So, back to her being out cold on my sofa: she was sleeping and sleeping, perhaps working off months of the Lambrini in her system, perhaps recovering from whatever damage the car had done when it hit her. For a time, I moved around her laid-out body in the lounge, sort of wafting in and out, clattering a bit, washing things up, hanging some laundry in the box room – generalised fussing which got louder the more I wanted her to wake up. I began wondering if it would be all right to leave her on her own or if it was all a ruse and she'd leap up and steal all my stuff the minute my back was turned. The more time went on, the more unlikely this seemed – perhaps I got used to her and so feared the stranger in her less. I went downstairs and opened up the shop, thinking that she couldn't leave the flat without passing me at the till. Things were pretty quiet. I popped up a few times to check on her, but nothing.

It was kind of boring waiting for her to wake up, so I had this idea that I should go and buy her a towelling robe for when she came round. She'd be wanting a bath, I reasoned, and you can't step out of a nice hot bath and immediately Goth yourself up, can you? It's quite mad what you think of when you're out of your comfort zone, and someone being in my flat was way out of my comfort zone.

I could have gone to Primark which is right by the Payless on the Kilburn High Road, but I'm quite tight by nature, and what the fuck was I doing buying a complete stranger a bathrobe anyway? So I headed to the British Heart Foundation shop by Argos.

I'll tell you the most annoying thing about being fat – the weight! No, I mean the actual weight: carrying it around.

42

Walking anywhere does me in. If you're not heavy, you cannot imagine what it feels like for your limbs to pull you down with every step. Imagine lifting pillars of concrete each time you place a step. Imagine gravity being such a force in your life that you're pulling against it with every movement. That's what it's like being me. I'm lugging myself places. Before I'd even crossed the road outside Poundland, I was out of puff.

I got this bathrobe – pink, a bit scratchy but serviceable – in the British Heart Foundation shop. I know she would have liked a black one, being a Goth, but how many black towelling bathrobes do you see in the shops? I like looking in charity shops, browsing, but I can never find anything to fit – everything's tiny. I see it as evidence that everyone else is expanding, too. I am not alone, if the charity shops are anything to go by – full of size 8s and 10s, but no lovely roomy upper sizes. No one's shedding the size 20s as far as I can see, because taking weight off? It's easier to broker peace in Syria or get to grips with quantitative easing.

Once I got into the flat, I was surprised to see the sofa empty and I looked at Tony, as if to say, 'What've you done with her?' I thought I was stuck with a size 10 towelling robe which I wouldn't even be able to get one arm into, but then she appeared, her face seeming bruised from sleep, her hair matted to one side of her head.

'How are you feeling?' I said.

'Better,' she said, but she was walking gingerly, a hand to her side.

'I think you should see a doctor,' I said.

'No.'

I could see she was in pain because of the way she was holding herself. Movement was causing her to wince. *Perhaps she's broken something*, I thought. How could a car hit you and not cause a fair bit of damage? I'd want a doctor to look me over. I'm at an age where death is more a distinct possibility than a distant dream.

She sat slowly, lowering herself by increments down onto the sofa.

'I'm Birdie, by the way,' I said. 'Bernadette, but everyone calls me Birdie.' I don't know why I said 'everyone' – not as if I've got an entourage.

'Angel,' she said, but I didn't believe that was her name. I mean, who is called that in real life? Also, it was as if she was saying it for the first time.

'Cup of tea?' I said. 'Or would you like a bath? I bought you a bathrobe.' And I held out my charity shop plastic bag.

'That was kind of you,' said Angel, peering into the bag reluctantly, and I wished I hadn't bothered.

Her black hair hung in wet rats' tails. She was back on the sofa, with her feet up. The bathrobe, now I could see it in a better light, was more peach than pink and had an unfortunate Care Bear on the pocket.

I could examine her face, too, without all that black muck around her eyes. She was a corker – I mean, not mildly attractive. I mean a proper looker, top class. Pale skin without a single blemish, and gas-blue eyes that you couldn't help doing a double take over. Black was definitely not her hair colour, not with eyes like that. I'd say she'd be auburn or maybe even redhead. Her peach-coloured lips were what the term 'bee-stung' was invented for – they gave her a slightly teary look. She was maybe not supermodel beautiful, but she could definitely get paid to do a catalogue or the Marks & Sparks website.

Another thing I knew for sure at that moment: she wasn't

44

a proper Goth. No offence to Goths, but they're quite often minging.

She was looking around my living room – the velveteen sofa on which she was curled, tobacco-coloured with ruffled seams; the two recliners, facing the telly; the nets, which were not grey because I'd soaked them in Vanish only the day before; the swirly carpets, gas fire, knobbly Anaglypta on the walls. I'd not noticed before that my decor was rocking an elderly vibe, though I'm only in my fifties myself, which I had probably inhaled from Nanny Fielding. I love my lounge: it's the perfect place to sit in front of the television and pop things in your gob.

'Why've you got a picture of Tony Blair on your wall?' Angel asked.

'Because I love him,' I said. 'I'm the last person on earth who still thinks he's marvellous.'

Oh he has his faults, it's not that I don't realise that. For example, although he's even more handsome than he used to be, now that he's grey and perma-tanned from the Middle East, he's always travelling and that'd get me down, him being away all the time.

So I'm not blind, I know he's not perfect. The God thing, that makes me uneasy, and towards the end he let it be known how irritated he was by the general public and that was probably a mistake. And he's partial to making a bob or two, but which of us isn't? The whole B-Liar thing, though: the epic righteousness of it would be enough to send anyone postal.

And in his heyday, my goodness! He united everyone. He didn't make you hang your head in shame. All those years the Labour Party suffered with the bad comb-overs, the stumbling on the beach and then Tony came along, our shiny straight-talking saviour. We almost couldn't believe he was left wing.

45

He made me feel safe: I could sleep well knowing his hand was on the tiller. Three terms he gave us and now it's as if that was a crime.

I got up and kissed my two fingers, then planted them on Tony's lips. His cross/stern eyebrows seemed to raise at this and he appeared to smile, in that way that said, 'Let's not let this go too far.' A bit Presbyterian, a bit hair shirt.

We sat in amiable silence, then I said, 'I'm not being funny, but have you ever thought of modelling?'

She pushed some wet hair over her face and sucked on a strand. Perhaps she was embarrassed. 'Yeah, I have. Ages ago. It's not a good business for girls. Makes them vulnerable. You can get caught up in things.'

'What things?'

'Dodgy stuff. There are blokes who hang around models like, well, like hyenas round meat.'

'I wouldn't know,' I said. 'The modelling scouts appear to have passed me by.' The self-deprecating joke – safe haven to fatties everywhere.

'Actually, plus size is a growing area,' she said and I flushed. I wasn't prepared for her to acknowledge the elephant in the room quite so readily. 'Sorry,' she said. 'I don't mean . . . You're not big.'

'Thanks,' I said but the atmosphere had darkened and she got up off the sofa.

'Better get dressed,' she said.

'Shouldn't we talk about what happened?' I said. 'About the car accident. About going to the police?'

'Nothing serious,' she said. 'Not worth making a fuss.'

Angel opened the bathrobe and showed me her torso – the left side. She had a huge bruise – deep red, black in places – from her bra strap down to the waistband of her knickers.

'It's feeling a lot better,' she said.

'I just don't get it,' I told her. Then I went to the kitchen to wash up our tea mugs. 'You were hit by a car and you don't want to tell the police about it?'

Angel moved to stand at my bathroom mirror, in order to re-Goth. My flat is tiny, so it's easy to talk across rooms.

I said to her, 'What if the bloke was drunk and he goes and hits a child next?'

'It was probably my fault,' she said. 'Maybe I wasn't looking where I was going. I think I stepped out without thinking.'

'CCTV will show what happened,' I said. I had come out into the hall, drying my hands on a tea towel and watching her layer awful black pencil all over her eyelids. Crying shame, shading over such a lovely face. 'I don't think there's anywhere on earth with more CCTV than Kilburn High Road. And anyway, even if you did step out, it's still an offence to drive away from an accident. He should've stopped at the very least to make sure he hadn't killed you.'

'Yeah, well, he didn't, did he, so let's just drop it, OK?'

She'd finished with the kohl pencil and mascara, and was zipping up her makeup bag. She came out of the bathroom and was peering in at my box room – it had a single mattress on the floor and one of those concertina laundry airers, hung with stiff tea towels.

'You've got an extra room,' she said.

'Think calling it a room is stretching it.'

'Can I ask a favour?' she said. 'It won't be for long.'

She told me she wanted to stay a while, to get herself straight. I assumed she meant laying off the Lambrini, in which case I wasn't too sure my flat was her best bet, it being above an entire shop full of cheap spirits and tins of super-strength lager – killing the poor quicker and younger. Carlsberg Special Brew,

47

Tennent's Super and Skol Super 9%. They used to die at 65, now they die at 45, even though they look 65. But I digress.

Angel walked to the window in the lounge and lifted the nets, peered out at the street as if she was George Smiley looking for shadowy figures in doorways.

'Are you on the run from MI6?' I said, as a joke obviously, trying to change the subject away from latent alcoholism. I didn't actually think she was on the run. I don't think anyone is on the run in real life, but she turned, sharply, and said, 'Why d'you say that?'

'You're acting like you think you're in *The Bourne Supremacy* instead of sitting in a flat above the Killy High Road.' I was going to add, 'wearing too much eyeliner' but thought better of it.

'Look,' she said, still peering out from under the nets, 'there are people who would like to know where I am, and who I'd rather keep away from. That's all you need to know. I could do with a place to lie low. I could go, tonight, get a bag of stuff, if you don't mind me kipping in your box room for a while?'

I thought about saying, 'How long is a while?' But instead, I said, 'I'll think about it. Now, I've got to open up downstairs or my lovely regulars will be wondering where to get their tramp juice.'

Downstairs, turning my keys in the lock to open up, I thought about what it would be like later on, watching telly with someone there to pass the odd comment to, making a plate of carbonara for two and not eating it all myself. Asking if she'd like a bag of Frazzles and popping down to the crisp aisle. The drinking worried me a bit. I don't like drinkers, much as they are my core fan base. I don't like the feelings of risk and uncertainty they create. That said, we've all got our thing, haven't we – that zone where we're not in control? I'm quite safe around a bottle of Chardonnay. I've been known to yawn in the face of pornography. Show me a shoe shop and I can walk on by. But salty snacks? I will MOW. YOU. DOWN.

This'll shock you, but I own Payless. I don't lease it; it's not a franchise. About fifteen years ago, when I was in my mid-thirties, this lawyer managed to track me down and told me there was all this money held in trust for me and did I want to collect it, because I'd got to a responsible age when I wouldn't squander it and he was retiring, so there would be no one left who knew the details of my legacy. I guessed it was money from Mum and Dad's house, maybe from Nanny Fielding when she died. I didn't really ask any questions – like why it had taken so long to come to me.

I was working in Payless at the time, just on Saturdays – the rest of the time I was on the till in Primark and doing the odd shift on a street stall which sold lighters and knock-off Dove shower gel and the like, and so the next time I was in I asked Majid, who I worked for, how much he wanted for the shop and he laughed and laughed and laughed. And then he spoke very quickly in Urdu to his wife, and she split her sides laughing as well.

Anyway, once they'd stopped laughing, I bought it off them.

In retrospect, I realise I should've bought myself a hair-dressers. Firstly, because I've always thought I'd make quite a good hairdresser, and second because of all those surveys about professions and rates of happiness. Hairdressers are the happiest people: there's creativity, but only up to a point (too much, I've read, can send you demented; just look at poets). There's craic – plenty of chat, but not that much intimacy (intimacy being a most overrated aspect of human relationships). And hairdressing also garners a great deal of loyalty. I read that the average woman stays with her stylist for twelve years. The average marriage lasts eleven.

But primarily I should've bought myself a hairdressers because it would've limited my access to the crisp aisle.

Did you know Britain has been voted the loneliness capital of Europe? The Office for National Statistics found we have fewer friends and that we Britons don't know our neighbours and it's killing us. Loneliness is as big a health hazard as smoking fifteen fags a day, and not nearly as enjoyable.

I think it is the English way. We can't stand too much contact. We don't know where to look during intimate conversations. The web of connections, which is a comfort to southern nationalities, especially Latin people who love to hug and wail at funerals, pains the Englishman. I remember living with Nanny Fielding and all the kids at school were going on sleepovers or to each other's houses, but I didn't. I went home to my gran and we barely exchanged a word. She made baked apple with sultanas and custard and there were lace-edged antimacassars on the arms of her wing chairs. She used to smooth a tea towel across her knees, not sure why, as if she was about to dress a wounded foot or shell some peas. It was just a pointless act of fastidiousness, which annoyed me until I missed it so much. I think this is why I seem so much older than my years – the grannyish house and the solitary ways. I've taken in Nanny Fielding and I don't know any other way to live.

Anyway, without us having a conversation about it as such, Angel fetched a bag of stuff and installed herself in the box room, which started to smell of Chanel Cristalle because she sprayed it about like it was Impulse. Low-level drinking – she wasn't bladdered, but she was hugging the Lambrini pretty close. She spent a lot of time on the Internet, saving files and copying Wikipedia pages, and the rest of the time she was standing by the window, lifting the nets and watching the Killy High Road. She was furtive. When I said something, she jumped. And when I called her name, she didn't turn around.

I said, from the kitchen, 'Angel? Cup of tea?' But I had to walk into the room before she realised I was talking to her. I took it as proof that Angel was a made-up name. The question was why?

And what was her real name? What was with all the curtain twitching and mystery? And also, if I was going to make up a name for myself, I don't think I'd pick Angel, d'you know what I'm saying?

But she wasn't totally self-absorbed. I could see she was trying to make herself a pleasant house guest. A couple of days later, for example, she stood in the doorway, holding aloft two Sainsbury's bags and smiling. 'Thought I'd make burgers,' she said. 'I'm assuming you've got ketchup.'

'Do I look like the sort of person who wouldn't have ketchup?'

'You look like the sort of person who wouldn't have vinaigrette,' she said.

We decided to watch *The Hotel* on telly – one of those documentaries where people act like they're not aware they're being filmed, when in fact they're completely aware but pretending, and the programme's main aim is the Ring of Truth, as if you're peeping in unseen. Fixed-rig cameras is how they're made. Rigged and a fix, I call it. I love those shows. I love watching people without having to spend any time with them.

Angel and I had a recliner chair each, the sofa being too uncomfortable to spend an evening on. I keep it because it was

Nanny Fielding's. I have always had two recliners; I bought them as a pair from DFS. Don't ask me why – I think it seemed too sad to buy one. But there's never been anyone to sit in the second one. Talk about hopeful purchase.

In *The Hotel*, you are shown round the penthouse floor of the Carlton Mayfair, 'London's most exclusive establishment', according to the breathy voiceover. The penthouse floor has three marble bathrooms, including a 'rainforest showering experience' which plays the sounds of tropical birds and other wildlife while dappling you in a moving light show so you think you're in a glade. The penthouse floor has two grand living rooms, each with about six sofas; a cinema; a catering kitchen, should the restaurant not suit, and a treatment room for on-site massages and facials. The penthouse floor is home to Donald Trump when he visits, and the Sultan of Brunei. The King of Saudi Arabia books it for the entire month of August and installs his family, flying over his fleet of cars, which they park all over Knightsbridge and get parking tickets they'll never pay. They spend the month shopping at Harrods.

Angel and I were watching all this, the smears of ketchup hardening on our discarded plates, our feet up as if our legs were paralysed – which they were, I suppose. There is little in modern life more paralysing than the recliner chair.

'Been there,' she said, nodding at the telly.

'Yeah, right,' I said. 'Me too. Stay there all the time.'

'No, really, I have.'

I looked at her. 'You what?'

'I can prove it,' she said, pushing down with her ankles (you have to use some force, as if the recliner is unwilling to give you up) so that her chair moved into the upright mode. She left the room and came back with a bag full of Carlton Mayfair toiletries. Shampoo, conditioner, body wash. Even a pack of cotton pads and buds, which you're not supposed to put into your ears. I find it almost impossible *not* to put them in my ears.

'How come you've been to the Carlton Mayfair?' I said.

'On business,' she said simply.

'Right, yeah, business. What business would that be? Cleaning the rainforest experience?'

'No!' she scoffed, but she'd gone back to watching the telly and when I tried to ask another question, she shushed me.

Couple of days later, Angel went out – for longer this time than just to Sainsbury's, which is about a hundred yards away – and I was relieved to have the place to myself without her loitering at the windows or jumping out of her skin every time I made a noise.

I'm not sure I'm built to live with anyone. It annoyed me when she was in the bathroom or in the kitchen making herself a cup of tea. The squeaky noise she made when she opened the door to the box room annoyed me, even though it was my door – my squeak. It annoyed me that she was hardly ever out, that she liked Laughing Cow cheese. It annoyed me that I couldn't trump openly or walk from the bathroom in my pants. Sometimes the sound of her breathing was more than I could stand.

Anyway, I used the opportunity of her being out to go through her stuff.

Lots of things about this girl didn't add up. Firstly, her holdall was Chanel – with the linked ring symbol. Now, I know a knock-off when I see one, I used to sell enough of them on the market, and this holdall, which was leather, with some animal-hide areas, like a furry cow's back, was no knock-off.

Second, she had all these creams – Clarins, Crème de la Mer,

Kérastase shampoo. Posh bottles and lotions. How did she afford them? So while she was out, I took the opportunity to have a try – washed my hair with the Kérastase, tried the Crème de la Mer. I didn't use the Carlton Mayfair stuff because the size of the bottles would have made it obvious.

Third thing, I was patting through the pockets of her coat and I found there was something – the shape of a lighter but smaller – sewn into the lining at the hem. I felt around it and it was a neat rectangle. I pushed my fingers around the seam but there was no way in. Perhaps it was just a weight, to keep the fabric hanging nicely. But I doubted it.

Fourth thing (come to think of it, there was precious little about this girl that did add up): she had what can only be described as a stalker's dossier. It was a brown folder, the type that's open on two edges, and slipped inside were all these newspaper clippings, lots of them from the *FT* and the City pages of other papers. Pictures of Chinese blokes circled, names in the text highlighted. Printouts from the Forbes China Rich List.

DAVY

'I just can't believe it,' Ellie Bradshaw is saying.

They are in interview room one, Harriet and Davy across the table from Ellie, who is shaking her head, hair swaying. She's got nice hair – hasn't got Manon's ringlets. Instead it is wavy, to her shoulders, in a sort of honey shade. And it looks almost impossibly soft, like advert hair. Davy thinks it probably smells nice, of chamomile or lemon.

'So you were where, between 4 p.m. and 5 p.m. last night?' he asks.

'Me? I was home with Solly, my son.'

She's slim too, lovely dark eyes. Yes, Ellie is attractive; he can't deny that. Strange to be sitting in an interview room with her because she is so like Manon – the very same voice and mannerisms. Yet at the same time, not similar at all. Like the same pudding in a different flavour – you can enjoy the orange, but find the mint tastes a bit like washing-up liquid.

'Jon-Oliver was coming to see us – well, coming to see Solly. That'll be why he was in Huntingdon. He was due to come over today. I guess he was booked into the George Hotel last

55

night. It's only, I dunno, the fifth or sixth time he's seen our son.'

He frowns. 'Can you think of a reason why he walked in the opposite direction to the George, along the Brampton Road towards the hospital?'

Ellie is thinking. Davy can't take his eyes off her. *Maybe she'd be worried about the age gap* – Davy being ten years younger – *but if it was good enough for Susan Sarandon . . .*

'Not really,' she says. 'I mean, he knows where I work. Knew, I mean. Maybe he was coming to see me?'

'Did he know someone called Judith Cole?' Davy asks. 'Ever mention that name?'

Ellie turns down the corners of her mouth. 'Doesn't ring any bells, but Jon-Oliver knew a lot of women.'

'What about this person?' Harriet asks, placing a four-by-six photograph on the table in front of Ellie. The picture is of a blonde woman, tanned and manicured. Sunglasses on her head. The sort of person who might frequent Cannes or appear in *Hello!*

Ellie leans forward to look at the photo without picking it up. 'No,' she says.

'The photo was found on Jon-Oliver's body,' Harriet adds.

'Well it's probably his current girlfriend then,' says Ellie simply. 'She looks like his type.'

'His type?' says Harriet.

'Yes – stunningly beautiful, young, probably very bendy. And keen on cold hard cash by the looks of her.'

Bit bitter, thinks Davy.

'He didn't mention any names to you, talk about his personal life?' asks Harriet.

'We weren't really on those sort of terms,' Ellie says. 'I hadn't seen him for two years, then he contacted me out of the blue

56

last summer – July or August, I can't remember – wanting to see Solly. I was having none of it. It took me ages to get over him, and having a baby on your own . . . Well, I keep telling Manon, it's no picnic.' The reference to Manon is jarring. She is trying to remind them they're friends, Davy thinks with some irritation – all on the same side. Well, they're not. 'I had to agree to give him access. Jon-Oliver gives – gave – me money, you see.'

'He supported you?' Davy asks.

'Well, I work, but nursing doesn't make me rich. I need his maintenance payments, yes. Anyway, Jon-Oliver's on the birth certificate, so I had no choice. Since then, he's visited Solly once a month. The meetings have been awkward – Solly usually ends up crying because he doesn't know what to do with a stranger in a suit crouching on the floor next to him. Doesn't know what it means, y'know?'

'So you disliked him? Your relationship with Jon-Oliver was strained, would you say?' says Harriet.

Ellie nods. 'Strained, yes, that's fair. I didn't trust him, and I wasn't too keen on having him back on the scene. I didn't want too much involvement with him, that's how I felt – like I wanted to keep my distance. Maybe that's what made Solly cry. Babies pick up on everything in the room. But,' she gives a resigned shrug, 'I'm not the first woman this has happened to and I won't be the last. You do it for your child, even though every bit of you doesn't want to. You do it to give them the possibility of having a father. So yes, it was strained but we were trying to make room for him.'

'So you were at home the whole time, between four and five yesterday?' Davy asks.

'More or less,' she says, distracted by the bleep of her phone. 'Sorry, I just have to look at this in case it's the childminder.'

She reads the text message, then punches something into her phone – a reply, presumably. *Rude, and rather presumptuous,* Davy thinks. She looks up, saying, 'Sorry. Yes, you can ask Solly if you like. You won't get much of an answer – he's 2. Do 2-year-olds count as alibis?'

She is smiling as she says this and Davy struggles with how it might be intended – as a friendly joke?

He says, 'Did anyone else see you at home, anyone else who can confirm your whereabouts?'

'No,' she says quietly. 'Fly came home from school at about quarter to five, and I asked him to watch Solly so I could pop out. Listen, I've got to get back to my son. He's been at the childminder too long as it is.'

'Just a minute please – you had to pop out? Where to?' asks Davy.

'Oh, just into town. I had to pick up a couple of things.'

At that moment, when Davy wants to ask where and for how long, Gary Stanton enters the room. Davy cannot remember the last time the chief super came in on a key witness interview.

'How are we getting on?' Stanton asks.

Harriet's face is awash with confusion. 'Yes, all fine,' she says.

'I think if we're all done here,' Stanton says, 'we should have a quick departmental review upstairs. Shall we go? Thank you, Miss Bradshaw, for helping us with our inquiries. We will contact you should we need further assistance from you.'

'Why did he shut that down?' Davy hisses, so the department can't hear.

'I don't know,' Harriet says.

'She's a key witness and she's got no alibi. And he says, off you pop, no further questions?'

'Well, I'm not sure he was saying that exactly.'

'What was he doing in there? I mean, when was the last time the super came in on an interview? And where is he for this departmental review he was so keen to have?'

Various colleagues have gathered around them for the briefing. Harriet is glancing furtively at them and she says, 'Let's talk about this later.'

They perch on desks or at their computers, Harriet and Davy at the front.

'Right, Derry says we're not getting the PM results till tomorrow, so let's press on with other lines until forensics come in,' says Harriet.

'I did a bit of digging around at Dunlop & Finch,' Colin says. 'Head of the firm is one Markus van der Lupin, then beneath him are the two vice presidents, equally pegged as far as I can tell – Ross and this other chap, Giles Carruthers.'

Hariet nods, saying, 'So let's look closely at the structure there – any rivalries, fallings-out, that kind of thing. Very competitive, the City. Davy, you'd best head down there, interview Carruthers and the rest of the staff. Rest of you, priority is still our King's Cross chap. Who is he, where's he from and how can we collar him?'

Marie from reception has entered the room, and says, 'The Ross parents have arrived. I've shown them into interview room one.'

'Let's not keep them waiting,' Harriet says to Davy.

'I'm very sorry,' Davy says, 'for your loss. This must be a difficult time.'

They nod, but don't speak. Both are little; beady. Grey hair in a scribble above faces mottled with sunspots. They have cried, he can see that from the puffiness around their eyes, but he can see their reserve also, making them contain their grief

59

in front of strangers. Not like some he's done this kind of interview with. Some like to wail and holler as if volume proves how much they feel.

'When did you last see your son?' Davy asks.

'Last Christmas,' Mr Ross says.

Davy waits. They're not the sort to elaborate. Rural people, Harriet said.

'Right, so that's nearly a year ago.'

'He always said how busy he was,' Mrs Ross says. 'Said he'd like to come and see us more, but he couldn't get away from work. We live out of the way. Not easy to get to. He was due to come this Christmas again.'

'Did you know about the cruise?' Davy asks.

They look at one another. Shake their heads.

'He had purchased two tickets in your names for a cruise on the Crystal Serenity. Around the Caribbean. For two weeks in January.'

'Ah, no,' Mr Ross said, shaking his head sadly. They look down at their hands. After a pause, he continues, 'It's not our way. We're not fancy people. We don't like restaurants and cruises and all that kind of thing. Jonno was always buying us that kind of thing and—'

'We didn't want him to,' Mrs Ross says.

Davy had looked up the Crystal Serenity online, its £17 million refurb complete with retractable roof above the Trident Grill, its seahorse-shaped swimming pool and on-deck golf course, a seemingly endless roster of dining opportunities. Something about it had the ring of battery-chicken coop. He could picture himself pressing his face against the cabin glass and screaming to be let off. *'Enough with the langoustine fricassee!'* He couldn't picture these two, who seemed more the cheese-on-toast kind, browsing the on-board diamond emporiums.

60

Ross's father sighs. 'We're not . . . comfortable in those situations. It sounds ungrateful now I say it.'

Mrs Ross says, 'We felt he was always trying to impress us, to shower us with gifts and whatnot. We didn't know how to say that he was enough in himself. We were so happy to have him.' She doesn't gasp or sob, but the tears leak from the edges of her eyes. Her quietness fells Davy. 'You see, we thought we couldn't have any children. We were married for twenty years and nothing at all happened. We were devastated by that but we'd come to terms with another sort of life. Then, when I was 42, Jonno came along, out of the blue.'

Davy nods, swallows.

'But children are only on loan,' Mrs Ross is saying. 'You can't keep them. We hoped he would have his own child one day, so that he might realise what we feel . . . to love someone not because of what they do but because they *are*. That they exist is wonderful, they don't have to do much more to make you proud.' Mr Ross takes her hand. She is quiet, thinking. Then she says, 'But somehow – and we don't know how this happened – it was as if the way we were, the *sort* of people we are, well . . . it wasn't the way *he* was going to be. And all these gifts, all these luxury things, were his way of saying he wanted us to be different. Oh I'm not making any sense. I'm just trying to describe the place we were in, with Jonno.'

It is not Davy's place to tell them about Solomon Bradshaw, much as he would like to comfort them with a grandchild they are not yet aware of. That's Ellie's job.

Instead, Davy says, 'Jon-Oliver, as I'm sure you're aware, was a rich man. He had moved a sum of money, rather a large sum of money, into a company registered offshore. Do you have any idea who the beneficiary of that company might be?'

Mr Ross is shaking his head. 'I know he had a few bob, but

I didn't understand his work. I don't understand about wealth management, couldn't get to grips with what he did. I make furniture for a living. Tables mostly. I take pieces of wood, and I sand them and turn them and create joints, and when they're made, someone pays me for them, and they take the table away. And that I can understand. I used to ask him again and again, but his work stayed a mystery to me.'

MANON

'Oh God, you need wine,' Manon says, pouring Sauvignon Blanc into a glass and handing it to Ellie, who's sitting at the kitchen table pushing a balled tissue into a nostril. Her eyes are red, her lips cracked. She takes the glass gratefully. 'Hang on,' says Manon, making for the doorway, 'right back . . .'

Out in the hall, she calls 'Fly! Fly?' up the stairs.

No response. She can hear the bath running, knows what they'll be doing up there. Fly will be lying on his bed reading his latest Anthony Horowitz novel, imagining himself a teen spy, while Solly squats on the carpet constructing the same dinosaur puzzle he works at every night: repetition being a source of unalloyed joy for the 2-year-old.

'Fly!' she shouts, a notch louder and with more irritation.

She weighs up her exhaustion and desire to talk to Ellie versus the need to intervene. She very much doesn't want to heave her bulk up those stairs but knows that Fly's total immersion in his book means Sol could be drawing on the walls while the bath overflows. Her belly creaks, she yawns, thinks, *fuck it*. 'Turn the tap off!' she bellows, her parting shot as she returns to her sister, whose floodgates have re-opened.

These are feelings entirely not put to bed, Manon thinks, looking at Ellie's dissolving face.

'Sorry,' Ellie says.

'Don't be.'

'It's just . . . it's just . . . there's no chance of anything now,' she says in a watery voice, plucking another tissue from the floral cube beside her, 'for him and Solly. No chance of a father for Sol. That's going to be a loss all his life. It's a fucking tragedy.' She breaks down again. 'It, it, it can't be undone. I can't ever make this better for him.'

'His parents are here, did Harriet tell you? There's a chance to give Solly some grandparents. We should invite them to stay.'

'I did,' says Ellie. 'They didn't want to but they're coming to meet Sol tomorrow.'

'Is part of it,' Manon begins, girding herself, 'that there's no chance for you and Jon-Oliver now?'

'No. No, it's definitely not that, not even in my unconscious. I'd never have gone back to him. Jon-Oliver was a great one for fresh starts, saying he was going to change, but you'd have been a complete moron to believe him. You know, when he first reappeared in the summer in London, he said, "I want to be good. I want to be a good father." And I said, "Right, and you think Solly's going to make you good? That's a lot to ask of a 2-year-old." He said, "I just think I can be a different person if you and Solly were in my life."'

'So he wanted you back? What did you say?'

'Told him he could leave me out of it.'

'Are you hungry?' asks Manon. 'I could make the tarragon chicken thing.'

'Christ, is that a threat?'

'Crisps?'

'Go on, then.'

In the getting up, opening a cupboard, emptying the Kettle Chips (sweet chilli flavour) into a bowl, Manon says, 'What was it like with Jon-Oliver?' Of course they'd discussed it in the past, but never in detail.

Ellie sighs. Sips her wine. 'He had this slept-in face – and my God he could be funny. Slightly dangerous-funny – irreverent, bit close to the wire. We'd come home from a night out, he'd mix some cocktails and then we'd go out again. And the sex—'

'Yes all right,' says Manon, shoving more crisps than seems feasible into her mouth, frightened it might be true – about all the sex she's missing out on.

'Anyway, he had all that rich boy's confidence, and I knew he was a bit of a player – you could just tell from his moves, and I'm telling you, his friends from the City were wankers, I mean boorish, sexist, the works. But Jon-Oliver . . . I suppose I thought if I was the one he settled down with, then I'd get all the sexiness and the money – the money was a really big part of it, I'm not gonna lie – and the other stuff he'd grow out of. Thought I'd be living in Holland Park and wearing taupe to yoga.'

'Nearly got there,' Manon says.

'Single mum living in Hinchingbrooke? Yep, not far off.'

'So what happened? Between you and him, I mean.'

'Playboys aren't fun when you're pregnant. They're the opposite of fun. First there was just a line over and over again on a bank statement he'd left out by accident. Awork. I Googled it. Adult work – a prostitutes' website. He came clean, said he was watching porn videos late at night, nothing more than that. But it's always more than that. The stuff they come clean about is only ever a fraction of it. To be honest, it was a disaster to have got pregnant and I say that with love in my heart for Sol.'

The thought of the unaware baby upstairs makes them both silent.

Ellie rotates her glass. 'To be honest, I'm not that surprised he's dead. I know that sounds awful, but the world he moved in . . . It was all glinting surfaces hiding God knows what. It wouldn't surprise me if he was trading for dangerous people. There was no heart . . .' Ellie is rubbing her fingers together, as if trying to assess a fabric. 'Nothing real to it, you know? He was a man without any substance. Every now and then, he'd deny himself – no coke, no prostitutes, back to the gym, kale in his NutriBullet, a really superficial bout of CBT. And then he'd rebel against the clean slate so hard it was terrifying. Jon-Oliver liked a cold kind of pleasure – sex without a relationship. I'd say it was some Russian bitch he was shagging. That'll be who stabbed him.'

They are silent again. Ellie sips her wine. Manon wishes she could have some.

'He told me some insane stories about the City. Champagne, hotels, piles of drugs, piles of girls. He told me about one party they had where they hired a whole floor of a London hotel and it ended up being a sea of naked bodies.'

'Don't get much of that in the police,' says Manon. 'Not on cold cases, certainly.'

'No, there's not much of it in nursing either. I mean there's bodies, and they're often naked, but not in a good way.'

'In general,' Manon says, 'if you're after the orgiastic experience, public sector isn't really the way to go.'

She is struck by a drip on the bridge of her nose. She touches it with her fingers, looks at the wetness, looks up at the ceiling. There is a small gathering of drips, trembling on the ceiling, waiting to fall.

'Fuck!' says Manon. 'The fucking bath!'

She gets up and makes for the hallway with every molecule of haste she can muster and generates all the speed of an 80-year-old. 'Fly! Flyyyyy! Pull the flipping plug out!!!'

Upstairs, the water is tumbling over the edge of the bathtub – rather beautifully, she notices, like an infinity pool at a posh hotel. She turns the tap off and pulls out the plug, wetting her sleeve and hearing the gushing of water down the waste pipe. The sound prompts an urgent need to pee. She grabs all the towels hanging on hooks on the wall and flings them onto the floor to soak up the wet; sighs, closes the bathroom door.

Only five months pregnant. Is it possible she will become still more ungainly?

When she emerges and walks into Fly's room, he predictably hasn't lifted his face from the page. Solly is squatting happily in his nappy. 'Dine-soar,' Solly says, pointing with his little pointy finger. He sets the universe in order with the naming of things with the pointy finger and she hopes he never grows out of it.

'Right, so thanks for flooding the bathroom, Fly,' Manon says.

He doesn't look up.

'Fly, *listen*. There was water coming through the ceiling in the kitchen. *Really! Jesus, Fly!*'

Was he this disrespectful when they were in London, or is his disdain part of her punishment for uprooting him? For being pregnant? She snatches his book away. He is forced to look up.

'What?' he asks, genuinely nonplussed. It's as if he's been in a bubble, the outside world on mute.

'You flooded the bathroom.'

'Oh my God, sorry. Did I?'

She is furious, but he genuinely didn't notice.

67

DAY 2
16 DECEMBER

MANON

They cannot take their eyes off Solomon, especially Mrs Ross.

All movement and talk swirls about them in the lounge; offers of tea, *isn't it awful, you must be devastated*, but Mrs Ross doesn't take her eyes off Solly.

Sitting forward, on the edge of the sofa, she drinks him in as he plays with his Duplo, making a tower in order to knock it down. He is delighted by knocking things down.

Fly is at school (Manon hopes). She has been tempted to walk him in each morning, to make certain he arrives, but stopped herself. The headmaster didn't think it was a good strategy either. 'You want to rebuild trust, not infantalise him,' he said.

For everyone else in the room, with grief as with illness, normal service has been suspended, hence the midday tea party.

'Isn't he like Jonno?' Mrs Ross whispers to Mr Ross. (They have not offered their first names – not, Manon suspects, because they are formal, but because the moment has passed and they are not smooth operators who can re-route the social flow.)

A smile plays about the corner of Mrs Ross's mouth as if she dare not find happiness at a moment such as this.

'The very spit,' says Mr Ross.

Their voices have a lovely Welsh song to them, but subtly and not all the time.

'We never met you,' Mrs Ross says, looking up at Ellie as if she is confused by the way in which Ellie and Jon-Oliver had this child, without marrying or meeting the parents.

'Where are your people?' Mr Ross asks. He holds his tea with one hand under the mug's base. Thick hands.

'Our dad's in Scotland,' Manon says. She is about to say, 'With our stepmother Una,' but it is all wrong. There is nothing of the mother in Una. Instead she says, 'Mum died when we were kids – teenagers.'

'Oh how terrible for you,' says Mrs Ross.

'Yes, it was,' says Manon.

Mr and Mrs Ross have gone back to drinking Solly in, as if they can soak up enough of him to take back to Wales.

'You'll have to visit us,' Mr Ross says. 'We've got a tractor, Solomon. Do you like tractors? I could take you on a ride in it.'

Sol looks up at his grandfather. Manon has been observing her nephew and he seems to have got around the difficulty of this social occasion by ignoring these elderly interlopers entirely. But the tractor is too much. He is awed by chunky vehicles. Manon has become accustomed to screeching to a halt in the car and bellowing, 'DIGGER!' She's even found herself doing this when no one is strapped into the back seat.

'Yes,' Mr Ross is saying, and his whole face crinkles in a most kindly way, 'a real tractor. Brum brum! Would you like that, Solly?'

'Trac-tor,' says Solly. He swills words, like a wine taster.

69

'Too-day' and 'birf-day' and 'Babe Buntin' when they're reading *Each Peach Pear Plum*.

'Trac-tor,' says Mrs Ross, with a look of wonderment. 'Oh he's wonderful,' she says to Ellie. 'You are wonderful,' she says to Solly.

Ellie smiles at them but Manon thinks it is brittle. Then Ellie leaves the room. She has not sat down since they arrived, first making the tea, searching for biscuits, asking where they'd like to sit, plumping cushions, offering to open or close windows, put the fire on. In and out of the room. It has reached such a pitch of fidgetry that Manon is concerned her sister is being rude. As Ellie makes for the door, she hisses, '*Can't you sit down for one fucking minute?*'

'Fresh pot,' Ellie says.

Manon frowns, nods at the olds. Perhaps it is next to the Rosses' stillness that Ellie seems manic and incapable of contemplation.

'She's off again!' Manon says to the room, as Ellie bustles out with the teapot.

Sol starts to fuss and whine. Mrs Ross immediately pitches onto her knees on the floor next to him, proffering him another block for his tower.

'You really should stay here with us,' Manon says. 'It'd be no trouble.'

'We don't like to be a burden,' says Mr Ross. 'It's a nice place, where we're staying. Mrs Linton, she cooked a full English this morning. Not that we felt like it. We'll go home tomorrow, I think. Police – well,' he nods at Manon, 'you'll know better than me. But they can't see a reason for us to hang on.'

The double meaning of those last words seems to suspend in the silence that follows.

Solly's whining is increasing, harder to mollify because really, he needs a nap but doesn't always take one (Ellie and Manon are clinging on, resolutely putting him to bed at lunchtime in the vain hope of retaining their midday hiatus). Sol is doubly exhausted by all the tension between the adults; tired from being lapped up by his grief-stricken stranger-grandparents.

'I'm going to have to put this one to bed in a minute,' says Ellie, bustling back in with the teapot.

'I think we'll go back for a nap too, Gareth, shall we?' says Mrs Ross. 'We didn't sleep much last night.'

'Won't you have a fresh cup first?' asks Ellie.

'No thank you,' says Mrs Ross. They have risen. 'I wish I'd brought him a present. I didn't know . . .'

'No need for presents,' Ellie says, stiffly.

'You will let us see him, won't you?' Mrs Ross says. 'We don't expect anything from you, only to see him and to get to know him. We can help you, in holidays and things. It can't be easy, having him on your own. Although I know you've got . . .' She trails off.

Ellie blusters her way through the departures, avoiding eye contact. 'Well, it was nice to meet you.'

Busying herself with Solly.

Hiding behind Solly.

Manon cannot understand it. These are visibly good people in search of a connection.

'What the fuck was that all about?' she says, after the front door has closed and after a respectful beat of silence so the Rosses can be safely out of earshot.

Ellie has Sol on her hip, stroking his forehead.

'*Language*,' Ellie says. 'I'm going to put him down.'

'My not tired,' says Solly, through the oval of a yawn.

71

DAVY

He's standing in front of a Georgian townhouse with a polished brass plaque saying *Dunlop & Finch*. The black gloss door is adorned with a wreath of greenery and red berries. Davy thinks it looks like a traditional Christmas card image. His two detective constables flank him and Davy presses the buzzer.

They are buzzed into a hallway with black and white floor tiles. An enormous ornate mirror hangs on one wall. An oversized vase of white lilies fills the air with heavy perfume. The DCs – two lads who have been seconded to him from team two and whom he barely knows, follow him into reception. On the train, Davy was anxious to brief them thoroughly. 'You're looking for strains and pressures on the victim, any fallings-out, office politics which might've got out of hand. Any backstory which colleagues were aware of – girlfriends, friendships gone awry.' The DCs were too relaxed to his mind and he didn't want to join in their banter during the rest of the journey, preferring to read his case file or gaze out of the window; making notes in his hardback notebook when questions occurred to him that he must not forget.

72

They are met with hushed tones from the receptionist. 'Ah yes, of course, take a seat.'

Davy remains standing and is annoyed when his DCs take up chairs.

A woman in a pencil skirt and tucked-in shirt comes to fetch them, leading them up a carpeted staircase with a polished banister. 'It's so terrible,' she says as she leads. 'We're all in shock.'

After some preamble and apportioning of interviews, Davy takes Giles Carruthers.

He is shown into a bright room with a large desk in front of the window. Around the fireplace is an arrangement of deep armchairs at the centre of which is a square coffee table set with a silver coffee set.

'I'm in shock,' Giles says. 'We all are. Can't believe it to be honest.'

He wears an impeccable suit of darkest navy and his white shirt shines brightly against it. Cufflinks. A slight tan. After some generalities about his friendship with Ross, their positions in the firm, Davy says, 'Was there much rivalry between the two of you? I understand you held equal positions as vice presidents, below van der Lupin.'

Giles says, 'I wouldn't call it rivalry. Look, we were up against each other but it was all friendly stuff. Coffee?'

Davy demurs. He doesn't like to take anything from anyone when he's on the job, not so much as an orange juice. Even coffee, with those sugar crystals that are all different shades of brown, like semi-precious stones. When his dad had taken him out once as a kiddie, Davy had rolled them against his teeth secretly.

'Markus – van der Lupin, our boss – he likes to foster a bit of competitiveness. Thinks it gets the best out of us. Happens all the time in the City. Jon-Oliver and I were your classic public school boys, you know?'

Davy nods. Smiles. *Not a clue*, he thinks.

'We couldn't play a game of squash without wanting to thrash each other. All good fun. But he was my friend. I'm gutted. Still can't believe it.'

Having met Ross's parents, Davy would be very surprised if Ross had been privately educated. Giles Carruthers is working hard to insinuate Davy into a world that couldn't be more alien to him. Above all, Davy doesn't like him. Is this political? Is it class? Is he stereotyping? A bit of all three and a gut response.

'Where were you on the night Mr Ross died?' Davy asks.

'At home,' Giles says quickly. He has one hand on the arm of the chair, which is boxy and leather. The other hand lifts and smooths his tie a noticeable number of times. 'I got a Chinese takeaway and I ate it in front of the telly by myself. Rock 'n' roll, eh?'

'Which takeaway was that?' Davy asks, pen poised.

'The Lotus Blossom, Upper Street.'

At the end of the interview, they stand and Davy asks to speak with the office manager, a woman called Linda Kapuschinski.

'Not sure she's relevant,' says Giles. 'Leaving us this week, sadly.'

'Think I'll interview her all the same,' Davy says.

'Fine. Why not use my office? The coffee's there, you can use the comfortable chairs. I'll just sit over here and get on with some work. You won't even know I'm here.'

'Ah,' says Davy, looking at the proximity of Giles Carruthers' desk. 'That's jolly kind of you, but we'll need a private space. One of your meeting rooms, perhaps.'

* * *

Linda Kapuschinski is giving him nothing. Yes/no answers, pulling at a lip of skin to the edge of her thumbnail. Pulling at it so it's getting red.

'You'll do yourself an injury,' Davy says, nodding at her hand. He leans back in his chair, taps his pen onto his pad. 'Look, I don't know about you, but I'm starving. What would you say to going out and grabbing a sandwich? We could carry on chatting while we eat.'

Two blocks away they find a café with steamed-up windows and, with the churn and spit of the milk warmer filling the air, Linda starts to relax.

'So,' he says. 'Pastures new.'

She nods.

'Got another job to go to?'

Linda has health problems, she tells him, brought on by stress at work. Insomnia, alopecia, she says, touching the underside of her hair. She lifts a clump of it and he sees a bald patch beneath.

'Gosh,' he says.

'I've had some compassionate leave but . . .' She pauses. 'It was never going to work. This place, the City . . . well, they don't believe in looking after people, put it that way. I'm surprised they've allowed me to work my notice. Probably because I'm only back room. Front-room staff are out without warning. The executions.'

'Sorry?' Davy says, alarmed at the word.

'That's the term for firings – executions, or the cull. Most people who've been culled aren't even allowed back to their desks. They're marched out by security.'

Davy blows out through pursed mouth.

'Last week it happened to my friend Emma. She called my mobile and said, 'Can you get my coat and bag?' She was out on the pavement with a blocked security pass. You think you can get hardened to it, but it has an effect on people, that culture. No one feels safe. You feel powerless.'

'What about Mr Ross and Mr Carruthers, how did they feel about the cull?'

'Jon-Oliver? Indifferent I'd say. Teflon man. But Giles thrives on it. He's the master of executions. He's always saying how it keeps the organisation lean, keeps people sharp. I think the opposite is true. It makes people not themselves, twisted with anxiety. It's also a massive disruption to the work – people's projects are halted midway, handed to someone new. Takes a while to hire new people. It's a macho thing; it doesn't make us efficient. Giles is wedded to it. He's always going on about how he came from Goldman Sachs but my guess is he was culled at Goldman Sachs and he's somehow playing it out, forever.'

'You don't like Giles then?'

'I don't dislike him. I just think he's the most damaged person I've ever come across.'

'Damaged how?'

'He can't be contradicted, he can't listen or change position. He's vengeful. If you cross him, you're out.'

'Did Jon-Oliver cross him?'

Linda shrugs. 'Jon-Oliver was his equal. Giles couldn't touch him.'

'How does the cull work?'

'Every autumn they fire their worst-performing staff. They do it in autumn to avoid paying Christmas bonuses – means there's more in the pot for everyone else. Happens all over the City. It's normalised, as if you shouldn't be a cry baby over losing your job.'

'How was Jon-Oliver's relationship with the boss, Markus . . . ?'

76

'Van der Lupin. He's very softly-softly as a person, everything unspoken. He'll say something vague in a meeting, like "Brazil, rather untapped for us. Any leads?" And he'll leave it hanging, undelegated, so that everyone falls over themselves to solve the Brazil problem. Giles and Jon-Oliver were at the top and there was an unspoken rivalry – they were both after the top job, as deputy chairman to Markus, but he left them to fight it out. Jon-Oliver had more or less blown Giles out of the water by signing the Chinese billionaire, Xi Ping. Now Giles will get his clients. And his bonuses of course.' She stops.

Davy turns his cup in its saucer a fraction. Waits.

'I've got some part-time work at my local health food shop.' She says this to Davy defiantly, as if he might deride her about it.

'That'll be good,' he says. 'Change of pace.'

'From success to failure, you mean? I thought I could change myself to fit into the culture here, but now I realise you have to make yourself cut off to do that. Stupid thing is, a part of me still wishes I could've made it work.' The end of her sentence tilts upwards as if it were a question.

'Natural, I suppose,' says Davy. He considers offering Linda another coffee – *cappuccino for Kapuschinski?* – but he has glanced at his watch and it's getting late. He wants to hug his public sector pension to his chest. In his job, there might not be brass plaques and lilies, but there was none of this culling or execution abomination either. You could put an awful lot of feet wrong before you were sacked from the police.

He escorts Linda back to the black gloss door in the gathering dusk and picks up his DCs for the journey home.

On the walk back to the tube station, his constables chatting away behind him, Davy notices how the Christmas lights of Mayfair are almost exclusively of the white pin variety –

understated compared to the winking green, red and yellow cacophony above Huntingdon town centre; love hearts and sleighs.

While walking, he takes out his mobile and calls the Lotus Blossom but is unable to get to anyone with enough English to answer his questions about Carruthers' takeaway.

'You wan order?' a girl keeps shouting, over the hiss of frying.

He should visit the place in person, but not tonight. He is anxious to get back to Huntingdon tonight. Doesn't want to spend it in a Premier Inn.

On arrival at Huntingdon station, he says goodbye to his constables, who are heading off for a pint together.

'I'll see you lads. I'm going in here to get myself a sandwich,' he says to them, before heading into the station buffet.

After paying, he slides the receipt alongside others in his wallet, thinking how these jobs put a serious dent in his efforts to eat his five a day. It is with relief that he sinks into the seat of his car, throwing his sandwich onto the passenger seat. Cars at night are lovely – warm and easy.

Headlights sweep past him both ways, illuminating the smears on his windscreen, then returning him to darkness on Hinchingbrooke Park Road.

He is within sight of Judith Cole's house. He can see her front door, but his car is under the shadow of a tree and as good as invisible. If she's lying – and that's the consensus in the department – then he wants to know why, even though he has been denied authorisation for any kind of trace or surveillance.

Another wash of headlights. Her front door opens, a slice of yellow light from her hallway. She pads outside to put a bulging bin bag into a black bin to the side of her driveway. She's wearing slippers. The front door closes again as she goes back in.

Anyway, this isn't surveillance. He's just parked here, in the dark in an unmarked car, eating a cheese sandwich for his supper.

The darkness of the car is soporific. He yawns, brushes the sandwich crumbs off his lap, checks his mobile. He Googled Giles Carruthers while on the train and apart from the Dunlop & Finch web pages on which he was featured, with its expensive profile photography, Davy unexpectedly found a Wikipedia page. He had the urge to check the IP address, on the suspicion that Carruthers had written the page himself. He was a boarder at Gordonstoun from the age of eight; his father was a stockbroker, his mother a housewife who went on to become a magistrate and active in the local Conservative Party. As mentioned by Linda, Carruthers had been on the Goldman Sachs training scheme before joining Dunlop & Finch.

Davy is so tired and Judith Cole is wearing slippers so his hunch hasn't paid off. He looks at his phone again out of boredom – looks at it far too much, like it's an addiction. When he's not looking at it, he's thinking about looking at it.

Yawning, he accepts he might be wrong about Judith Cole. The idea had come to him in the middle of the night; made him sit bolt upright. It was the moment Judith Cole's husband had said he was 'unexpectedly working from home' on the afternoon Ross was killed.

Davy starts the engine. Tonight his moment of inspiration has proved a dud – that can happen with ideas, he finds. They need to be road-tested. But he'll stake her out again, just in case.

BIRDIE

I can see his portrait on the wall from here, the Rt Hon. Blair. Tony has always had the courage of his convictions, whereas I don't have any convictions. I flip-flop between varied feelings. I'm all up and down and side to side. I can be full of mean-spirited thoughts, like wanting Angel out of my flat, wanting to be alone yet needing her to stay.

And when I feel happy, as soon as I notice it, then I'm not happy any more. It's like a fleeting ghost that disappears if you catch sight of it. One must notice happiness only by stealth, whistling, as if it doesn't matter at all – which it doesn't, I suppose. I'm going off the point again, into generalities.

My roof began to leak. In my box room, water was gathering in the join between the ceiling and the wall. I got a chap in – Jacek – chap I always get in for bits and bobs around the shop like extra shelving or fiddling about with the alarm. He's really good and when he's here, I feel insulated from some of the more irksome aspects of life, which must be how it feels to have a handy husband. I can say to him, 'That light doesn't work; you couldn't take a look, could you?' And he'll fit it in around the main job. A hook on the back of the door. A bit of skirting filled and repainted. But the downside of Jacek is his quoting method.

To cut a long story short, any job quoted as £300 by Jacek will come in at about a grand, not because he's ripping you off, but because the first quote has been rendered insensible by his desire to please. So one must ignore Jacek's quotes. Or add a couple of thousand to them.

I knew the roof would come in at about £2k because Jacek had said it was a quick job that shouldn't take more than an afternoon and would cost about £500. And I didn't have £2k. I was talking to Angel about this, explaining the situation, and she said, 'I can give you the money. Least I can do.'

She gave it to me in cash, just like that – great wads of twenties rolled in a ball and held tight with an elastic band. She didn't seem bothered by the amount and there was no mention of me paying it back. It was as if she'd handed me a fiver. She said, 'If you wanted to get Jacek to give the flat a lick of paint, I could pay for that too if you like. In lieu of rent.'

At the same time as she was generous, Angel was also annoying the hell out of me. She was forever in my space – never going out. The further we got into evening, the more slurry she became. And I was becoming more and more curious about the money, the posh toiletries, the stalker dossier I hadn't yet had a chance to look at properly. I was waiting for her to go out again, for long enough to have a more satisfying snoop about in her things.

It was the first week of December – about two to three weeks after she'd first moved in – she told me she was going out. She was jittery, kept going from room to room, another spray of perfume, checking her makeup. I asked her where she was going, all dolled up, but she said, 'You don't need to know.

Something I've got to do.' Then, as she was leaving, she said, 'Wish me luck.'

When she came home a couple of hours later, her hair was hanging funny and she avoided my eye – scuttled to the window and lifted the nets to look out, like she always did.

'Everything all right?' I said, quite confrontational as it happens, and trying to get eye contact because I was gearing up to tell her to jog on. I couldn't take it any more: didn't want to share my space. Her being out made me realise how much I wanted my flat back. I'd had a bath, watched TV in my bathrobe with my feet up on the recliner, and it'd been bloody marvellous.

She didn't reply.

'Angel?' I said, without trying to keep the irritation from my voice.

She turned then, to look at me. The first thing I saw was the tear tracks down her face – trails of mascara like black rain. The second thing I realised was that she'd been beaten up. The skin was split on her cheekbone and her right eye was closed up.

'Shit a brick, what happened to you?'

'Nothing,' she murmured, all watery and wobbly.

'That's not nothing.'

'Just got . . . jostled a bit.' She put a hand up to her cheek but didn't touch it, just let the tips of her fingers hover shakily over the cut.

'You don't get cut like that being jostled. Who the hell were you jostled by?'

'Didn't see their face.'

'Well, I s'pose you should sit yourself down while I dig out the Savlon.'

The bruise on her cheekbone started to fade, from red to purple, shading yellow. We kept the cut clean – fresh plasters every day and regular Savlon. She didn't go out again, even kept away from lifting the nets at the window, which was frustrating because I was feeling pretty claustrophobic as it was.

'*Hotel*'s on tonight,' I said to her. This was on 16 December – about ten days after she'd had the shit kicked out of her. She had the telly on. I noticed when I popped up from working in the shop that there was a lot of daytime telly being watched – *Bargain Hunt, Escape to the Country, Come Dine with Me, A Place in the Sun*. Angel seemed genuinely interested in the price of haciendas in obscure parts of Spain.

'Angel?' I said.

No response.

'What d'you fancy for dinner? Thought I'd get burgers and buns. Or would you rather have M&S lasagne or microwave turkey dinner?'

I knew what she really fancied for dinner was a couple of vodka Red Bulls. She was staring at the screen, legs hoisted in the recliner chair as if they were strapped in splints.

'Thought I might get a Christmas tree from Poundland,' I added.

I'd been thinking a lot about a tree – wanting one of those ready-decorated pink plastic ones. I noticed how having Angel staying made it worthwhile getting one, when in the past it seemed a childish indulgence just for one. Of course I had a cardboard box full of tattered foil accordion chains for the shop, but they never meant anything to me. At the same time, I hoped she'd hop it before Christmas Day, so I could really let myself go – watch telly all day and not say a word to anyone. Except I usually opened up the shop – people really need to get bladdered on 25 December.

'Right, won't be long,' I said.

Kilburn High Road was heaving with shoppers picking up

all the unnecessary detritus that goes with Christmas: boxes of baubles from M&S, reindeer-antler deely boppers from Poundland, and garish green tinsel and bulk boxes of cheap chocolate like Kinder and Oreos.

I got back to the flat with my Sainsbury's bags and she was still there, watching the telly in the recline position. I'd seen some mince-pie-flavoured liqueur on offer in M&S and I picked up a bottle for her, mainly because I wanted to have a taste. I mentioned to her that I'd bumped into Nasreen and had a little chat and that Nasreen, as usual, had questioned me closely about all aspects of my existence, looking for ways in which she was winning in the game of life. I'd mentioned, by way of a little boast, that I had a house guest this Christmas.

'What the fuck did you do that for?' Angel said, pushing into upright but initially failing. The chair is strong. 'I'll have to leave now.' The drama of her flounce, however, had suffered at the hands of the DFS recliner.

'Why?'

'Because they'll know where I am, thanks to you.'

'They? Who's they? Nasreen? She's not very dangerous. Boring and competitive, yes. Criminal mastermind? Hardly.'

'Dark forces.' But she was already a bit bladdered, so it came out 'ark forshes'.

I snorted at this. 'You're paranoid,' I said.

'Paranoid maybe, but alive.'

She'd got up off her chair and was marching about collecting her stuff, throwing it into her holdall. I'd spent all this time wishing she'd hop it, but now that she was going I felt panicked.

'What about the burgers?' I said, following her towards the box room and standing in the doorway while she balled up her pyjamas and stuffed them in her bag. She stopped, gave me a weary look, then carried on packing.

'Look,' I said, 'aren't you better off being with someone? No one's going to hurt you with me in the room. If it is "ark forshes" as you say, then they'll already know where you're hiding. They're not going to call Nasreen at the cash and carry for confirmation. At least together, we can keep an eye on each other. Stay tonight at least, and see how things are in the morning.'

I wanted to say, 'And anyway, you're half cut.' But she was well sensitive so it was best not to mention it.

She looked towards the window. It was already dark, the traffic roaring along wet tarmac, the winter night cold and long. She saw that she'd picked an impossible moment to storm off. Perhaps her thoughts ventured towards the burgers and that evening's episode of *The Hotel*.

'Put the chain on the door,' she said.

We moved around each other, making the burgers. They spat on the grill pan, bubbling and filling the kitchen with the smell of meat fat. Angel was squeezing ketchup onto the burger buns, saying, 'You can get a bar and a house in Spain for under £100k.'

'Is that what you're going to do?' I said. 'Move to Spain? Shall we have some orange barley water?'

I think my favourite moments in the whole experience of living are just before a feed. The moment the crisp bag is opened. The moment the burger patty is laid on the bun. The way a roast potato tumbles gently from spoon to plate. The splintered bridge of crispy duck across a pancake. When you're young you think happiness might be some kind of perpetual state of orgasm, but later, once the joints go, you realise it can be simulated with some cheese and a cracker.

'I've got this fantasy,' Angel said. 'A quiet place – dark inside, just a few regulars. Hot, dusty streets – you know, deserted during siesta. Trouble is, I don't speak any Spanish.'

'I speak Spanish,' I said and she looked surprised. 'I know – who'd have thought it? I was very good at school, as it happens.' I was filling two pint glasses at the tap. The water bubbled like soda on the surface.

'Why don't you come with me then? Sell up here – leave the rain and the dark. I've never run a business before. Could do with your help.'

She was shooting from the hip, just came out with it, and after that we were both quite awkward with each other, as if she'd blurted, 'Let's get married!' and now she couldn't take it back. We didn't know what to do with ourselves.

I loved the idea.

Not moving to Spain. I've never been one of those people who fantasises about moving country. I think it's just a ball ache, all the bureaucracy and not knowing where the nearest chemist is or when the bins are emptied. I know in my heart that when life feels like a big disappointment (i.e. most of the time), it's not going to feel any less so in Alicante. It'll just feel disappointing and also irritating because you won't know the Spanish for pile cream.

No, I loved the idea because I realised, after the prospect of her leaving, that I wanted the companionship that Angel had given me these last weeks, and because no one had asked me to move to Spain and run a bar with them before. I've never had a joint enterprise in my life.

I persuaded her to look at a hair salon for sale in Fuengirola for a mere £50k.

'D'you know anything about hairdressing?' she asked.

'About as much as I know about bartending,' I said. 'I've always fancied it. You'd have to drop the Goth get-up.' She smiled at me and it was the first open acknowledgement that this might be a disguise. 'And you'd have to tell me your real name,' I said.

She looked at me, thinking for a moment, as if deliberating on whether she could trust me.

Then she said, 'Saskia.'

DAY 3

17 DECEMBER

DAVY

He is standing in front of an illuminated map of Hinchingbrooke Park, projected via PowerPoint onto the wall, and holding a pointer stick as if he is an army general preparing them for battle. And they – his squadron – are all looking up at him, awaiting his orders. Davy has important information to share and just at the right moment, Gary Stanton idles in and perches on a desk at the back of the briefing.

'Our victim gets off the 4.13 p.m. train from London, walks through the car park as you'd expect, but instead of turning right into town and his hotel room at the George, he turns left, here,' pointer again, 'onto Brampton Road, following it until he can hang a right onto Hinchingbrooke Park Road. The question is, why? Was he heading for the hospital to visit his ex Ellie Bradshaw, who is a nurse on a medical ward?' He points to a line of dashes traversing the open fields of the park. 'As you all know, this is a footpath into Huntingdon and his body is found opposite the secondary school, at the start of this footpath.'

Davy nods at Stanton, kindly father figure, and Stanton

smiles back as if to say, 'That's the way, Davy my lad.'

'So the big development, the game changer,' Davy tells the room, 'is the forensic postmortem on Ross's body, which has just landed. Ross died from a single stab wound to the heart. Derry Mackeith has stated that the nature of this wound means that Ross could not have walked any distance at all after he was stabbed. In other words, he was stabbed either where he fell, or extremely close to where he fell. So this is our crime scene.' Davy circles the wooded area on the map with his stick. 'Now, at the scene there are a series of blood spots.' Davy uses his pointer to mark them. 'Here, here and here along this footpath leading to the car park. The blood spots go on for a distance in excess of what Derry reckons the victim could have walked. We must therefore assume that the spots came, not from the victim, but from the assailant – or assailants – leaving the scene. They could have dripped from the knife – as it was carried away, for example.'

Stanton slips from the room.

'Surely if he's stabbed and then falls, then Judith Cole would have seen whoever did it,' Kim says.

'Possible. But it's also possible that the assailant stabbed Ross, fled, either across the park or along the road, then Judith Cole comes ambling into the wood a minute or two later and Ross falls in front of her.'

'Is there any CCTV pointing at the scene?' Harriet asks. 'I thought we'd gathered all footage.'

'We've found a temporary camera, which was set up by the Friends of Hinchingbrooke Country Park to monitor antisocial behaviour. We're getting the footage off it,' Davy says.

'And when's that CCTV going to land?'

'Person who normally manages it is in the Algarve,' says Davy. 'We've made it clear there's a rush on this, but they're not the most . . . well, they're a bunch of volunteer pensioners trying to find someone who can burn it onto a disc for us. Additionally, there is a partial footprint in one of the blood spots, so we'll be looking to match that.'

'So this changes things,' Harriet says. 'It puts our King's Cross chap out of the frame. He got off the train at St Neots and then travelled directly back to London, don't ask me why, but he wasn't in Huntingdon at the time Ross was stabbed. It also takes the pressure off Giles Carruthers.'

They've lost the King's Cross chap anyway. His ticket paid for in cash, no trace on other CCTV cameras around the station. Davy still wanted to interrogate Ellie on her alibi, or lack of it, but Harriet was reluctant to authorise re-interview when Stanton seemed set against it. She hasn't told Davy why this is. Perhaps she doesn't know.

Davy says, 'Still haven't confirmed Carruthers' takeaway.'

'There's no evidence he left London on the fourteenth of December,' says Harriet. 'What we are looking for is the person who was as close to that location where Ross fell as possible, at the time in question.'

One week in
21 December

Manon

She stands at the entrance and lifts a basket from the stack – one of those with an extendable handle you can wheel along. The green signs and oak flooring and abundant flower displays cater for the well-to-do.

She hovers, unable to begin. Her vision swims. She wonders if she might need a sit-down, but instead she approaches the 'entertaining' cabinet – shelf upon shelf of canapés for the festive season. The supermarket urges a life of largesse; Prosecco parties, nibbles arranged in those bowls with partitions, warm finger food involving prawns or filo pastry or both.

Nearby are stacked enough boxes of chocolates to bury a tired woman.

Manon is all sunk in on herself and ungenerous, trussed up in her anxiety like a Christmas turkey. She turns, ready to put back her basket, thinking, *I don't have to do this now.* And also thinking, *is this happening because I didn't talk to Fly about the baby, avoided that conversation until the baby was self-evident?*

'Hellloooo!' says Ann-Marie, one of the school mums she barely knows.

Manon tries to erase her slack-jawed existential crisis face.

'Hi,' she says.

'Got fifteen coming for dinner,' says Ann-Marie, nodding at her trolley, which is groaning with booze and raw ingredients, venison probably.

Manon nods.

The headmaster had said, 'Take a seat,' when she was summoned to his office this morning. The last day of term, the atmosphere raucous and loose. From this, too, she was excluded. She heard shrieking out in the hall.

'I'm rather concerned about Fly,' said Mr Jenkins. She was grateful he'd removed his Santa hat. A mince pie sat on a napkin beside his keyboard. 'He got into a fight yesterday with the Cole twins.'

'A fight?'

She wanted to say, '*Well he won't have started it, that's not like Fly. It must've been the twins.*' But these days she's not so sure. Not in his current state. She's not sure of anything, in fact.

'A member of staff – Mr Mitchell, geography – had to pull him off,' said Mr Jenkins.

They both looked at the mince pie.

'What was it about?' she asked.

She couldn't figure out whether she wanted to wrap her arms about Fly and tell him how sorry she was that life had taken a turn for the worse. Or box his ears and shout that he needed to man up and pull himself together. Some confusing mash-up of the two was the likely outcome.

'Hard to tell,' Mr Jenkins said. 'All I got was a load of "he started it". You know what it's like.'

'He's finding it hard to settle here,' Manon said.

'Mmm. Everything at home . . . ?'

What? She wanted to ask. Everything at home dysfunctional?
'How does he feel about the baby?'

'He hasn't said. He didn't want to leave London. This was my idea, coming back. I wanted to give him a fresh start but it's not really panning out that way.'

'In that case we need to keep a very close eye on him,' he said kindly and she wondered if he was single and might sleep with her. 'Perhaps the Christmas break will do him good. Allow him some time away from school. It's very difficult to switch at his age, friendship groups tend to get established in Year Seven. He'll probably come through it.' She'd wanted Mr Jenkins to say, '*I'm sure he'll come through it*' but he wasn't sure, evidently. 'I'm not going to punish him for this. I don't think it's in his best interests. He's been under strain, we all know that. But you might want to talk to him.'

'Sore head tomorrow!' Ann-Marie is saying now, as the refrigerators hum beside them, pumping out cold. Shakin' Stevens' 'Merry Christmas Everyone' is being piped through the store. This woman is gurning away, searching Manon's face. What does she want, a fucking round of applause? 'Honestly, when our lot get together it gets *messy*.'

'Sounds exhausting,' Manon says.

'Ah no, it's a great laugh, a big party.'

Needy Ann-Marie pushes her trolley on, seemingly fortified by the bereft expression on Manon's face.

Manon puts her basket back on its stack.

DAVY

Here he is again, in the darkness of his car, this time with a tray of six mini pork pies, a jar of Branston Pickle and a teaspoon. He is bound to drop the odd brown cube of pickle into his lap in the act of spooning it onto the meat of the pie. He doesn't care.

Exactly one week since Ross was stabbed; same time, same place. He is taking a chance on Judith Cole being a creature of habit, though it's a bit of a long shot – who sticks to their routines on 21 December? Isn't normal service suspended? Still, there's no harm in sitting here eating pork pies, just in case.

At the sight of a man approaching Judith Cole's front door, Davy squirms more upright in his seat, drops his pie paraphernalia onto the passenger seat and gets out his phone, readying the camera.

The front door opens. No slippers this time. High heels in fact.

He photographs Judith Cole letting a man who is not Mr Cole into her home. Arm about the man's shoulder, glances out to the driveway, towards the neighbours. Is that a kiss on

94

the lips Davy sees, as she draws him towards her over the threshold?

Enough to bring her back in for interview, put the photograph before her and ask her to recap the events of 14 December with her memory somewhat sharpened. He pictures her outraged face. 'Where did you get those? Who took those? Have you had me followed? On what grounds have you been watching me?'

Davy will have to have a strategy for this one. An hour after the man's arrival, the stranger leaves Judith Cole's house.

Day 9
22 December

Davy

The following morning Davy is straight on the phone to the forensics lab.

'The DNA on Judith Cole's clothing,' he asks a lab technician. 'Was there anything unusual there?'

'Hang on, let me get the file,' she says. There is a delay, some rustling, laughter in the background.

'Right, here we are, um . . . Yes, so there was her own, and the victim's as you'd expect from her proximity to him at his time of death. And we found a third strand, in her underwear. Not the victim, not her husband. We ran it through the database and got a match, actually.'

'Right,' Davy says. 'Who is it?'

'Chap called Jeremy Mitchell, geography teacher at Hinchingbrooke School. He was swabbed years back in relation to the disappearance of a pupil; no involvement, just routine inquiries. But it's his DNA.'

'You say in her underwear . . .'

'D'you want me to spell it out, DS Walker?'

'No, no. It's fine, thanks.'

'I really don't know why I'm back in here. I've got a shocking amount to do to get ready for Christmas – supposed to pick up the KellyBronze from the butchers today,' Mrs Cole is saying, looking at her watch. Her voice is hard; her gaze to the side, not meeting Kim and Davy's, who are across the table in interview room two.

'I'm sorry to bring you in again. There's just a couple of things,' Davy says, 'that we need to clear up. Some confusion—'

'About the dog,' says Kim.

Enough with the dog, he thinks.

He says, 'We are not sure you *have* told us everything about the evening in question. In particular why you chose Hinchingbrooke Park and, as my colleague says, whether you were in fact walking the dog. I want to stress, Mrs Cole, that we are not investigating you or your personal life. Your . . . *intimate circumstances* are not of any interest to us. However, this is a murder inquiry and it is vital you do not obstruct the course of our investigation. I would hate for you to end up in court yourself. So . . .' He looks at her calmly, pauses. Lots of eye contact. 'The truth, if you don't mind.'

He has the confidence, so well armed is he, and as Mrs Cole looks into his face, he thinks she can see his knowledge about Jeremy Mitchell written there. Her eyeballs flicker. She is pausing, evaluating. Somewhat startled; perhaps the fight or flight response is generating some adrenalin in her body.

'We are retrieving additional CCTV from the woodland path, so we'll be able to ascertain whether the dog—' Kim begins, but Davy places a hand on her arm to stop her. He's got Mrs

Cole where he wants her, doesn't need Kim kicking her into touch.

Mrs Cole takes a deep breath, the tips of her fingers on the edge of the table. 'I was meeting Jeremy,' she says at last.

'Jeremy?' says Davy.

'Jeremy Mitchell. He's a teacher at my sons' school. We've been . . . Well, I don't need to go into details, do I? I mean it's none of your bloody business. I usually meet with Jeremy at home. Wednesdays, my sons have tennis club, but my husband—'

'Was unexpectedly working from home that day?' says Davy.

'Yes, so I told him – Jeremy, I mean – not to come. I texted him to meet me across the road in the park. At the time I saw Mr Ross, Jeremy'd gone, we'd . . . finished. Then I saw Mr Ross fall, and the rest you know.'

'So you would've been facing the opposite way. Your original statement says you were walking away from home, towards the park,' Davy says. 'But in fact, you would have been walking back home.'

'Yes, yes I suppose so. Look, please don't say anything to my husband. I can't bear for him to find out.' Her voice is quiet and sad. 'I've made such a mess. But I've never had any intention of leaving him – Sinjun, I mean. He's a good husband. I just . . .'

'Just to return to the crime scene. So Mr Ross was walking towards you when he fell. You were facing each other?'

Mrs Cole nods.

'For the tape, please,' Davy says.

'Yes, I was facing Snowdonia Way; Mr Ross was walking towards me, facing me when he fell. There is one other thing,' she says. 'I saw someone. I saw someone in the wood. I saw a boy. A black boy in a hoodie.'

BIRDIE

'Out of interest,' I said to her, 'why the name Angel?'

'A while ago, I met a child called Angel. At first, I thought what a cheap name, like calling your kid Chardonnay or Mercedes. But this girl was so feisty, she had so much kick in her. And this was a kid who'd had it rough. For me it became a charismatic name, because of that kid. And then I thought, I'll call my own daughter Angel.' She shook her head and turned away, whispering, 'But that didn't happen.'

'Angel suits you,' I said.

'Why, because I'm not one?'

That evening, we watched *The Hotel* – whole minutes of interview with the hotel florist, the teams of chefs. A giant televisual puff piece but worth it for the glimpse of unbridled luxury – tellies set into the bathroom mirrors, jacuzzi baths in the bedroom, that sort of thing. Then came seemingly spontaneous chat between chambermaids about the lost items they'd discovered behind the headboards. All the way through, Angel was tutting and letting out these bitter asides. 'This is a joke. You should see what really goes on in that hotel.'

'What sort of thing?' I asked.

'Depraved stuff.'

I looked over at her and she was scowling at the screen.

'Like what?' I asked again, but the news was coming on and Angel had pushed down on her footrest to take the plates out.

Fiona Bruce was standing there in a white trouser suit of the kind only worn by television presenters, giving the news headlines, when I heard the plates clatter to the floor. I turned to see Angel in the doorway, staring at the screen.

'Wha—' I said.

'*Shush.*'

Fiona was saying, 'Police investigating the murder of a City banker in Huntingdon, Cambridgeshire, are appealing for information. Jon-Oliver Ross, 38, from Holland Park, died from stab wounds. His body was found in parkland in the Hinchingbrooke area a week ago.'

Angel was pale, staring at the telly.

When the item was over, she sort of slid to the floor in the corner of the room, knees up to her chest, her arms hugging them. She was rocking a bit. I asked her what was up, did she know the chap on the news? Was he a friend of hers? It seemed to me from her reaction that he'd been more than a friend.

She just rocked, staring straight ahead.

I went to the kitchen and got a box of M&S mince pies, which had been reduced because they'd got bashed up. I pulled out the plastic tray, which made a loud crackling noise, and tore off the cellophane bag. I offered her some of the rubble of pastry and brown mincemeat but she shook her head. The sugar on top was in large, crunchy grains.

'Cup of tea goes nicely with these,' I said. 'Shall I make you one?'

She shook her head.

'Shall we talk about Spain?' I offered. I knew talking about Spain made her happy, but the truth was, it made me happy too.

'It'll be so hot, we'll wear nothing but loose dresses and flip-flops,' she whispered, as if she was looking at the scene in her mind. 'We'll walk down paths covered in pine needles, down to the sea for a swim when the salon's shut for siesta.'

'I'll be so thin,' I sighed and we both laughed.

'You won't be thin, but it won't matter. You'll be brown all over and your skin will be smooth from the salt and the sand. We'll be as unworried as children,' she said.

'Not like now,' I said, and her eyes filled with enormous tears, her lips trembling.

'This is all my fault,' she said, her voice wobbly. 'I went after them and now they've killed him.'

I could see she was panicking, so I said, 'How will you make the hairdressers different from all the other hairdressers?'

She swallowed, looking at me earnestly. 'I would never charge people for a blow-dry on top of the price of a cut or colour. I mean, that's just criminal.'

I nodded. I don't really go to the hairdressers, so I'm not one to judge.

'And when customers are waiting – like under the heat lamp while their colour takes, they'll get a nice hand massage or manicure if they want it, instead of just sitting there doing nothing.'

'Very good idea,' I said. 'Those little extras make all the difference.'

'And we'll have a proper stack of magazines, not a couple of falling-apart ones from six months ago,' she said.

'All the latest about Peter Andre,' I said.

I took her hand, put it on my knee and patted it there. We

were both looking ahead at nothing, sat there on the living-room floor, up against the wall.

'They're going to kill me as well,' she said.

'D'you want to tell me from the beginning? Was he your boyfriend?'

SASKIA

He was a client, one of many. But he was good – Jon-Oliver wasn't rough. He had loads of money, didn't go at us like a butcher and I wanted to get out. True love.

I was a hooker. I *am* a hooker. My name is Saskia, Elle, whatever you want. *Une pute de luxe.* Escort to the rich and powerful. One of Titans' girls. This is what these ageing, priapic, bald men call themselves: Titans, Emperors, Gods. The club that is run for their pleasure is called Titans VIP. It's like an addiction. They can't travel and not have girls.

They are foreign dignitaries, politicians, arms dealers, Saudi oil billionaires, Chinese businessmen. They're in finance or global retail or property. They run countries. I once had the head of the Kazakh police, nasty piece of work. They fly in private jets and they take escorts with them – beautiful girls, like racehorses. The girls they buy are models, dancers, they speak languages, they have PhDs. You would not believe how beautiful they are. They're all natural, dressed in Chanel, Isabel Marant. Perfect bodies, gorgeous faces, and they can bang all night.

103

I got into it through modelling. I was modelling for catalogues and this guy came to a shoot, Lebanese guy called Moukhtar but everyone called him Moukie, told me I could earn £5k if I had sex with him. I was disgusted, told him where to get off, but it planted the seed. My mum had a new boyfriend and he chucked me out, I had rent to pay and there were too many models and not enough work. Next time Moukie came back, I asked him to tell me more. Turned out he was a fixer for Titans – he tried out the girls, gave them a diamond rating according to how much fun he had.

That first time, with Moukie, was the worst, but after that it got easier. Actually he was a nice guy. I mean not at a deep level – at a deep level he'd break both your legs. But to meet and chat to. Big smile, friendly face. He called us 'beautiful' and 'darling', complimented us if we bought a new dress. Sometimes he seemed a bit camp. '*The red really brings out your colouring.*'

Moukie looked after us, sorted stuff out for us, made sure we were OK. He made sure we knew not to mess with him, too. One girl was chaotic, missing appointments with clients, maybe she was drinking or taking drugs. Moukie kept warning her. Then he took her son away, God knows what he did with him – rumour was he handed the boy to social services. Well, that was one of the better rumours; you don't want to hear the other ones. Then Moukie sent her to one of the Arab clients – the ones we used to dread, the ones they normally reserve for the two-star girls. Those guys lock you in a room and do crazy shit to you.

Here's what Titans is like, right? The website is all sexy photos, black silk and grand pianos boasting about what a classy service it is, foreign languages spoken and business degrees, but it operates out of a room above a taxi office called

Speedy Cars in Seven Sisters. The guys who run Titans, they're gangsters. Bit of drugs, bit of trafficking, dodgy as.

To begin with, Moukie gave me three diamonds. So I decided to up my game – I had to be perfect, perfectly manicured, healthy, beautifully dressed. I was sent to Paris – which sounds glamorous, but trust me, it wasn't – to learn everything there was to know about positions; reverse cowgirl, the longest blow job, how to keep going and going, how to stay clean, how to look like you're enjoying yourself. Because that's what you're there for: to do the things their wives won't do.

Titans girls are told to take no liquids for twelve hours before a booking – you can lose a lot of weight that way, by drying out. I ate no solid foods for nine weeks to get into perfect shape, worked out twice a day. It's incredibly hard to maintain. But the money these men are paying, they won't put up with any wobbly bits. You have to have the body of a Victoria's Secret model.

If you get a good rating – and in my prime I was up to five diamonds – you make more money. Ten thousand pounds for one night, forty thousand for a weekend. That was then. Prices have come down since the global downturn, and since more girls are choosing it as a career. If you're smart, you invest in a pension and property; get them to buy you jewellery, like something from Tiffany – that's an investment too. Best of all, you marry one of them. At the very least, you get out as soon as you've made enough to retire on. Titans clients are on the Forbes List: powerful, powerful men, and often they're very fucked up. The girls are fucked up too, but they're generally from very poor backgrounds, except for the university kids who are fucked up in a different way and trying to shock their fathers. But generally it's the very rich screwing the very poor. Isn't that how the world's going? It's separating, like oil from vinegar.

105

If you're a Titans girl you have to read *The Economist*, know about world events, look like a girlfriend on his arm. These guys, these sad old rich men want to look like they're going out with a model. That's why Jon-Oliver was such a catch – good-looking, nice to fuck, generous with his money. If I married him, I could get out.

Titans provides 'women of exceptional beauty, intelligence and sophistication'. You can't be, like, 'My name Svetlana. My fada work in factory.' No, none of that, though that is what lots of their backgrounds are like. The girls are numb: they don't care about their clients. They've got hardened by life. Let's just say there's a reason they're doing what they're doing. Like Jade.

To get to the root of all this, I have to go back to Jade. Jade changed me.

Jade was new, never done a Titans gig before. Moukie brought her to my flat, asked me to look after her, which is code for 'tell her everything, about keeping clean, keeping going, all the tricks'. Jade was 15, but seemed younger. She was so beautiful – she had freckles across her nose, a gap between her front teeth, huge dark brown eyes. She was like a young Kate Moss. She was into loom bands, d'you know those? Little elastic bands they make bracelets out of. She kept making me glow-in-the-dark bracelets. She had a teddy. She danced around to that song, 'Call Me Maybe'. We went shopping together for clothes for her, had manicures, pedicures. I did her hair, her fake tan. I looked at her and it broke my heart, knowing what they were going to do to her, so I kept trying to put her off. I thought, if I could just get her out of her first gig, she'd be all right. If she never went there, she might stand a chance.

We were getting ready at my flat. I told her I'd cover for

her, say she was sick. I told her to stop before she got really damaged.

She said she had no choice. She'd been in care, some really rough council-run children's home. This was her way out.

'I never had nice things,' she said. 'I never been in the Carlton before.'

'Doesn't look so good when you're on your back,' I said. 'Go and get some GCSEs.'

She said she couldn't go back to the care home, didn't say why but I could sense it was serious. She wanted to buy herself a home, she said. I could see what she really wanted to buy herself was a safe place in the world.

'Isn't that why you do it?' she asked me.

'I didn't do it when I was 15,' I said. 'These guys – they don't play nice. They can do what they like to you, even if you're crying.'

'I won't cry,' she said. 'I'll be smiling up at the ceiling, thinking about the money.'

She smiled at me. Fake bravado. That pretty face, so much in need of protection. She was bright and there was no one to protect her, not even me. I felt so much rage at that moment, I can't even begin to tell you.

It wasn't just Jade that caused a change in me. Two weeks earlier, I'd done a pregnancy test and it was positive. I was pretty sure it was Jon-Oliver's, and I started having all these thoughts about marrying him, having a family, thinking about that baby and who it might be. Anyway, five days before the Carlton party, I bled. The baby was gone.

Jade and I were booked by Dunlop & Finch with some other girls for a night with an important Chinese delegation – some billionaires they were hoping to sign. They were getting the full works, this group: limos, champagne, fine dining, girls. We

107

were often booked in groups for parties. This one was fairly intimate, just the Dunlop & Finch guys – Jon-Oliver, Giles Carruthers and the boss Markus van der Lupin. And the Chinese lot, about six of them. It was at the Carlton Mayfair. First of all there was some business chat around a polished oval table. Some of us girls were in there with them, handing out property brochures, refilling glasses.

After the meeting, there was a gourmet meal, prepared by that bloke off the telly, Yulio something. The girls were still pretty low-key at that point, just a bit of draping and cleavage. There was a lot of champagne: Krug 1998. The Chinese are weird about sex, very embarrassed. Not much looking, lots of bowing. Then, once they get going, it's hard to get them to stop. Guess that's what they're like in business too: relentless with a strong undercurrent of shame.

Anyway, everyone moved to the lounge for coffee and for quiet lines of coke in dark corners. I told Jade not to touch the drugs. 'Get pissed if you can't get through it any other way.' The drugs is how they kill you. There was a cocktail bar, music on. Some girls were dancing in a sexy way. Couples started making out, discreetly at first, sometimes two girls to one man.

In the Carlton Mayfair that night, I looked around to see where Jade was, to check on her. I looked into one of the bedrooms and through to the bathroom and there I saw a man, I don't know who it was, handing her a rolled-up bank note and her bending over the sink and snorting a line.

Jade died that night. Cocaine overdose. Bleeding through the nose on the floor of one of the bathrooms. A few people began to gather around the doorway, someone thudding away on Jade's tiny chest, trying to resuscitate her.

I said, 'She's only 15. She's only fucking 15.'

I had the feeling I was underwater, watching Jade's body being pummelled on the bathroom floor. Everything was slow and muffled. I'd had too much booze.

Jade was dead. They stopped giving her mouth-to-mouth. Jon-Oliver came up behind me and took my arm. He said, 'Time to get out of here.'

We ran, him and me. It was raining, but summer rain, a break in the humidity and it was like we were being washed clean. London seemed deserted. It was as if we had the city to ourselves. We hid under some railway arches, I don't even know where because I followed where he led me, and we had sex there. It was so warm and the rain had made the air fresh and soft.

Afterwards, I said, 'The police will come, right? And investigate Jade's death. It'll lead back to Titans.'

He shook his head. 'They'll cover it up. The firm won't allow its connection to Titans to come out, and the Chinese won't do business with us if they're dragged into some seedy police investigation, which brings shame on their families. No way. And her being underage? That just makes it worse. No, they can get rid of her body. Titans will deal with it. They've got connections with people who clean up that kind of mess all the time. All part of the discreet service.'

'But they can't – it's not . . . *right*,' I said. 'She was just a child and they killed her.' I was crying so much I could hardly speak.

'*Come on*,' he said. 'You've worked for them long enough; this can't be the first thing you've witnessed. You know what they're like, what Moukie's like.'

I couldn't explain it to him, and I didn't try – how I had a connection with Jade, how I saw her ruined by them, and in her I saw myself, my inability to get out. I saw that they had killed an important part of me, the part that could protect myself, the part that could fight for a good life. Jade had changed things.

'I have to stop them,' I said to Jon-Oliver.

'Good luck with that,' he said, and it was glib, a joke – like everything was with him. Nothing mattered. I hated him so much at that moment. I thought, you don't care because you're a man and none of this will ever happen to you. You can't care about it like I can. It'll never be your body or your daughter's body.

DAVY

A man wearing a yellow pastel golfing sweater has finally furnished them with footage off the temporary cameras in the park, which takes in the spot where Ross fell. Two cameras, two angles.

The team is gathered around Colin's monitor.

Kim points at the grey grainy shot of the path. 'So there were blood spots here, here and here, on the path,' says Kim. 'Right?'

'Right,' says Harriet.

'And according to Derry Mackeith, the victim could not have walked any distance with his injury. So the blood drips, rather than coming from the body, must have come from the weapon – from the assailant.'

'Right,' says Harriet. 'So who've we got on the path?'

'Watch this.'

A hunched figure ambles across the screen with his hood up. 'Well, I can't tell who that is,' says Harriet.

'Wait a minute, the camera will switch to the one angled from the car park and then you'll see his face.'

111

Harriet watches; they all watch in silence.

'*Fuck*,' she says. 'Play it again.'

They watch.

Harriet says, 'OK, so before we all go crazy on this, he's not in any hurry. He's not rushing away. He doesn't seem . . . pumped, like he's just stabbed someone. Let's look at it again.'

They are silent as Kim rewinds the footage and plays it again. They watch Fly Dent walking the path with a lolloping gait, half-rabbit, half-rapper.

'He does not have the look of a boy who has just stabbed someone,' Kim says. 'And anyway, what possible motive could he have?'

People have returned to their desks, still stunned from seeing Fly on the CCTV.

'I've literally never looked at financial records like these, it's blowing my mind,' says Colin.

'How d'you mean?' asks Davy.

'Too many zeros. The sums involved – they're beyond comprehension. He had half a mill in his current account. Nought point two five per cent interest.' Colin shakes his head at this, as if it is incomprehensible that anyone would store money on this kind of bank rate. 'That was his loose change. He moved £9million into a company called Pavilion Holdings, incorporated in Nevada, beneficiary unknown. Registered in the Cayman Islands so tax free.'

'There must be a way of finding out who the beneficiary is,' Davy says.

'There really isn't,' Colin says. 'Shell companies are notorious for this. The beneficiary is listed as some lawyer in Nevada, which will be the guy who set it up for him. True beneficiary is hidden until we find out the status of his will. Likely he died intestate, given his age, so it'll take an awful long time for that information to come to light.'

'Can I have a word, Davy?'

Davy jumps at the sound of Stanton's baritone.

He follows the boss into his office. Harriet's already perched at the side of the room.

Stanton closes the door after him. *Is this a secret meeting of some sort?* The door is normally left ajar.

Stanton goes to the window, looking out to the car park. 'Think we need to focus. We've potentially got an armed assailant out there.' He turns. 'Look, there were texts between Ross and the Dent boy, so there was a relationship. That goes to motive. You need the Dent boy's mobile.'

'How did Ross even have the boy's number?' Harriet asks.

'We'll need to find that out,' Stanton says. He pulls out his chair and sits at his desk. With the movement, Davy catches a whiff of chlorine mingled with shower gel. Stanton's started exercising. Rumour has it he's been spending a fortune on hair loss treatments from some Harley Street trichologist.

Harriet says, 'I just don't think Fly ... It doesn't seem possible. I know him. He's a good lad.'

'If you ask me,' Stanton says, 'the Dent boy's good for it.'

Why does he keep referring to Fly as *the Dent boy*? He hadn't been *the Dent boy* a year ago, offering Stanton peanuts at the Christmas drinks.

Davy says, 'To be fair, there are a lot of avenues which need exploring. Ross's £9million shell company might also go to motive. Or the blonde – the photo on the body – who might be another ex. And Ellie Bradshaw: there's a seven-hour hole in her alibi which hasn't been interrogated and she's a key witness. There's an array of potential motives.'

'Hardly think Ellie Bradshaw is a danger to the public,'

Stanton says. 'I just don't buy it, do you? A nurse stabbing her ex?'

What the hell is this, an episode of *Guess That Perp*? They're not supposed to go on hunches; the HOLMES database was invented to prevent all that. Trace, interview, eliminate. Every single line. Why isn't he telling them to be all over Ellie Bradshaw's alibi? Is there an instruction coming from above Stanton, or does he know something about Ellie and is leaving Davy out of the loop? He didn't even realise there was a loop. *Is there a loop?*

Stanton says, 'Look, Derry's PM shows Ross was stabbed where he fell. We've got a lad on camera at the crime scene, at the time of death as good as dammit – a lad from a not great background. I'm telling you, the Dent boy's good for it. There's been an additional statement from Giles Carruthers describing animosity between Ross and the Dent boy. Ross told him the boy was menacing.'

'*Menacing*? Fly?' says Harriet, and Davy feels similarly incredulous. They have both been around the boy. He's a good kid.

'When did this come in, this additional statement?' Davy asks.

'Phoned it in, yesterday,' says Stanton.

This is not right, something's not right. There are forces in the room that are not being talked about, invisible as magnetic fields, pulling the investigation in a direction it doesn't want to go.

'Apparently,' Stanton continues, 'Ross told Carruthers that he didn't want a boy like him around his son.'

'A boy like him?' says Harriet.

'Well, him being . . .' Stanton says.

'Black?' asks Harriet.

'Not just that, is it? The boy's had a hard life. Would it

114

seriously surprise you if a boy like him went down for something like this? Whatever, we need to see those texts. There might be threats, abuse. Motive. You need to arrest Fly Dent.'

A boy like him. Davy doesn't like it. His blood is swirling, stirring up nausea like ocean sand.

'Couldn't we just ask to see his phone?' Davy says. 'The effect of an arrest on him, on Manon . . .'

'Arrest gives us power to search and seize,' Stanton says. 'I think it's time to go through the house, too. We don't know where that knife is. Longer we leave it, the more evidence'll be lost.'

'I don't think that's necessary,' Harriet says, quietly, but her voice is wavering. She raises herself from perching position to standing, and Davy can see she is braced. 'I don't think there's evidence to justify an arrest. I think there are other avenues—'

'DCI Harper,' Stanton says, 'I don't want you to lose sight of this investigation because of personal feelings of loyalty. You really have to try to remain impartial. If you can't, I will have to reassign this case to a team without close ties to Manon Bradshaw.'

'I'm not losing sight of the case. But I am not turfing a pregnant woman out of her home three days before Christmas and arresting her son,' Harriet says.

'She shouldn't get special treatment,' Stanton says.

'She's my *friend* and one of our own.'

MANON

'Flyyyyy! Turn the tap off!' she bellows up the stairwell.

No response, as per.

The winter days have been over-warm, building to a crescendo of humidity and as she stands there, she feels the air around her thick as wool. It needs to rain.

She's not about to allow another infinity pool to leak through her kitchen ceiling, so she takes a firm hold of the banister and attempts to haul her body up the stairs.

When she has reached approximately step five, the doorbell rings. Manon calls to Ellie – 'You get that!' – while continuing her huff-puffery up the stairs. She has only mastered another three steps when Harriet appears in her hallway. 'Hello, this is a surprise. Have you come for dinner? I'll be down in a minute. Just have to smother a couple of children with some pillows.'

She turns the taps in the bathroom off, glances into Fly's room where he is predictably lying on his bed reading, while Sol squats doing his dinosaur puzzle on the floor.

Panting, Manon walks back down the stairs. 'To what do we owe this honour? Something to do with Jon-Oliver?'

Harriet is wearing a pale rain mac, on which are spatters of darkness at the shoulders. Rain. At last. *Good*, Manon thinks, as if it might wash away the congestion around her organs.

Harriet looks strained.

'I need to talk to Fly,' Harriet says.

'Fly? Why on earth would you want to talk to Fly?' Manon looks behind her and yells up the stairs again. 'Fly? Fly! Can you come down?' Then she smiles at Harriet. 'He should be down in a day or two. Glass of wine?'

'No thanks.'

'Crikey, you're a bit serious.'

'It is serious. I need to take him in.'

'Sorry?'

'I need to take Fly in. Question him at the station.'

'No you fucking don't.'

'Yes, I do, Manon.'

'He's a minor.'

'I know he's a minor and I'll make sure he has an appropriate adult.'

'Why can't you ask him stuff here, with me and Ellie?'

'Because there's evidence I need to show him and because I need it on tape.'

Fly has descended the stairs and is standing on the bottom step behind Manon, who is at ground level, eyeballing Harriet. The bottom stair is making him seem taller than he is and Manon curses her hormones, which are causing a swell of feeling.

He is only little. He is only little though he looks big. He's a baby, and she bobs up onto his step. 'Don't look so grown up,' she whispers, her cheek against his, in an effort to hide her tears, and he gives her a confused look.

'Do you mind coming to the station with me, Fly?' Harriet says.

117

'I don't understand . . .' he says.

'I just want to ask you a bit about your movements, in relation to the death of Jon-Oliver Ross,' says Harriet.

Manon gives Harriet her most withering look because this is why she left Kilburn. This is why she took Fly out of London; because he was getting stopped every five minutes by coppers who couldn't see past the colour of his skin.

'I don't know anything,' Fly says.

'No, well, we can sort it all out down the station,' says Harriet.

Fly is sitting on the bottom stair, pulling on his enormous lace-ups.

Ellie, having disappeared into the kitchen for a time, has rejoined them, leaning against the banister, watching Manon make a show of bending to gather her bag, getting her coat.

'I'm not sure, in your condition . . .' Harriet says.

'Yes,' says Ellie. 'I can go with Fly, you stay here with Solly.'

'Can you all stop talking about my fucking condition? My condition is I'm Fly's mother and I'm going with him.'

'You can't be his appropriate adult – you know that, right?'

'We can talk about that on the way in.'

Manon has swivelled Fly round by the shoulders and is following him out through the front door, past Harriet, into the spattering rain and the relieving oxygen of the night. She can picture what Harriet is thinking: *She's going to be a royal pain in the arse.* Well that's right, she is.

'And you're not keeping him in,' Manon says now that Harriet is following her down the path. 'He's coming home with me tonight.'

'What did they ask you?' Manon says.

They are walking back from HQ through the darkness. The wind is in the trees, loud and strong. It is the kind of wind

118

that seems portentous. Fly has been questioned for an hour, while Manon waited, feeling increasingly persecuted by her own powerlessness.

Fly shrugs. He is hunched, his hands in his jeans pockets.

'This really isn't the time to be the secretive teenager,' she says.

She's reminded of the article she read only a day or two ago, about the teenage brain, how it is nothing like the adult brain. It is open and suggestible, an ideal sponge for learning but also in grave danger from risk-taking: that explorative impulse seemingly indiscriminate. Children, essentially, are idiots, and teenagers are children driving adult bodies, while blindfolded by hormones. The article likened them to Ferraris capable of terrifyingly high speeds with no experience of the roads and no inbuilt sense of caution. *What has he done?*

He sniffs.

'Doesn't matter how still I am, how quiet I live. The world's still gonna throw some shit in my face.'

'Right, so I can see you're enjoying a pity party but you need to tell me what their line of questioning was, so we can close it down.'

Trust him, she tells herself. *Trust him.*

He says nothing and they trudge, listening to their shoes on the pavement. They are lit by a car's headlamps momentarily.

'Is there anything you want to tell me?' she asks into the silence he is maintaining. All her doubts swirl about them like the winds that rough them up.

'How do you mean?' he says.

'I don't know. I know you've been unhappy and things have got . . . You can tell me, that's all I'm saying. You can tell me anything and I won't go off the deep end. Well, I might, but I'll still love you and defend you and help you.'

'Tell you I stabbed someone?' he says. 'Tell you I stabbed Solly's dad?'

She stops. 'If you needed to.'

'You think I'm capable of things I haven't even thought of.'

'No, no, Fly, I don't.'

She ought to trust him, she ought to know that this is a mistake and yet, she knows Harriet, Davy, Kim and Gary Stanton, officers she has worked alongside for years. She has sat with them in cars through the night. Job after job. She knows how they operate. They wouldn't bring him in without evidence. They would be even more reluctant to bring him in because he's her son. They must have evidence, something strong.

Another thing she knows: that we are all capable of anything.

'Fly, slow down, will you? Look, you need to tell me, at the very least, what their line of questioning is. You need to tell me, so I can knock it down.'

'Kept askin' me what time I came home from school – was it 4.23 or 4.49 or whatever, like I keep track of the minutes. I said I didn't know. I left school after tech, walked across the park, like I always do, and went straight home. Ellie said she was popping out so me an' Sol watched some CBeebies, played *Temple Run*. Then you came in.'

'What've they got? What evidence did they show you?'

'They showed me on CCTV walking through the park, that's all. But I never said I wasn't in the park – it's my way home. I don't understand it. Why would I have anything to do with Solly's dad?'

'You haven't been arrested, don't forget. It hasn't got to that. They're probably eliminating you and this'll be the last you'll hear of it.'

'They took my phone,' he says.

120

'Right. And is there anything on your phone that we ought to be worried about?'

He shrugs.

She wants to interrogate who he is at this moment – entirely the wrong moment – so she says, 'You never told me what the fight with the Cole twins was all about. That's not like you, to get into a fight.'

'Nuffin.'

'Didn't sound like nothing. Mr Jenkins said you had to be pulled off by some geography teacher or other.'

'Sleazy Mr Mitchell. Always defending the Cole Nazis.'

'Nazis?'

'They're not very nice kids,' Fly says.

'Did you know their mother, Judith Cole, is the one who found Jon-Oliver dying on the heath? Cradled him while he died?'

'I didn't know that,' Fly says quietly and he looks at her as if he's in shock all over again.

Two weeks in
28 December

Davy

When you're on your own, mid-week can seem better than a
Friday. Plenty of occupation and company. Weekends are a
problem; Christmas has certainly been a problem (though
now he's through it). Just him and his mum in her bungalow.
Her obsessional studying of the *Radio Times* for the television
schedules; the way she often said, 'It's hard, being on your
own. Very hard. Old age is not for the faint-hearted, David.'
This refrain, he senses, is going to amplify with the years, given
she's only 57.

He's over the bloody moon to be back at work, having been
off since Christmas Eve. She kept asking him to go to the shop
to pick up this and that, then telling him he'd got the wrong
thing. 'This isn't the cream I asked for, David. I wanted *pouring*
cream.' She made him peel all the sprouts, then boiled the life
out of them. By the time they reached his mouth, they were
pale and mushy, disintegrating on contact.

After four days with his mother, a complex murder inquiry
with an over-involved super seems to Davy like a walk in the
park, though Harriet's expression is doom-laden as she

approaches his desk. Fortunately, she's not one to ask how the festivities went, a question he dreads and prepares for in advance. ('Ah brilliant, thanks. Too many sprouts,' with an accompanying pat of his stomach.)

'I need you to warn Manon,' Harriet says. 'Better coming from you. I can't hold Stanton off, not after the phone work. If I don't make an arrest, he's going to assign this to another team and then I *really* won't be able to do anything for Fly. Tell her to instruct Mark Talbot, he's the best.'

Fly's mobile phone gave them the texts they were looking for, the ones Stanton said would be there. Going through the data, Colin said, 'They're all pretty much in the same vein, sent by Ross just before each visit to the little fella – Solomon, is it?'

Coming up to see my son tomorrow.
Make yourself scarce, there's a good lad.

Time to go do one, laughing boy.

Off you pop.

'Was there a similar text for this last visit?' Davy asked.

'No, there wasn't. Bit strange, isn't it?' Colin said. 'Also, there is nothing in return from Fly. Doesn't respond. Unless . . . unless he finally had enough of being told to get lost.'

Davy picks up the receiver on his desk handset. Puts it down again. Digs into his pocket for his mobile phone and walks out through the double doors of MCU to the stairwell, where he hopes it'll be quiet enough.

MANON

'Davy!' she says into her phone. 'Just on my way in.'

'Shouldn't you take the holidays off, have a proper rest?'

She's in front of her bedroom mirror, despairing at finding anything to wear after her Christmas expansion.

Television is what got them through it. They watched everything: *Downton Abbey* special, *Strictly Come Dancing* special, *Midsomer Murders*, Bond movies, *Chicken Run*. Manon bought a tin of Quality Street and kept on digging her fist into it just because she could, her feet up on a pouffe. The heating was on a smidgen too high and the grazing never ceased: turkey sandwiches with cranberry, crackers and cheese, more Quality Street. Ellie said, 'I think you're going to give birth to a strawberry cream instead of a baby,' to which Manon replied, 'Now that's a delivery I could get behind.'

When Ellie brought out a box of posh chocolate-covered ginger, they all groaned, then dug in. Solly played with his vast plastic car park with a car lift that made an infuriating noise. Fly was constantly on his phone, watched anxiously by Manon who wondered if he was fixing a drug deal or exchanging lewd photographs with girls of ill repute but when she sneaked a look, found he'd been playing Scrabble on a site called Wordfeud. They tolerated the obligatory Christmas Day phone call with Ellie and Manon's dad in Scotland, in which they exchanged all the non-news of the season. 'Yup, sausages round the bird. Got to go, *Paddington*'s coming on.'

She has a single pair of black trousers that will cover her bump, giving her a snug feeling. She's also discovered some wonderful reinforced pants, enormous and belly-hugging, designed for post-operative wear. She has purchased ten pairs. The whole front section of her body, from her breasts to her pelvis, feels tight – both braced and straining, rather as if she is the prow of a ship moving stately forwards.

'I'm pregnant, not terminal,' she says to Davy, though as she says it, she wonders. Pregnancy is strange, the body so deeply occupied, so furiously at work. Seems incredible that one manages anything else bar a lot of sleeping. 'How are you, anyway?'

'Fine. Look. Things have developed, I'm afraid.'

'Things?' She has a hand on her hip; she looks to the ceiling, her heart rate accelerating.

'Harriet says you should instruct Mark Talbot.'

Mark Talbot is the cleverest defence lawyer they know, which isn't saying much because they view most of the briefs who frequent the station as at best annoyances, at worst obstructive idiots. Talbot is different. An extremely bright do-gooder, who seems to undertake only legal aid work, though how he makes a living at it is anyone's guess. He is diligent, sartorially shambolic. Manon finds him wildly attractive though she appears to be alone in this. Nothing new there.

'Don't do this, Davy,' she says. 'I'll come in, we can talk about it. I'm sure it's all a misunderstanding. Don't do this, he's . . . he won't deal with it. We can work it out without putting him through this.'

'It's not up to me, Manon.'

She senses there is something else he'd like to say.

'Yes, hello, I'm wondering if you'll take a case for me. It's DI Manon Bradshaw, Cambridgeshire MCU.'

She is making the call from her desk at the office.

'Sure, but shouldn't you go through the call centre? Why are you ringing me directly?'

'It's, it's someone . . .' Her voice wobbles uncontrollably. 'It's my son, you see.'

'Are you all right, Manon?'

'Not really, no. Listen, Mark, please take this case. You're the best solicitor I know. I really need' – up into the higher octaves, almost as if she's singing – 'your help. They did initial interviews before Christmas. I thought it might not escalate, y'know, that it was routine inquiries, but they're taking him into custody today and they're going to search our house.'

'You shouldn't have let him do an initial interview without representation.'

'I know. I know I shouldn't, but he hadn't been arrested you see, so I didn't think. . . It's not the same when you're on the other side, you don't think straight. This is like a fucking ambush. Can you come?'

A deep sigh at the other end of the phone. 'Let me shuffle things about here. I'll see what I can do. What's the charge likely to be?'

'Um,' quavering again, 'murder. I think it's going to be murder. Manslaughter maybe. He's 12.'

'Right, I see. I'd better get to you quickly, hadn't I?'

She is unable to answer that one.

As Manon puts down the phone, Harriet stops by her desk and takes in the tears falling and the trembling, twisted mouth.

'Why don't you go? Rest up at Bryony's,' Harriet says. 'You can't do any good here. I can't imagine you can think about anything at all right now, can you?'

Manon has her fingers on her lips and shakes her head. Swallows.

'No,' Manon coughs. 'No, I want to be here. In case—'

'In case what? You're not allowed to eavesdrop on the case. You know that. Look, I want you to see the police doctor.'

Manon looks up at Harriet with brimming eyes. 'Fuck you,' she whispers.

'Yeah fine, but I still want you to see the police doctor.'

The doctor doesn't look up when she enters the room. Manon is busy trying to stem the crying. When she is not crying, she looks angry, so perhaps crying is better, but that's not how it feels.

He is writing on a pad. Are doctors always writing on a pad, or is this a message about importance and the patriarchy? She once had a DI who would make her stand beside his chair for minutes on end before he would look up from his computer screen and acknowledge her presence; so rude, yet tolerated in the passive-aggressive environs of office life.

'I think you should take a leave of absence, officer . . .' He starts rifling through papers for her name, rank and number. Manon has lowered herself into a chair.

'Detective Inspector,' she says. 'Manon Bradshaw.'

The doctor still hasn't looked at her. 'I can sign you off for a month.' At last he looks up, and takes in her bump. 'In your condition . . .' he says, nodding at it.

'You can be pregnant and in the police.'

127

'You may find it hard to keep your mind on policing,' he says.

'My tiny pregnant mind, you mean.'

She doesn't know why she's doing this. She won't be able to concentrate on anything except getting Fly out, but to get Fly out she needs to be on the inside, not stuck at home, and then she remembers she can't go home. Home will be swarming with paper suits, the bath panels off, toilet cisterns dismantled, covers off the drains.

'I can't go home,' she blurts. 'I mean, I need to be on the shop floor. Take my mind off it. Otherwise I'll go crazy.' She forces a smile for him.

'I'm sure DCI Harper has explained the seriousness of you having any contact with the investigation, so I'll just reiterate it here. There is an exclusivity notice on this case. I'm sure you know what that means. Officers are not permitted to divulge any information and you, in particular, are not permitted to talk to officers about your son's case. Also, you are forbidden from searching computer files – these searches would show up on your computer, and your computer will be checked. Is that clear?'

She wants to say, '*Yeah, yeah, whatevs,*' as Fly would, but she remains silent. Which is like him, too.

Way back last July, when Manon saw the second line on the pregnancy test, the first person she wanted to tell (after her dad) was Bryony – her oldest friend, still in Cambridgeshire, stranded on Disclosure; mother of two, straining at the work–life–exhaustion balance. ('I can make it work,' she told Manon, 'I'm just not sure I can stay married.')

Bri's role is known as Officer in the Case, which makes Manon think of *Doctor in the House*. The case file in any inves-

128

tigation starts out as a slim dossier of the primary evidence against the suspect, growing by the time the case reaches court to Disclosure – as many as 3,000 documents (witness statements, CCTV footage, forensics, pathology reports, expert witness statements) which are shared with the defence. Disclosure is the evidence that serves the prosecution case. Secondary disclosure is all the rest – the evidence that's either deemed irrelevant, or more controversially, doesn't serve the prosecution case. Police and defence lawyers see secondary disclosure very differently.

Anyway, there was a lot of numbering of documents involved, Bri said. You had to develop a love of foolscap. After the pregnancy test result, Manon punched away at her phone:

I have big noos.

DON'T LEAVE ME HANGING.

I am With Child.

Hahahahahahahahahahahahahahaha.
You are going to be so tired. Hahahahahahahahahaha.
Who's the lucky fella?

No one you know. Due April.

Oh please come back to Huntingdon. My auntie skills are primed and ready *kisses the guns*

Working on it. Have baggage these days.

Also, I want to laugh more at how tired you'll be, haha-hahahaha etc, esp as mine sleeping through the night, *does victory dance* *falls asleep*

'This is really good of you,' Manon says, heaving over Bryony's threshold a brown wheelie suitcase in which she and Ellie had thrown, without folding, everything in their sightline which had seemed grabbable and useful – toys, vests, nappies, shower gel – while a uniformed officer stood guard.

The house seemed barely theirs. Manon felt its disarrangement at cell level; all wrong, strangers everywhere. Possessions, which had been connected to them – toys, cosmetics, condiments – severed from them at the disdainful hands of SOCO. She tells herself to remember this feeling when she's handling a search at a suspect's home in future.

Fly's arrest was conducted with the utmost quietness by Davy, with lots of muttering about 'just a formality' and apologies and 'nothing to worry about, Fly' and 'I'm sure this'll all be over soon'.

Manon kissed Fly, saying into his ear, 'I'll sort this.'

Ellie follows Manon over the threshold of Bryony's house. Solly is tangled around their legs, trying not to enter.

'It's a pleasure to have you,' Bryony says, brisk bosomy mother, her arm about Manon's shoulders as she kisses her. 'We have vast amounts of extremely dry turkey meat to get through, so don't think this is going to be any sort of holiday. It's fun for us, isn't it, Bobby?'

Bobby stands on the bottom stair wearing a Batman cape. He is 5. 'Is it time to watch TV yet?' he says.

'You see?' says Bryony. 'We are the perfect hosts.'

Sitting around the kitchen table, they can hear Dora the Explorer's squeaky saccharine tones emanating from the lounge while various-sized children including Bri's 3 year old daughter, little chubby legs splaying from the sofa unbent, watch open-mouthed.

'Fucking love TV,' says Bryony. 'Like taking their batteries out.'

'What'll it be like when we're allowed back in?' Ellie asks.

'Like you've been burgled,' Bryony says.

Manon is shaking her head and putting a grape in her mouth. 'Won't be that bad. No fingerprinting, so it's not like it'll be covered in soot. They'll pull it apart a bit – down the drains, under floorboards, tops of cupboards, that type of thing. It won't look like the cleaner's just been.'

'They're supposed to leave it as they found it,' Bryony says.

By the time the children have had their tea, Solomon has taken to following Bobby around the house like a salivating groupie. Bobby has found him a superhero cape and he wears it, naked but for a nappy, with a stretch-fabric eye mask.

'If only Fly could see you now,' Manon says to him upstairs, waiting for the bath to run.

Solly stops at the mention of Fly, looks at her, then shouts, 'Bobby!'

'Judas,' says Manon, even as she grabs him and gives him a squeeze. She is in need of it, feels watery on the inside and she holds on to Solly like someone drowning. His body is comforting, warm and ever so soft. He struggles free.

Downstairs she can hear Ellie and Bryony talking about potty training.

'I don't know when to begin,' says Ellie.

'Try when he's about ten. I'm not gonna lie, it's a long road. Boys just love that warm squishy feeling. Girls are like, *Bring me some pants, I've got a busy day at the office!*'

* * *

Manon lies in Bobby's single bed, beneath his Minion duvet, his moon and stars projector light throwing moving shadows onto the wall. The bed smells sweet, like warm bread, with traces of Vosene. Bobby is sleeping in with Bri and Peter. Ellie and Solomon are down the hall in the spare room, Bobby and Solly's requests to share a room having fallen on very deaf ears.

Manon thinks of the tape that might be wrapped about her house, setting the neighbours muttering over fences and down telephone wires about the boy they already glanced at with suspicion as he curved about their cul-de-sacs on his bike, long-limbed, standing up on the pedals. She wonders how long before his name is leaked, how long before aspersions turn into certainties, backed up by righteous indignation from people who claim they have been at risk.

A tear rolls down her cheek. Where is he now? Curled in a foetal position in his hard cell? The mattress a wipeable gym mat. The blanket scratchy, sliding off his thin body. Is he crying for her? She knows he is frightened, alarmed. Is Davy looking in on him through the square window in the door, then slamming it shut? What possessed her to bring him here, away from everything he knows?

DAY 15
29 DECEMBER

DAVY

On Manon's front lawn, he has an out-of-body moment, as if he is looking down on himself from above.

Normally, he'd be high-fiving his nearest officer or, if no one was to hand, just whispering, '*Yessss.*' He'd be on the phone to Harriet, saying, '*Got him.*'

Instead he walks over to her, heavy through the flat, shadowless day. Hands in his trouser pockets, he says, 'There's a knife block.'

Harriet looks grimly at him. 'Go on,' she says.

'There's one knife missing from the block – we've searched the kitchen for it. The proportions of the missing knife match the blade size given by Derry Mackeith for the murder weapon.'

'OK, that's still circumstantial,' Harriet says. 'Might be coincidence. The knife might be missing for some other reason.'

'That's not all,' says Davy. 'The trainer – the print in the blood. It was in Fly's room. And his hoodie.'

'The fibre snagged on the bush?' says Harriet.

Davy nods.

'Right,' she says. 'I don't think we have a choice now, not

133

with the postmortem and the phone work. We need to put the allegation to him in interview, see what he says, then call the CPS, see what they think about charging him.'

Davy has tried to contain the Bradshaw barrage by ushering her into interview room one and closing the door.

'I hope you're looking at all the other kids who would've been in the park that day. The park that's right opposite Hinchingbrooke School? There's barely an inch of that park that doesn't have a teenager in it at some time of the day.'

Less a mountain range, he's thinking (looking down at his case file to avoid Manon's tirade), *more a volcano, molten and spitting.*

'I hope you set up a roadblock to ask for witnesses. Did you, Davy? And house to house, did you do house to house? Because no one came to our house, Davy. Didn't I teach you anything? What about people who walked up from Huntingdon station? I take it you've captured all CCTV off transport.'

'We've got evidence,' Davy says quietly.

'What evidence?' she says.

'I can't tell you that, you know I can't tell you that. You'll find out when prosecution papers are served on the defence.'

'That's weeks! You're going to let my son rot in custody for weeks, without telling me what you've got on him?'

'Enough for the CPS.' In interview, accompanied by his brief Mark Talbot, Fly answered no comment to questions about what he was doing in the park at the time Ross was stabbed and whether he did it. 'I can't tell you what we've got, you know that perfectly well, Manon. I'm not doing this to hurt you, I'm following normal procedure where there's a case to answer. Same as you would do if it were my son. What d'you want me to do – ignore the evidence?'

134

'I'm not asking you to ignore it. I'm asking you to consider that you might be wrong. I'm asking you to look at the whole picture. Maybe, you've narrowed your main lines too early, Davy . . .'

'Because of the evidence that's come to light.'

'No, because you want it to be Fly. You want it tidy. And because you hate me for coming back.'

'Hate you?'

'That's right. I've ruffled your feathers and now you want to show your sugar daddy that you're up to the job. Well, you're not up to the job, Davy.' This comes out as a watery shout. 'You're not!'

He smarts. Colours up.

Harriet has come into the room. She casts Manon a guilty look.

'You've told her,' Harriet says to Davy.

'That you're charging Fly? Yes, he's told me. But you wait till I see your evidence. I'm going to knock it down, every shoddy brick of it,' says Manon.

'I'm not even supposed to discuss it with you,' Harriet says, glancing towards the door and going to close it. She turns. 'Ross gets off the train at 4.13 p.m. right? Takes him ten minutes to walk the Brampton Road, he turns into Hinchingbrooke Road at 4.23 p.m., he collapses and dies at 4.27 p.m. Fly is on the CCTV at 4.32 p.m. He walks over the blood drips that were found on the path. You explain it to me, Manon.'

'Fly doesn't dispute going through the park. It's his route home. Can you see him stabbing Ross on the film? No, I didn't think so. So, what, you're wondering how Fly didn't notice a man dying right next to him? He's in a bubble, that's how. Have you ever witnessed how many times I have to say things to get Fly's attention? It's like he's got his own time–space continuum. He's in a dream world. Santa could fly past on his sleigh and Fly wouldn't notice. Did he have buds in his ears? Because if he did, there's even less chance of him noticing. I often wonder if he's deaf or mentally subnormal but actually, he's just a *boy*.'

'The knife, the murder weapon, fits the dimensions of the knife missing from your knife block.'

Manon is pacing. 'Jesus, we moved house four months ago. I haven't located the cheese grater either. Or the garlic press.'

Harriet is silent. She has one knuckle on the table, the other hand on her hip. 'D'you want to come with us to Fly's detention room? Be there with him?' she asks.

They let Manon go first, lumbering in front of them along the corridor to the room that's closest to the custody sergeant, reserved for the young and the vulnerable. Mark Talbot is already in with Fly.

The atmosphere is like that surrounding a death, silent and grave in the moments before Harriet utters the words. Davy feels like an executioner. All those years he's spent volunteering at youth centres, mentoring vulnerable teenagers, and here he is with a square of black cloth on his head, sending a child down.

He looks at all the adults standing; dark suits, jowl-heavy grey faces like some sombre oil painting from the past. Davy sees that something irrevocable is about to take place. Just at the moment it wounds Davy most, Fly starts to cry: unashamed, terrified tears, looking at Manon and saying, 'Mum.'

'You are charged with the following offence,' says Harriet. 'That on the fourteenth of December at Huntingdon, you did murder Jon-Oliver Ross contrary to common law. You do not have to say anything but it may harm your defence if you do not mention now—'

136

'Mum,' Fly says, holding on to her.

'Don't do this,' says Manon.

Davy cannot look at her.

'—something you later rely on in court. Anything you do say may be given in evidence. Have you any reply . . .'

The rest passes in a blur, Davy aware only of the cold bubble of guilt travelling up his spine and the desire to get away.

'Fly will remain here until we can get a youth court sitting for his remand hearing,' Harriet is saying.

'Give us a moment, will you?' Manon says. 'Me and Fly.'

MANON

'I'll get you out,' she says to Fly. 'It's been a mistake and I'll get you out.' He looks so wounded, she is struck by her failure. *Our only job is to protect children from the shoddiness of adults and I've already failed.* She feels deeply implicated, a part of the world that has let him down. The police force has always for her been about protection, but it wreaks havoc also. 'I'm sorry this has happened, Fly.'

She holds him close. At first he is limp, too dazed to embrace her. Then his tears come again and he holds on to her, full of fear.

She takes his face in her hands, looks into his eyes.

'I'll get you out, Fly. You have to trust me. I know this is awful but just . . . hold your nerve. I will get you out.'

Mark enters the room, sits down at the table and opens his file.

'Right, I've seen the charge sheet and as per usual it's telling me nothing. Jon-Oliver Ross stabbed, etc, we think your client did it.'

Fly turns to Mark and says, 'No wonder they charged me,

138

after all that no comment business. You made me look guilty. If I'd just talked to 'em, told them everyfink, I wouldn't be in this mess...'

Mark is shaking his head. 'I advised you to go no comment because we don't know what they've got, right? Fly? Look at me. We don't know if there's a witness who could identify you, we don't know if there's forensics, we don't know if they've got a weapon. And they weren't about to tell us anything. Which means you could've given them information without meaning to, without even realising you were giving it to them. It was crucial not to say anything that might've inadvertently helped their case, right? And as we didn't know their case, not in any detail, the chances of that happening were quite high. So I was right to advise you to go no comment, and I'm sure your mum will agree with me. Even though she's a copper.'

He has a dense beard and cowlicks of grey hair, as if electrified. Heavy, black-rimmed glasses. He is smiling at Fly to try and reassure him.

'They are not going to release you on bail, so it's likely you'll be sent down from court, either tomorrow or the next day, to a children's secure home. Arlidge House would be my guess.'

She can see the terror in Fly's eyes. So can Mark. 'It's not a bad place,' he says, 'more like a youth centre than a prison.' Manon is watching Fly's face, watching him try to take in all the things he has never considered – that he would be sent to prison without any room for argument. Yesterday double maths, today custody.

'The only thing I can do for you during this period,' Mark is saying, 'while we're waiting for disclosure – that's the evidence to be shared with us – is to take lots of detail about your background, how you're doing at school, any health worries you might have. The Youth Offending team are going to be in

139

doing the same, I'm afraid, to make sure you're properly looked after in custody. I need you to sign this – it's a confidentiality waiver – so I can discuss all aspects of the case with your mum.'

As Fly signs, the drips of his tears wet the paper.

Outside, Manon leans her back against the door. She is panting, cannot draw breath. 'I can't leave him here. I can't . . . Someone has to be kind to him. No one's being *kind* to him. I was supposed to protect him from stupid adults and look what's happened.'

'Come on,' says Mark. 'We'll go and have a cup of tea. Talk it through.'

As they take the stairs down to the canteen, it's as if he's already forgotten her sensitivities, because he says, 'We've got to hope the press don't get hold of this. You can imagine what the tabs will do with a black 12-year-old charged with the murder of a white banker from the City. It'll be mayhem, even if they can't name him.'

Sitting across a Formica table from one another, like fugitives from the officers sitting at adjacent tables, she wipes a new set of tears from her face with a napkin, saying, 'You don't need to worry about Fly. He's super bright, top of his class, great reader. He'll understand everything you say to him.'

'Any history of self harm?'

'No.'

Mark gives her a sceptical look.

'Look, if there had been, I'd have been all over it,' she says.

'Any involvement with the police prior to this?'

'No; well, me – I'm the police. He was stopped and searched a lot when we lived in London. It was one of the reasons I wanted to get him out, move him here I mean. Bad move, huh.'

'Background?'

She braces herself to tell Fly's story, her efforts to bridge the gap between the bald facts and the nuanced reality. How things sound versus how they are lived. Fly's story always seems to come out the same. Damage equals guilt, but nothing could be further from the truth. How should she describe the boy she has come to love without sounding delusional, blinded by maternal faith?

She tries to tell Mark how losing his brother Taylor was far more significant for Fly than losing his mother, who died six months after Taylor from stomach cancer, though both losses rolled together into a year of turbulent rage and depression, in which she feared she would lose him altogether or that he wouldn't emerge and she wouldn't cope.

'Sorry, your relationship to Fly . . . ?' Mark says, looking up from his furious note-taking.

'I was investigating Taylor's death. Fly and I formed a bond. When Maureen died, I came to London to look after him, and also to be with my sister and nephew. Things just sort of . . . carried on. I wanted a child and he wanted a mother. A year ago I formally adopted him.'

She watches Mark lean back in his chair, as if there is some sort of fait accompli in his gathering notes. She is pricked by anger, that he is appraising her and Fly's relationship, picking at the strands that have them so deeply – or tenuously – attached.

'What, you think you know his story now, is that it?' she says. 'It looks bad on paper, this difficult life he's had, and I'm not going to lie, we've had our moments. He's definitely felt his losses. But the thing about Fly is that isn't the story. He's all there. He's all connected up. He loves Solly and he loves me. Just because he's been through bad things, doesn't mean he's incapable of leading a good life.'

141

'It increases his predisposition towards crime and involvement with social services.'

'Does it now,' she says.

'You know it does.'

'Maybe I know it does in the main, but in this case it doesn't because it's Fly.'

'Can you tell me how he felt about the baby you're having? Was he threatened by you having a biological child?'

'No, he was fine. He is fine. Everything is completely fine about the baby.'

Six months earlier
London

'How come you're still in bed?' Fly asked, setting the cup down as he always did on her bedside table. He was wearing a polo shirt and grey school shorts, the heat of the day already building around them. Most days, she'd be in the shower by now, and the coffee he made her each day would be waiting on the table. Most days, she'd wait to hear the click of the front door to know he'd left, before tipping his coffee down the kitchen sink.

'I've got a doctor's appointment,' she said, and regretted the word 'doctor' immediately; too sleepily preoccupied to prevent it slipping out.

'Doctor? Why?' he said, alarmed.

'Nothing serious, routine in fact,' she said, propping herself up in the bed, taking a sip of the coffee and trying not to visibly grimace. Brown water.

Fly was staring at her, rigid.

'I'm fine, Fly. Honestly. I'd tell you if I wasn't.'

He sniffed. Nodded. She recalled all the advice from counsellors, therapists, education welfare, social workers – about the terrors he carried with him. She was aware he'd been crippled by loss. Yet she could not shake off some irritation at the persistence of these shadows over them both.

'Another scorcher by the look of it,' she said. They were in the midst of a grimy heatwave which cooked the bins and baked the pavements. 'I'm really fine. Go on, you get on. Wear a cap, yes?'

She heard him leave and wondered how she could do what she was about to do when her mind was so full of him. Wasn't one child enough? Yet each time she road-tested the idea, she was surprised to encounter excitement, not fear. She was taking the bull by the horns. *Or the testicles*, more accurately.

She couldn't stand to wait any more.

She couldn't bear the waiting: to meet the right man, get to know him, find he (like all the rest) was afraid of commitment; to do her best not to put the pressure on so that she became a cauldron of internalised pressure fit to burst; to have the relationship go wrong and be so enveloped in grief, a rolling together of multiple griefs along with self-recrimination and dread of the future and to have her mind already calculating: when could it begin again and how long could it take? This way, she wasn't waiting. She was no longer contingent on the questionable emotional register of a man she hadn't even met yet. She'd considered the options: freezing an egg, freezing an embryo, but it all just seemed like more waiting, more contingency. No, she had decided and in the deciding she'd felt unexpectedly released. Elated. As if an enormous weight – or wait – had been lifted.

For £500 she had secured her initial appointment at the fertility clinic in Harley Street, grateful for the country-house lamps and Persian rugs that made it seem like some kind of luxurious spa treatment she was giving herself. Pedicure. Exfoliation. In-utero insemination.

'What is it you want, Miss Bradshaw?' the doctor said. He was in his fifties, silver-haired.

'I want a baby,' she said simply. 'I don't want to wait any more.' And it seemed so clear and straightforward, she wondered why she'd spent the last decade making such a meal of it.

He nodded, consulting the piece of paper. 'You are 42, is that right?'

'Yes, my ovaries are probably sitting in rocking chairs, knitting!' she said. She'd rehearsed this joke on the tube and as it came out, you could tell.

'We'll take a look at them now, see what they're doing. Run some tests to ascertain your fertility.'

Smearing the cold gel across her tummy and looking at the screen, he said, 'Lots of eggs. You seem quite fertile.'

And she'd had to hide the roar of delight inside herself. 'Turkey baster it is then,' she said.

As she walked out of the clinic into the searing light and heat, her phone rang. Havers – DCI Sean Haverstock, her boss and a dickwad of the first order. He said there was a body being hooked out of the Welsh Harp lake. Could she make her way there pronto? Yes, he was aware it was her day off but he didn't have anyone else. She was to meet Melissa Harcourt at the scene.

Melissa effing Harcourt.

Nemesis.

Melissa effing Harcourt was new to Kilburn CID, the handy hook on which to hang Manon's rivalry. The search beam of Bradshaw envy had tracked the passage of Melissa's suits and tottery shoes across the office floor. 'How's she going to run in those?' Manon muttered to a DC standing next to her, but he'd just frowned at her as if she was the bitterest object he'd ever seen.

Day upon day of Havers puffing himself up as he marvelled at Melissa's potential.

'She manages up,' Manon told Ellie. Ellie hadn't responded to this patently not-casual remark.

Melissa effing Harcourt had an engagement ring that sparkled as it caught the light. She wasn't hugging an extra stone. She had a spring in her step, which indicated she was not, as yet, beset by *the heaviness*. Did Melissa's feet balk at the re-stacking of Melissa's body above them of a morning? They did not.

Manon would've liked Melissa effing Harcourt to suffer illness or a breakup or even a Reg 14 misconduct notice.

The heat was beating out the smell of rotting flesh.

In the blinding light of the day, squinting and with tissues held over their mouths, Manon and Melissa stood at the edge of the reservoir, a vast oval of open water straddling Brent and Barnet, and a magnet for corpses; they were forever hooking cadavers out of the Welsh Harp.

This particular body was bloated and blue, traces of blood crusted black around the nostrils. The stench of it was like a putrid wall and Manon's body recoiled: her gagging reflex in full swing with the rolling away of her insides.

'We don't have an ID yet,' said Melissa, her tissue still over the lower half of her face.

'She looks young,' Manon said. 'In this weather, gases will have made the body bob up to the surface of the water quite fast. My guess is she died within the last couple of days. We'll need an ID from fingerprints. And we'll need to capture all the CCTV around the reservoir, see how she got in the water.'

'Probably a jumper,' said Melissa. 'Blood around the nose looks like drugs.'

Manon looked Melissa in the eye. 'We don't know that,' she said. 'Melissa? We don't know if she's a jumper or a drug addict, OK? No assumptions. Even if she's both, she deserves a proper investigation.'

That evening, at her laptop, Manon purchased a father with a simple Add to Basket and the inputting of her card details online. For £850 she secured the sperm of a Dane, a nationality that seemed to carry a neutral air. You couldn't *hate* a Dane. Catalogue number 4063. She knew nothing more about him than the following:

Skin tone: Caucasian
Eye colour: Blue
Occupation: Doctor [impossible to resist]
Skills: Speaks Danish, English and French. Drawing, maths
Height: 176cms

That was it. The rest – the pessimism, the envy, the brown ringlets perhaps, lack of sporting ability, the love of carbohydrates, the yawning ability to find fault: these riches would come from her. The Danes, she learned, are prolific exporters of Lego and sperm.

His sperm – the Danish doctor's – would be delivered in a test tube, encased in some polystyrene, to the Harley Street clinic where it would await defrosting at the right time.

She hadn't discussed the idea with Ellie because she didn't want to be dissuaded. In Manon's mind, Ellie had become the harbinger of practicalities: the workload (all those broken nights, no respite); the finances (supporting two kids on a police salary; covering the rent on maternity pay); never going out, always being tired. Manon preferred to turn away from these so she left them pinned on an imagined-Ellie's worried face.

And she hadn't discussed it with Fly. She flushed at the very thought that she hadn't discussed it with Fly, her guilt escaping in thoughts which came to ambush her at unexpected moments. She hadn't discussed it with Fly because . . .

Because she was a coward.

Because it was painful to think what Fly might feel. Displaced. Replaced. His position challenged by a gurgling white baby who shares her DNA. At the same time, she couldn't give up her right to a child of her own. There was some ruthlessness in this. At the same time – back it goes – she couldn't stand the thought of Fly entertaining insecure thoughts so instead she waited, maintaining the status quo.

Why tell him when it hadn't happened yet? Might never happen. Why upset him with what was – at her age – only a slim possibility?

The day after the body in the Welsh Harp and the online sperm purchase, Havers called Manon into his office.

'Welsh Harp body?' he said. 'She was called Jade Canning – ID came in from fingerprinting. Right, so, yes, I'm giving Jade Canning to DS Harcourt, testing her mettle. She's a very bright officer. Going places. Let's see how she does as SIO.'

'You're making a DS the senior investigating officer in a potential murder? Without a DI overseeing?' Manon said. 'Sorry, have you suffered a blow to the head?'

'I doubt it's a murder, not from the looks of it. Yes, it's unusual but a) I'm 99 per cent sure it's a druggy lowlife who jumped and b) I think Harcourt's got what it takes. And I've always said, how can young officers learn except on the job?'

Manon looked at him. Wondered if they were shagging. You'd have to be really desperate to shag Havers.

SASKIA

After the Carlton Mayfair and the railway arches, we went back to Jon-Oliver's house in Holland Park. He said I could stay a few nights, get myself straight. I suppose we were both a bit shell-shocked by what had happened, though he was pretending it was all part of life in the fast lane.

Jon-Oliver's place was like a hotel or a show home – everything new and unlived-in. He'd hired interior decorators and given them the keys and a massive budget, then left them to get on with it. It was all done out in a palette of greys, white and black, with massive chandeliers and identikit bathrooms in Italian white stone. The kitchen was full of new Miele appliances, untouched. The smell of paint and packaging. The film was still on the oven door and I peeled it off from one corner.

The living room had dove grey walls and black velvet sofas that no one had ever sat on by the looks of them. It smelled of new carpets. That's a lovely smell. Jon-Oliver wanted more sex – fine, I didn't care, part of the job – but first we had to remove twenty-one scatter cushions from the bed. Imagine what those designers spent on those stupid cushions. He went straight off to sleep but I couldn't sleep, so I went wandering round the house.

I kept thinking about Jade, where her body was and what they were doing to it, walking through the faceless luxury of Jon-Oliver's home. I ran my finger over the quality fittings and materials. I imagined what it would be like to live in a house like this, to have whatever you wanted, whenever you wanted it.

Then I went to his study, sat down at his desk, nudged the mouse and his computer screen lit up, so I had a nosy around his files. I read up about the Chinese delegation, and the investments Jon-Oliver was lining up for them. One email mentioned plans for a lavish Christmas drinks party to celebrate the signing of contracts. Much of it, I didn't understand – the stocks and shares stuff was a complete mystery. But I understood the property investments: four Thames riverside penthouses at £3 million each, in a skyscraper mostly owned by offshore shell companies.

At that moment, I realised a couple of things. I realised that the Chinese deal was very important to Dunlop & Finch. I realised there was no way of threatening Titans about Jade's death. Titans, and Moukie – or whoever's behind Moukie – those people don't have a reputation to protect. They're pimps, gangsters. They've got links to organised crime. They're like the Russians – couldn't give a fuck what anyone thinks of them.

But Dunlop & Finch? They're bona fide. Markus van der Lupin considers himself a man of business, part of the establishment. A City firm paying directly for escort girls as part of client hospitality? It would lay waste to their respectable veneer, to Lupin's dinners at Mansion House, his ties to the Chancellor of the Exchequer. Jon-Oliver said Lupin loves the British establishment, takes his wife to Ascot every year. He has left the Latvian sprat factory of his ancestors way behind.

And I realised he was right about them not allowing a police investigation to take place. The Chinese would view it as a stain, as would all those other clients who banked on discretion and anonymity.

At that moment I saw a way out, and it was a whole lot more realistic than waiting for Jon-Oliver to marry me. I saw that if I had enough information about Dunlop & Finch and their clients, I could get money from them – a lump sum that would set me up in Spain. I started the dossier.

I got the printer going, client after client, while drinking an array of macchiatos and hot chocolates from his unused machine in the kitchen. I printed off the details of a shell Jon-Oliver had set up called Claybourne Leisure, which is the front for Titans. His firm and the escort agency were 'in it together' as the saying goes.

I started blackmailing them, that's why I started getting hurt. At first I was sending demands by email from an Internet café. I wanted £1million or I'd go public with the connection to Titans and start naming clients like Xi Ping. It took a whole lot of courage (and some Lambrini) to send that email, but I told myself £1million was small beer for them.

My guess is that Van der Lupin told Moukie to sort it. I was hit by that car outside the Payless. I knew it was too dangerous to go back to my flat. They had me really scared and that made me drink more, which made it worse.

I was really nervous on the night of Van der Lupin's Christmas party, so nervous I had to drink just to get through it, to brazen it out. D'you know what it's like to bluff your way into a party you're not invited to? Then add to that, a party being held by people who'd quite like it if you were dead. Dutch courage doesn't even begin to cover it.

Van der Lupin's place was like a giant doll's house; white

stucco and double-fronted, with pompom-shaped trees on either side of its front door. There were white pin lights everywhere – in the trees, in a canopy over the path. It was like a Hollywood film set. It made total sense. Van der Lupin is all about veneer – respectability, Englishness, propriety. Underneath he's a gangster.

I took a deep breath and slid into the party in a huddle of guests, banking on everyone being too genteel to challenge me. Even so, I started getting some looks. It was probably the Goth makeup – I thought I'd toned it down, gone more 'smoky eye' – but the heavy kohl eyeliner helped me, as if it masked me. Stupid, huh – like a toddler putting its hands over its face and saying, 'Can't see me!'

Anyway, I hadn't toned it down enough because I started getting looks from people.

There was a Christmas tree at the centre of the hall that reached up three storeys, with the staircase behind it and garlands up the banisters. I spotted a couple of the Xi Ping delegation and could see this party was all for them. You know what the City's like – it rests on confidence.

Then Markus van der Lupin saw me – the look of horror on his face! He was greeting new arrivals. He quickly excused himself and came over to me. Just his look made me feel like a tramp.

He ushered me into a side room which turned out to be a library and which closed with a very heavy door – double thickness because it was panelled with books and this must've sound-proofed it.

He asked what the hell I was doing there. I was trying to be cool, running a finger along a shelf of books, as if I was some kind of Bond villain. I felt as if I was going to vomit.

He was furious, his face pink with it. I wondered if Valerie knew what he got up to with Titans girls, but I figured she probably didn't care, so long as the gardener was paid for. She might even have been an escort, once upon a time.

I told him I wanted to be paid off. I couldn't look at him while I said this, couldn't believe I had the balls. I told him Dunlop & Finch had plenty of money and they'd have to pay me to keep quiet about what had happened to Jade at the Carlton Mayfair.

And then I said, and I was really winging it at this point, high on adrenalin and vodka Red Bulls, 'Maybe your Chinese billionaire is going to think twice about signing with you when you're all over the front page of *The Times* in a sex scandal.'

I looked at him then.

Normally, there was no trace of Latvian in van der Lupin's accent, but it came out when he spat in my face.

'Don't fuck with me.'

The door opened and Jon-Oliver came in.

'Saskia, what the hell are you doing here?' he asked.

Van der Lupin picked up the phone and started speaking very fast in Latvian, then two big guys came in and they escorted me out.

They beat me up.

So what? They beat me up; it's nothing.

But they *killed* him. It must be the reason why Jon-Oliver's dead. Oh and I thought he was nice, an OK guy. It's my fault. They thought he was in on it with me, or that his connection with me brought them trouble.

MANON

She has clung to the office like an environmentalist to an endangered tree, unwilling to let go of the place where Fly is being held. When she is forced to leave, late in the evening, she loiters around his cell door, around the custody sergeant.

'Anything he needs? I can always pop back . . .'

She must wrench herself away, so alien is it to sleep in a building away from him. She wants him down the hall. She wants to fold his clothes while he sleeps. Cut him up an apple to eat after supper. She misses tending to him.

The energy she cannot use for this, she directs instead towards gaining information by subtle and ingenious means.

'C'mon Kim,' she whispers. She has cornered Kim in the third-floor toilets, having checked the cubicles first to make sure Harriet isn't lurking. 'I need this. I wouldn't ask, I'm not asking for, y'know, actual material.' She catches sight of herself in the mirror, puffy-eyed from crying and lack of sleep. She's trying to keep it light but notices, in her reflection, that she's leaning in somewhat menacingly. 'Just a quick look at the file. . .'

154

Kim is washing her hands, looking at Manon in the mirror. She pulls at the paper hand towels and a great wad comes out of the dispenser, which she balances on the side of the sink.

If only Manon had rubbed along better in the past. If only she was the type to confide, to hold people close. The only person she confides in is Bryony – someone she's known for twenty-odd years. When people demand of her an intimacy that she doesn't feel, she must force her face into calm, suppressing the urge to flee. But at this moment, she regrets her reserve. At this moment, in the cold echo of the toilets bright with daylight, she wishes she were a different type of person entirely. False, sugary, whatever it takes.

'Love your top, by the way,' she says. And Kim looks at her like she might be deranged.

Oh, and she was never a generous colleague or friend – never one to remember someone's hospital appointment or stressful meeting and call to say 'good luck'. Not the sort to offer childcare (Christ – she'd recoil) or help in a crisis. Some people pride themselves on these touches, seem to advertise them as an emblem of their goodness. Manon is not one of those.

How she regrets her mean-spiritedness now, when generosities could be recalled and paid back. She cannot pressure Kim, because she's never done anything for her.

'You just need what?' Kim is saying now, arms folded across her chest. 'Just need me to risk a gross misconduct report? You think I should lay my job on the line for you? You can fuck right off, Manon. And if you ask me again, I'll tell Harriet.'

She is more at ease sidling up to Colin, on a different tack this time, pedalling a swivel chair up to his.

'So, Col,' she says. 'Got a minute?'

155

'Mmm,' he murmurs, without taking his eyes off the screen where he is examining TripAdvisor's top ten hotels in Croatia.

'So I've got this new iPhone, right.'

He finds this irresistible and glances her way.

'But it won't back up onto the Cloud. Can't make head nor tail of it myself. Would you take a look for me? To be honest, I don't think I'm using half the features I could be—'

'The answer's no.'

'Why?'

'You must think I was born yesterday. Now hop it. I don't want to be seen talking to you.'

Harriet looks up from her computer as Manon closes the door to the boss's office.

'Are you all right?' Harriet asks.

Manon has come armed with a whole set of rehearsed arguments about Harriet's malpractice, the team's institutional racism or clod-hoppery or mistreatment of old friends, but instead of presenting these with barrister-like precision, Manon bursts into tears.

'Sit down,' Harriet says. 'Oh God I'm sorry, this must be agony for you, especially with the pregnancy. Everything OK with the baby?'

Manon nods, unable to speak, remembering her love for Harriet. They solved the Hind case together, have long held each other in high esteem. Of all police officers, she trusts Harriet most deeply.

'How far along are you now?' Harriet asks.

Manon puts her fingers to her lips, swallows, nods. 'Five and a half months. S'posed to be the best bit – the middle trimester. Y'know, glossy hair, lots of energy, rampant sex drive. Before your ankles swell up and you become an elephant.'

Harriet nods and Manon wonders if this conversation is painful for her, Harriet never having had children. They'd always bonded over that – singleness and childlessness.

Is that in ruins now?

'Please, Harriet, just tell me what we're facing. You know that it's weeks of waiting before the prosecution papers are served on the defence and in that time, what, Fly's just supposed to rot in Arlidge House? I have to be able to do something. I can't just sit and watch this happen to him.'

Harriet is looking at her. Her expression is both concerned and remorseful. 'If I could have it any other way, you know—'

'You can. You can talk to me about the case, like we've talked about a billion other cases. I'll never ask you for anything again. We've worked together for years, Harriet; we've worked on murder after murder. You can discuss this one with me and I promise you on my life, on my baby's life, that no one will ever find out that you did.'

There is silence in which Harriet thinks and in which Manon dare not speak in case she disrupts a decision in her favour.

'Come with me,' Harriet says, rising from behind her desk. She opens the door to her office and they walk through the department, as people look up from their computers and watch them pass.

Whispering, once they are on the stairwell, Harriet puts a hand to Manon's elbow: 'I'm going to show you something. But you better keep it quiet. I could get sacked for this.'

Down on the second floor, they take up seats in the dark video room, which smells of warm bodies, the trace of someone's korma. Harriet fiddles about with some footage, rewinding what Manon can tell is transport CCTV. 'I thought you should see this,' Harriet says, getting to the right spot on the film, then sitting back.

Manon looks at the screen. She sees Fly, little beloved figure in a sea of strangers, and she wants to reach out and touch him. He is quietly alone, her boy, in the big world. He is crossing the forecourt at King's Cross, then the footage flicks to him descending an escalator in St Pancras. She looks at Harriet.

'This is when he was supposed to be at school. We matched the date to when the head told us he'd failed to turn up. Took the train to King's Cross, then the Thameslink overground to Cricklewood. Here.'

Harriet pushes some buttons and a different machine plays on an adjacent screen. Manon sees Fly on Cricklewood Broadway, just standing. His face is slack, his sadness simply the absence of animation. He stands with his rucksack on his back, his thumbs beneath the shoulder straps, chest height. *He'll have the book he's reading in that bag,* she thinks sadly.

She can see he is outside the flat he used to live in.

Fly crosses the road to Momtaz Shisha Café.

'Then this,' Harriet says, pushing another play – this time the screen shows council CCTV which takes in Momtaz. Fly is sitting with a man – bald, in his fifties, soldier's build.

'Paddy Driscoe,' Harriet says. 'He's a dealer.'

She leaves it hanging there, while the hot fury burns at Manon's temples.

'Can I see him, please?' she says. 'If you could show me to Fly's detention room, I'd like to kill him.'

'We're looking into this chap,' Harriet says, 'seeing if he has any links to Jon-Oliver Ross, who we know was an enthusiastic coke user. Look, I'm not showing you this to say it's definitely a part of our investigation. All I wanted you to see is that Fly – well, he's been going through something, involved in stuff. And, y'know—'

'Come on, Harriet, it's not like you to fluff about at the edges. Come out with it.'

'You might not know him as well as you think you do. You might not know what he's involved in.'

Manon thinks of all the mothers she has said this kind of thing to. Mothers who didn't know about the glue, didn't realise the spots weren't adolescent acne. The mothers playing catch-up, who hadn't realised that Minecraft had turned into pornography. *And now I am that fool.* She looks at the paused tape of Fly standing on Cricklewood Broadway, the striations of the pause cutting the screen through the centre with white lines, and all she can see is the face of a stranger. A sad, lost 12-year-old boy whose mind she doesn't know.

Murmuring voices swim in and out of her thoughts, slippery fish. Bryony, Peter and Ellie still talking downstairs, or perhaps it's the television. She doesn't know if Fly did it, whether he is involved or innocent. It is almost impossible to stay fixed in not knowing. Instead, she ricochets. She watches Bobby's moon and stars rotate stupidly around the walls. How are children supposed to be comforted by something so coldly mechanical? She closes her eyes.

No one has told her that becoming someone's mother would lead her to imagine the catastrophic end to her motherhood. Her rehearsals of Fly's demise usually involve car accidents; the idiots on the road when her nonchalant child crosses the street daydreaming or worse – with white buds in his ears. Occasionally, those dark imaginings involve Fly being in the wrong place at the wrong time. Outside a pub when a fight breaks out, that kind of thing. Innocence rolled into violence.

Not this. She hadn't foreseen this.

She had become accustomed to feeling about the contours

of her love, feeling for areas of danger. She talked to Ellie about it and Ellie said she did the same with Solly: imagined him tottering drunkenly into a road or drowning in an ornamental pond. Ellie said she feared pushing her buggy in the park towards a dog of unknown provenance, pit bull on a string, which might attack Solly's beautiful face. It was a reminder to be vigilant, Ellie said. Danger was everywhere. Manon wondered if her fears contained something darker, some element of maternal ambivalence.

This is more complex even than that: her son contains mysteries, corners into which she cannot shine a light. He is a closed, separate person. You have a child, you hold him close and he becomes an unknown quantity, a dark taciturn presence in your house.

Sleep chased away by her attempts, over and over, to reality-test what she knows about Fly versus what she knows about her colleagues and the procedures of the police – the burdens of proof necessary to arrest and charge. If they didn't have evidence, he wouldn't be locked up. The CPS wouldn't agree to charge him. Who is her enemy, his offence or her office? Where is she supposed to draw the lines so that she might act? Harriet has shown her evidence of how little she knows about her son. She closes her eyes and thinks back to their Friday nights in Kilburn – the pretend naughtiness of those evenings, when they would come home from school and work, both excitable, shiny-eyed, impromptu hugs, 'It's Friiiiiday! Woo-hooo!', dancing around the kitchen to some Taylor Swift song.

Beloved days when Fly was free to be silly – *what joy* – performing some ridiculous dance which involved shoulder shrugging and eyebrow raising. They would venture out to the multiplex on the Finchley Road, and for something to eat at Nando's or Pizza Express. When they got home they would

160

watch a chat show on TV, unwilling for the pleasures of Friday night to end. Why did she rip him away from all that?

She opens her eyes. She has to turn in the bed, so the baby she no longer wants won't press too hard on her organs. She tells herself to calm down because her breathing is starting to feel shallow, as if there isn't enough breath to gasp.

Truth is, Fly's secrecy was mounting, even then back in Kilburn – accompanying his advance into adolescence. He was self-contained in a way no child should be. On Saturday mornings she would hear the washing machine on at 9 a.m. – his charlady act in full swing.

'I can do your laundry,' she said to him on more than one occasion.

'Why should you?' Fly said.

She wanted to shout, *because that's what people who love each other do* – they intertwine, like the embrace of dirty tops in the basket, over and about themselves. They take each other for granted, messily. This tidying of himself and his needs saddened her.

She turns in the bed again. The baby seems to be awake, squirming and pushing on her bladder.

Fly will have a bed, at least – his own room in Arlidge House – while they sit out the interminable wait for disclosure. Eight weeks minimum, perhaps twelve, before they can look at the evidence and interrogate it, offering alternative explanations, hiring their own expert witnesses to tell the court the Crown is wrong.

Fly will have meals, she tells herself. He can survive. All he has to do is keep it together until she can investigate, as she has investigated so many other cases.

He must not make any sudden moves, not allow his anger to get the better of him, not make a noose from the sheets, not take any of the razor blades that will certainly pass under his door. She hopes he can withstand the feeling that the world is accusing him. She is less sure she can withstand the oscillation in her mind, or the waiting, because what if the end point is Fly with a knife in his hand? What if the end point is one child in prison while another is wailing in her arms?

She thinks of Fly's empty room at their house, turned over now – drawers open, clothes taken, books flipped through. She thinks of Solly, who before having his head turned by the potent glamour of 5-year-old Bobby, would run to the door every time it opened, saying 'Fi?'

Her belly creaks like the timbers of an old ship, the baby saying, *I am inexorable*. She finds it hard to remember the yearning she felt for her own biological child, like the missing square in a tile puzzle: the space that haunted the picture.

She sees this was the gap that allowed the other tiles in their arrangement to move. Now they are stuck in their allocated slots. She should have left it at that – a spacious, unfulfilled longing. Isn't everyone haunted by a child they don't have? The window of fertility missed or deliberately passed by. The wished-for girl in a house full of boys. The dreamy baby when the older ones have gone to school. Shouldn't she have accepted her melancholic thoughts about unborn children, instead of acting on them?

At 4 a.m. she unpeels her eyelids. Like a zombie, arms outstretched for the door, she shuffles across the room only to find her palms against blank wall. She's forgotten that she isn't at home, the landscape of this house unfamiliar. On the toilet, she knows she won't get back to sleep for a couple of hours. This gnawing time – whatever she's working on, whatever's misaligned in her universe, these are the hours when she'll go at it like a knot she's working loose, like a pebble she can't stop fingering in her pocket. *Paddy Driscoe.* What's he been doing with Paddy Driscoe? Has Driscoe taken advantage of Fly, treated him not as the 12-year-old he is, but as an adult?

Fly's phone . . . if she could just call one or two of his London friends, they might know what the Paddy Driscoe angle is. But his phone will be zip-locked in an evidence bag; besides which, she always treated his friends with barely concealed suspicion. Or one of her old informants from her days at Kilburn CID? She arrested her fair share of dealers – not that they'd feel they owe her anything, especially not now that it isn't her beat. Harriet's probably sitting on Paddy Driscoe's number, yet a wall has gone up between Manon and 'them'. They are set in opposition, when they've always been on the same side. She could search the criminal intelligence database when she's back in the office, but she'd be breaking every protocol about interfering with Fly's case. The search would show up on her computer and she could be sacked for it.

She must get to Paddy Driscoe.

DAY 16
30 DECEMBER

DAVY

Davy squints up through the top of his passenger window, needing a glimpse of sky if he is to breathe, but all he is met with is a heavy lid of porridge-coloured cloud, which seems to press down on the roof of their panda car.

His arm is aching.

He's been holding it in the same position, out from his body, his hand resting on the central back seat, for a while now. Handcuffed to that hand, is Fly's: daintier than his own, black at the knuckles, his neat nails peach-coloured and matt with pale half-moons. Fly, too, is looking out of his window so that he and Davy form a parting V. Davy can feel the vibrations of Fly's emotion through the cuffs, like the tugs of an insect caught in a web.

Perhaps it's the valet air-freshener that's making Davy feel sick. He feels a judder through his arm and turns to look at Fly; sees the boy's shoulders going with his tears.

'Are you all right?' Davy asks.

Fly turns to him, his eyes huge, lips trembling. 'I want my mum,' he says.

'You'll be all right,' says Davy. 'Won't be as bad as you think.'

The car has stopped at an entry gate, uniformed guards stepping out from their sentry hut and taking details from the driver before they will open up the gates.

Davy turns away from Fly's damp face to look up through the top third of his passenger window once again. He wishes the fencing wasn't quite so high, its uppermost panels bent inwards to prevent scrambling children scaling over the top. He wishes the sense of incarceration wasn't so apparent to the terrified boy beside him. The car starts to move again along a wide river of tarmac towards a series of low-slung new builds. Square Lego-like buildings, somewhere between a uni campus and a medical centre. Not unlike Cambridgeshire HQ in fact.

Arlidge House. Home to sixty boys charged with everything from murder and rape to burglary and assault. You could spend most of your life pretending a place like this doesn't exist, ignoring the children inside it who've had rubbish lives from the off.

Can he really be responsible for putting Fly in here? Will the state take care of this child, once Davy hands him over?

He shuffles over towards Fly's end of the back seat, so they can exit the car together. Reception – reached after a copious unlocking of doors and disabling of alarms – is bright at least. The word 'Welcome' is writ large across the wall in lots of different languages and in different-sized fonts, which seems a case of over-thinking, seeing as most of the kids in here won't have shown up to school, let alone be saying '*willkommen*' in German. Flat foam sofa bases, which remind him of the youth centre where he volunteers, are the only place for himself and Fly to perch while they await the processing of reams of paper-work. They must decide how to sit, the cuffs giving them little leeway, so they sit forward, elbows leaning on their knees. And through it all, Davy can feel the trembling of Fly's apprehension.

'See?' Davy says, his cheery sing-song voice an irritant even to himself. 'Not so bad, is it? Feels a bit like a youth centre.'

It doesn't feel like a youth centre.

They are approached by a big man – shiny-headed, wearing waist-hugging combat trousers (macho pockets, yet camply tight around the buttock area) with a tucked-in T-shirt and carrying a clipboard. Around his belt are clusters of keys on various chains and crackling black radio handsets.

'Right, Fly is it?' he says in thick Yorkshire, holding out his hand. 'I'm Neil, your care worker. We don't have guards here, right? This isn't a prison. We call it a college.'

Davy thinks of the term for custodial sentence where kids are concerned: DTO (detention training order). He wonders how much 'training' there will be.

'Let's show you to your room, shall we?' says Neil.

They walk down grey carpeted corridors which have the feel of a sixth-form college but they are stalled by the relentless locking and unlocking of doors: ten between reception and Fly's room.

'Why is there a toilet?' Fly asks, standing at the centre of a stark bedroom. 'In the middle of the room, I mean?'

'Your own private facilities,' says Neil. 'I'm sorry it's lidless and there are no walls. It's for your own safety, you see.'

'I don't understand,' says Fly.

'Kids can pull lids off, use them as weapons. Attack the staff.'

'Still,' says Davy, that jaunty upswing irrepressible, 'it's a nice room.' He drags Fly over to the window to look at the view, which is of a small empty yard with some sort of chequerboard tarmacking surrounded by high fences. The sky, low with dense white cloud, is sharply bright. A pigeon sits on top of the bent-in fencing.

'Now,' says Neil, 'here at Arlidge House you're a resident, not a prisoner. This is your room, your home, not a cell.'

'Except you lock me in it,' says Fly, looking at Neil's keys. 'Are there any books?'

'Books?' says Neil. 'First time anyone's ever asked me that! What kind of thing?'

'Maybe if you could bring me what you've got I can choose. Or is there a library?'

'Not as such. I think there might be a trolley somewhere that I can wheel your way. I'll need to check if you've got to earn your good behaviour points to qualify for a book.'

Christ, thinks Davy.

'The system will be explained to you,' says Neil. 'Everything you do here will be assessed with a point system, one to five, and good behaviour is rewarded with treats – takeaway on Friday night, movie on the telly, that kind of thing. Rudeness to staff will not be tolerated. Nor will violence of any kind.'

Fly's trembling has increased, Davy can feel it up his arm. Delicate and fragile. He wonders if Fly is going to cry again.

Walking away, Davy rubs his unencumbered wrist and tells himself this is procedure. Fly has potentially committed a serious offence and it is their job as police officers to see that justice is done. He gets into the waiting panda car, winds down his window and gasps for air.

'Let's go,' he says to the driver.

MANON

'You need to eat properly, you know – you can't neglect your body, not at this stage,' Bryony says, coming into the room with a stack of files and looking for somewhere to deposit them.

She finds the only inch of bare surface on the kitchen dresser. Bri's house takes clutter to new teetering heights – Lego on every window ledge, pens with lids off, half-made paper planes and scraps, of the sort with scribbled lists on, propped behind vases. On the dresser are bowls of various sizes containing family detritus – rubber bands, bits of toy, erasers shaped as snowmen or burgers, a battery or two (spent or new, nobody knows), paper clips and Nerf gun foam bullets. Yesterday, Manon had to finger through several of these bowls looking for Bri's iPod headphones. She came up with four sets; none of them worked.

'Jesus,' Manon had muttered. 'Is my house going to become like this?'

'Like what?' Bryony asked.

'I'll make you some toast,' Bri is saying now.

'No, I'm not hungry.'

'Any news on the house?'

'We can go back in this afternoon. Get out of your hair.'

'You're not in my hair. Jam or Nutella?'

'Marmite if you've got it.'

Bryony makes a disgusted face as she opens the jar. The toasted bread leaves beads of buttery moisture on the black granite worktop, which Bryony ignores.

'Is it kicking?' she asks, looking at Manon's bump. Manon looks down to see a bulge protruding from the top of her belly – an elbow or a foot, flexing against its enclosure.

'So weird, isn't it?' Manon says.

'Like harbouring an alien,' says Bri. 'I remember after mine were born, I missed the feeling of having them inside.'

'I won't,' says Manon, putting down the toast, nausea sweeping through her – the first of her pregnancy coinciding with Fly's arrest.

'Yes you will,' says Bryony. 'You can get through this.'

Tears roll heavy and slow down Manon's face. 'It's even worse for me to feel like this – I mean, I'm the one who longed for this baby. I'm the one who went to such lengths—'

'You think because you wanted the baby so much, there won't be times when you hate having it?'

'Just seems the ultimate selfishness.'

'Don't pile that on yourself,' says Bri. 'Did you know, rates of post-natal depression are way higher with IVF babies? The pressure to love every minute. S'just not possible.'

Manon sniffs. Nods.

'Let's get Fly out, shall we?' says Bri, coming to sit at the table with Manon. 'Who have you instructed?'

'Mark Talbot.'

'Good, he's good. Why haven't you been signed off work?'

169

'I have, but I'm not having it – what good would it do? I need to be on the ground. I need to stay close to the investigation as far as they'll let me.'

'Which isn't very far I'd imagine. Look, sorry about this, but it's gone a bit quiet upstairs. Better check on the kids, make sure they're not necking Calpol or something.'

Manon is pricked by irrational hurt, the child being left in her hour of need.

'You have all these pleasures to come,' Bryony says. 'Not being able to finish a sentence, like ever.'

Fuck's sake, thinks Manon, *and patronise me as well why don't you?* Bryony nods at the pile of cardboard files she's deposited on the dresser. 'No peeking at my paperwork, otherwise I'll be in deep shit, all right?'

'No, fine,' says Manon, barely listening. She has picked up a spiky crust from the table and is pressing it between her fingers, feeling it crumble onto the tractor oilcloth.

'Manon?' Bryony says. Manon looks up to where Bri has turned in the doorway. 'I'm serious. No looking at my files, you know that, right?'

Manon frowns at her. They have worked together for years and know about one another's work. Why is Bri emphasising the confidential aspect of her files? 'Yes, all right, I think I've grasped it,' Manon says, wondering what Bri is trying to tell her.

'I'll be a while upstairs. Make yourself a drink or whatever.'

Bryony gently closes the door on the kitchen and Manon rises, approaches the dresser. There on top of the pile is a denim blue folder, stuck with a white adhesive label on which has been printed: *Fly Dent, Case file,* followed by various dates and reference numbers.

It is a slim dossier in Manon's shaking hand, too early in

the investigation to encompass the 3,000-odd pages that will eventually be served in court. Just an OIC report, the case summary sent to the CPS along with the bare bones of the evidence they have at this stage. Manon takes out her phone and photographs every page: witness statements, pathology reports, paperwork familiar to her and yet her hand shakes as the phone's camera attempts to focus. Click after click after click. It's not illegal, exactly, but Bri is laying her job on the line. They must use this on the quiet. Manon doesn't waste time reading. She closes the file and lets herself silently out of Bryony's house.

Out in her car, she is forwarding image upon image to Mark. He calls her in the midst of it.

'How are you getting all this?'

'Doesn't matter.'

'Have you done something illegal?'

'Look, we can make a start. This means we can start knocking down their case.'

'Will I be disbarred for using this material?'

'Who's going to know? We get served this stuff eventually. We're just seeing it six weeks early, is all.'

He pauses on the line.

'Give me a chance to read it all and I'll come back to you.'

Evening. Her head back on the armchair, case files spread across her knees. Sleep threatens to overcome her, but only briefly. She knows that, come 4 a.m., she'll be working at the knot again.

She has never been a solid sleeper but her broken nights have worsened with age. She's sure she should accept them, but the exhaustion mounts and makes the days harder. In ordinary times, her thoughts would churn like washing in the machine: mundane rotations, domestic in theme but with morsels of self-recrimination.

Put salt in the dishwasher.

Bring up Fly better.

Eat less. Detox. Get into interesting salads.

Send Internet purchase back via post office. Remember to get receipt.

Stop buying cheap tops on the Internet. (Often, she would text Bryony an image of said top with the words 'Nice?/Not nice?' And Bryony would invariably try to dissuade her – 'Hot flush waiting to happen' or 'SAME AS EVERY OTHER TOP YOU OWN'.)

Stop eating, stop fucking eating, Jesus, and bring up Fly better.

Get Fly more books, go and see Fly's teachers.

Stop Fly and Solly watching so much television, as this only creates window in which to buy cheap tops on the Internet.

Become Zumba instructor?

On and on and on until she falls into a deep sleep seemingly moments before her alarm goes off and then digging herself out of bed is like the exhumation of a corpse.

Not tonight. Tonight she'll be nostalgic for the petty recriminations of the past. She hears Ellie enter the room and raises her head. Ellie has on her woollen coat, buttoned up, and a thick red scarf about her neck which has brought out the flush in her cheeks. She carries a black leather handbag gathered in folds at the clasp.

'All right?' says Ellie, breathless.

Manon doesn't reply.

'How's Fly? Is he in Arlidge House? I was wondering if I could take Solly in to see him. D'you think they'd let me?'

Manon doesn't reply.

'Solly give you any trouble tonight?'

172

'Solly's not the problem.'

Ellie looks nervous. Manon knows she can make people tense – that it is her specialist skill. She contains ruthlessness.

Ellie has unwound her scarf and is squeezing it on her knee with her fist. Manon frowns at her. *Sometimes*, she thinks, *the people she hates most are the ones who deny their ruthlessness.* They view themselves as blameless in all turbulence, thinking they can't be cold. Forgetting, for example, a seven-hour hole in their alibi.

'How did Jon-Oliver have Fly's number?' Manon asks.

'I wondered that. I guess he must have got it off my phone when I was out of the room.'

Manon nods. Then frowns.

'Isn't your phone passcode locked?'

'Well, either he knew the passcode – maybe I told it to him, I can't remember – or he got it off my phone just after I'd used it, y'know, before it'd re-locked itself,' she says.

'How could he send Fly those horrible texts? They're horrible. He's mean and nasty, telling Fly to get lost.' She's aware she's saying this to Ellie as if *she's* sent the texts. Manon is finding it hard to separate Jon-Oliver from Ellie. She's finding it hard not to attack Ellie.

'I haven't read them,' Ellie says. 'He wasn't a very nice man.'

Ellie still wears her coat. She's perched on the edge of the sofa, as if she'd like the option to make a run for it.

'I'm just wondering,' says Manon, 'where you were for seven hours on the night Jon-Oliver was murdered.'

'I don't have to tell you.'

'Yes you do.'

'I was with a man, OK? I was with a man and I don't have to tell you about it. I have a right to a private life.'

'It might have a bearing on the case.'

'It doesn't,' she says. 'The police are happy with that, why can't you be?'

Manon wonders *why* the police are happy with it. When have they ever been happy with a seven-hour hole in a key witness's alibi? She notices she's thinking 'they' instead of 'we'.

'Why should it matter if I know who it is?' Manon asks. 'What's the big secret?'

'No big secret. It's just . . . not serious, that's all. It's no big deal. I don't want to go into it, with you or with anyone else. Why can't you understand that?'

'Because I don't think your privacy matters as much as Fly.'

'Who I was shagging is not going to have any effect on Fly's case, I'm telling you that now.' Ellie leans forward. 'He won't go down for this,' she says. 'He didn't do anything, so he won't—'

'He better not,' Manon says, and she's hard as nails, she can feel it. 'But I wouldn't be so sure that the truth will out. You think people don't go down for stuff they didn't do? You're fucking deluded.'

Their *entente cordiale* hangs by a thread. Old jealousies, happy to rouse themselves. Part of Manon wants to cut the ties now, because Ellie's son is sleeping in a room upstairs while Manon's is in Arlidge House. All their life they've been like this – a double helix curling together, then away.

'I hate this house,' Ellie says quietly and they both look around them, at the half-open drawers, the cushions badly rearranged by SOCO. There will be worse upstairs – clothes spilling out of chests of drawers, wardrobe doors open, duvet covers turned inside out as they were pulled off, this disarrangement like their innards exposed. The hands of strangers all over their personal things, except Manon prob-

174

ably knew a few of the SOCO team, which only seems to make it worse.

'Me too,' she says.

The next morning, once she has heard her sister's departure from the house, Manon sits on Ellie's bed. The curtains are still part-drawn, so the room is in darkness apart from a bright plank of sunshine down one wall. The air is laden with moisture and the scent of Ellie's shower gel from the en suite. A damp towel lies on the lower half of the bed.

Manon looks around the room, at the shoes banked against the wardrobe, the clothes strewn on the chair by the window. She wants to pry, but without a mobile or computer (God alone knows where Ellie's laptop is) she's not sure where to search. She goes to the doorway of Ellie's bathroom. Makeup all over the Ikea sink unit. A bottle of CK One, lid off. A blue eyeliner, which Manon has long coveted though she can't be bothered with daily makeup. Beside the toilet, a box of Tampax. Tights strung from the little radiator.

Manon returns to the bedroom, sits back down on the bed and opens Ellie's bedside cabinet. In its cavity is a bottle with a tumbler upturned on its neck. Manon lifts it out. A dusty bottle of The Famous Grouse, half empty. Manon remembers seeing it in some out-of-the-way cupboard in London, alongside never-used napkin rings and some defunct fairy lights. It was packed for the move, she can't think why ('Well, doesn't go off, whiskey, does it?' Ellie had said); the remnant of a long-gone Christmas.

Manon smells the glass, breathes traces of whisky. Has Ellie taken up drinking? And why hasn't she discussed it and given Manon the option to bail in (pregnancy not withstanding)? She replaces the Famous Grouse, closes the cabinet door. Above

175

this is a small drawer which she opens and pats about inside. She lifts a bundle of paper: receipt from Primark, receipt from Starbucks (Ellie must've emptied the scraps from her purse in here), and then a blister pack of pink pills. She turns it over and reads the word Xanax. Half the pack has been popped.

Downstairs Manon Googles Xanax, unsure what it is. 'Commonly used for the treatment of panic and anxiety disorders. A sedative, or sleeping aid, which can cause dependency, not to be used during pregnancy [another pleasure closed to her] or lactation.' Easy to buy online from the looks of her Google search, but Ellie can probably come by them fairly easily at work.

Is it her upset over Jon-Oliver's death that's making her pop pills and knock back whiskey?

DAY 17
31 DECEMBER

MANON

'Right, so I've read through the evidence file that has mysteriously landed in our lap,' says Mark, giving Manon a disapproving look. Then he begins attacking his eggs with gusto.

'Yes,' she says, eyeing his plate and wondering where her own eggs have got to. She's not even peckish but has ordered anyway. For the baby.

'And their primary case, their scenario if you like, is this: Jon-Oliver was stabbed in the heart. If you're stabbed in the heart, so Derry Mackeith has it anyway, you cannot walk anywhere. There are blood spots on the path leading away from the body, which must have come from the assailant. Fly is on CCTV walking over those blood spots. Fly is therefore the killer. His trainer print is in one of the blood drips; that puts him categorically at the scene. And the fibre from his hoodie.'

'Wait, so Fly is supposed to have dripped the blood *then* trodden in it? Is that even feasible?' Manon asks.

'I suppose it is, if he's holding a knife away from his body. But it's a bit contorted as a theory. We should look at that,' Mark says.

'And their witness – this Mrs Cole woman – has identified Fly,' Manon says. 'But the thing is, Fly doesn't dispute being there – it's his route home from school. All their evidence puts him at the scene, fine, we're not arguing with that. Doesn't mean he did it.'

'Jon-Oliver was texting him, telling him to hop it, while he visited the son,' Mark says. 'That's presumably the motive, such as it is.'

Manon has been telling herself to think about the whole case dispassionately. Think of it as the start of any old investigation.

'Let's say we agree with them,' she says. 'The blood spots are critical to solving this. So we need to go back to the blood spots, we need to do an inch-by-inch search of the crime scene ourselves. Widen it, show exactly where the spots are coming from or where they lead to.'

'What else?' he says, chewing his food while leaning back and looking at her. 'Let's say you are SIO – what evidence would you go for?'

'Send the CCTV to forensic analysts, sharpen it up, see what I could see. I'd get back-up testimony from cardiac experts to firm up Derry's theory as it's central to the case. And I'd look at character witnesses, evidence of motive.'

He is nodding, swallows. 'Which brings us on to this statement by Giles Carruthers.'

'Wait, I've missed this. Show me.'

He rifles through his file for the right witness statement.

Saying, 'Right, so Carruthers is a wanker, I'm sorry BANKER, at Dunlop & Finch with Ross. They worked hard, played hard—'

'Earned hard,' Manon says.

'Very much so. Ross just landed a mega client, Xi Ping. Chinese billionaire. He's signed with Dunlop & Finch for all kinds of wealth management, setting up shells in Panama, buying London properties, a portfolio of investments. That client alone would bring him a bonus of £3million.'

'How many clients did he have?'

'Ten, maybe fifteen. One of them was a Libyan guy, member of Gaddafi's cabinet, who bought some hotels in Scotland.'

'What did Ross actually do?'

'Investment fixer. Middle man. He arranged everything when these billionaires came to London looking to put their money into a safe economy: made sure there was a limo and champagne all the way – viewings of Kensington mansions via posh estate agents, or incorporation of shells by dodgy lawyers in Nevada, or tax status in Turks & Caicos. He greased the wheels. Anyway, his mate Giles has given a statement saying Ross was frightened of Fly.'

'You *what*?' she says. 'Frightened of Fly? It's literally impossible to be frightened of Fly.'

Mark, through another mouthful, reads. 'This is verbatim from Carruthers' statement. "He wanted to see his son but there was this teenager hanging around the child who was, well, 'menacing' was the word Jon-Oliver used."'

'Menacing?' she says. 'And they're talking about Fly? *My* Fly?' Her eggs arrive but she can no longer stomach them. 'I can't think of anyone less menacing than Fly. Barely audible sometimes, yes. But seriously, he's the most gentle boy I know.'

'You may not know him as well as you think you do.'

This seems to be everyone's narrative – that she doesn't know Fly.

Eventually, she says, 'Doing anything nice tonight?'

'Nope. You?'

'Supposed to be going round to Bri's to watch *Jools Holland's Hootenanny*. Not sure I can be fucked, to be honest.'

DAVY

At the front of the main major crime room Davy coughs into his fist, but no one stops talking.

He can smell brewing coffee, reminding him he's tired – of the office lighting and the broad white desks. Behind him, Harriet claps – just once, and not even that loudly. Everyone snaps to attention.

'Thanks everyone,' he says, more uncertainly than he'd like. 'So to update you, we have had forensic analysis back from Videotrue on the CCTV of the footpath close to where Mr Ross's body was found. The analysis shows a red colour on Fly Dent's hand, which could be blood where he is holding, or has held, the murder weapon.'

He stops. His face is prickling with something like an allergy. He's done this enough times. Why's his nerve giving way this time? He's put away plenty of murderers, heard plenty of desperate tales, sob stories, people with no luck, no money. No love in their lives.

This one's different.

Colin is eating an apricot Danish. Kim Delaney is looking

181

at the whiteboard that's just behind him. Harriet is watching him, her arms folded. He can't throw his voice to the room, can't lift his chin. He's ashamed of his main-lines-of-enquiry list, of his badge, of the dirty job he's got to do. He is alone, up here at the front. Is he alone in fitting up a child because the boss wants it tidy? He recalls Manon shouting, 'You're not up to the job, Davy. You're not!'

He swallows, then says, 'We are prioritising cardiovascular pathology reports to back up Derry's, the timeline of Jon-Oliver Ross's travel to Huntingdon, witness statements. Non-sensitive documents – Colin, I'm directing this at you – like phone records, historic bank work, emails, they need to be moved out of the way, into the general folder on the O drive. Finally, I want to talk to you about the press. We do not want Fly Dent's name or age to come out in relation to this homicide, OK?'

'They already know a 12-year-old has been arrested,' says Kim.

'Yes, but there are comprehensive reporting restrictions all over this case. Please be mindful of that everyone, OK? Can I also remind you that it might be New Year's Eve, but it is still a full working day and this is a murder investigation, so no sneaking off early everyone, OK?'

Three weeks in
5 January

Manon

Head down, scrutinising the tarmac and moving forward only when she has examined every inch, just as she was trained at Shotley in the art of hands-and-knees search. The best she can manage in her current unwieldy state is a stooped-shuffle search, wearing a headscarf that must make her appear from a distance like a bowing babushka. Tiny lumps and bumps, the weeds, a crisp packet, mud. Focus, focus on finding blood spots.

She planned on tackling it this morning, in the to and fro of coffee and cereal. Told herself just to come out with it. 'So, the pills and booze, Ellie? What's all that about?' But in the event, she bottled it; hadn't the courage for a confrontation, Manon being more the type to fester in silence. She enjoyed festering in silence: people falling below the standards she silently set for them. Besides, Manon felt sure Ellie would brush her off, tell her it was none of her business and perhaps she was right. Blood spots. Focus on the blood spots.

This morning, in the kitchen, as Manon bolstered herself to say something, she watched as Ellie bustled about in her nurse's

183

uniform, getting Solly food and a drink, standing and eating a bowl of cereal herself while reading something on her phone. Then Ellie put the phone down on the counter and pounded up the stairs to her bedroom. Manon quickly picked up Ellie's mobile and looked at the screen.

'Mummy phone,' said Solly, and Manon looked him in the eye, a finger to her lips.

Don't worry, we'll talk about it later.

The contact was named 'G'.

Who is G? She is turning this over again now, looking at tarmac but failing to focus on the blood spots. Gerald, George, Gino – she can't think of anyone whose name begins with G.

While she gazed at the text in confusion, half an eye on the toddler truth-teller in the corner, the screen had dimmed and locked. Manon didn't know Ellie's passcode. '*Shit*,' she whispered, quickly replacing the phone on the worktop as Ellie re-entered the kitchen.

'What are you doing?' Ellie said, looking at Manon's hand and its proximity to her phone.

Solly chose that moment to fling his bowl of Weetabix off the table and they were both distracted by picking up clumps of what felt like wet papier mâché, and wiping him down.

Manon has followed the paths that tickle into the woodland along Hinchingbrooke Park Road, inching along and arguing with herself because she cannot keep her thoughts fixed. They skitter from Ellie and the secrets she keeps, to Fly in Arlidge House, and then having to go back and do that stretch of tarmac again. And then to her body. She needs food and sleep, neither of which is in plentiful supply. Her feet and hands are cold; the wind whips about her face. The baby pushes and squirms; pelvis under strain. She longs to sit down.

Keep your mind on the blood, she tells herself. Will she even see it, on grey tarmac, three weeks after the murder? She tries to recall how much it has rained since Jon-Oliver's body was found. She is nearing the Brampton Road. She goes back a yard – she hasn't been concentrating on the tarmac, she's been thinking about Fly. A car without a silencer on its exhaust roars insolently past her, and she's infuriated by it, wants to shout 'Wanker!' just as she feels her handbag vibrating. Mark Talbot.

'Mark,' she says, breathless.

'Found anything?'

'Not yet,' she says. 'Think I've become blood-drip blind.'

'Why don't you head home? I'll take over.'

'Are you sure? I've got an appointment actually at the hospital. Also, I've been thinking. We have to find the girl in the picture – the blonde. She'll be a jilted ex, from what Ellie says about Jon-Oliver. Plenty of motive.'

'Dunno,' he says. 'Something about that photo doesn't smell right. I mean, if you were going to carry a photo of your loved one—'

'I haven't got a loved one,' says Manon. 'Partner,' she corrects, realising Fly is her loved one. 'I mean I haven't got a partner.'

'Right, but if you did, you'd carry a little picture in your wallet – I mean if you were going to carry anything at all. Most people don't any more – they have photos on their phones. They have screen savers.'

She wonders what photos Mark Talbot carries – a glossy brunette wife, freckled and makeup free, two lovely children. A dog, perhaps. He's never said.

'What are you saying?'

'It's just the photo – a four-by-six photo. Seems a bit . . .'

185

planted to me. Odd. I'm wondering if he had it for some other reason.'

She passes the dressing-gowned smokers in wheelchairs and the slipper-shufflers trailing their catheters outside the double doors to Hinchingbrooke Hospital. NHS staff, Manon finds, are often brisk-cheery-busy. Perhaps it's the simple pleasure of being purposeful – the job of making life better for other people. Wasn't this why she joined the police? And when she's on the cold cases – which Harriet had told her she'd hate – she has a satisfying sense of being needed. So many mums, dads, sisters and brothers, stranded in a state of not knowing, so that mourning can't begin. The perpetual dusk of postponed grief. When she visits them to ask questions, they fall on her with needy gaze, wanting to revisit with a stranger the only thing that occupies their mind.

She walks down squeaky reflective corridors, through over-ripe smells of hospital food, looking up for signs to the ante-natal department. She couldn't be less interested in this baby and she wonders if it can tell. Can a foetus pick up on maternal ambivalence in utero? She has seen posters saying stress is bad for babies and thought, what could induce more stress than DON'T FEEL STRESS IT HARMS YOUR BABY. Besides, she's not sure she believes in 'stress' entirely. Surely turbulence is the ordinary rhythm of life?

In the corner of her eye, halfway down a corridor to her right, she sees a familiar figure – perhaps it's Ellie's stance that draws her. Her sister is leaning on a door frame, her arms folded, chatting to someone. Manon smiles, walking towards her, but when Ellie spots her, she straightens and frowns. There is a man with his back to Manon, an arm high on the door's architrave. He's leaning over Ellie, as someone might at a house party. *You will always find him in the kitchen at parties.* He turns to discover what Ellie is frowning at.

'Boss,' says Manon, wrong-footed. 'I didn't know you knew each other.'

'Knee trouble,' says Gary Stanton, patting his. 'Your sister is taking very good care of me.'

Manon says, 'Oh, right. You never mentioned it, Ellie.'

Ellie shrugs.

'Right, well, I've got a scan so . . .' And she turns away from them.

'Everything been feeling all right?' the sonographer asks briskly. 'Bit of a cold feeling now,' she says as she squeezes jelly onto the bump. 'Lots of kicking?'

'Yes, everything's fine,' says Manon, her mind like a jumping bean. She has to forcibly stop herself leaping off the bed with all the activity in her brain. *Let's just get this over with*, she thinks, yet she hopes the sight of the baby might calm her into feeling a connection.

Fear also.

What will the sonographer find, as she sweeps her rounded joystick over Manon's skin. A reptile? An alien? Two heads – one of them Gary Stanton's, the other Ellie's?

A grainy black and white image appears on the screen.

'So everything looks good,' says the sonographer, lining up measurement points on her screen. The baby is hammock-shaped, curled over its own protruding stomach. Giant-headed. An unfurling bean. Manon feels . . . curiosity. A scientific type of interest: so this is how new people are made. A perilous path – cells migrating, limbs lengthening – that miraculously goes right more than it goes wrong. Nevertheless, there is a gap, between the picture on the screen

187

and the watery tugs and pushes inside her body. Is she supposed to feel love?

She can feel her phone vibrating inside her handbag.

'Sorry,' she says, without moving but digging into her bag. 'I just have to . . . Mark?'

'I've found something,' he says. His voice is urgent, excited.

'What?'

'I think I've found one or two spots, on the steps down to the station.'

'The station? But that's a long way from the scene. Are you sure they're related?'

'Nope, we'll have to get forensics out. But there's a chance it's Ross's blood. And if it is, it's a game changer.'

'I'll be right there, OK?'

'Aren't you having a scan?'

She cups a hand over the phone, saying to the sonographer, 'Everything's broadly OK, isn't it?'

'Looks like it.'

'So I can get up?'

'Yes,' the sonographer says, as Manon takes some paper towels, wipes the jelly from her bump and heaves herself upright. 'You don't want to know the sex?'

'Not really,' Manon says. She is halfway out the door, doing up her trousers.

'Photo?' the sonographer calls after her but she is too far away to reply.

She waddles towards him, shifting her handbag from one shoulder to the other. He hasn't looked up from the step he is examining. He is making notes in a pad. A gust of wind blows his forelock over his glasses and as he pushes it away, he sees her.

'Here,' he says, pointing. 'There's one blood drip here, and then another right on the other side over . . . here.' He has descended a couple of steps. 'And then a third, over on this side again.'

She looks out across the car park, the rows upon rows of commuters' cars lined up outside the train station. 'What brought you all the way over here?'

'Long shot. I thought of routes away from the body, getaway routes.'

The steps lead from the edge of the station car park, up a tree-covered slope to the busy Brampton Road and above it, the thundering concrete hulk of the A14 flyover. The steps' yellow paint has been trodden away so that it is only visible at the edges.

She says, 'We need to get CCTV off this car park. I can see two cameras from here. That should show who was walking down these steps, leaving this blood trail.' She's breathless, heart thudding. 'This is it, Mark. We've got him.'

'Well, hang on a minute. Unless it isn't Ross's blood – might be a commuter having a nosebleed. And unless the person walking down these steps is Fly. You might need to prepare yourself for that possibility.'

'It isn't Fly,' she says.

'I would guess DS Walker didn't even request car park CCTV.'

She smiles at him. 'Come on,' she says. 'This is good. This is how we knock down their shitty case.'

'How was the scan?' he asks. 'Everything all right?'

'My sister's having an affair with Gary Stanton. Detective Chief Superintendent Gary Stanton.'

'Good news,' says Mark, in a flat monotone. 'We can get the case thrown out on that. Perverting the course of justice. What evidence do you have?'

'A text.'

'Saying what – great shag, let's do it again tomorrow?'

'Well, no. Saying "talk about it later". He was in for a hospital appointment.'

'Not exactly incendiary, is it?'

'No, but I saw the way he was leaning on the door frame over her – it was . . . pervy.'

Mark looks at her over his glasses.

'They're shagging,' Manon says, 'I'm telling you.'

'I'm not going to court for a dismissal based on your dirty mind.'

She calls out to the hallway from the kitchen, hoping to reach Ellie who is upstairs. Manon is holding Ellie's mobile phone.

'I've deleted Angie's number off my phone by accident,' she yells, glad her face cannot be scrutinised as she says this. 'What's your passcode and I'll re-send it to myself. Is it under child-minder or . . . ?'

Ellie is nearer than she suspected, and now she is entering the kitchen, taking her phone off Manon and eyeballing her crossly.

'I'll do it,' she says.

'Are you shagging Gary Stanton?' Manon says.

'What? No! Of course I'm not.'

'Only he seemed quite, well, flirty at the hospital.'

'You know him better than me.'

'Because you do *not* want to mess with Pam Stanton, let me tell you now,' Manon is saying as Ellie goes to the sink to drink a glass of water. She sets the glass down, then says, '*Fuck*,' with a high-pitched squeak, as if she's cut herself.

'What's wrong?'

Ellie turns. She is crying. *Here we go*, thinks Manon.

'I'm just sick of . . . everything being so *shit*,' Ellie says. 'D'you know what happened at work yesterday? HR called me into a meeting and said they've overpaid me £5,000 because of an administrative error and I need to pay it back. I told them I haven't got £5,000 but they said that's irrelevant, I still need to pay it back. I told them it was their error, not mine.' She *has* cut her hand and she turns, holding it at the wrist as further evidence of all the injustice stacked against her. 'They said I could pay £50 per month for like, all eternity. Can you believe that? All the shifts where I don't take a break, when we're understaffed and the patients are furious because they've been sent for the wrong scan or they've come in without having had the right tests, and we suck it up.'

Manon looks at her, knowing there has been a cover-up. But she says, 'Sorry. That's rotten.'

Evening. She is looking at Mark beyond the French windows, his hand in a trouser pocket, smoking and hunched against the cold. He is brash-lit by the outside light.

He is working at her house because there is lots of evidence they need to look at together and it makes sense to sit at one computer. Not only that.

'What about your office?' she asked.

'Come with me,' he said.

He led her out to the kerb where a navy Vauxhall Astra, about fifteen years old and heavily rusting, was parked.

'Do you show this to all the ladies?' she asked. 'Because I hate to burst your bubble, but it's a Vauxhall Astra.'

He pointed to the back seat and she peered in through the window to see pale concertina box files in place of two children.

'This is my office,' he said.

'Wow, this is filling me with confidence.'

191

He shrugged. 'It's impossible to make enough on legal aid work to rent an office, so I work out of my car. It's either this, or I take on private driving offences and licensing.'

He went on to list the pittance he'll make working through evidence, fifty quid for every hour of CCTV viewed. And nothing for secondary disclosure – the reams of material deemed by the police to be irrelevant. If a case doesn't go to trial – as she hopes Fly's won't – because the CPS drops the charges, then he doesn't get paid. 'Not ideal,' he said. 'You want a jury to acquit, because then you get the trial fee. Even though that fee doesn't begin to cover the hours of preparation that a trial requires, especially a murder trial.'

Looking at him now, she takes in the shirt that is hanging out of his suit trousers at the back. The loafers that have seen better days and have the hint of Cornish pasty about them. His hair sticking up at mad angles. His fingers are stubby. His suit jacket, draped over the chair beside her, has concertinaed into creases at the back, where he's sat on it. He is self-absorbed. Dishevelled in the way of clever people. She wonders if he has ever noticed her, in *that* way.

There are cracks in the case against Fly, she can feel it. It must be this chink of hope making her giddy but she should not confuse Mark Talbot's attractiveness – which is probably simply maleness in proximity to her hormones – with the fact that he is helping her. He is on her team, though his legal experience means he refuses to be drawn on Fly's guilt. Perhaps he is a pessimist by nature, or perhaps dealing day in day out with criminals has worn him down.

Anyway, all his monied private-school-educated guilt is being launched in her and Fly's service. He has shaken his head in disgust at the memory of the Thompson and Venables case – the youngest murderers in British criminal history; the 1993

192

trial in which two 10-year-olds were convicted of killing a toddler; the way the public, supported by the tabloids, bayed for their blood forgetting they were children. Thompson and Venables continue to be in danger from vigilantes twenty-five years on.

Mark has used the term 'institutionally racist' on more than one occasion to describe the police and she has flinched, thinking of Harriet, Davy and Kim and feeling that the wrongs Fly is now suffering are probably more shabbily accidental than that. She might even be wrong about Gary Stanton and Ellie. Shagging a key witness is sackable, after all – the very essence of gross misconduct for a police officer. Stanton – who is not only married but within sniffing distance of a very sizeable pension – would not be so stupid.

No, there are no conspiracies. There is only bad luck and the very variable abilities of human beings, be they teachers, doctors or police officers. So many brainy detectives in books and on telly, and yet a great number of the officers she's come across in twenty years in the force are, frankly, challenged in the deducing department.

Mark told her people consistently mistake black kids for being older than they are by about four years. 'They don't afford a black boy the same presumption of innocence or the same need for protection as they do white boys.'

She knows this from experience rather than from any study and she feels it sadly, rather than as a lefty crusade, as he seems to. She cannot change this difficulty for Fly, the way the world mistakes him time and again. How fraught with peril life will be for him. All she wants is for him to survive despite it and prosper. She'd had to have 'the conversation' with him, back in London, when he was repeatedly being stopped and searched: her sermon on how to behave with the police. Don't get their backs up, don't disagree, don't be impolite, don't question their authority. And she'd thought, as she said it, that what she was really saying was, 'You cannot be fully yourself in this situation. You must reduce yourself, because the justice system that protects me is a risk to you.'

After that chat, after he had gone to sleep, she'd crept into his room and kissed him at the temple.

Yes, it is the prospect of cracking this one that is turning her head in Mark Talbot's direction, nothing more, though sometimes he smiles at her in a way that seems keen. (She feels guilty even thinking this; even more so at how exciting the thought is.)

When the car park CCTV comes in, they will see the real killer and she can march into MCU to Harriet and Stanton and say, 'What about this then? This knife-wielding lowlife jogging down the station steps to board a train? Huh?' She can hardly wait.

Ellie comes in to make a cup of tea. She's been watching television in the lounge.

'How's it going?' she asks.

'Fine,' Manon says.

Above the surge of the kettle, Manon hears Mark's mobile ringing beyond the glass, watches him stoop over it, looking at the ground; talking while the smoke escapes his mouth in a white river. She must not fall for this do-gooder, whose personal life is after all a mystery. What she must remember is that people like herself and Mark Talbot – people in their forties – have Heathrow-sized carousels of baggage. They have weathered too much disappointment. Bad sex, illness, less money than they ever thought possible. Verily the tawdry Bagpusses of disappointed dreams.

She is kicked in the bladder by the baby, just in case she's

194

forgotten this small but mighty impediment to her allure. And what will this baby leave behind once it has made use of her flesh? Ellie, who is now padding out of the room with her tea, had jiggled the empty sacks of her own breasts in front of the mirror, allowed them to fall like deflated balloons and said, 'They don't tell you about this on the breastfeeding posters.' In a bid to keep hope alive, Manon sometimes clicks on Internet articles about women who get 'the best body they've ever had' in their forties (*there is still time*), having taken up radical exercise or some kind of raw-food juicing diet, and are grinning with maniacal intent, like they've just had an enema and all the bile from their recent divorce has shot out of their anus. *'As a special treat, I have six grapes on the weekend!'*

Most of us, she thinks now, observing Mark Talbot's rotund middle and finding him no less winning for it, *are carrying extra pounds which are hard to shift or lift, even in the service of humping.*

Stop thinking about humping.

Pens in a Tupperware box, several with their lids missing, some with fabric nibs fraying where Solly has pressed too hard. She watches Mark take one, lacing it between his fingers as he rolls out a truculent piece of white card, pushing the dome down. He tries to make a sweeping line across the white but the pen he has chosen, a dark teal, is all dried out. His line is a whisper.

'Try this one,' she says, handing him a navy, and in the attempt to be quick and elegant about it she drops the pen and his outstretched arm brushes the underside of her left breast.

Oh the agony of it all.

The navy is strong and dark. He draws Hinchingbrooke Park Road, the scrubland opposite Fly's school where Jon-Oliver's body was found, the footpath and the blood drips on the footpath. Then the sweep of Brampton Road, the underpass, the steps down to the station car park and the blood drips found there. Soon the station CCTV will come in, she will be able to iron out this current wrinkle, and things can return to normal. She will have Fly home and she will make it up to him with an excess of top-quality mothering.

'Hang on,' she says. 'Why've you got three blood drips on the footpath? I thought there were only two.' She is frowning at his triangulation of Xs.

'This one here,' he says, circling the X on the left-hand side of the footpath, close to the body, 'doesn't fit with their theory because Fly didn't walk over it. So my guess is, it'll be left off disclosure when the paperwork has been properly sorted. But because this isn't proper disclosure, it's just the case file, it's currently still in there. At trial, we'll need it to look as if we found out about it through painstaking trawling through secondary disclosure, right? Anyway, Fly would've been weaving all over the place to go from this blood spot over to this one.'

Her first thought is, it's not going to get to trial, she won't let it.

Her second thought is, he's right about disclosure – about the omissions and obfuscation, the way the defence is left to wade through secondary disclosure – hours and hours of CCTV deemed not to be relevant, sheafs of documents, all of it taking time (and money) and containing clues, often. How many times has she made decisions about what evidence is pertinent and what needs to be disclosed to the defence?

How often are we selective in life, she thinks now, looking at Mark Talbot – selective in what we reveal to friends ('the holiday was bliss') or loved ones ('it didn't cost that much'/'I was held up at work'). How often are we selective in what we

196

take as proof of reality? We choose. We are all constructing a prosecution case in one way or another.

She starts to cry. 'How the fuck am I supposed to get him out?'

Mark is watching her cry, which feels good, an audience to her suffering (ever the narcissist).

'Have you been in to see him?'

She shakes her head. 'The AV paperwork hasn't gone through yet, takes an age, with the holidays and everything.' She lets out a guttural sob. 'I miss him so much.'

'You're a good person,' he says.

'No I'm not,' she says, stopping her tears with a tissue and a deep inhalation.

'I'm checking on him,' Mark says. 'I'll chase the AV paperwork when I'm next in there seeing him.'

She nods. 'Shall we pin your artwork up on the wall like two sociopaths building a shrine?'

BIRDIE

What did I think as I walked down the stairs from my flat, on my way down to open up the shop?

I thought, she's a prostitute, can you really rely on what she tells you? I thought, yeah, these girls come from not-great backgrounds, like she said, so how far do they tell the truth? I thought, that story showed her in quite a favourable light, victim of the rich and powerful. I've never even met a prostitute before and I was surprised how harshly it made me feel towards her – as if she was damaged goods to be kept at arm's length.

I thought a few hours away from her, doing normal stuff like stocking up on Magners and John Player Blues, and serving my usual alkie fan base, would help me to get things straight in my mind. Because if what she was telling me was true, then someone connected to Titans or Dunlop & Finch had got a 15-year-old girl's body out of one of London's most exclusive hotels. And the threat of a leak – of information about the connection between the bank and Titans – might have led to murder.

I started to ask myself – as I always did when a particularly knotty dilemma presented itself – what would Tony do? I went back upstairs to have a good look at his portrait hanging in the lounge. Angel was having a lie-down in her room.

I looked at him: the grey hair at his temples, the steel grey eyes, boyish ears, emphatic mouth, and I wondered how this man, the most successful leader we've ever had, has been so roundly demonised. This man that I have loved since he first became leader of the party in 1994, who seemed the sensible yet stern father after all those weak and shambolic fathers of the past, has now come to represent deceit and villainy and all his achievements swept away, as if winning was something to be ashamed of.

Did we expect too much in 1997 when the landslide took place and we couldn't believe our luck? Did the love affair founder because no one could deliver the socialist perfection we dreamed of?

Looking up at him and feeling very sorry, it seemed to me that we live in an age of sanctimony – it is the fashion to pass judgement on people, to refuse to acknowledge context or accommodate nuance, and this made me think about the judgements I had passed on Angel only moments ago downstairs at the till, while serving people their tinnies and tobacco, their sugar and scratch cards. I looked at Tony and asked what he would do, in a whisper because I didn't want Angel thinking I was some kind of loon.

And Tony said, *Go to the police.*

He didn't really say it, obviously. His lips didn't move. I don't hallucinate, but his eyes hinted at it. Who could fail to listen to a terrified hooker-turned-Goth and the morbidly obese owner of the Payless Food & Wine?

I shouted to Angel, rattled her door. Nothing. Silence.

'I have a plan,' I yelled through the door, shuffling next door to the kitchen to put the kettle on. 'It's all going to be all right.'

The door opened and she emerged groggy with matted hair, saying, 'What?'

'Cup of tea?' I said.

'I can't go,' she said. 'They'll definitely kill me if I go.'

She was watching me eat my second Penguin while eating nothing herself, as per. I was starting to catch on that slim people might actually deny themselves. This concept is completely alien to me.

'But we have to tell someone,' I said. 'We can't just let this carry on, you being terrified, Jade's death, all that? I mean, what are you going to do, hide forever?'

She smiled at me, laying her hand flat on the table towards mine, though we didn't touch. I was contemplating another Penguin when she said, 'I'm going to live in Spain. Thought you were coming with me.'

'I am,' I said gently. 'I am coming with you.'

'Why don't I buy a flight today and you can sell up here, lease out the shop, whatever you need to do, and join me when you're ready?'

'D'you want to spend your life looking over your shoulder?' I said.

'I won't be, not in Spain.'

'I think you will,' I said.

I ate a third Penguin and it tasted even better than the other two. 'You never told me,' I said, 'what happened after, with you and Jon-Oliver.'

'After the Carlton and those few nights at his house, he said he was going abroad on business so I had to hop it. Then he stopped taking my calls. He changed his number I think, because when I texted him on the number I had, they pinged back with 'number not recognised' and if I rang it, the number didn't work. I cut my ties with Titans. At that time, the end of last summer, I was staying on a friend's sofa, or sleeping outside. I disguised myself – dyed my hair black, did the Goth makeup, all that. Thinking about it now, it's not really a disguise being a Goth. I mean, it makes you kind of noticeable, but I looked very different to how I looked as a blonde, so that gave me a feeling of safety I guess. As if I had become someone else.

'That's when I started drinking – you remember? – coming in and buying a bottle of Lambrini. I followed Jon-Oliver a bit, saw him go into a flat round the corner from here – some woman and a kiddie. I'm guessing it was his kid – not like he was the type to get friendly with someone else's. I was drunk, watching him with her and I was so jealous I could've killed them both. She was normal. Natural-looking. Not a hooker like me.

'I got in the way of this builder and he shouted at me and that brought Jon-Oliver across the road to me. He said he wished I was dead and if I ever came near him again, he'd make sure I was.'

'He's sounding like a keeper,' I said.

'Yeah well, he's dead now, isn't he?'

DAY 23
6 JANUARY

MANON

There he is, most familiar stranger. He looks so much older here than he has ever seemed at home and so much lonelier. His face elfin; the huge dolefulness of his eyes. He sits opposite her in the empty room, just the two of them on blue plastic chairs and the guard, back to the wall.

Fly's head is bowed; he is slouched forwards, legs apart. Only 12 and he's perfected the manspread.

'So, this room's full of charm,' she says, seeking him out with a smile.

Silence.

'Are you all right?'

He shrugs.

'I've brought you books.' She reaches down towards her bag but the guard has simultaneously taken two strides to intercept her contraband. 'I'll need to take those,' he says.

She hands him the stack. Looks at her son who will not meet her gaze.

'How's the food?' she asks.

He shrugs. 'Lot of chips.'

'I can imagine – every cloud, eh? Are you sleeping OK?'

'Not really. How is Solly?'

'Oh, you know. Unreasonable. I made him toast this morning but before thinking, I cut it in half so he went ballistic.'

'How could you?' Fly says and she sees his first smile. 'Did he shout, *mend the toast?*'

Nodding, she says, 'I deserved everything I got. That toast was unacceptable.'

'I miss him,' Fly says.

'I miss you. Anything for you to do in here?'

'Not much.'

After what she deems to be a decent pause, she launches into the thing that's troubling her: 'I need to ask you something. I know you travelled to London on the train when you were supposed to be at school. The day you bunked off.'

He shifts with palpable irritation.

'I just want to know what you were doing,' she says.

'You think that means I stabbed him?'

'It means you've been keeping things from me. What else don't I know?'

Silence.

'What else, Fly?'

'You want to know? You really want to know?'

'I really want to know.'

'I missed my home. My flat, where I lived with Taylor and Mum. I missed the guys in Momtaz, the broken biscuits from Buy Best. You took me away from everything – all my friends at school.'

'They weren't a good influence—'

'At least I wasn't the only black kid in that school. At least I wasn't treated like some kind of danger, like a bomb – don't go too near, y'know? You ripped me out of that place to this

203

. . .' He sweeps his arm to show her. 'This *dump*, so I can watch you have a baby. Your own flesh and blood when my flesh and blood are dead.'

'A clean break. I thought a clean break would—'

'Who the fuck is a clean break clean for?'

She knows better than to pull him up on his language, though it is an affront. Has he learned it in here? She's never heard him speak like that.

'Did that make you—?'

'I did *nothing. Nothing*, you hear? Just cos you think somefin's good for me, doesn't mean it is.'

She nods. 'I'm sorry,' she says. She is finding it hard not to cry.

'Too late,' he says.

In the sweep of his arm about the room, showing her the dump she has put him in, his sweatshirt sleeve has ridden up. She looks now at his forearm and the cross-hatching there made by a razor blade.

'What's that?' she says, grabbing his wrist before he can remove it. She lifts the sleeve higher, holding him tight. 'What are these?'

The scratches, red lines over red lines, beaded with dried blood, go on right to the crook of his arm.

He pulls his arm away. 'Nothing. It's nothing.' He tugs his sleeve downwards and has got up off his chair, nodding at the guard to let him out of the room.

'Fly! We can talk about it.'

But he is gone and the sound of repeated unlocking and locking goes with him.

Neil is sitting at his desk, combat trousers tight as ever. Neil holds all the keys.

'How can I help you?' he says, wearily swivelling on his swivel chair – the puffed-up wheels of little Napoleons every-where.

Neil has the look of a man who knows he must be seen to have an open door but hates every millimetre of it.

'He's been cut,' she says.

'Have a seat,' says Neil.

'I don't want a seat. Fly has been cut. He's not safe here.'

'It's unfortunately not uncommon for new students to harm themselves in response to their situation.'

'He's not a fucking student and he didn't harm himself. He's been cut. You're not protecting him from the others.'

She wishes her voice would stop wobbling into the upper octaves. She doesn't know he's been cut by others – *of course* she doesn't know that. But the thought of him doing it to himself brings with it more guilt than she can cope with.

'I know this is hard for you,' says Neil. 'Particularly given . . .' He looks at her bump.

'No. No, it's not. It's hard for *you* because I'm going to have to launch an investigation now into duty of care at Arlidge House.'

'What evidence do you have that he didn't do this to himself?'

'He didn't have any razor blades when he came in here. So how did he get one? Who from?'

She looks away from him. On the floor is a collapsed Tesco bag containing a ready meal and tomatoes. Neil's damp towel is draped over the radiator. *This is just a job for you.*

She shifts her handbag over to the opposite shoulder and registers the sudden, violent urge to pee.

'Excuse me,' she says, pelting from the room.

When she returns, Neil is no more helpful than before, though he does pass on her request to see Fly again.

Fly says no.

Beyond the dogged push of her wipers is a great thumb smudge of cloud and the slate-like lowering light, cold and wet. The droplets across the windscreen cast a haze around the red brake lights of the cars in front, and the red orb of a distant traffic light. Yellow junction box lines on the tarmac, seen not through tears but through eyes dry with fury. Her foot pressing on the accelerator, held at bay by the clutch. Hand to the horn. At the first movement of the car in front, she cuts it up, swerving recklessly to the right towards Huntingdon station car park. By the time she parks, at a wilfully obstructive angle, it is fully dark.

She hurries towards the ticket barrier, shoving her police badge into the face of a sleepy member of staff and barging through the turnstile when he waves her through. *Fuck the barrier, fuck the baby.* She is scanning the ceiling, the corners of the walls. Before her is the entrance to the station 'buffet' – a grimy room, high-ceilinged and smelling of churned milk. Above the counter, its oversized clock appears to have ticked its last sometime around 1953. Scanning and scanning: pale mint walls, a yellowing picture rail hung with framed prints of ancient locomotives. Dusty pot plants. Manon scans wooden racks filled with the usual magazines (breasts, teeth, more breasts); greetings cards (puppies, cats, flowers, *Birthday Girl, Goodbye and Good Luck!*).

A blast of noise and air blindsides the room, lifting papers and making the smattering of customers flinch – the fast train from Cambridge to London blowing through the station. Behind the counter, the serving woman's movements are unruffled – she has been blasted by that horn so many times, she barely registers it. Behind the woman, Manon searches shelves of spirits, an industrial fan, a whiteboard saying *Bar Tariffs*, too faded to be legible. Mini Cheddars, Hula Hoops, Werther's Original, a fridge full of Lucozade and then – hallelujah – there it is: a little yellowing camera, once white, the size and shape of a spotlight, trained on the counter.

'Hi there,' Manon says to the woman, holding up her badge.

The woman shifts uneasily.

'Your camera work?' asks Manon, pointing at it.

The woman nods.

'I wonder if you remember seeing this chap, came through the station mid-December?' Manon says, reaching into her handbag for the photograph of Jon-Oliver Ross that is always with her. Such a long shot. There is every chance Jon-Oliver did not sample the delights of the station buffet.

'Middle of December, you say? We get loads of people coming through here.' She takes the picture from Manon, peering at it. 'I do remember him as it goes. He came in and bought a Twix or something like that. Only because I clocked him, y'know? Bit of a looker!' She winks at Manon, who notices a gold tooth.

'Can I look at the film on that?' Manon asks, pointing at the camera. 'Will it show December the fourteenth?'

The woman nods. 'Twenty-eight-day turnaround on that one, so yes, you'll still be all right for December. I'll have to get my husband to burn it onto a CD for you. Is that all right?'

'I'll wait,' says Manon.

When she lets herself in, Mark is already at the kitchen table, under a cone of light from the pendant, scrutinising his laptop, his back to her. Ellie must've let him in. She can hear water running upstairs. Solly's bath.

At the sound of her clattering her keys on the side, and without turning round, Mark says, 'Car park CCTV.'

She sees dead coffee cups, the surface of their liquid clouded with cold milk. A side plate with crumbs from demolished toast. Pens with their lids off.

'And,' she says, dropping her bag to the floor, 'I've got CCTV from the station buffet. Turns out Jon-Oliver bought a Twix when he got off the train.'

'Great, that'll be fascinating to watch,' says Mark, still without looking up at her. He is jabbing the arrow button to inch forwards on the CCTV timeline. 'What we need to see,' he says, pausing his words as he presses the key, 'is who came up or down those station steps leaving those blood drips. Not that your Twix footage isn't riveting, obviously.'

'Yes, all right,' says Manon. 'Your CCTV is better than mine. Think it might be wine o'clock. Want one?'

He doesn't reply as she opens the fridge, looks at the wine, realises sadly that she doesn't feel like it, then closes the fridge again. She pulls a chair next to his, looking at his screen: 4.19 p.m. on the timeline. As Mark leans back to stretch out his arms above his head, she says, 'Woah, there! There. Look at that.'

A figure in a long woollen coat, weaving across the car park towards the station steps. He appears steady at first, but then his course becomes more haphazard and on the steps he stumbles.

Mark straightens, squints at the screen, then rewinds the footage by a minute. The figure weaves up the steps unsteadily once again.

Mark is at such close proximity to Manon that they are touching, thigh to thigh. She can feel him breathing, the woody smell of cigarettes surrounding him. He presses pause on the CCTV, then looks at her. They are silent, frowning.

208

'Play it again,' she says.

They watch Jon-Oliver Ross walk across the station car park then climb the steps towards the underpass.

'Why is he weaving?' she asks.

'Is he drunk?' Mark says.

'No, the PM said coke but not alcohol.'

They watch Ross grab the handrail at the side of the steps and stop, head down, for a moment. Then he climbs again.

Manon and Mark look at one another again. She rewinds the footage and they watch him again.

'Wait, go back,' says Mark. 'There, on the steps, that's exactly where I found the blood drips – exactly in the path he's weaving. There was a drip on one side of a step, and then right over the other side on the next.'

'So what if the blood is coming *from* him?' she says. 'What if he has already been stabbed at this point? Did we get a result on the blood analysis?'

Mark nods. 'It's Ross's blood. So – what? – he's just walking up the stairs with a stab wound to the heart? Come off it.'

'I know,' Manon says, 'And the pathology report says he couldn't walk anywhere, I know. And if he'd been stabbed in the station there would be about a zillion witnesses. We need something where we can see the expression on his face, get a sense of why he's unsteady.'

'Get your Twix footage out then, smarty pants.' And he smiles at her in a way that makes her light up inside.

This time they are at Manon's laptop, Mark beside her.

She watches and watches. Jon-Oliver approaches the counter of the station buffet. The camera is angled on the till and she can see Jon-Oliver's face. He puts a Twix on the counter, rummages in his trouser pocket and hands the woman what looks like a two-pound coin, takes his change, puts it in his trouser pocket. Something in his movements is odd but she can't work out what it is. His face seems impassive.

He isn't brisk. That's what it is.

'It's an absence of briskness,' she says.

'That's a bit subtle,' says Mark. 'Try slowing it down.'

'How do I do that?'

'Here,' he says, nudging her so that she moves aside. He sits at her laptop and clacks about too quickly for her to discern the keystrokes. They watch, together.

'I can't see anything on him. No marks. On his body, I mean,' Manon says.

'You mean there isn't a knife sticking out of him anywhere?'

'No, I mean, there isn't a wound. Face looks fairly normal too.'

'Yes but his coat—'

'Wait,' she says, 'look at his chest – there.' They watch him pick up the Twix again, from the trays of chocolate in front of him, place it on the counter silently. Jon-Oliver and the woman behind the counter do not exchange a word. His chest is rising and falling, his breathing is laboured. 'He's panting,' says Manon. 'He's fucking *panting*. We need to get this to an expert,' she says, but her phone is skittering across the kitchen table. The screen says Bryony.

'What is it?' Manon says irritably. 'I can't talk right now – can I call you back?'

'You need to see something,' Bryony says. 'And I'm putting my arse on the line even telling you about it, let alone letting you see it. But something's come into Fly's case file which is a bit of a game changer.'

'What?'

'Open your email. But delete the bloody email as soon as you've downloaded the statement, OK? Otherwise I'll be on traffic for the rest of my life.'

DAY 24
7 JANUARY

DAVY

'So, we've had a cell confession,' he says almost in a whisper, then coughs into his fist. 'Excuse me. Can you settle down please? I said we've had a cell confession from a lad at Arlidge House – he says Fly Dent boasted about stabbing Mr Ross while they were working in the poppy shop together.'

His voice keeps trailing off, as if he cannot puff the bellows under it. Truth is, he wishes this cell confession hadn't come in, and not just because he's been feeling more and more uncomfortable about which side he's on in this investigation. Even without that discomfort, cell confessions stink. Made by professional liars who are desperate to commute their sentences, they are about as reliable as drunk witnesses. Everyone knows it, and yet the trade in them by the Crown Prosecution Service is brisk to say the least. Every lowlife in the clink is eavesdropping on true renditions of crimes committed, if you believe the statements coming into the courts. He looks at the sheet that is jittering in his hand.

Statement from Conley Woodchurch
Age 15
Arlidge House, 5 January
DTO number: 5360CW
Length of sentence: indeterminate

I was working in the poppy shop with Fly Dent on Wednesday afternoon, 4 January. We were snapping the poppy petals onto the black centre and attaching the green plastic stems, and putting these in cardboard boxes. He was silent most of the time – he's not much of a talker, is he? I was asking him this and that, what he was in for, who the guy was that he knifed; why he did it.

He said, 'Bloke was an arsehole, had it coming.'

I said, 'How did you do it?'

Fly said, 'Just pushed the blade in, didn't I? Went in smooth as butter.'

This is a fair and honest account of the conversation that took place between us. No one else was present.

MANON

All the myriad things that used to irritate her: tripping over
his enormous shoes, left at angles like discarded bricks outside
the bathroom or, more perilously, on the stairs; the lid left off
the toothpaste, flecks of it on the bathroom mirror where his
electric toothbrush has sprayed on exiting his mouth; the things
he broke, like door handles, with his unaccustomed strength
employed in the mindless opening and shutting, the *fiddling*.
No one had ever warned her how much children fiddle:
bouncing a ball, flicking a pen, kicking a shoe/wall/bag.
Standing on your handbag for no other reason than that it has
found itself under their trainer.

All this she misses. Any part of his disruption, she longs to
have back. The house lacks his untidiness. It is still disarranged
daily by Solly – Duplo and fire engines and Peppa Pig figures.
But there isn't Fly's more grown-up detritus as an extra layer.
Hoodies on the backs of chairs, schoolbag right in her path,
books splayed in the bathroom. How could she ever have
resented the things that told her he was here? He wasn't even
like other teenagers, fought mostly to tidy himself away so that

his imposition would be less, but even the slither of his head-phone wires on the kitchen worktop, she feels nostalgic for. She would gladly have him leave the butter out after making toast – would be grateful for it.

What she knows now, driven by her regret and guilt, is that the cell confession is bullshit, a small additional lie in a sea of lies, the author of which is DS Davy Walker. And she must knock down every shoddy last one of them. Mark is searching the Internet for a pathologist who can analyse the café CCTV and hopefully make sense of the panting. Was Jon-Oliver on something? Had he been beaten up?

She parks outside Arlidge House, slams her driver door; is cowed by slanting rain. Daytime but barely light, the car park grey and freezing. Inside reception she is at the counter and without meaning to make it so, her voice is brusque to the point of rudeness. 'I want to see Fly Dent,' she tells the woman behind the counter.

'Are you on his AV list?' asks the dreary monotone on the other side of the counter. The woman, now Manon takes her in, looks like a toad whose head is melting into her neck. A string of large fuchsia beads nestles in her neck fat.

Manon nods. 'I am, yup.'

She casts about the reception area while Toad shuffles through interminable lists on clipboards or inside cardboard files. Manon shifts her body (her expansion, at six months pregnant, seems visible daily). Transfers her handbag over to the other shoulder.

'No, I'm afraid you're not,' says Toad.

'What?'

'Fly has removed you from his AV list. It is his prerogative.'

A watery sensation rises in Manon's chest. *Don't cry don't cry don't cry.*

214

'Are you sure?' she asks.

'Quite sure.' Toad purses her lips as if to say, *Not my fault he doesn't want to see you.*

'Right,' says Manon, swallowing down her tears. 'Well, in that case . . .' She is rummaging about in her handbag for her badge, thrusting it in Toad's face. 'As I can't ask him myself, I'll need to see a schedule of all his movements since he's been here, in particular the time and date of any sessions working in the poppy shop.'

'Why would that be?' asks Toad. 'Are you part of an official investigation, DI . . . ?'

'Bradshaw. Yes I am. I am investigating a cock and bull story told by one of the lowlifes you have in this institution, a fabricated cell confession which isn't worth the paper it's printed on.'

Manon has leaned so far over the counter that she can smell Toad's Impulse-type body spray, and its excessive chemical overlay causes a wave of nausea.

Her demeanour must've successfully communicated the *'Don't mess with me because I am on the very edge'* vibe, because Toad hands over Fly's entire case file.

DAVY

'He was never in the fucking poppy shop!' Manon shouts. She's been pacing about and pointing quite a lot.

'What?' says Davy. He and Harriet have escorted the bellowing egg-shaped Manon into Harriet's office to prevent a scene.

'Your cell confession is bullshit.'

'How did you even know about the cell confession?' asks Harriet.

'Never mind that,' Manon says. 'Fly has never done a single shift in the poppy shop. He does cooking. He likes cooking.'

'Perhaps Conley Woodchurch was mistaken about the location of the confession,' says Harriet. 'Which should never have come into your possession, by the way.'

'Fly told me about the cell confession, because Conley bragged to him about it,' Manon says, thinking she must not forget to protect Bri in all of this. 'Yeah, it's possible Conley was mistaken, or he's a LYING TOERAG who made it up to get himself out of Arlidge House, which by the way is not a "cool youth training college",' Manon says, making quotation

216

marks in the air, 'but in fact an irredeemable shit hole.'

'It's not the only evidence against Fly, you know,' says Harriet gently. 'In fact, I'm going to tell you about something else, Manon, because you're clearly finding it hard to accept that Fly had anything to do with the murder of Jon-Oliver Ross.'

'I am, yes, because he didn't.'

'Videotrue has examined the CCTV footage of Fly and the expert has stated that there is red on his hand. He is willing to testify that it's blood,' Harriet says.

Davy feels an air pocket rise beneath his ribs, like heartburn or wind. It spears him and causes him to shift position in an attempt to dislodge it without making a rude noise.

'Are you joking?' Manon is saying.

'I'm not joking, no.'

'You can barely tell who it is. That footage is so grainy it could be Kim Kardashian in a hoodie. And anyway, you know full well that CCTV forensic science is the biggest load of bullshit since, since . . . You might as well consult some crystals. There's no red on his hand, you know that, Harriet. Don't do this. Don't go down this road. Fucking hell.' She is backing away, breathless, she starts to cry.

Davy's heartburn is worsening. She's right – Manon is right. Forensic CCTV analysis is dubious at best; at worst, it is guesswork destined to fulfil the needs of whoever commissioned it. Some expert witnesses in the States, so he's heard, have even started asking police, 'And what would you like us to find in this evidence?'

He knows where it can lead, that expert witnesses set great store by being experts and that their grip on righteousness can become vice-like in the face of doubt. The more their expertise is questioned, the more staunch they become. You only have to look at that shaken baby fella, Sir Roy something, and the way he put grieving mother after grieving mother in prison. You only have to look to America, where you can hire anyone to be your 'expert' and pay them to lay before the court their smoking gun. Davy is not happy being on Harriet's side of the Videotrue evidence.

'Anyway,' Harriet is saying, in the same hush used by under-takers when handling the bereaved, 'I'll leave you to think about it.' She goes out, leaving the door ajar. Manon slowly picks up her bag from the table at the edge of the room.

'Wait,' says Davy. He closes the door.

'What?' she says. 'D'you want to arrest me under some fabricated charges as well?'

He has perched against the desk, his elbows bent behind him.

'Something about this case isn't right, Manon,' he whispers.

'No shit Sherlock.'

'I'm feeling . . .' he says, and he can't look at her, instead fixes his gaze on his shoes, 'I'm feeling unsure about certain aspects, that is to say, certain elements—'

'Fuck's sake, Davy.'

He looks up, meets her eyes. 'I think we've narrowed too early. Stanton was very clear that Fly was good for it, that it was tidy.'

Manon is silent, waiting for him.

Davy whispers, 'I think there are other avenues which haven't been looked at. Stuff to do with Ross's work in the City, his firm Dunlop & Finch. There are these emails, right, about a Chinese delegation coming to London and they're wining and dining them, to get their business.'

She has perched next to him. 'Go on.'

'Just before he dies, there's an email from his boss, van der Lupin, saying, "Vis-à-vis what happened at my house last week, it better not happen again. I'd strongly advise you to cut those ties." Well, if that's not a threat, then I don't know what is.'

'Yes.'

'Then there's another email, saying, "Xi Ping minded to sign with us provided the Carlton problem has been dealt with." I think, at the very least, we should've found out what the Carlton problem was, don't you?'

'Where is this material?'

'The emails have been pushed aside because they're not relevant to the prosecution case against Fly. They're in the low-priority folder on the Operations drive. You know, they're not even going to be included in disclosure. So if you, y'know . . .'

'Had a little rummage?'

'Yes,' whispers Davy, glancing at the door. 'Well, you wouldn't be breaking any protocols because you have access to the O drive anyway, don't you? I mean, you'd be working on the O drive for your cold-case work so that's not going to raise any alarm bells if they check your computer.'

She puts a hand on the top of his arm and lets it rest there.

'What about Ross's relationships?' she asks.

'You can look at the call data, that's on the O drive too,' says Davy. 'There are lots of calls, between Ross and Ellie – very high frequency. There is also high traffic to another number, unknown 618. '

'I'm so sure it's a relationship thing. He was the world's biggest love rat. It's not Fly – you know that, right?'

'I don't know anything any more,' Davy says.

'You know *me*,' Manon says.

'Yes, I know you.'

Davy smiles at her.

'I need to ask a favour,' she says and at that moment he'd

do anything for her, so guilty does he feel. 'Can you watch Fly for me? I know you won't be his favourite person but he's taken me off his AV list, whereas you can just barge in without asking him. He's got cuts up his arms.' This causes her voice to swell and she wobbles out the words, high and tender. 'They say he's done it to himself. That Neil guy is a dick—'

'A massive one,' agrees Davy.

'That place is eating into him, destroying him. I'm really worried. Will you go? Keep an eye out, make it clear to Neil that you're all eyes on Arlidge House, duty of care, all that. Make sure nothing bad happens while I sort this out.'

'Course,' Davy says, and it makes him feel better to be able to do something for her.

MANON

'Look for the affair,' she mutters, clicking on the O drive. Manon has checked her area is deserted before getting into the Jon-Oliver Ross folder. On the A4 notepad beside her keyboard, she has scribbled *Xi Ping? Emails? J-O ex-girlfriend?*

Experience tells her the ex will go to the heart. The ex will know everything. The ex might even be their perp. She is trying to suppress mounting panic about the Videotrue evidence. She and Mark must send the same footage off to their own expert, so they can knock it down, tell the court what she knows: there is no red on his hand.

The first thing she notices is the volume of calls between Ross and Ellie, perhaps because she knows Ellie's number off by heart and so the number leaps out from the grey lines of call data. A couple of the calls have lasted twenty and thirty minutes, late in the evening. What were they discussing at such length? Solomon?

She works her way through the call data, line upon line, through December, November, October, September. As she works backwards, she sees another number take over in

221

frequency from Ellie's, like batons in a relay. Unknown 618. Look for the affair, this is the affair, she'd put money on it. But the calls fade out as Ellie fades in. She must locate this person, ask her why. She texts Davy.

When did you last update the trace on unknown 618? Can you renew?

She prints a couple of documents to take home, the printer humming contentedly as her mobile vibrates. A text from Davy.

Yes, was going to do this anyway.

The call data lines have given her a headache. She's too exhausted to sit at this desk into the night. Her decision to go home has nothing whatever to do with the fact that Mark Talbot is working at her kitchen table. She can neither bear to be within his orbit, the sexual tension being so . . . tense, nor out of his orbit, when the lack of tension causes her to be immediately asleep.

Mark is outside having a cigarette.

Manon frowns, down the lines of Ross's financial records, printed off the O drive. The difficulty with going through this material is its greyness; numbers, references which don't mean anything to the reader, line upon line upon line. A lot of police work is grey these days: phone work, ANPR, digital data, and hours of CCTV.

She yawns.

Payments were made on Jon-Oliver's company credit card to a Claybourne Leisure under the reference 'Ents', all in the high thousands. Eight thousand six hundred, nine thousand.

Over and over again, Claybourne Leisure appears. More than a gym or club membership. More than restaurant food. Was he throwing relentless corporate events? What form of entertainment could 'Ents' be?

She hears the muffled sound of Mark's mobile phone through the French windows. She can't hear what he's saying.

She Googles Claybourne Leisure. Not a single hit. A few results about domain names and registering your company. How can a functioning business have no web presence whatsoever? It must do something, sell something, provide something, surely. She tries again, wondering if she has the spelling wrong, but Google will usually offer a 'showing results for'. Nothing. Claybourne Leisure does not exist on the Internet, and if you don't exist on the Internet, do you exist?

She glances again through the French windows, relieved to have some distance from him. She's exhausted by her feigned detachment, when every molecule in her body stands to attention when he is near. She is so tired of it, so fed up with her libidinous self. Sometimes, she must escape to the downstairs toilet to check herself, to breathe deeply, let out some wind and get away from the intensity of being in his orbit. She stands now to get away, as he re-enters the room – goes out to the cool of the hallway where the loo is situated under the stairs.

They pretend, they pretend.

Or is it only Manon who is putting on this charade of disinterest? Perhaps for him it really is nothing after all. She doubts it. She thinks there is collusion in the 'working from her home late into the night' set-up. He could get out of it, potter off, but he doesn't.

She looks in the toilet mirror and sees the marionette lines like open and close brackets on either side of her mouth, the sagging jowls which make her look miserable even on the rare

223

occasions when she's not; lopsided eyes, brown sunspots mottling her cheeks. She is becoming invisible, pushing her trolley up and down the aisles of Waitrose towards oblivion, picking up some grapefruit-scented all-purpose surface spray on her way there. Her desires exhaust her, her inability to act on them. She is too obedient, too ready to tidy her needs away into the cupboard under the stairs.

What would she think of herself, what would the world think, if she were to hurl her haggard self at Mark Talbot, lay her Francis Bacon body at his feet? Or pinch the bottom of a younger man next to the photocopier in the office; to deny, as men do, the ageing of her flesh? Why can't she, as men do, say: yes, I am pot-bellied, wrinkly-bottomed, short-sighted, but I will make a play for that 28-year-old nevertheless? Why should she hide her desires inside the acceptable consumption of table lamps and Boden cardigans and heritage tomatoes as if this is compensation, when what she wants is callous and vivid?

Obedience. She dries her hands on the damp lavender hand towel, sniffs the Baylis & Harding hand-wash – it, too, pretending to be classier than it is. Jon-Oliver Ross answered all the requests of his flesh – for coke, sex, money, more sex with someone new, someone younger and firmer – and did he ever wonder if other people would think that was all right? He is dead, to be fair, so things haven't worked out all that well for him.

If she has a girl, she thinks now, laying a hand on the tight drum of her bump, she will try to inculcate her with a sense of rebellion. At the very least an ability to throw off the shackles of duty (unless, of course, that duty is to her own mother, in which case it should take precedence). She vows to teach her daughter disobedience, within acceptable parameters of course (one doesn't want to raise a sociopath); make her into a woman who can go her own way (though only up to a point, obvs).

Obedience: is it drummed into girls or is it hard-wired? She was always slavishly obedient about schoolwork – always a day early, even if the work would've been better a day late. She longed to be one of those dishevelled types burning the midnight oil, but was too ruled by fear of censure, as if she mustn't cause a wrinkle in the smooth running of anyone else's life. She's the same now, even at 42 – if the teacher at Fly's school ever asked where that permissions slip for the school trip had got to, she grew breathless, panicked. 'No, I *did*, I *did sign it*. There's been a mistake.'

She returns to the kitchen, a glance at Mark: mop-headed, lovely glasses. Writing on his pad. The kitchen clock says 11 p.m. She settles back down. She must interrogate this Claybourne Leisure, see what Companies House has to say about its incorporation.

'How can a company not exist on the Internet? Ross paid tens of thousands to this Claybourne Leisure but it appears not to do anything.'

'Probably a shell company,' says Mark, without looking up from his writing. 'Didn't he set those up for a living?'

'So how do I find out who owns Claybourne Leisure or what it does?' she asks.

'You can't, would be my guess. Shell companies are notorious. Lots of governments want to put a stop to their ownership being hidden. Creates a massive window for money laundering. Think the Cayman Islands aren't keen though.' He smiles at her. Oh joy.

Back to the grey lines of the Ross bank statements.

'Is it me,' she says, yawning, 'or is it stuffy in here?'

He hasn't looked up. They still have a pile of case-file documents to get through. The table is strewn with crumbed plates, mugs with rings of cold tea and coffee. Wine glasses (not hers) with puddles of red at their base; a plastic carton of olives with feta cheese, its film lid ripped and oil from the olives dripped across the table. She's too tired to clear it all up.

'I'm going to sit somewhere more comfy,' she says, moving to the kitchen sofa – a blue and white striped affair from Ikea, with low white coffee table, at the far end of the room.

'Right you are, DI Huevo,' he says, under his cone of light, still looking through sheaves of papers.

'I won't always be this preposterous shape, you know,' she says, heaving down like a weighty pebble. She lifts her legs stiffly onto the coffee table, noticing that her ankles are swollen. The position forces her to lie back.

'Have you ever read anything by Saul Bellow?' he says, writing on his pad. She loves this, working together, late at night, talking about disclosure, about prosecution and defence, about Saul Bellow. Flirty intellectuals.

'Urgh,' she says. 'Hate Saul Bellow. Really boring.'

'Oh right. Was thinking of trying him. What did you read that you hated?'

'Dunno, something with "Rabbit" in the title. Man, it was boring.'

'D'you mean *Rabbit, Run*?'

'Yeah, that one.'

'By John Updike?'

'Yup.'

'So have you ever read anything by Saul Bellow?'

'I don't think so, no.'

The next thing she knows, her hair is being gently smoothed across her forehead. He has her slippers in his other hand.

'You're brave holding those,' she says sleepily.

226

'I know. Well, slipper emergency. Shall I take your shoes off for you?'

'Oh my God, would you? Only bending—'

'Say no more. You certainly know how to snore.'

'Yeah, right. I wasn't even asleep.'

'Must've been the boiler,' he says. 'You didn't fart either.'

He is jimmying off her shoes, which seem to have become wedged onto her swollen feet. Why does pregnancy make everything swell up? Fingers, feet, ankles, neck, face. It's so ungainly. She has shut her eyes again, simply because it is impossible to keep them open, and is horrified to feel him massaging her feet. She wonders if they smell or feel sweaty in his hands, but then the sensation takes over and it is so erotic, the release of pressure up her legs and along her spine, that she groans.

'Where did you learn to do this?' she asks.

'Law school,' he says. 'You must be exhausted.'

'Doesn't even begin to cover it. I dream of mere exhaustion. How much more evidence is there to get through?'

'Tons.'

She is quiet, thinking about the kneading of her feet and the line he has crossed and why he has crossed it. He is putting on her sheepskin slippers and she says, 'Oh, is that it?'

'Afraid so – cuts to legal aid and all that.'

'I hate austerity Britain.'

He has got off his perch on the coffee table and has come to sit on the sofa next to her.

She wonders what he intends.

He takes her hand in his. 'We should talk,' he says.

She closes her eyes. *Here we go*, she thinks. Another fuckwit who will announce he's in love with someone else, or he likes petite women, or flat stomachs, or he likes men, or he really

likes space, lots and lots of space, in which to shag other women
. . . Her heart has sped up and her breaths are shallow. No
more. No, she will not go down this road with him, not in her
condition, not with Fly to think about. She opens her eyes and
makes them cold.

'It's OK,' she says. 'There's nothing to talk about.'

He looks disappointed.

'I would get up and march briskly away,' she says, smiling
in order to appear conciliatory and ever so grown up. 'In a
way that would be forthright but also wildly attractive. Except
I can't actually get up and anyway I'm too tired.'

'I think you are wildly attractive,' he says. He has laid his head
back on the sofa cushions, like hers. His body is turned towards
her. Their foreheads are almost touching. She can feel the warmth
of his breath, its sulphurous smell making her feel vaguely sick.
She wishes pregnancy hadn't made her so hyper-sensitive to
odour – they could use her at crime scenes in place of sniffer
dogs. Pregnant women on leashes, leading forward on all fours.

Still, she's not about to exit a moment where someone finds
her wildly attractive, even if it involves a touch of nausea.

'Is it the chins?' she asks. 'Is that what's turning you on?'

'It's the whole egg-like package.'

She nods, looking down at the mountainous undulations of
her body. 'I can see it's pretty irresistible.'

'Can I kiss you?' he asks.

'Well, fortunately for you, I am rendered immobile.'

He leans in and kisses her and an arrow dart of excitement
shoots down the length of her body, her tiredness evaporating.
She awakens, pushing herself upright and kissing him back,
now leaning over him, clambering on to him. The bump has
disappeared, so wonderful is it to be close to him, to smell
him. She feels like a teenager making out, her clothes hot and

constricting, her face burning from his stubble. After what seems like hours but is probably only twenty minutes, she straightens away from him and leans back, sighing. The bump's edges have become impossibly tight.

'Pregnancy makes you so horny. Think it's the blood flow to your privates. I've spent the last five months dry humping my pillows.'

'Wow, I feel so special right now,' he says.

They sit there in silence, holding hands, heads back on the sofa cushions.

'Whose baby is it?' he says.

'No one's.'

'That's medically impossible.'

'Not these days it isn't.'

'D'you not want to tell me? You don't have to.'

'Look,' Manon says, and she can't believe she's saying this, 'I just don't think we should talk about either of our situations, that's all. You've had too much to drink to drive home. Come on, let's go to bed.'

He is reading Knausgaard, he says.

'That's a bad sign,' she says.

She has returned from the bathroom wearing her Marks & Spencer nightie, long-sleeved with polka dots, which might as well be a placard saying, KEEP AWAY ALL MALES. She wonders if M&S aren't specialising in this line and should make it one of their labels, like Autograph.

He holds her throughout the night – her hand, her arm – or wraps himself around her like a co-parachutist, falling. For the first time since Fly's arrest, she gets a decent night's sleep, not uninterrupted, but not the usual tortured thrashing with hours of vigilant wakefulness.

This is not a thing, Manon tells herself when she rouses groggily at 4 a.m., stumbling to the bathroom for a pee, before the free-fall of dreaming takes her back down. It's just a temporary diversion. He is very silent and still in his sleep and this quietness holds some secret about him, but it doesn't matter. It won't go anywhere. She stares at his tufts of hair in the grey early light, his crumpled face, pale and featureless without his heavy-rimmed glasses.

Is he a serious person? Can he be trusted?

The next time she wakes, she can smell shower gel and he is sitting on the edge of the bed, suited and booted, holding out a cup of coffee for her.

He says, 'I'm back on the hunt for a pathologist today. You?'

'I'm digging about for more on Claybourne Leisure. You defend, I'll prosecute,' she replies, drinking. It is wildly delicious as only the first coffee of the day can be – smoky, strong and thirst-quenching after the dry deserts of the night. She smiles at him.

'Gis a kiss,' he says.

DAY 25
8 JANUARY

'My God, you are MASSIVE,' says Bryony admiringly, lugging one of those giant zipped bags favoured by the dispossessed across the threshold of Manon's front door. 'Like a great galleon of womanhood. I want to worship you.'

'Fuck off,' says Manon, closing the door after her, a coffee in one hand and her slippers on.

'Baby clothes,' says Bri, breathless, nodding at the bag. 'Nought to three months. There's about ten more where that came from.'

'I don't want them now, I'm not due till April.'

'No, I know, but by March you'll develop an overpowering urge to fold small vests and that bag is full of small vests. I'm telling you, it's primeval or primordial – whatever the word is. What I mean is, it's what mammals do: they turn around on the spot and burrow into straw. The human equivalent is folding small vests and becoming laundry obsessed.'

'I still don't want it.'

Bryony looks at her in a way that is too much, puts an arm

around her. 'Don't want what?' she asks, kindly. 'My baby vests, or the baby?'

Manon's eyes fill with tears. 'I don't want it, Bri. I just want Fly. And Mark Talbot if I'm honest, but that's a whole other story. I've been so stupid and selfish. I haven't protected Fly. He's got cuts up his arms and he won't let me see him. All these horrible lies,' she gasps, 'they're building around him. What the fuck am I doing having a baby? All I want is Fly. I just want Fly out of there and safe and reading his books in his bedroom.'

'I know,' Bri says. 'I know you want Fly. Look, there's still time. Sounds like you and Mark are building a case and you can get him out. And I can carry on risking my entire career by feeding you case-file documents.'

'Harriet's suspicious about how I got Conley's cell confession, by the way,' Manon says, over Bri's shoulder. She smells Bryony's skin – warm sweetness, like caramel or bread, the absence of anything artificial such as perfume. 'I told her I got it from Fly.'

'I'll say the same then. Look, like you say, you're not due till April and Fly will be out by then and things will be back to normal. Anyway, more urgently, I need to hear about how you've thrown yourself at your defence solicitor. Was it unbecoming?'

'Very. Come through, I'll make you a coffee.'

'Excellent,' says Bri, rubbing her palms together.

While the coffee machine bubbles and churns, and Bryony hangs her handbag on the back of a chair, Manon says, 'I'm so worried about Fly.' Bryony is silent, leaving the space for her to carry on, while Manon gets the milk. One of the many things Manon loves about Bri is the way she listens. 'I still don't know what the visit to London was about – him skipping school and going to Momtaz. I don't even know if it was just one time, or more than one.'

'Might be nothing,' says Bryony. 'Might be nostalgia.'

'Nostalgia can be very dangerous,' says Manon. 'And hanging out with that lowlife Paddy Driscoe? I mean, what's all that about?'

'He's a dealer, isn't he? Is Fly experimenting with drugs? I don't mean in a hairy scary way. I mean, you don't need to go off the deep end about it.'

Manon is shaking her head. 'Fly's actually quite moralistic about drugs. Got that from Taylor, his brother. I think their mother was so out of it, they developed a hatred of anything that makes you lose control. He's the same about booze. Weirdly, I'm more confident about him not doing drugs than I am about whether he stabbed Jon-Oliver.'

Manon places a cup of coffee in front of Bryony, then says, 'Thank you. For the baby clothes, for the documents, for everything.'

'Pleasure.'

'He won't let me see him in Arlidge House. He's taken me off his authorised visitor list.'

'He sounds very hurt,' says Bri.

After she has spilled the beans on making out on the sofa with Mark, Bri says, 'Oh it'd be wonderful for you to be settled with someone!'

'Knew you'd say that,' Manon says.

'What's wrong with wanting you to find someone?'

'Nothing, it's just . . . it won't go anywhere. I can't see it being the happy ever after. I can't see anyone taking on me and my motley collection of children and I don't want – well, I don't want to hope for it really.'

'Why ever not?'

Manon has got up and is opening kitchen cupboards. 'I haven't got any biscuits – trying not to buy them. Ryvita?'

'Christ, no thanks.'

'I've bolstered myself to do this alone. I have to have my backbone in to manage it, I can't just collapse in a heap the minute a man walks through the door.'

'Could he get struck off? Mark, I mean. Does it go against some kind of defence solicitors' code to cop off with the client's mother?'

'Dunno. We haven't talked about that. We haven't talked about anything actually. He wanted to tell me his "situation" but I said I didn't want to hear it. And I think my situation is fairly visible.'

'Oh, don't push him away, Manon,' Bri says with feeling. 'I mean, you might as well see where it goes.'

DAVY

He's unable to turn his head; woke this morning with a crick so tight and excruciating that even throwing his head back to take down the Panadol was nigh-on impossible. It's as if a band is looped between his right ear and his right shoulder blade, preventing any range of movement. They are twenty-five days in. He knows this without consulting a calendar, as if the sand in every investigation's hourglass has become a part of his body clock and it's down to its final grains. At twenty-eight days, CCTV film usually gets wiped, a watershed of sorts. If there is evidence they haven't gathered yet because they've gone down the wrong road, there are only a few days left to get it.

He turns his stiffened upper body at the sounds of unlocking – bolt after bolt getting nearer on the inmate side of this visiting room, which smells of cleaning products overlaid with institutional food. A vat of shepherd's pie in a metal tray, perhaps. The smell is hospital-like, wipe-down; loveless.

The door opens and a boy walks in but he is barely recognisable. He has been so badly beaten that his left eye slants

235

downwards, inflated and closed. There is a cut to his lower lip. His hands are cuffed in front of him.

Davy's heart is knocking. 'Fly,' he says, standing up.

Fly has sat in the chair in front of him, on the other side of the table, in a leaned-back position, legs spread, a 12-year-old's attempt at saying, 'Fuck you.'

'That looks nasty,' says Davy. 'What happened?'

Fly shrugs.

'Guess there's no point asking if they're treating you all right in here.'

Again, no response.

'I brought you chewing gum, a selection of flavours – look, there's Tropical Burst. I've tried that. It's good. Thought you might be fed up of getting books.'

Fly doesn't reply but he shifts his body subtly in what might be a slight receptiveness.

'Your mum sends her love,' Davy says.

'She's not my mum.'

'Manon, then. She'd really like to visit you.'

Silence.

'It's not her fault, you know, all this.'

'I'm not being funny but why are you here?' Fly asks. 'I mean, is it official, are you here as a police officer, or is it, like, personal? Did she send you here? And whose fault is it, all this? Yours? Because it sure as fuck isn't mine.'

Davy colours. 'I don't know,' he says. 'In answer to your earlier question, I'm here on both counts. I'm here because Manon asked me to check you're all right and I'd also like to ask you something, actually.'

Fly has slouched back down.

'This visit to London. The one where you skipped school and went back to Cricklewood. Is there anything you'd like to

236

tell me about that – for example why you were meeting Paddy Driscoe?'

'There's nothing I'd like to tell you about that,' Fly says. 'Is that everything? Because I think I've got basket weaving right now.'

'D'you want me to talk to anyone, here I mean, about that?' Davy says, indicating Fly's face. 'I can do something about it, get them to look into it, take action against whoever did it.'

'Oh yeah,' says Fly, getting up. 'That'd definitely make things better for me in here.'

'He's been fighting,' says Neil, swivelling around on his wheelie office chair. 'That's why we've had to cuff him. He's got into trouble. A lot of trouble. Conley Woodchurch, mainly.'

'Did someone tell Fly about Conley's cell confession?' Davy asks.

'I think Conley told Fly about that. And to be honest, you think Fly looks bad, you should see Conley's face.'

Davy thinks about saying, '*Yeah, well he had it coming,*' but knows he can't. Instead, he says, 'Right. So what are you doing to separate Conley and Fly? To calm the situation down?'

'It's up to Fly to control himself,' says Neil, wheeling back to face his computer. 'Conley's done nothing wrong, he's only reported what Fly said to him. I've known Conley a long time. He's not a bad kid. There's a culture here; your lad has to learn to fit in.'

What sort of culture? Davy thinks. *A violent, racist, threatening culture presided over by Neil's blind eyes?* The sight of Neil's back enrages him.

'Right, but Conley's been here a long time, he's established here. Fly's been here little more than a week and he's got razor cuts up his arms and he's been beaten up. I think you need to step up when it comes to protecting the new kid, don't you?'

'Thought you'd be pleased,' Neil says, smiling up at Davy. 'Conley supplied extra grist to your mill. He's helping your case.'

'I'd like an interview with Conley Woodchurch please,' Davy says. 'Now.'

Conley walks in sporting a black eye, with his arm in a sling. He sits in a blue plastic chair while Davy stands. Paces, in fact.

'Conley,' he says, then smiles.

Conley has short hair, almost a skinhead, but it is wet with some kind of gel so that his scalp glows white beneath the slicks. He is pale and spotty. No one cares whether Conley's getting his five a day.

'So,' Davy says, 'what's going on between you and Fly Dent?'

'He started it.'

'Did he?'

Conley shifts in his seat.

'I'm surprised to hear that. What was the argument about?'

'Weren't no argument. I told the coppers what he said to me in the poppy shop about stabbing that bloke, he's sore about it.'

'Right, yes, the poppy shop.'

Silence.

'Whereabouts were you in the poppy shop? I mean, front table, back table?'

'Front.'

'And what were you doing?'

'Fixing the petals onto the black bit, putting them in boxes.'

'How many did you do?'

'Bout 150.'

'And Fly?'

'Dunno, didn't count his.'

'Fly did none,' Davy says. He has stopped, leaning over the table at which Conley is sitting, glaring at him. 'Zero. Nought. Fly wasn't in the poppy shop. Fly has never been in the poppy shop, you lying git.'

Conley has sat more upright. Davy is feeling very much like a police officer from the Seventies and it is marvellous.

'*You* know he was never in the poppy shop, and *I* know it. Now either you retract your bullshit cell confession or I will personally make sure your indeterminate sentence never ends, you get me?'

Marching out of Arlidge House, he feels so macho there even seems to be a stirring in his trousers. Then he realises it's his mobile phone vibrating.

'How can I help you, Mr Carruthers?' Davy says, looking up at the porridgy sky.

'Just wondering if you've made any progress on Jon-Oliver's case.'

Davy remains resolutely silent.

Carruthers presses on: 'You know, we all want to see justice done, see his killer caught. Otherwise, well – what's the point, know what I mean?'

'Hmmm,' says Davy. His hand jangles his keys and coins in his trouser pocket. He waits.

'Can you tell me who your main suspect is? Is it the Dent boy? Because, I think I mentioned, Jon-Oliver always had his suspicions. Thought he was a wrong'un.'

First thing Davy does back at HQ is knock on Harriet's door, to which she shouts, 'Come.'

'Just had a strange call from Giles Carruthers,' he says.

She stops writing, looks up at him. 'Strange how?'

'Wanted to know about the progress of the case, who we'd arrested. Very keen to stress Fly Dent was a "wrong'un", as he put it.'

'Did he now.' She leans back, flicking her pen between two fingers.

'Look, boss, I'm not feeling so good about—'

'I know,' she says. 'The Ellie Bradshaw alibi.'

'I just don't understand it.'

'Well, I brought it up with Stanton again and he totally lost it, started shouting about the pathology and the footage at the scene, and saying why would you want to go off on some tangent following a nurse's trip to the Co-op or whatever it was.'

'Because that's what we do,' says Davy.

'I know. I'm just explaining how it went when I pushed it. Y'know, Davy, sometimes the top brass gets a bee in their bonnet over something and this is Stanton's. Best thing to do is accept it, to be honest. Later on, we'll find out he's had a steer from the commissioner or whoever's pulling his strings.'

Davy thinks of Fly's swollen face and swallows down a bubble of feeling, too much for him to express.

Harriet says, 'Doesn't stop you investigating the fuck out of Giles Carruthers though, does it?'

BIRDIE

Have you ever watched raindrops race down a pane? A single drop – clear bauble reflecting a world – can sit in its fullness for whole moments before it contains too much. Then it bursts and runs down, this way then that, until it is nothing at all.

One minute you have everything, not even realising that your life is at its fullest, and then it runs off to nothing.

I told Angel I thought we should go to the police – lay it all out there, tell them everything about the Carlton Mayfair and Jade. Let them investigate it all so that she didn't have to run any more. She looked at me with hollow eyes – an expression that said 'it doesn't make any difference'. Like she'd lost all her faith in the goodness of human beings, like no one would help her. It was my job to prove her wrong. There are lots of good people, aren't there?

I went to my local nick, couldn't think what else to do.

Reception was the colour of sick. Yellow floor, yellow walls. The desk was behind a sliding window, its thick frame painted blue gloss. An empty chair on the other side of the glass. I

241

pressed on the intercom. Eventually, someone said, 'Yes?' like I'd interrupted their favourite TV show.

'I need to talk to a police officer.'

'Have you called the main switchboard telephone number? It's there, on the wall.'

'Why would I do that when I'm here, in person?'

'What's it about?'

Well, how d'you answer that in a nutshell? A murder. A prostitution racket. The City and all its money. The death of a child. A cover-up.

'It's a bit complicated,' I said.

'Someone will be down soon.'

I sat down on welded-together seats that were stuck to the back wall. Took out my phone and texted Angel.

Everything in hand. You bought that salon in Fuengirola yet?

Not yet.

We could call it British Hairways.

Curl up and dye?

Are you feeling down? Have you eaten anything?

Haribo.

HAIRibo would be better.

I think we should call it Birdie & Sass.

That pulled me up short. She was putting my name first, even though she was miserable and scared and probably pissed seeing as it was past 11 a.m.

Still no sign of anyone, I wrote to her.

A little later, wondering if she was sleeping or watching TV, I wrote again.

This is taking ages. Mind if I pop to the cash and carry on my way back?

After an age, some pissed-off officer wandered into reception and asked me what I wanted the police for. I gave a short precis, during which he looked at me like I was a delusional fantasist, then he said, 'Well, you'll need to speak to a more senior officer. You can either go to a larger police station, such as Kilburn CID, or come back tomorrow when we're fully staffed.'

I'll be honest, I didn't have the energy. And I'd been out for long enough. I thought I would nip to the cash and carry for some crisps and then hurry back to Angel.

Manon

Davy has called her, saying, 'Right, so we've discovered Ross's iPhone passcode. We got his bank card PIN and tried that. Bingo. I'm sending you the file, OK? Delete the email after you've downloaded it.'

'Righto,' she says, logging on to her laptop and throwing her mobile onto the table.

The phone work shows texts from something called Titans VIP.

Meeting with Saskia confirmed.
Please contact us to rate your experience.

Payment received. We offer a discreet service.
The reference on your bank statement will read Claybourne Leisure.

She Googles Titans and the screen tessellates with images of pouting women, scantily clad, with diamond ratings beside their details. 'Tina has huge brown eyes and an incredible sense of humour. The Brazilian model is a student of international relations in London. She speak five languages and loves to travel.' She is also on all fours in a bustier, with a whip in one hand.

Manon searches for Saskia but nothing comes up. So, he used prostitutes – Ellie warned her as much. Back to the phone work.

Meeting with Kristen confirmed.
Payment received with thanks.

Texts between Ross and unknown 618.

Enjoyed last night, must do it again. J-O

I am here for your pleasure. With you it's different – special. We can make private arrangement if you'd like. Sass.

Busy guy. Then in late July, he texts:

Cut the shit. I mean it, Sass. These people do not fuck around.

A couple of days later:

I can't help you any more. Leave me out of it.

Look for the affair? This is the affair, an affair with a prostitute, which got him embroiled in something heavier than he wanted; drugs perhaps, or the violent world of pimps and gangsters – all too much for a suited City boy.

245

She calls Davy, who tells her to wait so he can take the call somewhere private. From the echo, she's guessing the gents.

'Where are the texts between Ellie and Jon-Oliver?' she asks.

'There aren't any,' he says. 'Either they didn't text, or they used something else, like Snapchat or WhatsApp, which can be erased.'

Shaggerapp, she thinks.

'Any luck with the trace on unknown 618?'

'Not yet,' Davy says.

While she is waiting, not knowing if the phone trace will give them anything other than the mast in London the phone last pinged off, she thinks about Paddy Driscoe and cooks. Browning mince, sweating onions, thinking about how to get to him. Tupperware boxes of homemade sausage rolls – Fly's favourite. Vanilla biscuits and meatloaf that tastes as good cold as warm. Manon is not an enthusiastic cook, certainly not one to pore over recipes from the colour supplements involving forty-eight ingredients. But certain basic signature dishes she has become good at through repetition. Beef stew, spaghetti bolognese, one-pot hearty casseroles. There is pleasure in tending to children with these.

She drives to Arlidge House and turns on the charm with Toad woman on reception, persuading her to deliver the food to Fly personally.

'Anything to report?' she said, pseudo-casually. 'Everything all right with him, as far as you know?'

'You're still not on his AV list,' Toad responded.

'No, right, well if you could make sure he gets the food.'

The next time she went, with tubs of tuna-sweetcorn-mayo, Toad said, 'The sausage rolls went down well. He cracked a smile.' She said this without looking up from her computer screen. Manon had to resist the urge to blow her a kiss.

'Bring you some next time,' she said.

She can't search Paddy Driscoe's name on the police database, because it'll show up on her computer. But anyone can look on Crimestoppers, gnarly-faced beauty pageant of the UK's most wanted. Expressions pale and undernourished against the grey police mugshot background. *Wanted on licence. Wanted for recall to prison. Absconded prior to sentencing.* Shaved heads and the weary look of recidivists: *must I go on with this depressing cycle?*

She types in Driscoe. Nothing. Types in Drisco. Nothing. Patrick, Paddy. Nothing.

Searches under drug crime, London. Three suspects whose whereabouts are unknown: Mark Liscott, Daniel Bowes, Dave Hargreaves, known as The Badger.

She takes a slug of cold tea, whirring through probation officers of the past, drug squad contacts from her CID days in her mind. She really doesn't want to call Dan Ashton (known to everyone as Ash) and not just because she used to sleep with him. Well, mostly because she used to sleep with him. She sees his shortcomings so clearly now; he is almost 100 per cent shortcomings. Why couldn't she see it then? Professional charmer, flirt in uniform, the vibe he gave off strongly was You Want Me But You Can't Have Me. He clothed himself in sensitivity, with a hint of the vulnerable, very good listener, laughed at all her jokes, but in reality he was a narcissist who scrolled through his phone every time he fancied being unfaithful to the person he was seeing and often came up trumps with Manon. She probably wasn't even the first he tried.

No, she's not in the humour to flaunt her swollen ankles in his direction, but for Fly she will do anything.

'Ash,' she says, at the end of a deep breath.

'Hello stranger.'

'Fancy a drink?'

Day 27

10 January

Davy

The Lotus Blossom takeaway in Islington is a broad oblong of window, bright yellow against the evening sky. Buses, cars and taxis thunder past. Roadworks nearby are jackhammering away. Horns toot, engines rev, people shout, some music blares from a passing car. London is a pair of boxing gloves beating Davy about the head via the ears and he feels glad he lives in unfashionable Sapley, with its deathly quiet new builds.

Inside the Lotus Blossom, there are just a couple of feet of linoleum and then a counter running the full width. Davy can hear the splash of wok frying and Chinese being shouted, and wondrous smells fill his nostrils. Sweetness and meat and vinegar. A couple of worn tabloids at one end of the counter, a menu laminated onto the counter surface, a pen on a chain. He wonders if, as he's here, and the smells are making his stomach coil snake-like . . . there is anything unprofessional about carrying a white paper bag, warm at the base, back to the Premier Inn?

He waits. Looks in his wallet to see if he has enough cash for a quarter crispy duck with pancakes. Waits some more.

Soon, his hunger becomes irritation.

'Excuse me,' he says, raising his badge.

A black-haired girl looks up, says nothing.

'I need to ask you some questions about a customer who came in before Christmas,' he says. As he says it, he's wishing he'd pursued this line earlier, on the day of the Dunlop & Finch interviews for example. Then he might have been in with a chance. Instead, he's asking them to remember a customer who picked up a takeaway four weeks ago. 'Do you recognise this man?'

He holds up a picture of Carruthers, a print-off from the Dunlop & Finch website. If Carruthers was a cat, he'd lick himself.

She shrugs at him, perhaps hasn't understood. She barks something in Chinese very fast over her shoulder towards the kitchen. A man comes out.

'Can I help you?'

'Yes, I was wondering if you remembered serving this man. It's a while back now, December the fourteenth. He says he came in for a takeaway.' Davy hands over the image of Carruthers.

The Chinese man nods. 'He regular customer, yeah.' Then he waits, looking at Carruthers' face. Looks up at Davy. 'He came taxi.'

'Taxi?'

'Taxi, yeah,' he says, nodding fast. 'He very stress. Make big fight in here. Say we no quick enough.'

Davy looks up at the camera, which points at the door. 'Any film in that?'

From Davy's purple-branded budget hotel room, he calls Kim and tells her to ANPR the number plate of the car carrying

250

Giles Carruthers to the Lotus Blossom not on 14 December, but on 13 December. Carruthers did not go to the takeaway on 14 December.

He's watched the film of Carruthers pacing the linoleum of the Lotus Blossom, checking his phone, looking anxiously through to the kitchen to see where his food was, complaining to the girl behind the counter. Davy watched an argument break out, rather like watching an old silent movie. Even without sound, Davy could see Carruthers was being rude – patrician towards the staff. None of his usual sleek confidence. Why was he so jumpy?

Lying on the bed, Davy pops the mini pot of Pringles he purchased at the bar. Pringles for one, sour cream flavour. The little pot of Pringles and the cool beer on his bedside unit are creating in him a firmament of pleasure in his solar plexus.

Of course Davy went straight to Carruthers with this rather significant hole in his alibi.

'You weren't at the Lotus Blossom on December the fourteenth. You were there the night before. The thirteenth.'

'Really?' Carruthers said. 'Are you sure?'

'Quite sure. Any thoughts about where you were on the fourteenth?'

They both behaved as if this was an easy mistake to make, and it was, except Davy had a hunch it wasn't a mistake. And yes, his training told him there should be no hunches in police work, but sometimes hunches went to the very heart. He knew Manon would agree with him. '*Nuance*,' she once said to him. 'And no, Davy, that's not another word for paedophile.'

Carruthers turned the corners of his mouth down, hands in his trouser pockets. 'Home, I guess.'

'Anyone who can confirm you were at home?'

'Not that I can think of. I live by myself.'

251

Davy pops a Pringle into his mouth, with his phone to his ear, listening to Kim say, 'Why're you pursuing a *not*-significant witness on *not* the night of the murder? Carruthers didn't travel to Huntingdon to stab Ross. He would've been picked up.'

'I still want to know,' Davy says. 'Want the name and location of the taxi rank. Harriet'll back me up.'

Sometimes, he wants to tell Kim, life takes you down tributaries and it's important to go with it – to allow the journey to an unknown destination. But Kim's not the sort to deal in abstracts.

'Can't see where it'll get you,' she says.

'No, well, there we are.'

'How's the Premier Inn?'

'Y'know, purple.'

MANON

She's caught the train to London, and in a gastropub over an early-evening drink, she says to Dan Ashton, 'I need to find someone, a dealer on your patch. Paddy Driscoe.'

'You look really beautiful,' Ash says, gently, quietly, as if it is an eternal truth that he can't help iterating. He looks really great with his shaved head and blue eyes. Shirt sleeves rolled up so she can see a hint of bicep. He has that police officer gym-bulk about him.

'Thanks,' she says, crisply. She wants to get on with it, get it over with. Return to Fly and the matter in hand.

'I'm serious,' Ash says. He blows out, as if the power of Manon's pregnant beauty has actually winded him. 'It's . . . you're so . . . radiant.' He's blushing. She's witnessing turbo-fuck-wittage in motion and she couldn't care less. It's like holding up a stick of kryptonite to Superman. 'I'm so glad you got in touch,' he is saying, while she laughs on the inside. 'I missed our friendship.' Big, howling single-lady laughter on the inside.

'Ah, thanks Ash,' she says. Then, after a decent pause, 'Anyway, Paddy Driscoe – d'you know him?'

253

He looks down, adorably, fingering a napkin. She considers heading for the toilet, just to cut down the amount of time she must spend in the presence of this idiot. The hubbub of the North London Tavern seems louder, New Zealand voices, then booming male laughter; cutlery on plates. The walls are navy and the tasselled lampshades ironically askew.

It *was* really good sex, she remembers, looking at him and marvelling at how boring he is. He is saying something about how hard it is to meet people with whom one has a connection and she's thinking, *yeah, especially when you're not remotely interested in who they are.* She wonders why she put herself through all that emotional masochism, the tears when he told her ever so regretfully he couldn't see her any more because he really was devoted to Natalie/Hannah/Meredith. Until his next lapse, of course, when Manon would open the door to him at 11 p.m. She realises he's a sad specimen. *It's not a crime,* she thinks now, *to be a shagger who pretends to like women but whose main aim is to make them miserable.* If only she could inform all girls at birth about men like Ash. She'd save them so much time.

He is yawning on. 'We had a connection, you and me, Manon. Y'know?'

'Sorry, I really have to get this,' she says, noticing Davy Walker lighting up the screen of her phone.

Out on the Kilburn High Road, the wind is unruly, whipping the rain up as if she's being spat at. Her coat flaps chaotically.

'Phone data's come in on unknown 618,' Davy says.

'Right.'

'Just been topped up. I've got an address.'

'Go on.'

'The Payless Food & Wine, Kilburn High Road. She might have only popped in there to top up, but there might be CCTV which could give us an ID, or the shopkeeper might remember her and to be honest, it's all we've got.'

'OK, I'm right by it actually. I know Payless. It's where I used to buy my Quavers. Did you go and see Fly? Is he all right?' Davy's voice is faint, intermittent. 'Hello? Davy? You're breaking up . . .' Perhaps it's the wind or her hair flapping about her head.

'I said yes, I went there. Yes, he's all right. Eating well, you know, following the rules. No need for you to worry. I'm on it.'

'Oh thank God. I'm so relieved to hear that, Davy. Davy? Hello?'

She frowns at the phone. Must've lost the signal. She notices she's down to one bar of battery, and she hasn't brought her charger. Still in her hand, the phone vibrates.

A text message from Mark.

Found pathologist at UCH. Showing him café CCTV tomorrow.

Back inside the North London Tavern, she sits again with Ash. Heart rate's up at the thought of Fly in Arlidge House. Bump tight as a drum. She must stop doing things that appear to be so physiologically exerting.

'So, you want to trace Paddy Driscoe?' he says, sitting up straighter. He looks hurt and defensive. Hasn't had enough attention, poor little baby. 'What d'you want him for?'

'He was in contact with . . .' Manon hasn't mentioned Fly, because – she realises, *revelation after revelation* – Ash has never been interested in anything about her. 'He's connected to a case I've got going on in Huntingdon.'

'Why don't you just look him up on the system?'

255

'He's absconded. Thought one of your contacts might know how to raise him.'

He nods. He's not going to help her. She can see that. She watches him tear up the napkin. Is that a tan mark left by a wedding ring on his finger?

'Sorry, I've got to go,' he says. 'I'll see what I can do. Can you claim this on exes?'

While she settles the bill, her phone dies. What if Arlidge House needs to reach her? No, Davy said Fly was fine. He is probably, at this very moment, making the most of all the woodworking and cookery and literature appreciation courses on offer.

What if her colleagues need to reach her? She's not on duty. This is not official police business, there are no pre-existing protocols for this situation. She doesn't allow herself to contemplate whether danger lies ahead or whether her baby might put in a very unwelcome appearance. No, being without a mobile phone is OK. It's the modern malaise, this inner quaking at being out of reach for a nanosecond: not having a phone to check is like being a baby without a breast.

What if she misses the call that would tell her Fly has been released, that the case has been dropped? Can't happen, even in her wildest fantasies. Only a judge can throw out this case and Fly won't go before a judge for weeks. She remembers Mark telling her he preferred an acquittal to a case being thrown out, because at least then he gets the trial fee. Their best interests not quite aligned. Sometimes, processes are set in train, which cannot be derailed even by good sense. *Curse you*, Harriet Harper.

She wonders, then, whether Davy has been telling the truth about Fly being fine in Arlidge House. She wants it to be true, but she wonders whether it is possible for Fly to keep his

256

equilibrium – to manage under the strain of being wrongly accused. She knows what a terrible feeling it is to be held inaccurately in the mind of others, taken as baser and meaner than you are. She is thinking that this sensation is particularly awful for children, who rely so much on the good opinion of powerful adults.

She thinks of Ash and realises she has stopped caring about the good opinion of idiots, which is progress of a sort – like stepping out of some really uncomfortable clothing that one doesn't need to wear any more.

She has turned, is walking to the lower part of the Killy High Road, towards the Payless Food & Wine. As she walks, a conversation with Mark comes to mind from last night. He came home late from the police station (home, he had called it himself, as if they were playing at a new situation without talking about it); pulling his tie side to side to loosen it and telling her about the client he'd just seen. Then he said, 'I'm shattered. Can we watch a bit of telly before bed?' And she had felt content/cautious/overjoyed/exhausted. All at once.

They slumped together, bodies glued side by side on the sofa in front of a dating show in which a 40-year-old man told the camera that his longest relationship had lasted a couple of months.

'Rings alarm bells,' said Manon.

On the television show, the man's date asked him what he was looking for in a woman and he said, 'Someone easygoing, Just y'know, someone who's a laugh, someone to hang out with, who's really easygoing.'

'That's the second time he's said easygoing,' said Mark. 'Think we've identified why he's single.'

Manon looked at him and Mark had pointed his wine glass at the telly. 'Anyone who says he wants a relationship with someone easygoing, doesn't want a relationship with a real person,' he said.

The bell rings above the door, which opens into a grey grimy place stacked with boxes of crisps, the usual humming fridge filled with sugar-laden drinks and corner-shop milk, racks upon racks of chocolate bars, sweets, fizzy pop and snacks of a more international flavour: Japanese rice crackers, Bombay mix, cashews and pistachios.

Behind the counter is a large woman of indeterminate age wearing massive Deirdre Barlow glasses. She has curly brown hair, cut short and with a fringe (a haircut with the whiff of a DIY job). She is struggling for breath over the fat. Manon shows her police badge, she doesn't know why – habit, to give her the authority she feels she doesn't actually have.

'Can I ask you some questions?' she says to the shopkeeper.

'Fire away.'

'Do you know this woman?' Manon shows her the photograph of the blonde that was found on Jon-Oliver's body. She is fairly certain the woman in the photo is the owner of unknown 618.

The shopkeeper looks at Manon. Pauses. It is clear from the weight of the silence and the pause that the shopkeeper does know this woman.

'Is she a friend of yours, or a regular?' asks Manon.

'Who wants to know?'

'I showed you my badge, I'm from Cambridgeshire Police.'

'Yes but why are you asking about her? What do you want to know about her?'

'This photograph was found on the body of a man who was murdered in our area,' Manon says. 'I have reason to believe her mobile phone was topped up here recently.'

'You'd best come with me,' the shopkeeper says, waddling out from behind the counter. 'My name's Birdie, by the way. Birdie Fielding.'

'Manon Bradshaw,' she says, while Birdie locks the shop door and flips the Closed sign.

Birdie shuffles around the packed aisles and pads her way to the back of the shop, taking a packet of custard creams en route. Manon follows her to a staircase, at the foot of which is a dark stain across the linoleum. The type of stain Manon has seen numerous times before.

Birdie pushes a rectangle of plastic matting with her foot to slide it back in place, covering the stain. She begins to climb the stairs; heavy stomps, breathless, saying, 'If you follow me we can have a chat up here nice and quiet. Just a minute while I get my keys out. Ah, here we are. Come in.'

They enter a hallway papered with white-painted Anaglypta – Seventies striations – and brown carpet on the floor. The place smells homely and clean.

'Through here,' Birdie says.

The living room is the kind that should house two grand-parents watching *Countdown*. Brown recliners and a sofa with ruffled seams arranged around the television; net curtains and glass figurines on the gas-fire surround. 'Have a seat. I'll just make you a cup of tea and then we can have a nice chat.'

Manon sits on the edge of the velveteen sofa, knees together, handbag on her lap. She pushes into it with a hand and feels about for her mobile, casting a glance at it out of habit, but it has not miraculously sprung back into life. She tries not to think about what she might do were she to need back-up, tells herself the worst she'll be faced with here is some trans fats. The congestion about her middle – the size of the bump and its tightness – causes her discomfort. She needs the toilet, as always, but decides to wait for a bit.

'Here we are,' says Birdie, returning to the lounge carrying two mugs of tea. 'I'll just get us some biscuits.'

'Nothing for me,' calls Manon.

Once Birdie has heaved down into one of the recliners with an 'ooof', and has opened the packet of custard creams, Manon says, 'So you know the woman in the photograph?'

Birdie nods. 'Think so, yes. She didn't look like that when I met her, mind. More of a Goth. Told me her name was Angel, though I didn't believe her. She stayed here for a bit. Why're you asking?'

'We – I – think she might be able to tell us more about our victim, Jon-Oliver Ross, and who might have wanted to harm him.'

'And you're one of the detectives investigating his murder, are you?' says Birdie, smiling at her with unnerving focus through those glasses, like two windscreens.

'Sort of,' says Manon. 'How long did she stay here?'

'Not long,' says Birdie. 'I can show you her room if you like. You're the first to come, the first to ask about her, so you can go through her stuff.'

'Where is she?' Manon asks. 'I was hoping to talk to her.'

'Come through,' says Birdie, getting up. 'Over here.' She leads the way out to the hall. Manon sets her tea down and follows. Birdie is nodding at the box room, adjacent to the kitchen. 'That's where she stayed. You'll see her holdall in there if you go in. Like I say, you're the first I've allowed in, so no one's seen that, her holdall and that. It might be good for you to go in and perform an examination, so to speak.'

Something strange in Birdie's sentence construction. In Manon's experience, the more contorted a person's grammar, the bigger the lie. You see this most clearly when you're being dumped by a boyfriend who is lying about his reasons – leaving out the other person he's shagging, for example. Manon has heard all manner of mangled verbiage from the mouths of lying gits.

Yet out of some mindless obedience coupled with curiosity, Manon enters the box room. She and Birdie are in its doorway, Birdie's heavy breath at her shoulder. 'Further in,' Birdie says.

'Look, I'm not very good at getting down on the floor,' Manon says, taking in the dishevelled mattress at her feet. 'It's the pregnancy . . .'

'Hold up, I'll get you a chair,' Birdie says, huffing and puffing out towards the small galley kitchen.

'Why don't I just bring it out to the—'

She is about to say 'lounge' when she turns to find the door to the box room closing and a key being turned in the lock.

'Hey!' Manon shouts. 'What are you doing? Birdie? What the . . . *fuck*!'

Manon rattles at the door, heavy slams down on the handle. She bashes her palm onto the door itself. 'What are you doing? Why have you locked me in here? Let me out! You can't imprison a police officer. Do you know what you'll get for this? Let me out right this minute.' Thud, thud, thud. Rattling. Banging, bashing. A sharp arrow dart of pain right down the side of her bump, like a lightning bolt. *Oh please God no, not this moment. Don't let it be now, locked in here.* Manon winces, clutches at her side with her hand. Tries to massage the pain away. It subsides. A one-off perhaps.

'Have you calmed down yet?' says the voice from the hall. 'If you calm down, then I can tell you all about it and I'll know you're listening good and proper. Because I've been given the brush-off up to now, you see, so I needed to make sure you'd

261

stop and listen. Make yourself comfortable and I can tell you how I first met Angel. I can tell you everything that's happened up until now.'

Calm, Manon tells herself. *Keep calm, listen to the old bint and then I can get out of here.* The dart of pain has subsided to a dull throb, so she heaves herself down onto the mattress on the floor, leaning her back against the wall. The sooner this woman tells her what she wants to tell her, the sooner she'll unlock the door.

'It started when she was knocked down by a car on the Kilburn High Road, see. I came out just like anyone would – like Nasreen did from the cash and carry – to see what all the tooting and commotion was about . . .'

BIRDIE

After that pointless trip to the police station, I popped in at the cash and carry. So when I opened up the shop, my face was mostly behind a huge Walkers Crisps cardboard box. I was balancing the box on one arm while I pushed the keys into the shop door and fell in, dropping the box to the floor. Angel had stopped texting me back at the police station, but I figured maybe she was asleep or watching telly.

I felt for the lights, and they blinked. In the plink-plink on and off of the strip lights I could see snapshots of her body, twisted at the bottom of the stairs, and then the room went dark again. Then light again. Plink, plink. Eyes open, neck snapped. And dark again. My heart went to my feet. Even in those seconds I could see she was dead.

You don't fall down the stairs and die. You just don't. When the lights were fully on, I could see there was a pooling of blood around her. Her body was lying the wrong way up, legs higher than her head. As I said, her neck was twisted along the floor. Eyes staring out of her blue-tinged face.

I didn't move. I got my phone out and dialled 999 and in

263

what felt like an instant, they came, blue lights sweeping the room from out on the street. I was standing stock still, staring at my friend, when an officer grabbed my arm quite roughly and said, 'If you wouldn't mind coming with me, while we secure the scene.'

I was 16 when Nanny Fielding died. Her legs were skinny and bowed in the plywood coffin the mortuary used to cart her off. Charlie Chaplin legs.

She had a low walnut sideboard with sliding doors. In it were boxes of chocolates from Christmases gone by. Dark violet creams. Chocolate-covered orange peel, like stubby worms. They had a white bloom from age but they tasted all right. I sat and I ate them all, as if I could have Nanny Fielding inside me. I went downhill after that.

I'd taken her for granted. I hadn't realised she was the pin that kept my life together, and that without her I would flutter to the floor. I thought Nanny Fielding was a bit of a bore. I didn't want to sit with her unless the telly was on. I didn't want to listen to her tales, which were so long and all about the past. Mourning someone is hard work. It's so hard it brings with it a tiredness you can't even believe. You keep thinking you can sleep it off but you just get more tired as it goes on. I was blindsided by the guilt. I missed her so much and yet all I could remember were all the times I found her tiresome and decrepit and wondered idly what it would be like if she died, so it was as if I had ushered in her death.

The police got very quickly to work, taking a statement from me, cordoning everywhere off with their yellow and white tape. I was taken up to my flat by a lady officer who insisted I drink tea with sugar in it and who was glancing around for Angel's stuff. She put me in the lounge, and she went through to the box room, went through her holdall, her toiletries, all her things. I'm guessing that officer took Angel's phone, because I haven't been able to find it since. But they didn't know about the USB key, you see. They didn't think to look in the seam of her coat.

I kept trying to tell this officer about Titans, and the recent attacks on Angel, but she kept undercutting me, asking how long I'd known 'the victim' and what was my relationship with her like, and had there been an argument between us. 'So you were close, and yet you didn't know her real name?' she said. And these hints and inferences, about what Angel and I were, what we did together and meant to each other, seemed to back me into a corner. 'You were just friends?' and 'How long had you been friends?' 'You'd only just met and yet you started living together?' 'And did she sleep in the spare room or did she share your bedroom?'

They kept me in the flat for hours and hours, told me they didn't want me to 'contaminate' the scene.

'Is it murder then?' I asked.

'We don't know yet.'

It was the following day before I was allowed back down to the shop. They'd wanted me out altogether, but I told them I had nowhere else I could go, unless they wanted to pay for a B&B and evidently nobody did. So I stayed holed up, upstairs, wondering what was happening to her down there.

Next day, her body had gone. There was just an outline where she had lain, and the stain on the lino. The lady officer told me the body had been taken away for a postmortem to find out the cause of death.

I said, 'Well, it wasn't falling down the stairs, was it?'

MANON & BIRDIE

On the other side of the door, Manon's bump feels hard, as if braced for something. Braxton Hicks contractions? She asks, 'Did you call the coroner, find out what the cause of death was?'

'Oh, you can speak, can you? I was wondering if you'd passed out in there.'

'I'm still here.'

'Yes, I rang the coroner. I rang him five or ten times. I rang and rang, I was put on hold, I was played every variation of Vivaldi there is. When I finally got through I was asked, "Are you a relative?" and when I said no, they said, "Then I'm afraid we cannot give out that information."

'I said, "She's dead, who's it going to hurt?" To which they said, "I'm sorry, I don't make the rules, I just follow them."

'I said, "Well there must be a public record of how someone died. What if she was killed?" And they said, "If there were suspicious circumstances, or concerns raised by the post-mortem, the police would investigate." So over to you, Detective Inspector Smarty Pants, if you're so clever.'

'Let me out – let me out before I give birth and we can work something out.'

At last – and it's been a good couple of hours in the box room – Manon hears the key turning in the lock. She scrambles to get up off the mattress.

There is Birdie, her jailer, in the doorway.

'Sorry about that,' Birdie says. 'Needs must.'

Manon decides not to speak until she is safely out of the box room. She strides for the lounge, taking up her handbag from the sofa. She feels about for her badge.

'I am arresting you for the false imprisonment of a police officer. You do not have to say anything—'

'Oh come on, there's no need to be like that. You can see why I had to do it. I needed you to listen.'

Birdie is trying to give her a stern look, similar to the one Nanny Fielding used to give her when she was a girl – opprobrium with just a twinkle of forgiveness in it. This police officer is proving to be more trouble than she's worth. And the pregnancy – well, that's all anyone needs in the current situation. Not only will it make her less nimble on her feet (though to look at her, was she ever nimble?) but Birdie has always found pregnant women to be overtly pleased with themselves. *Oh yes, let's all admire your sodding fecundity.* She has done all this – the imprisoning, the confession – on a whim. Misguidedly perhaps.

'Anything you do say may be given in evidence,' Manon is saying.

'Shhhh,' Birdie hisses. 'Listen.' She is frozen, a finger pointing upwards.

Manon stops, listens. She can hear movement downstairs.

'Someone's in the shop,' Manon says.

'I locked the shop,' Birdie whispers.

The footsteps are audibly on the stairs heading up to the flat's front door.

'Through here,' Birdie whispers. She is making for the kitchen where she pulls up the sash window and straddles the window sill. Birdie has climbed out onto a metal fire escape clamped to the exterior of the building. 'Come on,' she hisses at Manon.

The outside air is freezing after the old-age-pensioner dry heat of the flat. Manon swings her legs over the sill, onto the fire escape with Birdie, who closes the sash and pulls Manon's body away from the window and against the brick wall, out of sight. Birdie has a finger to her lips.

Manon wonders if she's being played for a fool again. Is she going to push me off the fire escape? *All the king's horses and all the king's men.*

They are pinned to the wall. The great swag of cloud above them vibrates with thunder and the rain comes down in sheets. Manon inches her head forward to peer in through the kitchen window. Water is bouncing off the metal of the fire escape, off her head. She sees the edge of a brown leather jacket, the back of a bald head, an earpiece.

'*Tur ir nekas,*' the man says, or something that sounds like that. Russian or an Eastern European language?

She hears objects clatter to the floor. Are they emptying drawers? A search for something, a ransacking of Birdie's flat.

Manon's teeth are chattering, water pouring down her temples. She wonders how much more her poor body can take. How have these people got in? Did they have a key?

She glances at Birdie – her big glasses, like two Seventies television screens, steamed and spattered. Her hair is bedraggled, stuck to her forehead. Manon can taste the rain running into her mouth. What if Birdie and Angel are right? What if dark forces are at work and Fly is the collateral damage?

268

Birdie pulls her cardigan ineffectually across her bosom, the drops sitting atop its synthetic yarn like mercury. She's certain she locked the shop, locked the back door. *How have they got inside her flat? And what do they want?* She pictures the USB key, still sewn into the hem of Angel's coat.

She and Manon dare not speak. Birdie fears they are going to freeze out here on the fire escape. Or slide away, like human dinghies over the edge of a metal waterfall. A helicopter hovers loudly overhead, treading water in the clouds above them. Deafening. Are helicopters supposed to be up in storms?

'Think they've gone,' Manon whispers.

They crane their necks slowly. The flat looks like it's been burgled. Kitchen drawers upturned, cutlery and utensils across the floor. Emboldened, they stand at the closed window for minutes, taking in the ransacking of Birdie's flat. 'They' – whoever they are – have turned the place upside down.

Eventually, they muster the courage to lift the sash – a brutally loud noise.

No one comes for them.

Encouraged, they clamber in through the window.

They stand and look.

'Loving what they've done with the place,' says Birdie.

Manon rubs Birdie's shoulder. 'Won't take us long to clear it up.'

There is much shaking down, fetching of towels, sloughing off outer layers. Gas fire lit. The guttural noises which accompany coming in from the cold: brrrr, and ooof, and aaaaagh. Birdie checks various rooms in the flat.

'You know what they've taken?' she says to Manon. 'The Carlton Mayfair toiletries. Now why would they do that? What would a bunch of gangsters want with some shower gel and shampoo miniatures? Didn't take her Crème de la Mer, mind.

Just the hotel stuff. And why now? Why didn't they take it when they pushed her down the stairs?'

'Well, we don't know she was pushed down the stairs,' says Manon. 'But also, if you want it to look like an accident, best not to ransack the flat at the same time.'

Birdie slides the chain across the front door and then feels along the hem of Angel's coat. The tiny lighter-shaped rectangle is still there. She pushes her nose into the folds of fabric, closes her eyes. It smells of her perfume – citrussy – but mixed with Angel's personal smell, the one which arises from the cells of a person's skin and which is unlike anyone else's. Birdie reminds herself – forcefully, like sticking a pin in her own hand – that she will never see Angel again.

'Are you all right?' Manon asks, recognising the look on Birdie's face. She remembers those moments of coming up against death and having to shock yourself with the permanence of it. The hollow sensation of actively loving a person who cannot love you back because they are dead. And wondering who you are, if the you who was loved by them isn't being loved by them any more.

All the hug-less years since she died. Manon's mother was the person she most wanted in the world, the person who held Manon's happiness and security in her hands – the person she wanted never, ever to die. And she died first, when Manon had taken on the physical form of a young woman but was deeply, needfully, a child – just 14. Manon wearing terrible, wobbly eyeliner. Manon slamming doors. Manon in the throes of hating her mother, in a state of constant criticism of the woman her mother was, the type of woman Manon would never be.

In the midst of Manon's ordinary tussle of love and hate, her opponent died. If she could only tell her, now, how happy she is to have inherited so much. And yet her mother frowned on

270

overblown emoting. She could show affection via a casserole or a Lemsip but not in speech or with direct eye contact. In fact, if Manon is really honest about it, she can recall all the unrequited feelings that bounced off her mother's blank wall, the way she found Manon a bit much. Histrionic. *'Oh do stop exaggerating.'*

'They weren't speaking English,' she says to Birdie. 'Sounded like Russian to me – or Eastern European.'

Birdie is ripping at the hem of a coat hanging by the front door.

She lifts up the USB key, saying, 'This is what they were after.'

They work slowly and mostly in silence, replacing whisks and peelers in drawers, folding tea towels, winding tights, restoring toiletries to an upright position in the bathroom cabinet. Except when Birdie says, 'You're not going to arrest me then?' To which Manon says, 'That can wait.'

When they have the flat back in some semblance of order, Birdie microwaves two macaroni-cheese ready meals to a scalding temperature. Manon blows at a gloopy white tube and asks if she might stay the night. 'I can't go home now, it's too late.' She doesn't mention that she's on the brink of physical collapse.

'Yes, righto,' says Birdie. 'I'll just put out a hand towel.'

Manon asks to borrow a mobile charger so she can call Mark, but inevitably it's the wrong kind. She wants to let him know she's all right but realises she doesn't know his phone number: it's programmed in, not memorised. On Birdie's phone, she tries her and Ellie's landline, knowing that they never pick it up – it's only ever a relative or a computer banging on about mis-sold PPI. Sure enough, it rings out. She can't remember Davy's number.

She will solve this problem tomorrow. For now, all she can do is answer her body's urgent request for sleep.

DAY 28
11 JANUARY

DAVY

On the Victoria Line to Seven Sisters, he takes in adverts saying *Tired of Being Tired?*

He looks from the ad to the commuters, grey-faced with ennui, and wonders if anyone looks at that ad and thinks, *not me!*

He might be tired but he cannot be lured by the ad saying *Hello Flexible Working* because he loves his job, even with the pressure and the politics; Stanton behaving erratically, Harriet holding the line while fudging it, as all middle managers do, and Manon his touchstone, on the outside of this one. She would break it open, expose the nut. Perhaps she still can. And he thinks about phoning her when he surfaces, to tell her where he's going. It would be back-up of sorts. Slow, ambling back-up.

He waited around most of the day, sitting in the Premier Inn bar on his laptop until Kim rang to tell him the ANPR on Carruthers' taxi tracked it back to Speedy Cars in Seven Sisters on the night of 13 December.

This is where Davy is exiting from the tube station – onto

the four-lane Seven Sisters Road. Learn English for £30, indoor market, 7-Sisters Appliances, Ria Worldwide Money Transfer.

A really crazy-looking African guy, jittery because he's on something, is leaning into a pram and bothering the baby inside while the mother looks away, smoking a cigarette. Davy is assaulted by smells from the fish shop, as well as over-ripe fruit, soap, incense. The early-evening sky is slate blue and all the shops are glowing. Mobile phones and luggage.

Davy wonders if he'll be robbed, yet he is opened up by a surge of curiosity – eyes wide, nostrils sensing. What would it be like to live in this stew of nationalities, all the different foods and smells and languages, instead of among the traffic-less cul-de-sacs of Sapley where all the pensioners are paranoid? He thinks of his mother and how much she'd hate this place, her mouth twisted with suspicion and fear. This thought seems to boost his interest.

Groups of men sit outside cafés, smoking. He hears them greet each other. 'As-salamu alaykum.'

An Asian lady walks past him carrying two enormous bottles of vegetable oil, each dragging down an arm. An alarming number of shops boast 'mobile phone unlocking' in neon.

He turns left on to West Green Road to where Speedy Cars is located, its signage lit up and phone numbers in big lettering around the window, with prices for airport transfers. The lobby smells of tobacco, with a patch of unstuck brown carpet laid on the floor, curling at the edges. Behind a dirty window is an office of sorts. A Middle Eastern man is on the phone.

'Sixteen pounds. Ten to fifteen minutes, OK?'

Davy waits.

The controller comes off the phone. 'Can I help you?' he says. Davy has his right hand to his jacket inside pocket. He is

273

lifting his badge out, about to flip it open without thinking. He glances to the back of the office room. That's when he sees him.

Bald, muscled, wearing a bomber jacket. The man from the King's Cross CCTV. The man who looked at Ross like he was dinner. Davy carefully places his badge back inside his jacket pocket. He scans the ceiling corners. There is a white unit with a glass dome beneath it containing the camera. If he declares himself, the bald guy will make a run for it. Or there'll be a fight, which Davy won't win. Both, possibly. Someone will unplug the CCTV hard drive and jump on it, smash it with a hammer, or plunge it into water so that he can't seize its contents. These people are not going to give up their secrets willingly. He cannot take out his badge.

'I've . . . sorry, I've changed my mind,' he says, smiling at the controller, and stepping outside onto the pavement.

Hand shaking, he dials 999 on his phone, keeping his voice low but urgent. 'This is DS Davy Walker, officer 634, Cambridgeshire force. I'm at Speedy Cars at 62 West Green Road, N15. I need to urgently arrest a suspect in connection with a murder. I'm single-crewed and I've got no personal protection equipment.' He tries to prevent the swell in his voice at this. He pictures the woman typing this into the system and it being simultaneously read by control who will probably have dispatched units before he's even finished speaking. 'I need urgent back-up, repeat *urgent back-up.*'

He hangs up, knowing they will come fast, very fast. And they will send lots and lots of units.

He glances in through the lobby of Speedy Cars. All the men have moved to the front of the shop and are staring at him. Some of them whisper to each other. What have they heard of his phone call?

'How can we help you, my friend?' says a man, not the

274

controller or the bald man but someone with an expansive smile, who has stepped out to join him on the pavement.

'Oh, I'm . . .' Davy coughs. 'Fine thanks. Just, waiting for some friends.'

Davy hears sirens a few streets away, decides they might be his, steps back into the lobby and whips out his badge to the man behind the window. 'I'd like a word with—' Davy looks about the room for the muscled bald man but he has disappeared. A lot of talk breaks out in languages Davy cannot understand. Over the top of them, Davy says, 'Where is the bald guy that was there just a minute ago? Where is he? I want to talk to him and I want your CCTV hard drive. *Now.*'

Then they are awash with blue lights, the road filled with them.

MANON

They wait for the USB key to load on Birdie's extremely slow Lenovo laptop.

'Hi,' she says, pacing Birdie's living room. She has used a charger purloined from a market-stall owner of Birdie's acquaintance. 'It's me.'

'Oh thank God,' he says, 'I've been worried sick.'

'Yes, she says – sorry, my phone went dead. I've only just got hold of a charger. I had to stay in London a night to follow up a couple of leads.

'Anything good? he asks.

'Might be, can't tell yet, she says. Are you all right?

'I'm fine, he says, and in his voice is gentleness and affection. I'm hoping this pathology report is going to come through in the next day or two and it'll tell us what we need to hear.'

'That'd be good, she says. She wants to lay her head on a pillow with him at her ear, but she casts a glance at Birdie and says, Right, well, I better go.'

'Clever girl,' says Birdie, reading the screen. 'She's saved the dossier on here. All the names – of the Chinese delegation, emails off Ross's hard drive, photographs of the City pages she tore out. It's all here, everything.'

Manon's phone vibrates. A text from Ash.

Hey, you.

Just like the bad old days, here he is: the Chris-de-Burgh lothario of West Hendon.

'????' she texts back, irritably.

One of my contacts came good on your Paddy Driscoe. Got a number for you. Fancy a drink?

I'm a bit tied up. Can you text it over?

'Is that Paddy Driscoe?'

'Who wants to know?'

'It's Manon, Fly's mum.'

'How did you get this number?'

'Look, don't hang up. I just want to talk, about Fly. Not as a copper. I'm not interested in what you've got going on, arrest-wise. Honestly. Fly's in really big trouble. If you care about him, just meet me. You can choose the place. I'll come on my own, I swear – no back-up, no badge, nothing. I'm in Kilburn. I can come up to Momtaz.'

'Yeah, I know your boy Fly,' he says, sunglasses on his bald head even though it's mid-winter. He's a body-builder type, wide-necked, with a lopsided smile and gold tooth. When she arrived, he appraised her physically in a way that did not mark him out as a new man.

'Why was he meeting you, when he was supposed to be in school?'

'Ah, now, calm down lady, his schooling's nothing to do with me, right?'

'No, but it is to do with me, so answer the question.'

'You're not going to bust my balls cos you don't like what you hear?'

Her heart starts knocking at the possibilities.

'Your boy,' Paddy says, 'he's not happy. Not happy at all. He wants to come home, back here to Cricklewood. I've known him since he was this high . . .' He levels his hand to the tabletop they're sitting at. 'Since he lived with Maureen and Taylor. Maureen was a fuck-up, useless mother, always out of it. He done better with you. But Taylor brung him up and Fly is good, like Taylor was. He's just a good person, y'know?'

Yes, I know, she thinks and all her judgements about Paddy fall away. They know Fly, both of them. Worse, Paddy is more confident in his knowledge of Fly's goodness than she has been. She feels weak and grateful, because she hasn't been sure of late.

'He arksed me to trace his dad. I found him, chap called Adewale Sane. Nigerian fella; actually he lives round here. Fly's hoping he can live with him, if he can persuade him. That was before he was locked up. I don't like his chances with Adewale – not really a family man, y'know? Into this an' that. Not into commitment.'

'This and that?'

'Ah, I'm not going to land him in it with a copper. I'm just not sure he's father material. Anyway, I was setting up a meeting between them.'

'Can you give me Adewale's number?' asks Manon.

'I could, but why would I? I mean, what would be in it for me?'

There follows a dance of sorts, a game of finding out what

278

charges Paddy is facing, which coppers are making his life difficult, what strings she might pull in exchange for Adewale's mobile number. She hasn't the means to promise half the things she ends up promising; she no longer has the contacts to pull the strings she claims she'll pull. No matter. She's got the number now.

She's walking back down the Killy High Road when she stops, bends double – winded. *Fly wants to leave her.* She betrayed his trust, mishandled his feelings so catastrophically that he wants to leave her, has been planning all this time to leave her.

He doesn't want to be her son any more.

'That's a strong look,' she says, appraising Birdie's mohair coat of lilac and pink broad checks.

'British Heart Foundation,' Birdie says. 'It's my best one.'

The coat's not going to help matters, Manon thinks.

Why is she nervous about approaching staff at the Carlton Mayfair? It's as if all her certainties are crumbling, her sense of who she is as a mother and a police officer. She is unsure how to play it, how brazen to be.

She finds herself on a border, straddling bluffs and evasions with a *Coronation Street* sidekick. Manon likes things clear, dislikes ducking and diving – not because she's so pure, it's more to do with clarity and confidence. Will they be stopped on the marble steps by a top-hatted doorman asking what, precisely, their business is? Their ability to blend has been greatly diminished by Birdie's coat.

'There's a dress code,' Manon says, reading off Birdie's laptop. 'We respectfully ask guests visiting the hotel to refrain from wearing baseball caps, beanie hats, ripped jeans, sportswear, trainers, flip-flops and shorts, in our restaurants and bars.'

'Wonder if that applied to Justin Bieber,' Birdie says.

279

'Nothing applies if you're rich enough.'

'Right, well I'm not wearing flip-flops or a baseball cap so shall we go?'

On the step above Birdie, going down the escalator to the Jubilee Line, Manon notices the bald patches between her curls. They have become accustomed to one another inside Birdie's flat, but now they are outside, they are strangers again. People have an atmosphere and Birdie's is one of stoic determination. *Here we are,* her demeanour says, *so let's get on with it.*

Rocking and knocking on the tube train, the black oblong window doubling back their reflections. Manon feels quite sylphlike next to Birdie, who spreads widthways beside her. The train whines, an upward siren song. Manon glances to the left: empty pram, and beside it, a toddler writhing in a woman's lap. Straight ahead: a man with wrinkles about the eyes, Egyptian-looking with a grey beard, gazes at his phone.

The next station is Green Park.

They follow white-tiled underground corridors, Birdie panting.

On the walk through Mayfair, Georgian townhouses rise up on either side, frilled with ivy in window boxes. Black gloss front doors, marble steps and shiny brass plaques with company names ending 'equity', 'capital', 'international' or 'private banking'.

Land Rover showroom, Jaguar showroom, Aston Martin car hire.

'Different vibe to the Killy High Road,' says Birdie.

Service vans are double-parked. One says 'Wine Cellar', another 'The Window Box Company', another 'Bronze Restorations'.

'Wait, look at that,' says Manon, who has been reading brass plaque after brass plaque, surprised that this world exists in reality, much as she knew about it in theory.

'Dunlop & Finch, private bank,' Birdie reads. 'How convenient – round the corner from the hotel.'

Two men hurry towards them in suits, one with a worried expression. 'Lunch with Snellgrave today,' Manon hears him say to his friend as they go past.

The top-hatted doorman outside the Carlton Mayfair greets them with a broad smile and a door held open.

'I'm going to talk to the concierge,' says Manon.

'Shall I get us a table over there?' Birdie asks, looking towards the lounge. 'A pot of tea won't do any harm, as we're here . . .'

'I'd check you can afford it first,' Manon says.

She parts ways with Birdie and approaches the sepia-mirrored concierge desk, behind which five suited men stand in a row, waiting to serve.

'How may I help you, madam?' says the first with a slight bow.

She shows her badge. There is a frisson along the line, like a row of pigeons lifting at the blow of a horn. They flap back down.

'I'd like to ask for some guest information relating to the night of July the nineteenth last year,' she says.

'Perhaps you would like to follow me,' says her concierge.

She is taken to a black door with yet another brass plaque, this one saying 'Manager'.

'You have *got* to try the toilets,' Birdie is saying ten minutes later, at a round table set with art deco cups and saucers, delicate in mint green with silver leaf; a sugar bowl with tongs.

'Have I?'

'It's like the most comfy living room ever: big armchairs, mirrors, lovely table lamps and fancy hand-wash – smell.' Birdie holds out the back of her hand for Manon to sniff.

'Mmm, nice.'

'Madam?' says a waiter bearing a pillow. Manon looks up at him, confused.

'He's going to plump you,' says Birdie. 'Lean forward.'

The waiter places a cushion behind Manon's back and she leans into it. For the first time in weeks, the small of her back isn't pulsating with pain. She is insanely comfortable.

'Wait till you taste the water,' says Birdie. 'So delicious – iced with lemon.'

Voices from surrounding tables lap at the shore of theirs, an array of accents: French, African, Russian, Estuary English. An effeminate voice says, 'I think we can make it very chic and coordinated.' She looks at its originator. He has tattoo sleeves and earring studs like chocolate buttons. *Fashion*, Manon thinks.

'I might sell Payless and stay here for a week,' says Birdie.

'And then what?' asks Manon.

'That would clean me out.'

'We would require such a request in writing,' the manager said, 'with your evidence for suspicion of criminal activity having taken place at the Carlton Mayfair. You understand, I'm sure, we cannot allow the police to go fishing, speculatively so to speak. Our clients are high-net-worth individuals who greatly value their privacy. They entrust us with their personal details . . .'

Manon just wanted to get away from the manager and his stupid dance. He was clearly adept at sidestepping, having sharpened up his non-compliance techniques. She rose and was backing out of the room, when she heard Birdie yell across the lobby, 'Mini Battenbergs! They've got mini Battenbergs!'

'I believe your friend is calling for you,' the manager said with an oily smile.

Birdie is taking one now, saying, 'And those round short-breads, they've got salt in. Amazing.'

'We're not getting anywhere here, except racking up a massive bill,' Manon says.

'It's not that big actually. Seven fifty for a coffee, with free biscuits. I call that a bargain. Sandwiches are thirty quid, mind. I've been chatting to Artem, the chap who plumped you? He said his friend Joaquín – not Joaquín Phoenix unfortunately – he works in the service bay. He'll have a chat with us when he comes on shift in twenty minutes. He's night staff, so he might remember something.'

'You know that Mr Kipling makes mini Battenbergs,' says Manon.

'Not like this he doesn't.'

'How I remember one night from six month ago?' asks Joaquín, smoking on the back lane outside the loading bay. Behind a congestion of white vans (one delivering catering supplies, another a plumber's called West One Bathrooms) are three metal garage doors which open to reveal the bowels of the hotel. Silver tubing, intestinal-looking, runs along the ceiling; crates line the wall. Manon casts about for cameras, out of habit, then remembers they are way outside the turnaround for CCTV.

She says, 'The people we're interested in booked the pent-house suite for a delegation of Chinese businessmen. This was July the nineteenth.'

'Chinese here all the time,' says Joaquín, sucking on his tiny nub of roll-up. 'I don't know who book penthouse, this not my area.'

Manon presses on, without much hope: 'That night, a girl called Jade Canning died in the penthouse and her body was removed from the hotel, probably through here.'

'We keep log,' Joaquín says. 'Vans she go in, out of back. Come.'

He opens the door to a tiny room and switches on the strip light. Just outside the door, Manon whispers to Birdie, 'Why is he helping us?'

Birdie whispers back, 'Said you'd help with his cousin's immigration papers.'

'You did *what*?'

Birdie shrugs.

Joaquín is flicking back through a lined A4 book with hard-back blue cover. 'July nineteenth . . . Oh – here. Early morning of twentieth. Van she is leaving 2 a.m. Registration KC55 YFY.'

'Can I photograph the page please?' Manon says, taking out her phone. She doesn't want the management getting rid of this.

'I remember this,' Joaquín says, looking down at the page with Manon. She scrutinises his face, but it is slack, without guile – as if he really has just remembered.

How can he possibly remember one vehicle at 2 a.m. six months ago, when he must see dozens go through here?

'I remember – I never see this driver and his friend before. We know everybody who come here – some suppliers, some trades. We chat, say hello. Know first names. Some are family. They stop, have smoke, drink, game of cards sometimes. The fruit guy, he my cousin. But these guy . . . Latvian I think. Or Russian. They put rug in back of van – Persian one, from hotel. Maybe it had stain or something. I say, "What in there, dead body?" This is my joke. I think, why you take rug out at 2 a.m. like emergency? I think, maybe manager want it back quick. Customer very fussy in this place. Maybe client want rug be cleaned in night. This kind of shit we deal with all the time.'

DAVY

'*Bez komentāriem*,' says the big fella, the muscle man, for the umpteenth time. He looks bored, big arms folded across his chest – so biceped they will only just cross. His gaze to the floor like he's just waiting. *Bez komentāriem.* No comment in Latvian.

His name is Juris. He was caught by the marvellous boys in blue, who crawled all over Seven Sisters like ants on jam.

'How do you know Giles Carruthers?'

'*Bez komentāriem.*'

'Have you ever met this man?' Davy slides forward a photograph of Jon-Oliver Ross.

'*Bez komentāriem.*'

'What is your relationship to the private bank Dunlop & Finch?'

'*Bez komentāriem.*'

Why they've bothered to shell out on an interpreter is beyond him.

Davy wonders what this guy Juris is thinking. Is he thinking about British prison, and how much better it would be than

Latvian prison? Better food, better beds, better guards. Because Latvian prison doesn't really bear thinking about, and that's where he'll end up, if this goes anywhere.

Except Davy's not sure they can collar him for anything. There's no weapon linking him to Ross's death. He wasn't near Ross at the time of death, and Derry's pathology report runs contrary to this hired hunk of muscle having anything to do with the stabbing. Yes he followed him onto the train to Huntingdon, but he got off the train at St Neots. The CCTV showing what he did at St Neots – his stepping off the train, and catching another one home – has already been wiped in the statutory twenty-eight-day turnaround.

However, there appears to be a connection with Carruthers, revealed on the camera hard drive which they successfully retrieved from Speedy Cars before anyone could tamper with it.

Davy and Harriet watched the footage together, watched Giles Carruthers talking to the friendly chap with the wide smile who gave his name as Moukhtar – 'Moukie' – when he was interviewed at the cab rank. Carruthers climbed the stairs with Moukie and this Latvian chump.

What was Carruthers doing going upstairs at Speedy Cars? What were they discussing?

DAY 30
13 JANUARY

DAVY

'I really don't see how me taking a taxi to a Chinese takeaway is of any interest to you,' Giles Carruthers says with utmost warmth and tolerance for Davy's puerile procedures.

So superior and relaxed is he that Carruthers has not as yet drafted in some exorbitant brief to tell him to say nothing.

Davy presses play on the CCTV from Speedy Cars.

'The chap you're talking to here . . .' Davy points to the Latvian, whose name he struggles with. *Juris* something. 'He boarded the same train as Mr Ross and appeared to be following him. D'you know anything about that?'

'No.'

'What were you talking to him about?'

'My fare to Islington.'

'What are you giving him in this frame?'

Davy freezes the CCTV. The image shows Carruthers handing a paper to the Latvian.

'Um, maybe it's the address.' Carruthers runs a hand through his hair. 'Look, it was a month ago. Yes, it was probably the address of the Lotus Blossom, with the postcode for the driver's satnav.'

'It isn't this?' Davy asks, sliding the four-by-six photo of the blonde that was found on Ross's body, across the table. 'We will of course sharpen this image to see what's on the paper.'

Carruthers shifts. His pallor has become a bit sweaty, Davy notices. Some moisture at his temples. He swallows. Dry mouth, perhaps.

'No. I've never seen that before.'

Davy presses play on the CCTV again.

'Can you explain why you are going up the stairs at the cab office? Wouldn't most customers wait in the lobby or out on the pavement?'

'I asked to use their toilet. I needed the toilet, you see . . .'

'And these two chaps decided to go with you? This Moukie chap and the Latvian fella?'

'They were showing me where it was, that's all.'

'Do you know these men?'

'No.'

'We'll need your phone, Mr Carruthers.'

'My phone? Why? I'm afraid I can't let you take my phone, it's vital for my work.'

'If you could drop it into this bag.'

Carruthers is making a big show of patting himself down. 'I . . . I can't seem to . . . I don't know where it is.'

Davy watched Carruthers arrive at HQ for questioning: on his phone as he entered the building. Davy took in the sharp cut of his suit, the shiny shoes; how Carruthers was giving off the Big I Am, doing his deals, arranging his meetings, a bit too busy for the police. He came into this building *on* his phone.

Davy walks fast from the interview room and pelts down

the stairs to reception. Two hands on the reception desk, he eyeballs the duty sergeant. 'I need a search of all the toilets in this building. Get everyone out of them. Suspect has tried to flush his phone.'

GARY STANTON

He is tapping the edge of a cardboard coaster on the table, waiting.

His other hand is around the coolness of his pint glass. He drops the coaster, in order to rearrange his tie neatly over the protuberance of his belly. When will she come? Will she look as attractive as she did the last time, when he couldn't keep his hands off her and all his decades of tiredness had fallen away? The black lace bra beneath her nurse's uniform. Will she overlook his paunch, as she appears to have done up till now?

This is the meat in his pie. The chase, the frisson. The triangle that gives life its vigour. Without these three points, the exclusion slash disapproval of one, the sense of how hurt she might be if only she knew, the naughty pleasure in her not knowing but perhaps finding out . . . Without his wife, the affair would drain of its energy.

He takes a sip. He's not sure he *has* sufficient energy. Should he go the way of his colleagues, put his feet up in front of *Location, Location, Location*? Order in the Prosecco for drinks with the neighbours? Have sex twice a year? It would be like water closing over his face as he goes down. It would be like the stupid nonchalance he'd felt as a child, thinking everything was solid – well, a bit tense, which was the grim-faced status quo in their house. His mother – a mood hoover at the best of times – harrumphing over some element of the domestic workload, as if she was lugging a laundry basket up the mount at Calvary in place of a cross. His father in from work, reading the paper. Each member of the family in their personal cube of unhappiness. Why did it have to change? No one was dying or getting beaten up. No one was in a dire state of suffering as far as he could tell. *Why couldn't they all just put up with the misery of family life?*

He remembers waking in the night for a pee and hearing arguing downstairs. The word 'sex' reverberated up the stair-well, and its radioactivity sent him back to bed.

When he was 11, he came home from school to find them sitting side by side in the lounge, which never happened. His throat contracted because just their positions meant bad news. Maybe Gramps was dead, or 9-year-old Trevor had been run over. He paused to enjoy this last thought, wondering if he might get to be an only child. He acknowledged there would be an irritating period of mourning for his younger brother, but after that . . .

'Gary, love, come and sit down. We want to talk to you.'

He ventured into the room and was disappointed to see his brother still alive and sitting opposite his parents. His mother's knees were together. She leaned forward, a balled-up tissue in her hand. It was like a business meeting but in fact, it was the moment the ground disappeared from under him. He didn't take in what they said to him at that sit-down family confer-ence. His mind just kept saying, *Don't do it, Don't do it. We can go back.*

His father moved out, without saying goodbye. Just an awkward ruffle of his hair and a 'See you, son.' He went to work in America, that's what their mother told them, though looking back he wasn't sure if this was an excuse for the lack of weekend visits, or a euphemism. Perhaps America was actually Audrey or Ann-Marie. These things were not discussed openly for fear of upsetting someone, he wasn't sure who – the children? He'd rather have had the facts laid out where he could look at them.

When his dad returned from 'America' three years later, his mother said to his father, as angrily as Gary had ever heard her speak, 'I've had them for three years, now it's your turn.'

And she promptly left. Gary hadn't realised looking after him had been such a trial for her.

They lived with their father then – no one really had a choice, certainly not his dad – and the best word to describe the following three years until Gary Stanton left home for good was taciturn.

He looks at his watch. It is 1.30 p.m. They agreed to meet at one, he has a room upstairs reserved for the afternoon, no luggage. You'd be surprised how *unsurprised* hotel staff are – how wearily disappointed by tawdry bedroom shenanigans. If she doesn't show up soon, he'll have to head back to the office.

He's sustained the happy-family illusion much longer than his mum and dad managed it: kids, wife – though he doesn't wear a wedding ring – promotions in the force, Ford Kuga SUV with heated seats and integrated satnav. It even has a built-in DVD player to keep the children entertained on holidays touring through France. But inside himself, he's always on his way somewhere, searching out the next diversion. So when he encountered Ellie Bradshaw at Hinchingbrooke Outpatients, it was not unlike him to ask her out for a drink.

He'd had a knee operation – the result of playing five-a-side while carrying an extra couple of stone – and after this his dressings needed to be changed twice weekly. At 55, his muscle strength and recuperative bounce-back are not what they were.

He said to her, as she was kneeling next to said knee, 'Hang on, you must be a relative of Manon's.' They seemed so similar, it was uncanny. And the 'Nurse Bradshaw' name badge was a bit of a clue. No flies on him.

'Sister. I'd shake your hand, but . . .' Ellie said, raising her latex-gloved hands which were clasping bandages in one and some sort of medical cream in the other.

'Gary Stanton,' he said.

They said nothing further. But he could see down her top – could see her bra beneath her nurse's uniform. It was rather jauntily like a scene from *Carry On Nurse*.

'There you are, all done,' she said when she'd finished the dressing. 'Might feel a bit stiff. But walking it out should help.'

It's not the only thing feeling a bit stiff, he wanted to say, embracing the *Carry On* theme.

He straightened and bent the knee, feeling for its aches and limits.

It wasn't out of character, after she had said yes to a drink, to text his wife to say a job had come in and probably an all-nighter as well. It was quite natural for him to book a room at the George Hotel and seduce Ellie there. Adulterous excitement: there was no better way to feel truly alive, exhausting though it was.

It was unfortunate that he'd been with Ellie on the night Jon-Oliver Ross was stabbed, she being a key witness. Unfortunate that he, the detective chief superintendent in charge of MCU, represented a seven-hour hole in Ellie's alibi – the subject of much irritable texting from her when she was being questioned ('I strongly suggest you get your arse down to interview room one and call your dogs off.'). More than unfortunate when he was within spitting distance of his pension. Once he'd started to cover for Ellie, there was no way to back out without a gross misconduct notice.

He'd managed to steer Davy away from interrogating that timeline too closely. Besides, it was irrelevant. What was he covering really? A harmless fling, which was no one's business but their own. Manon's lad killed Ross. Ellie's whereabouts had no substantive bearing on the case.

The gases are building in his belly with every sip of his pint and the problem with an extra-marital affair, or perhaps the bonus, is you never get to the farting stage. Everything – gases, stomachs, emotions – must be suppressed in the service of lust. None of the letting yourself go that happens in a marriage. In truth, he wonders how long he'll be able to keep it up (literally), what with his aching knee and his expanding girth and the way his heartbeats occasionally bunch up together when he gets excited or has too many Tassimos.

She arrives at last, disdainful of him (which is perhaps what turns him on), saying, 'Which room've we got then? Presidential suite?' As if he hasn't splashed the cash enough. Truth is, he's more than a little scared of her. It's not that she's threatened him explicitly, but she has a way of making clear that they are 'in it together' – 'that any investigation of her on the night Jon-Oliver was stabbed would quickly become an investigation of him.

Yes, she scares him, grabs him by the balls and doesn't let go and he's in it for the ride but what a fucking terrifying ride it is, all the while making him aware that she doesn't like him much but that their fates are entwined. Nasty sexy sex.

In between the margarine-coloured sheets of the George, a

twinge begins its journey up his left arm to clench its fist around his heart. *Just the climax*, he thinks, *just keep going, don't let her see it's agony*. He is looking at the watercolour above the bed, not at Ellie, lying beneath him, still wearing her bra. The fist clenches more tightly about his heart; his heart clenches back.

And then, what Gary Stanton experiences at the moment of his death, is the silence of the inside of his body, the same as the silence of a car when the engine has been cut but it continues to coast. The brain is last to die. The body has a hum, like that of a boiler, but now there is silence in his ears.

DAVY

Harriet stands over Stanton's body, which lies on the hotel room floor following the paramedics' attempts to resuscitate.

'Who was with him?' she says to the room, which contains a couple of constables and Davy.

'Reception says a woman, late thirties, light brown hair. Left before the ambulance crews arrived. She's the one who phoned it in,' Davy says.

Harriet nods.

'Well, we don't need to make a thing of it,' she says. 'Natural causes. Christ he's young, though. Fifty-five.' Harriet and Davy look down at him. They are both in shock.

'Death walks among us,' Davy says.

'Yes, you'd think we'd know that in our line of work.'

Stanton's body has grown waxy, the colour of the pale yellow sheets twisted on the bed. 'Pamela doesn't deserve to be left with this,' Harriet says. 'Stupid fucking man.'

'She doesn't need to know, does she?' says Davy.

'We'd have to rely on her not coming here to chat to the hotel staff. I know Pamela, and she will. She'll want to know if

296

he died alone, if anyone helped him – well, you would, wouldn't you? I want you to go through his data, Davy – texts and emails. Discreetly. Make sure there's nothing that might . . . upset anybody – shame him, or us. Know what I mean?'

Davy nods.

Join the force, get divorced. Wasn't that the saying? Not such a surprise that Stanton's marriage had been foundering. Common enough, and yet, if you could deceive your nearest and dearest, it spoke of other deceptions. Slipperiness. A lack of empathy.

Harriet is saying, 'He should already be ashamed.' But she has said it ever so sadly and Davy understands that Stanton is as big a disappointment to her as he is to Davy.

He looks around the room for Stanton's phones – work and private – and finds them among the folds of his trousers on the lady chair by the window.

Perhaps Stanton was looking for love, Davy thinks, pummelling down the stairs of the George and out onto the street. He notices how he's trying to sympathise with Stanton, to understand him, just like he always did with his father after he left his mother. Or is love a euphemism – a place to stop and lay your head? And why couldn't that place be alone? What's so bad about being alone?

Sometimes, his father said, being with someone can be the worst feeling in the world. Davy had plucked up the courage to ask him, during a visit to Whitstable where his dad lived with 'new wife' Sharon (though in fact they'd been married for fifteen years, 'new wife' being the term coined by his mother, said with disgusted mouth).

Davy felt he needed to know why their life, when Davy was a boy, had fallen apart. He felt he needed to know why he'd been left with a mother who didn't get up from one day to the next, so that Davy had to cook, clean, take out the bins, pull open the curtains with some platitude in a cheery sing-song voice – a tic that never left him. Desperate edge, of course.

Davy didn't say it like that to his dad, kicking at pebbles on the seafront. His dad knew what he was getting at, though, and was quick to leap to his own defence, as if Davy were not a son asking for help but a high court judge, passing sentence on fatherly failing.

'There was nothing else I could've done,' his dad said. 'I was going under.'

And Davy thought, yes there was. You could have stayed. You could have put yourself second, behind me, because I was only 10.

'Sometimes a marriage is so bad that all you can do is get out,' his father continued, and he had a skimmer in his hand, aimed at the sea, and he threw that skimmer with what Davy felt was more force than the stone quite demanded.

'And of course you had Sharon,' Davy said.

'Sharon was a comfort to me. Times were dark.'

Not as dark as they were for me, Davy thought. Maybe that's why he can't find a girl. *He really ought to find a girl*, he thinks now with the image of Stanton's body in his mind. Settle down, create something permanent.

Last wedding Davy went to – and he's attending quite a few, must be his age – was Conor and Savannah's. He wasn't sure they were strictly his friends, but he'd sat with Conor Cartwright during woodwork at school, both boys inept with a lathe though ironically Conor had gone on to work at Huntingdon Timber and Roofing Supplies. Davy didn't really know Savannah but her expression on her Big Day was a rictus of anxiety. She seemed to be scanning the room every time Davy looked at her, her skin radioactive with fake tan, visibly performing a mental inventory: chair covers with flouncy bows, glass pebbles scattered on the tables (Davy had popped one in his mouth, thinking it was a mint); little boxes of sugared almonds for each guest (which were

298

as much a danger to teeth as the glass pebbles). The whole thing must've cost an arm and a leg and Davy had immediately thought of a severed arm and a severed leg, someone they'd discovered in an attic a while back. Anyway, Savannah didn't look happy on her Big Day. She looked like someone going through an ordeal.

He watched the groom – hair wet with gel so he looked as if he'd just slid out of a drainpipe – laughing with the laddish gang from school. These were boys (shouldn't they be men by now?) Davy didn't really fit in with. He found them too . . . macho? Ungallant.

It was more than that. When he'd joined them on a night out in Cambridge wearing slippery shirts and cheap body spray, they ratcheted up the volume as if to cover the whisperings of all they didn't have in common. They were shouting over their lack of intimacy, and also the lack of confidence in themselves. There was a gap, visible to Davy, between the football scores and taking the piss out of the fatter one in the group (a lad called Digby Boxer, poor bastard) and beneath it, the absence of meaning: the way they didn't care about their jobs or their girlfriends, about anything at all. Davy felt beaten about the head by all the swagger, marinated in alco-pops, which seemed to stand in for masculinity. Nothing of his inner life was expressed by this group. There was nowhere, he felt, to put the quietly sad corners of his experience.

Now, walking towards HQ carrying God knows what in Stanton's phones, he realises he never actually liked Conor and he wonders why he hasn't been able to admit this to himself and move on. When Conor stood to give his wedding speech – chinking a fork on a glass and standing next to his perma-tanned now-wife – his eyes were on the table of lads near the front as he joked about how Savannah had forced him down the aisle with typical feminine connivance. He lovingly referred to her as 'the ball and chain'; said she wasn't the sharpest knife in the drawer but my goodness she could shop so he'd better sign up for overtime at the timber yard.

Davy balked at the laughter that rang out, particularly from the bride's Asti Spumante-infused parents. The thought flitted across his mind that Conor Cartwright might be homosexual but unable to express this, fearful of being beaten to a pulp and left bleeding in his slippery shirt in some Cambridge gutter.

How do women stand it? Davy wondered. It was as bad as the past, when the sexes were miles apart and couldn't communicate, only now there is this pretence. Conor's disdain, hiding in plain sight, told the congregation what he really thought of his wife, who seemed to have sweated blood organising this shindig. And the whole room was laughing.

Am I becoming not myself? Davy wonders now, jogging up the steps of HQ. Am I more suited to hanging out with Manon Bradshaw and the poncy Cambridge graduates who marry in jeans at register offices or not at all? The thought feels only like a loss – as if he has no place to put himself. Perhaps all he's becoming is a snob, looking down on all the people he's grown up with.

There is no need for Davy to cover anything up any more, and there are lots of reasons not to, like the idea that Davy himself might die, none of us being immune. Yes, Davy might die all of a sudden, and his legacy? Leaving a frightened 12-year-old incarcerated for something he didn't do.

'Look for the affair,' Manon always told him when he was her DC and she was his sergeant. Look where that had got Gary Stanton. His crimson bed had turned into the narrow bed.

'Least he died happy,' Colin says smuttily when Davy reaches MCU, to which Davy says, 'Not necessarily.'

There's an awful lot of sad desperation in extra-marital sex. And with this thought, he lets himself into Stanton's office to go through his data.

MANON

Back at the flat, Birdie sits on the sofa while Manon paces back and forth.

'So what have we got, evidentially?' Manon asks.

'Ooh, evidentially. Like it,' says Birdie.

'Jade Canning – well, I know about that, because I was there when she was hooked out of the Welsh Harp. It was investigated by a DS, someone I worked with called Melissa Harcourt. Unheard of to put a DS in charge of a potential homicide, don't know why they did that. Anyway, Melissa was very keen to wrap it up as a jumper. So we need to show that Jade's body was removed from the Carlton and that the van made a journey from Mayfair to the Welsh Harp. There won't be any CCTV but . . . Where's your laptop?'

'I hid it when we went out, just in case. I'll get it.'

Birdie comes back into the room carrying the laptop. They switch it on and wait for it to connect to the Internet.

Reading the screen, Manon says, 'I'm pretty sure ANPR—'

'What's that?'

'Automatic Number Plate Recognition – yes, here it is.

"ANPR data is stored for a period of two years. Data outside the 90-day time frame may only be accessed by a senior officer." Fortunately, I am that officer. If we track car reg YFY to the Welsh Harp, that's enough to re-open Jade's case.'

'What about Angel?'

'I've put in a request to the coroner for a copy of the PM report. I'll forward it to you as soon as I get it.' She leans back in her chair. 'Have to warn you though, PMs are often inconclusive. She might have died falling down the stairs and had loads of booze in her system, and the coroner might record an open verdict. An open verdict means the death is suspicious but there isn't enough evidence to know what happened.'

Manon thinks she should perhaps care about this and she realises that Birdie cares, but all she can think about is Fly. 'None of this helps my son.'

'Well, the murder of Jon-Oliver must be tied up in all of it,' says Birdie.

'"Sass" was the last thing he said before he died. No one knew what it meant.'

'I wonder *why* he was saying her name,' Birdie says.

'Maybe he was trying to . . . get a warning to her. Unless she was the one who stabbed him.'

Birdie is shaking her head. 'She was here, doing her curtain-twitching routine.'

'Can't be the Dunlop & Finch lot. Why would they get rid of one of their own, when he'd just signed their biggest client?'

'Maybe they thought he was in cahoots with Angel,' Birdie says. 'Maybe the boss guy, van der Lupin, was furious about her showing up at his Christmas drinks, blackmailing him, and thought she and Ross were in it together.'

Manon frowns. 'Doesn't make sense though. It's one thing to clean up the Carlton mess. They didn't kill Jade, remember, and we don't know what the involvement with Angel's death is, if any. I don't think they'd risk a job like Ross. Too high profile, too messy. No, it doesn't fit together.'

Manon looks up at the familiar building, seat of woe, which is now being spattered by fat drops of rain, the kind that splosh.

Her leaving do from Kilburn CID had been depressing. DCI Haverstock had the day off, so a desultory speech was given by a DI she barely knew. He made sparse jokes about her love of Quavers, unable to drum up any knowledge of significant cases she might have worked on. *That's because I didn't work on anything decent,* she thinks now, climbing the steps with dread determination. *On my knees with the law-enforcement dustpan and brush, not standing erect, like some of the male DIs, holding a long-pole litter picker. Oh, the refuse collection analogies we weave.*

The DI, whose name she can't even remember, had ended his speech with the words, 'To the pub!' which resulted in low murmuring among the gathering and a lugubrious threading of coats. Manon had longed to say, 'I'd love to but I've got something on.' Not really an option on that particular occasion.

It had all contrasted sharply with her leaving do from Huntingdon a couple of years back – a series of raucous in-jokes from Harriet, a litany in fact, all of it peppered with Gary Stanton's middle-management jargon, the source of much departmental mirth. 'She's an officer who knows how to deep-dive an alibi, she is no stranger to the helicopter view and she can open the kimono on key project deliverables.'

Harriet had also referenced all the perps they knew were guilty but who'd got off, prefacing them as 'The indisputably innocent . . .'

'Let us raise our glasses to the indisputably innocent Edith

303

Hind,' was one toast. Plastic crinkly cups, warm white wine. Manon had felt loved.

She shows her badge at the front desk. 'Here to see DCI Sean Haverstock,' she says.

'Not in,' says the desk sergeant. 'On holiday in Dubai, if you don't mind.'

'Melissa Harcourt then,' she says.

'Just a moment please.'

The Cambridgeshire MCU gift – they'd had a proper whip-round – was in stark contrast to Kilburn's. From this grey-hunkered office she's now standing in (the very smell makes her tense) she'd received a mug-and-handkerchief set saying 'I'm not always right, but I'm NEVER WRONG', which she'd dropped off at the Cancer Research shop on her way home. She's never understood why people like these Hallmark "witticisims".

From Cambridgeshire, she'd got £300 worth of John Lewis vouchers. 'As we all know, it is Manon's spiritual home,' Harriet had said. 'If Manon Bradshaw, never knowingly under-moaned, had not become a police officer, I think we all know which well-known Partnership she would have joined.'

'God, I love it so much,' Manon had said, red-faced and swaying. 'The table lamps!'

'Someone support her, she's having a giddy turn,' said Harriet. Then she'd looked out to the gathered faces, everyone smiling as Manon looks back on it. 'Manon Bradshaw does not only love a scone in The Place to Eat. She has a passionate hatred for parties where standing is involved. In fact, make that all parties. She owns twelve versions of the same smock top and has never missed an episode of *First Dates*. Manon Bradshaw is also the best detective I know. She has never shied from the dogged work that solves cases and secures convictions. I wish—'

and here Harriet's voice had audibly cracked ' — I wish Manon wasn't leaving the team because MCU won't be the same without her. But the good news is, London is about to become very safe indeed. So let's loop back offline, go forwards together and sing from the same hymn sheet: to Manon!'

'DS Harcourt will be down shortly if you'd like to wait,' says the desk sergeant.

Perhaps she should never have returned to Cambridgeshire; left it on that high note of affection. Perhaps coming back was the professional equivalent of shagging someone you'd binned off six months earlier. Is that why it all went so catastrophically wrong – why they turned on Fly?

'Manon!' Melissa Harcourt's shrill voice bounces off the gloss-painted institutional walls. She is too loud and too effusive. How does she have the energy to fake so much?

Manon notices the exhaustion that is dragging at her like an oceanic undertow. Invisible yet muscular, the pull downwards.

'Hello, Melissa.'

'It's soooo good to see you. Wonderful! How are you? Gosh, look at you! Can I touch it? I know pregnant women are supposed to hate this, but can I touch it?'

'Um, yes, OK then,' she says. And Melissa Harcourt bends in her tight navy suit and her nude patent heels and places her hand on Manon's body.

'Amaaaaazing!' she says.

'Thanks,' says Manon. 'I need to talk to you about Jade Canning.'

'Jade Canning?' says Melissa. 'Who's Jade Canning?'

'Body we hooked out of the Welsh Harp last summer. You and I. In the heatwave, remember? Really stank. Havers gave it to you, even though you shouldn't have been SIO on something that serious.'

'Oh yeah,' said Melissa, turning her face away. 'Yeah, vaguely. Why are you interested in that? She was a jumper, wasn't she? Tons of cocaine in her system, no suspicious circumstances, the usual with girls like her.'

'Ah, but she wasn't actually – a jumper, I mean. In fact there were an awful lot of suspicious circumstances. Jade Canning died at the Carlton Hotel in Mayfair while working as an escort. She'd been hired by a private bank to entertain a Chinese business delegation and her death was covered up by persons unknown. Body was taken out of the back of the hotel in a van which then drove it to the Welsh Harp and dumped it in the lake.'

Manon tries out a cloying tilt of her own with the attendant unpleasant smile.

Melissa is looking deeply uncomfortable. 'Why are you poking about in all this? It's not your patch any more.'

'Well, apart from a basic regard for professional standards, Melissa, I have an attractive proposition for you. You could allow me to take this to professional standards with my concerns about the inadequacy of your investigation and face a potential Reg 14 misconduct notice. Or there is another way forward.'

Melissa shifts on her tottery shoes. Manon's belly creaks in a way that is close to insupportable. Birth is supposed to be three months away. *Not now you little fucker. Stay inside.*

'Well,' Melissa says, 'just because new evidence has come to light now, doesn't mean I did a bad job.'

'Ah, but it does,' Manon says, 'because if you had covered the very basics of victimology, the first question you would have asked was: what was my victim doing, where was she doing it and who was she doing it *with* on the night she died? And the answer would have been, she was being exploited by some excessively rich people at a hotel in Mayfair despite being below the age of consent. And that, if you were a half-decent police officer, would have led you to open a murder investigation. See where I'm heading? So, here's my idea. You re-open the Jade Canning case stating new evidence has come to light, evidence which I shall furnish you with and which includes ANPR capture of the white van's journey from the Carlton Mayfair to the Welsh Harp. You mount a search for the Persian rug, which I would hazard is covered in Jade Canning's DNA. Your investigation spills over into an examination of that night at the hotel and the use of high-class escorts by a private bank for corporate entertainment. I have a file—'

'You have a file?'

'Yes, it's quite an interesting file. You may wish, in the course of your investigation, to share this file with, oooh, the Financial Conduct Authority and MI5—'

'MI5?' Melissa's eyes are wide.

'Yes and this way, you see, you change a misconduct notice into a rather high-profile investigation which gets you noticed by the top brass and you get your arse out from under that dickwad Havers. Unless you're shagging him. Are you shagging him? Because if you are, I really can't help you. This—' she wags her finger between them '—sisterhood only goes so far. Want to have a little think?'

The cramping sends an arrow dart down Manon's left side and straight into her groin. She buckles at the knees. 'I might have to sit down . . .' she says.

'Here,' says Melissa. She supports Manon's weight, leading her backwards towards the blue plastic chairs that are bolted together against the wall of reception. 'Are you all right?'

'Will be,' says Manon. She pants, waiting for it to pass. It's taking a long time to pass. It's as if everything inside her might fall out, as if her pelvis is a broken bridge, bulging and ineffective.

Her phone is going.

'Mark,' she says.

'Hi there. Are you all right?'

'I'm all right, yes,' she says.

'I think you need to come back. Fly's in hospital.'

Mint green walls. Blue linoleum which squeaks and shines with pools of reflected light. Outside the door is a police officer sitting on a chair.

Fly's neck has a white support collar around it. He is asleep.

'He should make a full recovery,' says Mark.

'Who found him?'

'An orderly. Very lucky with the timing. He came in on him only moments after he'd hung himself, which is why he's still with us. He'd made a noose out of the bed sheet.'

'*Oh God.*' She is holding Fly's hand against her forehead and her tears are falling onto his sheets. She is so sorry and this sorriness is flowing from her on a ribbon of tears. All she can think is she won't let go of his hand again. They'll have to prise her off him. She won't let another single thing happen to him.

'Shouldn't be any long-term damage,' Mark says. 'He's breathing all right and there's no damage to his spine.'

'Did he write a note?'

'Not that I know of. You look awful.'

She clasps Fly's hand, palm to palm as if for an arm wrestle. Her lips to his skin.

'He's only asleep,' Mark says. 'He really is going to be all right.'

'I'm not sure he'll ever be all right.'

'Actually, I think we can get him out. Read this.' Mark has

opened his briefcase and hands her a wad of A4 paper stapled at one corner.

She gathers herself, wiping her face on her sleeve and reads.

Expert Medical Report: Michael Fairbrother

Professor of Trauma Sciences

Consultant trauma and vascular surgeon, UCH

She scans the first page of Fairbrother's curriculum vitae. 'I have a particular academic interest in severe bleeding after injury.'

Next page, Jon-Oliver's injuries: 'A single stab wound to the right chest at the 8th intercostal space (between the 8th and 9th ribs). The wound penetrated the lower lobe of the right lung, right diaphragm and right lobe of the liver. The wound then penetrated the pericardium and then entered the right atrium of the heart. Mr Oliver died from profound cardiovascular shock due to the combination of severe blood loss and cardiac tamponade (collection of blood around the heart). I am of the opinion that blood loss is the most dominant factor leading to shock and death.'

'So he's written this based on Derry's postmortem and seeing the CCTV from the station buffet?' she asks Mark.

'That's right.'

The next line springs out at her as if pulsating. 'It is possible for people not to realise immediately that they have been stabbed. Mr Ross displays laboured breathing while in the station buffet which could be the result of ongoing blood loss at this time. Mr Ross went into traumatic arrest in Hinchingbrooke Park at 4.27 p.m. If he had been stabbed prior to going into the station buffet, he would have been bleeding internally for at least fourteen minutes. This scenario is consistent with his injuries.'

'How can you not realise you've been stabbed?' she asks Mark.

'Well, there are a number of possible reasons. If you've been

309

beaten up, for example, you might be distracted by other injuries. There was bruising on Ross's legs. Maybe he was kicked. Also, if you're drunk—'

'He wasn't drunk.'

'No, but there was cocaine in his system. Keep reading.'

She returns to the report. 'At the counter of the station buffet, he appears to have increased depth and rate of breathing. His respiratory rate is approximately forty breaths per minute while buying a Twix. Otherwise he does not appear particularly distressed. He walks across the station car park, mounting the steps up to Brampton Road. He is not hurried and does not appear distressed although his gait becomes unsteady. There is no sign of blood on his clothes.

'The amount of time a person can function normally after a stab wound such as this depends on the rate of blood loss (or collection around the heart) induced by the injury. It is possible and even common for victims to bleed at a slow or moderate rate so that they are able to talk normally and maintain their blood pressure.

'As blood is lost from the circulation, there are compensatory responses in the cardiovascular and respiratory system to maintain as much blood supply to the vital organs as possible. One of these responses is to increase ventilation, seen by an increased rate and depth of respiration. In the station buffet, Mr Ross does appear to have a markedly increased rate and depth of breathing. This is one of the earliest clinical signs of internal bleeding. It is consistent with his body going into haemorrhagic shock.'

Manon sits back. You can die two ways, it turns out – just like you can fall in love or go broke: gradually, or all of a sudden. Jon-Oliver was stabbed on the train. He was panting in the station buffet, buying his Twix. He was bleeding to death

310

all the way across the car park, up the steps, along Brampton Road, turning right into Hinchingbrooke Park Road, and then he fell, into the arms of Judith Cole, by which point he was bleeding profusely, panicked by the realisation that he'd been stabbed, and soaking her clothes with his blood.

'What do we do with this pathology report then? As it stands, it's just one pathologist contradicting the rest.'

'I want to show it to Derry Mackeith. I think if he reads it and watches the CCTV, he'll be persuaded it's right and will change his position.'

'Er, have you ever met Derry Mackeith?'

'Only in passing.'

'Just, he's not really a change position kind of guy.'

'There's a lot of evidence backing this pathology report. Firstly there's the CCTV showing him panting. Then there's the blood drips on the station steps, and car park footage that shows him weaving. And then there's the blood drips at the scene itself, which they claim came from Fly's weapon, but which patently – I'd argue at least – come from the victim himself. Hence the drip which doesn't fit their hypothesis.'

She leans back in her surprisingly comfortable chair, the kind relatives have to sleep in. She considers nodding off – the undertow dragging deep within her as if her brain is longing to go into shutdown mode, to evade the situation. She can remember this sleepiness from other high-stress situations – her Cambridge exams or key police interviews. The totally inappropriate desire to take a nap. Head back, she closes her eyes. The undertow is too much and she is being dragged under, her head lolling against the padded backrest of the oh-so-comfortable chair.

She has re-taken Fly's hand in hers. She and Fly, sleeping side by side, together like in the old days and not at war.

311

When she comes round, preparations are being made to move him.

'What are you doing?'

'We need the room,' says a nurse. 'He's out of danger so he can go onto a ward.'

'You should go home and get some proper rest.' It is Harriet, one hand on Manon's shoulder. Manon's eyelids are so dried out, they are slow to unstick.

'We're going to have to transfer him back to Arlidge House once he's discharged,' Harriet says.

'Are you fucking kidding me?' Manon says.

The room is full of people doing things; unclipping monitors, pushing down metal sides on the bed, un-hoisting tubes from around Fly.

'He'll be under close observation,' Harriet says.

'Like he was before, you mean? Have you seen the cuts on him? Who'll be watching out for him? Neil? Neil doesn't watch over anything except his own back. Have you been in there? It's not fit for purpose. I will never forgive you for this, Harriet. Never.'

DAVY

The sun sets, lurid peach bleeding up through pale yellow to light blue then dark beyond the window of Stanton's office. An electronic chord chimes out of Mark Talbot's laptop.

'Manon all right?' Davy asks.

'Not really,' Mark says.

Davy wonders if Mark is going to break down, but he holds it together enough to say, 'The stress – she looks so tired. Fly doing that to himself, that's broken her heart.'

Harriet and Derry enter the room. Brisk and suited and giving off the 'we really don't have time for this' atmosphere of middle managers everywhere. *Yes you fucking do*, Davy thinks. *You've put a child away, so you do have time to look at this.* He's surprised at how angry he feels, a hurricane of it blowing about inside him.

It's been there since he saw the contents of Gary Stanton's texts.

'Right, where's this footage you want to show me,' Derry says. 'Because I've got several stiffs on the slab, and they don't like to wait.'

'If you could take a look at this pathology report from a chap called Fairbrother at UCH. He's an expert in bleeding,' Mark says, handing copies to both Derry and Harriet.

The printouts are crisp, stapled at the corners. Mark Talbot has come prepared, Davy notices. Good that he's in Manon's corner.

Derry shifts as he reads. Davy scrutinises his face.

Derry is frowning, starting to look uncomfortable.

After a few moments, Derry says, 'Where's this CCTV footage then?'

They fan out behind Mark, who sits at Stanton's desk. They look over Mark's shoulder at his laptop on which he plays the station buffet CCTV.

Silence.

Mark plays it again.

'You can see on this—' he begins.

'Yes,' Derry says.

Davy is surprised to feel sorry for Derry – Derry who strides about HQ like some grim-reaper colossus; busy, busy, busy. Derry who depends upon minions falling on his expertise. Derry who wears bow ties as if he were a private school head-master. At this moment, he looks frightened and old.

'It seems I may have been wrong. I would like to show this to colleagues,' he says to Mark.

'Of course,' Mark says.

Davy steps out of the way and avoids Derry's eye on his way out, not wishing to add to his humiliation. It is very hard to climb down. The shame and then, waiting in a dank pool at the bottom, guilt.

After Mark and Derry leave the room, Harriet says, 'This puts the Latvian firmly in the frame.'

'Yes. Enough to release Fly?'

'I should say so. This changes the time of death. Fly was in school. Let's get a court hearing asap so the CPS can offer no evidence. Then Fly can be released straight from hospital – once he's well enough to be discharged, that is. Call Manon to tell her, or even better, go and see her.'

'What about Carruthers?' Davy asks.

Carruthers' phone was found, a black shadow in the bowl of one of the gents toilets, unflushed. Tech team had it in rice in an attempt to dry it out. Would they be able to get the data off it? Davy didn't like their chances.

'Carruthers can go,' says Harriet, though he hasn't been under arrest – insufficient grounds. Merely staying at The Old Bridge Hotel while he 'helps police with their inquiries'.

Linda Kapuschinski has retracted her statement, having been offered a generous severance package by Dunlop & Finch, which included a very comprehensive non-disclosure clause.

When Davy tried to call her, Linda wouldn't pick up. A few moments later, a text arrived from her.

I can't talk to you. They just fired Claire in HR. Try her.

'That Latvian chap did not kill Ross off his own bat,' says Davy.

'No.'

'He was paid.'

'Yes.'

'Carruthers paid him.'

'Maybe. Or Dunlop & Finch. Or persons unknown,' says Harriet. 'Least we get a collar out of it.'

Linda supplied a mobile number for Claire from HR and while Davy would normally hot-foot it to London for a face to face interview, on this occasion he'll make do with a phoner. He is anxious to get to her before Dunlop & Finch can clam her up with an 'enhanced' severance package.

'Tell me about Giles Carruthers,' he says.

'Um,' Claire says, with a long exhalation, 'well, classic City boy really, very alpha. But even by the standards of the City, he's the most competitive guy I've ever met. You know about the cull, right?'

'The cull?' says Davy. He knows, from Linda, but he wants Claire to tell him all about it.

'Every autumn most of the successful banks like Goldman Sachs and JP Morgan fire their worst-performing staff, no matter how much money they make for the firm. It's called the cull. So, usually a bank our size – listen to me, I'm still saying *our* – a bank the size of D&F would be too small for a cull, but Giles was *so* into it. He loved to cull. He used it to fire people he didn't like, people who threatened him in any way. There was a guy called Juan, who'd come over from São Paulo – really popular guy, big expansive personality, always joking. Everyone loved Juan, he was the life and soul. Anyway, one evening there was a "friendly" five-a-side football match. Juan played in the team against Giles. Massive mistake. I wasn't at the match, so I don't know exactly what happened; maybe he scored the winning goal, maybe he tackled Giles or crowed about victory.

'Anyway, next morning I was up at 5 a.m. to a text from Giles saying, *Juan's out*. When I got into the office, I talked to Giles. I said Juan was one of our most profitable employees. I also said he had a wife here and children in school. Giles said, 'Don't care. Execute.' That's the other word for the cull – executions.

'Juan was never allowed back in the building. His pass was

blocked. That's often the first people know – they can't get into the building. Everyone, and I mean everyone, was gutted about Juan. Such a nice guy.'

'Was that the first time Giles had behaved in that way?'

'Oh no, he always behaved in that way. Giles is not someone who can take things on the chin, you know? He can't laugh anything off, which means if he's ever the loser, he's so humiliated that he has to totally destroy the source. It's not an uncommon trait in the City, actually.'

'And his relationship to Jon-Oliver?'

'Well, Jon-Oliver had trounced him by signing Xi Ping and there was no way back from it. If I'd been Jon-Oliver, I'd have been terrified.'

'So why wasn't he?'

'Maybe he thought he ruled the roost, thought he had the boss's ear, he was going to be deputy chairman. He had the upper hand. He had reason to think Giles might be culled before too long.'

'All very macho,' Davy says.

'Yes,' says Claire. 'Being fired, it's part of the game. You can't cry about it. Juan did though. He was normal.'

Carruthers can go.

Harriet's acceptance of this ricochets in Davy's brain. *People like Carruthers always get away with it*, he thinks, but he cannot muster Harriet's resignation. Sometimes, the world order is too upsetting for acceptance – and this isn't like Davy at all, Davy's all for the status quo. Except sometimes, one must say no.

He runs along Brampton Road into town, across the mess of busy roads that have nothing but disdain for pedestrians and another stitch starts to pinch at his side. He really must get fitter.

317

In The Old Bridge Hotel car park, the light is orange from the street lighting. Carruthers has pointed his fob at his BMW and it has answered him with a top-of-the-range beep.

'Mr Carruthers?' Davy calls.

He looks up from placing a case in the boot. His expression moves from confusion to annoyance as he makes out Davy walking towards him out of the shadows.

What will Davy say?

The air is damp and he feels ridiculous.

How will he begin?

'I was just off—' Carruthers begins.

'Yes,' says Davy.

'Is there something . . . ?'

'Not really,' Davy says. 'It was just, I was wondering . . . Did you *leave* Goldman Sachs or did they, were you . . . How shall I put this?'

'Fired? How is that relevant to your case, DS Walker?'

He puts his final bag in the boot and pulls on its lid, which closes itself with a soft, controlled shunk. Turns to Davy with both hands now in his trouser pockets.

'I was thinking that if you were fired, it might have made you feel insecure and then when Mr Ross began to substantially overtake you in the competition to be deputy chairman, the ground you were standing on must've turned to sand.'

The muscle in Carruthers' jaw is going – clenching and unclenching – but he maintains a steady gaze.

'That's very far from how it was,' he says. Pauses, then smiles. 'I expect you're looking for promotion yourself, are you? Is that what this is all about? Everyone moving up a rung since the super coughed? Is that it?'

You would destroy me if you could, Davy thinks. Before him comes the image of Conley Woodchurch's spotty hopeless face,

Juris banged up. The headlines that will inevitably feature the word 'immigrant'. While this sleek cat will glide away.

'Ah, but the police promote on merit,' Davy says, not believing a word of it. 'Whereas your cull . . . What happened between you and Juan, by the way?'

'You've been listening to gossip, I see.'

'Oh no, it's a matter of record that you fired Juan. He says it was because he scored a winning goal in a friendly five-a-side. Doesn't sound very friendly to me.'

'How could you know that? Juan is back in São Paulo—'

'Never heard of Skype?' Davy asks.

'Look, DS Walker. I'm not sure what you're getting at, I'm really not. I believe I'm free to leave, and I'll be honest, I'm pretty keen to get back to London having spent quite a bit of time in this charming town of yours.' He opens his driver door, then turns to Davy. 'I'm not a perfect person, I know that. But I'm not the devil you make me out to be.'

Yes you are, thinks Davy, stepping back so that Carruthers can reverse his BMW out of its parking space. He watches the light pool on its black paintwork like oil, its red brake lights glowing.

No, it's never people like you who pay.

Day 32
15 January

Manon

She's bolt awake. Two a.m.

'I'm bleeding,' she says, waking him. 'It's not much, but . . .'

'Right,' he says, sitting up, blinking. Rubs his eyes before putting on his glasses. 'Right, come on then.' He gets out of bed and starts pulling on his jeans. She isn't doing anything. 'Why aren't you getting dressed?'

'It's probably nothing,' she says. 'Maybe we should leave it till morning.'

'Nope,' he says. 'Come on, we're going to A&E. Better safe than sorry.'

In the strip-lit waiting room, a urine-soaked tramp is singing Cher. *I really don't think you're strong enough, woah.*

Manon lays her head on Mark's shoulder.

Taking her hand, he says, 'They'll see us in a minute.' And she thinks, *you can't possibly know that,* but likes him for saying it.

'Why are you here?' she asks.

'To see if the baby's all right,' he says.

'No, I mean, why're you with me?'

320

'I don't know, really,' he says.

She lifts her head to look at him. If she could have written the line she least wanted him to say, that would've been it.

Oh, it doesn't matter.

Fly is all that matters. He will have been informed that he is to be released. Perhaps the worst is over. Perhaps.

Since she was told by Davy, it's as if the knot at the centre of her body has unravelled, a level of tension she hadn't realised she was holding inside her. Ellie exhaled when she heard the news, in fact she cried and Manon looked at her sister in shock. Hadn't realised she was holding a knot inside her as well.

'I'm so glad,' Ellie said, holding on to Manon tighter than was natural. 'I'm really so glad, Manon. I know you're going to be OK, now.'

Manon looked at her strangely. 'All right, you can stop being weird.'

'*You don't know?*' Manon says to Mark.

He shrugs. 'I'm here, aren't I?'

'Yes, but seemingly you caught the wrong bus and wandered in by accident.'

'I didn't mean it like that.'

She crosses her arms. 'D'you even know my name?' she says.

'Fun sponge,' he mutters.

'I beg your pardon?'

'Oh look, I'm sorry it's not more Disney. Maybe I'm a bit passive. This – situation . . . You and me. I want you and you come like this. And it only requires me to stay and join in.'

She looks at him and wants to cry. It is all so wonderful and so utterly disappointing at the same time.

A while back, his answer would've proved to her his irredeemable flaws: weakness, primarily. She would've poked at him with her critical stick – *passive passive passive* – until there was nothing else in her sightline. Now, though, it seems like rather a stroke of luck. Has she become so bovine she's lost her ability to find fault? She remembers, too, that the case being dropped against Fly has lost him trial fees of well over ten grand. He likes her that much, at least.

'You're not passive about work,' she says.

'No, it's almost entirely confined to my personal life.'

She thinks of all the dirty plates he hasn't placed in the dishwasher, the bin he hasn't thought to empty.

'What a terrible father you'll make.'

'No doubt.'

I don't like most people, but I do like you. You and Fly and this one in here. 'Don't you want your own children?' she asks.

'Probably. But I'm the sort of person who might not get round to it.'

'And it doesn't bother you, that it's someone else's baby?'

'It's not ideal. What do I know? I think loving someone is probably about getting to know them, whether you're a baby or not.'

'And what if it's horrible and we can't stand each other and you have to leave?'

'Then we'll join millions of other people who couldn't make it work.'

She bursts into tears. 'I want to know whether it's going to be all right.'

'Ah,' he says, prising her hand out from under her folded arms. 'No one can tell you that, my darling. Here's the doctor.'

'You can feel movement, is that right?' the doctor says.

'Yes.'

'How recently?'

'Now, it's moving now.'

'That's good. So, we're going to scan you, but just to warn you, I think we're going to want to keep you in for observation. D'you want to go home and get your wife an overnight bag?' he says to Mark.

'Bring the passion-killer nightie,' she says to Mark.

'That doesn't really narrow it down,' he says.

She surfaces to the sensation of push and fidget inside her belly, acknowledging it with gratitude. *Still there then, not dead.* With the knot at the centre of her unravelled, she can let loose her fondness for the baby. For the first time in Manon's life, she is not moving through the world alone. She has a companion tucked inside her, her favourite kind of human: silent.

She wonders if Fly has woken in his hospital bed with the knowledge that he is free. Might they wheel her down to him?

If she could only wake, if she could only come up into consciousness, dig deep for some energy, she could lift herself from the bed and scoop Fly up and escort him home. Look after him, engulf him in her protection. But every cell in her body longs to go back down, away from it all, deep into unconsciousness for hours and hours. Forever. This is not tiredness, it's the desire for oblivion. She has no right to be anyone's mother. She hasn't the *energy* to be anyone's mother. How can you be a mother and still feel like a child?

A hand on her hand.

She peels open one eye. Blurry light. A chair. Dark shoulder, a jacket. Mark? She squints, trying to focus.

No, Davy.

'Hello,' he says.

She manages a microscopic nod.

Davy talks to her while she's hoisted to a sitting-up position by a nurse and checked over, given a plastic cup of orange squash, which is too watery to give her any energy.

'Amazed at Derry,' she whispers, groggily. 'Never known him to admit a mistake before.'

'He blanched when he viewed the CCTV and read the Fairbrother report. It'll be the same with the other pathologists, once they see the breathing – it's pretty incontrovertible. I felt sorry for him actually. Derry's full of himself, but he's not bent.'

She has her head back on the pillow. She takes in Davy's sallow complexion, his disappointed expression.

'Are you all right?' she asks.

He shrugs, very unconvincing. 'I shouldn't have been so . . .'

'So?'

'So fucking naive. I don't know if you're up to this . . .'

'Up to what?'

'Stanton was having an affair with Ellie.'

'Ah,' she says. 'I had my suspicions. Hence the unchallenged seven-hour hole in her alibi.'

Davy has been tapping away on his phone and he now passes her the handset, saying, 'Have a read of these. Texts between Stanton and Ellie.'

Ellie: I strongly suggest you get your arse down to interview room one and call your dogs off.

G: Got us a room. No luggage. 😜

Ellie: Promise you won't want me to sing 'Five Little Ducks'?

G: None of that. But some of something else. 😜

'What is he, 12?' says Manon.

'Pathetic,' Davy says.

'Your idol has fallen.'

With her head back and her eyes closed, she tells Davy about Titans VIP and Dunlop & Finch, about Saskia and the Carlton Mayfair, Jade Canning, the cover-up. Her new friend Birdie.

'We're pretty sure Ross was stabbed on the train by the Latvian fella,' Davy says. 'Got off at St Neots. Too late to get any CCTV off the platform there, see where he dropped the weapon. We could have had the whole thing on film, in-carriage . . .' Davy is shaking his head.

'There often isn't in-carriage CCTV,' she says.

'Anyway, Stanton wanted it tidy against Fly. Didn't want it seeping into other areas.'

She feels the stirring of anger towards Ellie. How could she sleep with a man who was hell-bent on convicting Fly of murder? Even in the face of her anger, Manon's eyes are closing, the pillow so soft and welcoming. Is this what her unconscious is evading – all the myriad ways she blames Ellie?

'I better leave you to rest.'

She wants to say, 'No, wait.'

She wants to ask, 'Who was the beneficiary of that shell company that Ross set up, Pavilion Holdings?'

'Go down to Fly, will you? I can't . . .'

'Yes, course.'

The darkness comes in at the edges; she wishes someone would come and move her body for her. Being on her back is insupportable for any length of time, the press of the baby against her organs. She musters all her will to heave herself over onto her side, relieved at the lifting of pressure and grateful to the attendant squirm of the baby telling her it's alive.

She's aware that Davy is talking, *still here then*, as she tunes back into the room.

'I . . . I haven't got anything else,' he is saying. 'I've given everything to the job.'

'You need a girlfriend,' she whispers. 'Nice one this time, not like Chloe.'

Mark carries, not her, but her hospital bag over the threshold.

Amazing what you accumulate in hospital: paperbacks, *OK!* and *Hello!* magazines, boxes of meds, toiletries 'to make you feel more human' from Bryony. Apparently, all she needed was to sleep for twenty-four hours, her body's imperative so powerful it required hospitalisation. Her body had work to do, the small matter of growing another person's brain, and for that it needed total lockdown. She even had visitors, so the nurse told her, but she'd been blotto through the lot.

'Sleep, rest, stay away from stress,' the doctor said while discharging her.

Chance would be a fine thing.

'Why's it so tidy?' she asks, gazing around the kitchen, at the worktops now visible – clear of mounds of clutter. Where is all the detritus?

'Oh, I had a tidy-up,' he says, setting the kettle on to boil. 'You sit over there on the sofa. Are you hungry? Shall I make you something?'

'It's more than that,' she says, suppressing the buoyant surge of joy that he has undertaken *anything* domestic.

'There is something else. Let me just make you a cup of tea.'

Knew it, she thinks, *he's going to dump me so he's done the washing-up to soften the blow.*

He sits down next to her, putting the mug on the low coffee table.

'Ellie's gone,' he says.

'Gone? Where?'

He turns his palms up. 'Shipped out, taken Solly with her. Her room's empty, so is his.'

'She wouldn't have gone anywhere without telling me,' Manon says.

Did she come, to the hospital? Did Manon open one eye to see Solly on Ellie's hip, fingering her necklace, through the tugs of sleep? She doesn't know. *Au revoir, see yourselves out.*

'The probate information came back from Ross's lawyers. The beneficiary of his shell company and inheritor of £9million, is Solly. Incorporation took place in November.'

She is staring at Mark, open-mouthed.

He hands her the mug of tea. She drinks, absorbing.

'Well, I know what Solly'll spend it on,' she says.

'What?'

'Balls.'

'He does love a bouncy ball, it's true,' says Mark. 'Hard to burn through £9million in Poundland though.'

'How does a 2-year-old inherit £9million?' she asks.

'Via payments to Ellie, in a trust managed by Giles Carruthers. I think Davy wants a word, he's on his way over.'

'You don't think . . .' she says.

Mark shrugs.

Another draw on the tea. 'So she's gone abroad to spend more time with her money,' says Manon.

'How d'you feel?'

'Bewildered.'

'Want me to put you to bed?'

She shakes her head.

She gets up, and walks slowly up the stairs to Ellie's room.

The duvet, milk-coloured without its cover on, and the mattress with striped ticking exposed, and the door to the bedside cabinet swung open. All is emptiness. She sits on the side of the bed and runs a hand over the mattress. What has Ellie done? Where has she gone?

In the pendulum swing between fury and envy and betrayal, Manon lies down on Ellie's bed, her head on Ellie's pillow and misses her sister. *She would have left me a message. She would have explained.* She thinks back to Ellie's tears on hearing Fly was to be released. Was this the news that allowed her to ship out? Had she been waiting?

She wonders what Ellie might have done, how deep her ruthlessness might go. Manon feels the same capacity for coldness inside herself. This darkness doesn't feel 'other'. It feels like a part of herself.

We have parted before, we have had ruptures before.

We are our meanest selves.

DAVY

'Right, so if you could be quiet please everyone,' Davy says, and his voice is powerful and strong without him having to forcibly billow any effort beneath it. Has a reduction in the amount he cares given him more confidence at work? 'So Juris, our Latvian chap, has been charged with Ross's murder. CPS is happy with the evidence against him, even though we don't have a weapon. This is going to be a long one because evidence in our case is going to have to tessellate with the Met investigation into Titans and Dunlop & Finch, which is multi-agency – they've got vice and the FCA in on it. Even MI5, so I heard. Anyway, Juris is pretty happy with that, because he's getting cooked meals in Whitemoor instead of freezing to death in some Latvian hell-hole. The question, however, remains: who was pulling his strings?'

'Is there anything linking Juris directly to Dunlop & Finch? That's the question,' says Harriet, getting up from where she's been perching against Colin's desk. 'Ellie Bradshaw inherits £9million, that goes to motive. Ellie was with Stanton on the evening Ross died. Ironically, after everything he did to cover it up, Ellie's alibi is rock solid. They were at the George Hotel at the time Ross was stabbed.'

'The other person with a motive is Giles Carruthers,' Davy tells the room. He's not bothered now, about lines of deference to Harriet or anyone else for that matter. He's only interested in the work.

The rice worked its magic. Carruthers' phone dried out eventually and on it were texts between Giles and Ellie, a seemingly intense history of involvement between the two.

When Davy questioned him about this, he waved a hand as if it were nothing, saying, 'Oh, we met at a Dunlop & Finch do. She was there as his plus-one.'

Ellie: I think we should stop. I've had a change of heart.

Giles: Bit late for that, sweet cheeks.

Ellie: Don't call me that. Don't speak to me like that. I want to call it off. I want out.

Giles: Do you now?

Ellie: Why are you being like this?

Giles: Because it's so typical. Now that it's done, you want to wash your little hands clean.

'It was about the *money*,' Giles said. 'She was having a crisis of confidence about being the beneficiary of Pavilion Holdings, it being a shell, ill-gotten gains, tax unpaid, all of that. Bit of a lefty, Ellie. But how Jon-Oliver stored his money and what he declared to the taxman, that was his business, right? That's what I told her. She paid her dues and then some, working for the NHS. So we were arguing about the moral rights and wrongs of Solomon being the beneficiary and her being . . . well, exceedingly rich. Told her she should become a champagne socialist and stop worrying about it. You can be left wing and love money. Anyway, didn't bother me. Managing the fund for her, well – not a problem. Can do it in my sleep.'

'And you're now deputy chairman of Dunlop & Finch?'

'I am, yes.'

Davy addresses the room without a glance to check it's all right with Harriet.

'So Giles Carruthers gets his rival out of the way, and secures the job at the top of the bank. Ellie Bradshaw gets rid of an ex who is proving a thorn in her side, and comes away with £9million for herself and her little boy. She flew to Mexico City, we know that much, and tracing her whereabouts will not be a problem. The issue is evidence. Where is the evidence?'

Underage Girl Among Prostitutes Hired by Private Bank to Win Chinese Business, Police Say

Guardian.co.uk

- Culture of excess exposed during investigation into girl's death

- Dunlop & Finch hired suite in five-star hotel and escort girls to court Chinese billionaire

Police investigating the death of an underage call girl at a luxury hotel in London have uncovered a secret world of corporate excess surrounding the business deals of the world's richest men.

Wealth managers at private bank Dunlop & Finch provided a £5k penthouse suite at the Carlton Mayfair, free-flowing Krug champagne at £2k per bottle, and girls from escort agency Titans VIP, to entertain Chinese billionaire Xi Ping and his entourage. Senior partners Markus van der Lupin and Jon-Oliver Ross were hoping to win the contract to invest Xi Ping's

fortune in London property and a portfolio of other investments.

Police are investigating the death of 15-year-old Jade Canning at the luxury hotel on the night Dunlop & Finch was entertaining the Chinese delegation. Canning's body was removed from the Carlton Mayfair, preventing a police investigation into her death. 'We will get to the bottom of who engineered this cover-up, whether it originated with the bank, the escort agency or the hotel,' said DS Melissa Harcourt, part of the investigation team.

Senior partner at Dunlop

& Finch, Jon-Oliver Ross, was killed on 14 December last year, his death the subject of a murder investigation out of Cambridgeshire's major crime unit. A Latvian national, Juris Kalniņš, has been charged with Ross's murder and is being held at Whitemoor prison.

In a statement, Markus van der Lupin, president of Dunlop & Finch, said, 'I was not aware the girls were escorts. As far as I was concerned, they were guests. If they were escorts – and I have seen no evidence of this – then they were organised and paid for by our late colleague Jon-Oliver Ross, without the knowledge or consent of either myself or any other staff member at Dunlop & Finch. I have launched a full investigation at the bank.'

Xi Ping is worth an estimated 13.2bn dollars and is number six on the Forbes China Rich List. He made his fortune in smartphones. It is understood he has since withdrawn his business from Dunlop & Finch.

The private bank has changed its trading name to Regent Mayfair.

Sources close to the investigation have confirmed that a number of girls working for Titans have been offered immunity from prosecution in return for their evidence. The escort agency's client list is understood to feature a number of high-profile politicians, businessmen, members of the judiciary and police, as well as celebrities.

MANON

Torrential rain came down in hammering sheets as she looked out of the windows, waiting for Davy's car – waiting all morning for Fly to be discharged from hospital. At a court hearing in Fly's absence, the CPS offered no evidence and his judge discharged the case. Harriet had persuaded Manon not to attend. 'I won't let anything go wrong, you have my word. You need rest,' Harriet said. Manon spent the time fluffing about in his bedroom, laying out a selection of new books from the bookshop, smoothing out the clean bedding on his bed, plumping his pillows. She stopped short of putting flowers in his room, feeling this smacked of desperation. And anyway, young boys don't notice flowers.

'You're home!' she says, front door flung wide for him. Manon brandishes her monoboob like some mountainous harridan.

Davy shuffles behind Fly, into the house.

Fly, wet about the shoulders and head, still wears the white neck brace from hospital. The noise of the weather is deafening and she welcomes them in out of the rain.

She gives Fly a squeeze to which he submits but it is clear

he's not in celebratory mood; avoids her eye, hands in his pockets. He looks hunted, his face a cauldron of feeling.

'Ain't got a home,' he whispers. His mockney is ridiculous.

'It's not "ain't", it's haven't and you *have* – with me, your mother,' she says, her arm around him. Perhaps she can bluster her way through his bombed-out emotional rubble like some jolly wartime warden.

'You're not my mother,' he says, finding her face and in his look she recognises his need to hurt her, to hand over to her his most ghastly feelings.

'Anyone like a tea?' Davy asks, forging ahead to the kitchen.

She nods at Fly, pushing back her tears, like a hand pushing down on the lid of a full rubbish bin. She wishes her bump, now careering past the six-month mark, was not so enormous.

'Well, as far as I am concerned, this is your home,' she says. 'I am your home. I know I'm not your mother in the traditional sense, but I feel like your mother. I *want* to be your mother. Does that count?'

She shows him her tears, unable to close the lid on them. And why shouldn't he see that she is vulnerable also – that he can hurt her?

They sit, stiffly, at the white Ikea table, which Mark has incongruously wiped before he left for the day and this act of fastidiousness made her vaguely suspicious. 'Wiping the table – again?' she said.

'Right, well, good luck today. I'll leave you . . . to it,' he said, seeming to know she needed space to welcome Fly home without his complicating presence.

Fly focuses his wounded gaze on her once more. 'Won't be on your hands much longer,' he says.

'I want you on my hands – you're my son, Fly. I adopted

335

you. You agreed. You adopted me. You can't back out the minute it gets difficult.'

'Yeah, well, doesn't feel like that any more.'

She nods. 'I'm sorry for everything,' she says. 'I don't know what I can do to make it up to you, except say sorry. I'm sorry for all of it. I'm sorry I brought you here, I'm sorry about this baby. I'm sorry I was so stupid, not to see what I had. I went after this idea of having more children without thinking about the child I already had.'

'But I'm not yours,' Fly says, looking very directly at her. 'I'm not saying that to upset you, or because I'm angry. I'm saying it because it's true. I'm not yours and you're not mine. That's just the truth, no way round it.'

'But I want . . . I want to *try*,' she says, reaching out her hand. He moves his hand away before she can touch him.

'I want to be with my own people,' he says.

'I *am* your people,' she says.

'Three teas!' Davy says, coming to the table with his mugs.

Davy has put sugar in, even though they don't take sugar – it's something police officers commonly do for traumatised people.

Fly seems to open and relax. *Perhaps*, she thinks, *all he needs is time.*

'I miss Solly,' he says. 'Solly made me feel . . .'

'Happy?' she says.

'He made me forget myself.'

'Because he was such hard work.'

'It wasn't just that he was naughty,' Fly says. 'He was himself. I really loved him.'

'You still love him. He hasn't died.'

'Feels like he has. Did she not want Solly near me, like his dad didn't? Is that why she went abroad?'

'Oh God, no! Fly, *no*. Ellie loved your relationship with Sol, just like I did. We both thought you were great together.'

She is angrier with Ellie than she can begin to express, a great turning tornado of fury for hurting this lovely boy's feelings and not giving it a second thought. She turns to the stove.

She has made him a bolognese sauce, the kind she uses to hide vegetables: mushrooms, courgettes, peppers, celery, sometimes even aubergine if she's feeling risqué. Blended so the children can't tell what they're eating. When she makes it, she feels like a vitamin stealth bomber and this is what Fly needs after all those refined carbs in Arlidge House.

If she's honest, the sauce is a bit tasteless unless you add copious crystals of salt and a mountain of grated cheese.

'His name is Adewale,' Fly says, more expansive with a full stomach. With that name, the boy's face is lit with hope. She realises that he has spent his time in Arlidge House imbuing the name with meaning. This is the fantasy he's clung to, when all was lost. His face begs her to believe in his good news – that Adewale will become all the things he needs: a father and a family. 'All that time I was living in Cricklewood, he was only a few streets away.'

'It's a wonder he didn't find you sooner,' she says.

'He's a doctor, actually. So there's no need to be like that.'

'Have you met him?'

'Not yet. Going to. Paddy's setting it up.'

'Right.'

'Figure if things work out, I can go and live with him. You know, get to know him, live where I used to live, go back to my old school.'

She nods. 'What's his full name then? His last name, I mean – Adewale's?'

'No you don't,' says Fly, leaning back in his chair. 'You're not going to ruin this for me. I'm not going to let you start some bogus investigation on him, digging around, finding lies – that's all you lot do, isn't it?'

Davy and Manon glance at each other.

'Delicious!' Davy says, jabbing his fork at his remaining spaghetti.

Ellie

Wind ruffles the fronds of the palm umbrella, making shadows play over her feet.

Ellie squints out to a blue horizon, sunlight flashing like fireworks on the water. Solomon, wearing his bright orange UV vest, is playing beside her in the sand. Digging sadly with his spade, a rare moment when he's not crying, demanding 'home'. She's been run ragged by his beseeching looks, candlesticks of snot grey with sand on his upper lip; eyes pleading for Manon and Fly. All his conservatism has erupted, here in paradise. It is horrendous, to be alone with Solomon's heartbreak and to be the cause.

Resting on her brown, freckled knees is a pad and a pen poised. The breeze brings with it the scent of suntan lotion, coconutty, and behind it a delicious smell of fried snacks, chips or churros in a paper cone.

If she can just write this out, then she'll buy some for herself and Sol. Cheer him with sugar and salt.

But she can't write it out. Several attempts at a letter she can never send, her sister being not a priest in a confession box, but a police officer. A very angry police officer, one who has never been quick to forgive at the best of times. Impossible, unreachable Manon Bradshaw.

I was going to give you more space anyway. I was going to give you and Mark and the kids a chance to make it work as a proper family.

Christ, she sounds so patronising, trying to frame her abandonment as a gift. She crosses this line out. Looks at the page. Half of it is scored out: black, aggressive running-through.

Each bout of writing is driven by imagining Manon's recrimination.

Of course I tried to get Stanton to drop the charges against Fly! Ellie answers. *I stopped seeing him, I was so horrified at what he was doing. But he was driven by not wanting our affair to come out, especially not the night of Jon-Oliver's death. He was facing the collapse of his marriage and then, once he started covering up because of that, a gross misconduct notice. So then I went back to him, thinking I could persuade him more . . . well, persuade him gently rather than bully him. That was the day he died.*

She scores through this, also. The attempts to defend herself are so ugly.

You want to know why? she writes.

The pen stops on the page, at the bottom of the question mark's hook. Pokes into the sheet and bleeds there.

She looks out at the glittering water, the happy shouts of swimmers and windsurfers.

Paradise, she thinks. Paradise is an internal place. It is not this. She dreads Sol bursting into tears again for bringing him here, away from his toy vehicles on the kitchen floor and the people he loves.

From the beginning, perhaps . . .

Solly has had his third birthday here. It was a bit flat, just the two of us – he misses you and Fly so much.

I never fully told you what it was like when Solly was born. It was January – absolutely freezing. Snow everywhere. I was holed up at home with this newborn who didn't stop screaming. I got mastitis, so badly I was shaking and feverish. On my way to the GP I had to sit down on a bench in the snow because I couldn't walk the distance.

I was hit by this wall of grief for Mum. I wanted her so badly – to ask her what to do, to have her say it was all right, I was doing all right. I wanted her to take care of me – for someone to take care of me. I felt like a baby taking care of a baby. I didn't get dressed from one day to the next. Sometimes when he wouldn't stop screaming, I thought he'd been swapped, that he was someone else's child, unrelated to me.

One day a health visitor came and she was kind to me. It all came pouring out. I just cried and cried. After that things got better slowly. My milk supply improved, we got the hang of feeding. The more sleep I got, the more I was able to cope – even four-hour stretches made a huge difference. But it was one of the worst times of my life. If you think I've been down on your pregnancy and you having a baby on your own, it's because I don't want you to go through what I went through.

Then, last summer – during that heatwave, d'you remember? – when everything was good; we were living close to each other and Solly was great, Jon-Oliver reappeared. I told you how reluctant I was at first, how difficult it had been to get over him, but he went on a charm offensive, like he was love-bombing me. Looking back, I'm not sure if he was love-bombing me, or just getting round me to get to Sol.

I was reluctant for weeks, months even. That only seemed to make him keener. He was the very best version of himself, buying

341

stuff for Solly, delighting in Solly. That's the other thing about having a kid on your own – there's no one who delights in them as much as you do. So having his dad doting and sharing the good stuff. That was very . . . well, it was amazing. There was someone to text my photos to: pictures of him asleep – Sol is so beautiful when he's asleep.

Or texts about silly things he did or said. The feeling that Jon-Oliver wanted us, really wanted us, was overpowering. I just got to a point where I thought I'd be crazy not to give it another shot. No, I know I didn't tell you. I didn't want to tell you.

Our situation, Manon, you and me living together – I didn't want it long term. I didn't want to be married to you and bringing Solly up without a dad. I wanted someone to love me and take care of me. And when Jon-Oliver was charming, it was turbo-charged. He had mega-watt charisma and it was being launched right at me. You never saw it, you were always at work, but the three of us . . . fuck. It was heaven.

Thing is, when you've had your guard up as long as I have against Jon-Oliver; when you have been wounded as much as I have and then you let your guard down again, and then you're deceived again, it's five times as bad. I should have stayed hardened but I didn't. I knew what he was really like, yet I was stupid enough to fall for his charm again.

I made myself vulnerable, opened myself up, and look what happened. Not just that, I'd opened Sol's life to him. So when I found texts on his phone again – sex texts, texts from women saying, 'Are you hard?' or ones saying, 'Your appointment with Angel is confirmed for 11 p.m.' – I knew I'd fallen for the shit again, and that he'd only wanted me because I was reluctant, and now that I wasn't reluctant he was going to ride roughshod all over the both of us. I decided he wasn't going to get away with it.

342

D'you know what it's like to feel so angry you could commit murder, while having to sing 'Wheels on the Bus' and stay soft for all the cuddles and the stories that Solly needs? It was close to impossible. I was pretending with Sol, when inside I was boiling with rage. And that made me even angrier, that everything I had with Solly had been corrupted by him.

I didn't confront him. I pretended I didn't know about the shagging. And then, early November, he asked me to sign some legal papers. He was making Solly the beneficiary of one of his companies offshore, as a tax dodge. He told me it was only temporary, that he'd take Sol off the paperwork within six months. But for the time being, Solomon was the sole beneficiary of £9million held in a shell.

And at the same time I was being chased by the NHS for five grand I didn't have because they'd made a fucking admin error and overpaid me. I was working nights, watching Sol in the day; I was so dog-tired I could hardly stand, and he was jetting here and dining there and shifting millions about and every now and then he expressed these 'concerns' about the environment Sol was growing up in, the way I allowed him to watch telly while I dozed on the sofa, the amount of time he spent at the childminder, the fact that Fly was around.

He was an arsehole. He started to hint that he could provide a better life for Sol than I could: proper nanny, top-flight nursery, private schooling, everything money can buy. He could buy and own and go after the things he wanted, but he was incapable of loving anything.

He was erasing me. He was erasing my role as Sol's mother. I'm a lot of things, but I'm a good mother. I love that boy. I couldn't let him do it to me. I couldn't . . .

She squints out to sea.

Then scrubs across her writing with great loops from her pen.

Solly is patting the top of his sandcastle with the back of his spade.

How to explain her relationship with Gary Stanton, her relationship with Giles Carruthers?

She flips the page.

Me and Giles? We wanted the same thing, for different reasons of course. It cropped up one evening at a lavish bank function that all staff had to attend. Jon-Oliver was all over some 20-year-old in a low-cut dress, even though he'd asked me to go with him as his plus-one. Anyway, Giles and I had both had a bit to drink and we started watching Jon-Oliver and that led to each of us venting about him, I guess. Giles was pitted against him at the firm and it was driving him demented. Jon-Oliver had signed the Chinese billionaire and it had blown Giles out of the water. He said, 'We don't have to just take it, you know.' Giles is a narcissist of gigantic proportions. He cannot bear even a sniff of humiliation. It was Giles's suggestion to put one of the Titans guys onto it while Solomon was on the paperwork of Pavilion Holdings. A window of opportunity, he called it.

What did Giles get from me? A hand to hold, I guess, or maybe someone to hide behind. I did wonder if Giles was in it with me so he could pin it on me if things got rough. Or maybe he got from our collaboration the same thing people get from a stiff drink before an ordeal: Dutch courage.

Truth was, he would've done it without me.

She crosses this out, too.

She cannot send any of it to Manon.

She tries again but her back is so sore, a line of pain between her shoulder blades from the tension in her wrist and her rounding over the pad.

She gets up. Stretches out her back, bending each arm behind

her shoulders and pushing down on the elbow. Then she prof-
fers her hand to Solomon, saying, 'Quick dip in the sea?'

Sol rises from his squat and puts his tiny sandy hand in hers
and she thinks, *Oh please put your little hand in mine forever.*
It is the very best feeling, enclosing your child's soft hand in
your own.

Her writing pad is on the lounger, pen resting on it at an angle.

FEBRUARY

BIRDIE

It took a while for the body to be released from the coroners. Moukie was named next of kin on Saskia's passport so he's organised the funeral. DS Melissa Harcourt told me the date and time when I handed over my recordings to her for use in her investigation. She said I could email them to her as an attachment (as if I know how to do such a thing) or burn them onto a CD (again, bewildering).

I said, 'Actually I've got tapes. Little mini ones, you know, the type that go in a dictaphone. Quite a few of them. Shall I drop them off?'

'*Tapes?*' she said, as if I'd said 'parchment scrolls'. I suppose hers isn't a cassette generation, never having taped the Top 40 off the radio. She looked even more bemused when I handed her the little boxes.

'These will be very useful,' she said. 'I'll contact you if I need to fill in any gaps.'

I've got into the habit, now, of narrating my life. I do it all the time in my head.

Here I am at Hampstead Cemetery under a spattering rain,

at a graveside that resembles Robert Palmer's 'Addicted to Love' video.

Never seen so many long legs in sheer black tights, so many red lips, so many dead eyes. This is the sexiest funeral I've ever been to and I bet none of these giraffes will make a play for the sandwiches.

Your lights are on, but you're not home
Your mind is not your own.

People are being poked in the eye by other people's umbrellas but the rain is hardly rain, more like a fuzz of moisture held in the air. I don't bother with umbrellas because I don't have a hairstyle to protect.

People are looking at the coffin and thinking about her body. I know this, because it's what we all think about at funerals. The body, the state it's in, how the person you knew and loved, who moved about and laughed and talked and whose brain had thoughts is now an inanimate object inside a box.

I think about how she filled my flat with her complicated life, her drinking and her curtain-twitching and cooking burgers or macaroni cheese and watching *The Hotel* and how much I loved it. How quiet my flat is now.

And what's bothering me is not just her body but the fact that no one here knows who I am. I spent her final weeks with her, and no one knows about it. No one knows how much it mattered to the both of us, or about the plans we made, and I know it shouldn't be important – in fact it makes me sound like a baby, putting myself at the centre of the grief – but actually it does matter. The acknowledgement of the part you played in the person's life does matter.

I don't know anyone at the graveside and I don't know where the reception will be, or even if there is one, so I'm not going. I'm walking out through the high iron gates of the cemetery, onto

Fortune Green Road. Manon was right about the postmortem. Whatever they did to her, and I'm in no doubt she was killed by the Titans lot, was covered up by the booze in her system.

'Right, as predicted it's an open verdict,' Manon said on the phone. 'Basically, they found massive alcohol levels in her blood. Coroner's theory is she was hammered, she fell down the stairs, knocked her head on the skirting, was knocked unconscious and bled to death. It's possible the bleed was from the opening of an historic injury, maybe from when that car hit her. Anyway, they didn't do toxicology or anything. We've got the Latvian chap in custody here, so I'm trying to get some pressure put on him to confess. Y'know, say you did this one as well and we'll be more lenient about the other matter. That kind of thing. At the moment though, it's *Bez komentāriem* all the way.'

'Bez—?'

'No comment. In Latvian.'

'So if I hadn't sat there in that stupid police reception, if I hadn't gone to the cash and carry . . .'

'Don't go there, Birdie. Doesn't get you anywhere. We all could've done things differently.'

Past Tesco Metro and a strange bathroom shop, enormous and seemingly without any customers. The thought of opening the Payless fills me with tiredness. I can't be bothered. Moving to Spain like we planned, well it holds no appeal now she's gone, except the prospect of change ahead – that I miss. I've had a chat with a commercial estate agent, who said I could sell Payless easily, and he'd even look out for a small salon for me, let me know if anything comes up locally. Change doesn't have to be seismic, after all. It can be by degrees.

A going concern, as opposed to a joint enterprise, that's what I'm after.

It's downhill all the way to Kilburn from here and the gentle decline down Mill Lane and the Kilburn High Road would carry me along, like the flow of a river, but I wait for the 328 bus instead.

MAY

MANON

The baby was breech, born by caesarean section. In the hot post-natal ward, Manon was paralysed from the waist down, in support stockings and dry-mouthed. The baby slept in a transparent plastic box on wheels beside the bed. And slept. And slept. *I am a natural at this*, Manon thought. *Always knew I would be. So calmly maternal am I that my baby is sleeping through on day one.* She pitied the poor screamers in the next bay who did not have her knack. Mark brought her M&S mini trifles and while he was shopping, she tried to make herself look presentable to him, which was ridiculous after having abdominal surgery.

Day two and the baby still didn't do much waking. The hippy manuals she'd read claimed everything would happen naturally – the baby would ask to be fed, and would find the breast and suckle there, adorably.

Manon cuddled the baby a bit, talked to him, did a bit more expert mothering while he slept. The midwives, surprisingly disdainful and brusque, ignored the pair of them, only occasionally stopping by to dole out painkillers or empty her catheter. They seemed to her unkind almost to the point of contempt – was Manon over-sensitised by hormones, her feelings gaping like her abdomen?

It was on the second night, while she was still immobilised by the surgery, that the baby began to scream. He screamed and screamed, a bloodcurdling cry of torment, which turned him red with the effort of it. Manon held him, kissed him, forced herself up dragging the catheter. Perhaps this is what people meant when they described walking babies up and down in the night. When she tried to put him to the breast, the baby seemed to only half open his mouth, then fall off. And nothing seemed to be coming out.

'I don't know what to do,' Manon said to a midwife, but the midwife wasn't listening.

Then they were both crying, Manon and the baby. The midwives saw them and ignored them. This was not underfunding or being short-staffed. This was a culture of contempt.

'I'm sorry,' Manon said to the baby. 'It's all right.' Up and down the corridors, until a midwife said, 'You're not allowed to walk here.'

At discharge the next day, a kinder midwife (it was a low bar) said, 'He's hungry.' Manon had been told – by whom? The hippy manual or an NHS leaflet – that bottle-feeding was the enemy of breastfeeding. So the midwife fed the baby from a cup.

Back at home, she and Mark panicked. The baby and Manon proved an incompetent duo when it came to breastfeeding. Every time he went on the breast, he fell asleep. One ineffectual pinched-mouth suck, then lapse. Mark tried to cup feed him formula, but most of it went down his vest.

At her home check, ten days after the birth, the health visitor weighed the baby and called an ambulance. 'He's lost too much weight,' she said. 'I'm re-admitting you.' She gave Manon a form to hand in to the hospital. On it was written, 'Mother not feeding properly.'

In the hospital, the baby was whisked away to an incubator, a tube in his nose through which was poured pale yellow formula milk. Manon looked at her baby, wanting to hold him, worried the tube must've hurt going in, but she felt relief.

The nurses gathered around Manon's bed. You need to pump every two hours so your milk comes in, they said.

She pumped. She slept for maybe one hour forty minutes. It was as if the moment she nodded off, the alarm went off again. This was how they tortured people. She wanted to shout, 'Fine, I give in. No more!' Frrrr-pah, frrrr-pah went the pump. She wanted to shout, 'I don't care about the baby!' She'd give anything to sleep. No baby, just frrrr-pah, frrrr-pah and her eyelids closing.

Her milk came in. At home, with the help of a very expensive lactation consultant, she learned to feed the baby. Formula milk wasn't the end of breastfeeding. Stupid hippies. Stupid leaflets.

'What are you calling him?' Mark asked.

'Errol,' she said, looking at Mark for a reaction. 'Because he's so handsome, like Errol Flynn.'

Mark just kept on unpacking the shopping as if she hadn't said anything at all.

'Well?'

'I would hate to be called Errol,' he said.

She called the baby Edward. Eddie, Ted, Teddy Bradshaw.

In the numb, sleep-deprived early weeks, she thought the world would stop to give her time. She neglected to renew her tax disc and was fined. She cried on the phone to the DVLA, saying, 'But I've just had a baby, I can't even get to the chemist! I make a cup of tea and forget to drink it!'

Wasn't there leeway for stuff like this? Did the world expect her to keep up with admin and bills *and* look after Eddie?

How was this possible?

After a time it dawned on her that the world was full of catastrophically exhausted people on the borders of normal function – offices laden with zombie-parents who hadn't slept in years, never mind weeks; cars being driven by ravaged adults with barely enough energy to find their shoes.

The shock of this was immense: she must accept a new status quo more exhausting than she thought possible. She started to fantasise about retirement and being old. Going on a cruise maybe. Looking out to sea with a blanket over her knees and an all-you-can-eat buffet to look forward to.

JULY

DAVY

'So, been enjoying your time off?' he asks, surveying the dishevelment of the room: every surface covered in bits of white material (muslims, she tells him, but he doesn't know what the religious significance is). Baby bottles, baby bottle lids, dummies, toys, fabric books, teething rings, seemingly wet baby vests draped over the ends of the sofa.

She's really let herself go. The room smells slightly of sour milk.

She hasn't even offered him a drink.

'Time off? Are you having a fucking laugh?' she says.

'Well, no time sheets, no on-call.' He imagines she's been wandering about the park a lot in the summer sunshine. It's been lovely weather this last week.

'No sleep, Davy. You have no idea. This is round the clock.'

He is horrified to see her lift her top, unclip something on her bra and lob a tit out right in front of him. It bobs downwards like an escaping jellyfish, eddying with blue veins. The nipple is dark and enormous. He doesn't know where to look.

'It's a boob, Davy, not a bomb.'

'No, right, course.'

She's changed, he thinks. She's already told him all sorts of things he feels are not really fit for polite conversation: how it's a good job she's still wearing pads because every time she sneezes she does a little wee; about her bleeding nipples; the giant, reinforced caesarean pants she wants to wear forever. It's as if all her indignities have flopped out as well.

Yet he finds it impossible not to look. Edward's face is engulfed by bosom – it looms over him like a planet eclipsing a small, bright star. The baby opens his mouth wide, closes his eyes and embraces the breast with arms wide as if he couldn't be happier to be smothered. While he feeds, his little fist pumps Manon's flesh.

'He's lovely,' Davy says at last.

Manon exhales, shifting her position so she can relax. 'How are you anyhow? Still disillusioned? What's going to happen about Stanton?'

'The force are not minded to take it to professional standards, seeing as he's dead.'

'Ah,' she says.

He nods, then shrugs sadly.

She says, 'You know this about the police, Davy. We're a defensive organisation. In the face of criticism, our main aim is to cover our tracks.' She puts her little finger into the corner of Edward's mouth to break his suction-hold and adjusts her sitting position. Just as the baby is about to wail, a look of utter panic on his face, Manon clamps him back on.

'You look sad,' Manon says to Davy.

'Actually, I've started speed dating.'

'Ooh goody, now the shoe's on the other foot. You always looked down on me for this kind of thing.'

355

'Yeah, well, turns out being single isn't that easy to get out of.'

'Tell me about it. Go on then – depressing, was it?'

The experience had left him both ashamed and wildly hopeful. He'd looked at all the people in Commemoration Hall, lifting their white parcel labels off the trestle table and sticking them onto their chests, and he'd felt about as much spark as he did on public transport. People's faces were interesting: sad often, sagging, noble, exotic. But above all they were strangers.

Plastic chair after plastic chair and he'd felt nothing. Then he sat in front of a woman with a conker brown bob and a fringe, very straight and shiny. She was wearing thick-framed glasses, in fact she rather reminded him of Velma from *Scooby-Doo*, and she told him she was taking a whole new approach to dating conversations.

'Instead of saying, "This is weird, isn't it?" or "I've never done this sort of thing before, have you?" I'm going through the alphabet; so have you ever been to Texas?'

'No,' he said, 'have you?'

'No,' she said. 'Asked the last guy how he felt about salt.'

'What did he say?'

'He was for it, in moderation.'

'Seems sensible.'

They were momentarily silent.

'It's not really working out for you, the alphabet thing, is it?'

'Not really, no.'

He only had a couple of minutes, but for some reason he wanted to tell her the quandary he was in, that something had died inside him, age 28. Not every ounce of love for his job – he still found investigations fascinating, still loved the chase,

356

still wanted to nail their perp. He'd recently gone out to a scene with a younger officer who was breathless with adrenalin at viewing the stiff and setting off on his main lines of enquiry and Davy had found himself saying, 'Calm down. No need to get over-excited. You need to go about this methodically.' His voice full of weariness and restraint. Sad, really. *Do not hurry, do not rest* – whoever said that was bang on the money.

His faith in the meritocracy and the idea there might be an immutable space for him at work, that had ebbed, as he imagined it must for everyone except the most delusional or the most ruthless. He worked for an organisation, and organisations couldn't love you back. Occasionally, you got an allright boss; other times you got an arsehole. It was random.

He must've made a stab at explaining this to her, his date, though he doesn't remember what he said exactly.

'Why d'you think everyone starts wanting to get married around the age of 30?' she replied, matter-of-factly. 'Death of ideas. Birth of pragmatism, leading to compromise in choice of life partner, leading to procreation.'

'You make it sound so romantic.'

'True though.'

He looks now at Manon feeding her baby and thinks, *not just pragmatism*. It's wanting to get on with it. Wanting some change, wanting meaning – he shifts in his seat, wondering if he's sat on a wet babygro because his trousers feel damp – some of this chaos to rough life up.

'Actually I met someone,' he says to Manon.

'First time? You're fucking kidding me. That's not fair.'

She has lifted Edward onto her shoulder, draping a muslin there first, and is rubbing the baby's back. The boob just hangs there, pendulously. Edward lets out a belch which would put a man in a pub to shame, and Manon clips her breast safely back inside her bra – to Davy's relief – only to open the flap on the other one.

Mark walks in, looking like he got dressed in the dark this morning. His jacket has a white stain on the shoulder and his socks don't match. His eyes are squinty, his hair all over the place. 'Hello, Davy,' he says. He kisses Manon's and the baby's head and asks, 'How are you two?'

'Good,' says Manon. 'I didn't cry today.'

'Wow, that *is* a good day. Shall we celebrate with a takeaway?'

'Yes, but let's wait for Fly to choose. He'll be back from karate soon.'

AUGUST

MANON

She opens the door to Eddie's room, called there by his mewling; lifts his sugar-bag body out of the cot, overjoyed to see him even at 4 a.m. In the darkness, Manon can shower him with the adoration she feels she must tone down during daylight hours or in the presence of others. Secret lovers, glad to be back together. Loving Ed is physical – tingling in Manon's follicles, expansion in the depths of her lungs.

She especially doesn't want to love the baby too fulsomely in front of Fly, who is still with them but only just. A slow thaw.

The police intelligence system threw up numerous previous convictions for Adewale Sane, not least fabricating details of his medical training in Nigeria. Davy urged Manon to tell Fly, in order to dissuade him from investing in the relationship. Manon shook her head.

'Everything that comes from me is just further evidence of how the police try to pin things on people. If it comes from me, it'll push him further into Adewale's arms.'

Besides, she is confident Adewale will reveal his fecklessness to Fly soon enough. Adewale is exhibiting no keenness to house and feed a 12-year-old, which Fly explains to her with feigned confidence. 'He's between flats right now. He just wants to get himself straight before I go there.'

'Righto. Lay the table will you, kiddo?'

This and other lines like it, Manon uses to bluster across her uncertainty. She knows their status quo is fragile, that she cannot rely on Fly to stay; knows that he is emerging as a grown person in his separation from her and that she must let this happen.

It is enough, she tells herself, to have him here for now. She is aware life is at its fullest and, having been alone for so long that the loneliness had worked into her marrow, she does not take the fullness for granted. She knows, ever so sadly, that there will be a life after the children.

Slowly, slowly, they co-exist. Fly is still unhappy at school, though he has moved class – away from the Cole twins – and this has allowed him a fresh start of sorts. She must stop referring to things as fresh starts; kiss of death. His schoolwork is improving. Slowly, slowly. She is anxious not to foist the baby on him, though Fly does love a baby. Manon watches how hard it is for him to resist Eddie. The other day, they lay on their sides on the carpet, looking into each other's eyes. Then Ed tried to breastfeed from Fly's nose.

'Urgh,' he shouted, delighted. 'He's sucking my face.'

'Consider yourself honoured. He doesn't suck on just anyone's face.'

Actually, he really would. Eddie would suck on anyone's face.

In the past, she has tutted irritably at idiot-parents gurning over their offspring. Now she finds herself calling Edward 'the Gnu'. Mark calls him 'sausage'. They can't get enough of him.

She fells herself like a chopped tree onto the single bed beside the cot, holding the baby tight and opens her nightdress, already damp with leaking milk. Darts of responsiveness shoot towards her nipple as he latches on and then the feeling of spreading relief as he sucks, the engorgement of the night releasing itself. Then the flooding: her baby's satisfaction and her own. The here and now is at its fullest, she realises, and soon she will have to mourn it. *This is what happiness contains*, she thinks; *the awareness that it can't last.*

'Don't grow up,' she whispers to Eddie.

Lots of looking after him is tiring and difficult. In the early days, Manon cried daily with the exhaustion, the relentless servitude, the boredom, the confinement of their days, but the crying was ordinary. The care of Eddie is punctuated not just by crying (from both of them) but joy. Her son is the most fascinating and the most boring person she has ever met. His milestones bring back Solomon and she and Fly talk about Solly often. They miss his paddies, his effortful repetitions. If anyone needed to learn about dogged persistence in the face of incompetence, they should spend time with a toddler. There is no greater grit than in the short-legged, nappied person who keeps on falling down.

Life is easier without Solly, who required constant supervision of a most tedious kind. It is also easier without Ellie, who fills Manon's mind with complicated thoughts.

It's not that she cannot comprehend the *idea* of what Ellie has done. The idea, at arm's length, is easy. It's not as if Ellie turned the knife. And her reaction to Jon-Oliver's death – her grief, her agitation at seeing Gareth and Branwen Ross – must've contained guilt and horror at the loss she had inflicted. Ellie couldn't offer them Solly because she had harmed them too much. Did Manon balk at Ellie's ruthlessness? Yes, she was overturned by it.

361

Recrimination accompanies thoughts of Ellie; her mother's voice saying, 'You must look out for your sister.' Manon had, following their mother's death, been a surrogate parent protecting Ellie, always told to make allowances. This created in her both rebellion – *why should I?* – and terrible guilt. She imagines her mother's horrified face asking how Manon could have allowed all this to happen.

The swirling of guilt and recrimination makes Manon turn away, so that it has become efficacious to her internal world not to think of Ellie at all.

The baby's tiny fat hand lies on Manon's other breast, possessively. Recently, he's begun pulling off – rather painfully taking the nipple with him in his powerful suction-gums – in order to look up at her and smile. Huge gummy mouth, frog-like, eyes filled with delight. It's as if he is saying thank you for the milk, or something along the lines of 'Isn't this nice, we two?'

A flooding, that's what loving him is like – an inundation, out from her solar plexus to the follicles of her hair.

She hears the door to his room open.

'Shall I take him?' Mark says, sleepily, in the doorway.

'He hasn't finished yet,' says Manon.

She hears him turn on the bathroom light down the hall, a little later the toilet flush.

Mark wanted to be with her, and he has never wavered from it. He loves her in fact. How has she pulled off this feat, at 42 and in such haphazard fashion? They barely know each other and yet there is so much.

She'll probably fuck it up, she thinks, as she sits up and rubs the baby's back.

Acknowledgements

This book could not have been written without the help of DS Graham McMillan of Cambridgeshire major crime unit – my advisor on all things police-related.

I was also greatly helped by Daniel Burbidge and Mark Ashford, both partners at TV Edwards solicitors in Whitechapel. Where I have played fast and loose with police procedure or criminal justice, this is my doing, not theirs.

Certain events in this book were inspired by a real case in which two young men were falsely accused of stabbing Vitalijs Janovics in Bermondsey in 2011. I am grateful to defence barrister Tim Moloney QC of Doughty Street chambers, and solicitor Lionel Blackman, for talking to me about this case.

Thank you Stuart McWilliam of anti-corruption charity Global Witness for talking to me about shell companies, money laundering and global finance.

Thank you Nicole Toms for talking to me about the pressures and strains of nursing in the NHS.

I learnt about the culture of the City by reading *Swimming with Sharks* by Joris Luyendijk.

Thank you Susannah Waters for excellent editorial help. Thank you Tom Happold for reading my drafts more times than any reader should have to and for your enduring support.

Thank you Sian Rickett for your valuable insights. Christmas lunch at John Lewis is on me.

Thank you to my editors, Suzie Dooré at The Borough Press in London, and Andrea Walker at Penguin Random House in New York for the best editorial notes in the business and for cheerleading Manon every step of the way.

Last but not least, I would not be doing this without Sarah Ballard at United Agents and Eleanor Jackson at Dunow, Carlson & Lerner.